# SUVIA

# Suvia

## Alison Brett

Spiraling Compass Publishing

To my three brothers, my parents, my friends, and my love, who have shown their endless and unconditional encouragement throughout all of my endeavors.

# 1

# Two Red Dots

Zara gazed longingly at the black sky, counting the white specks which illuminated it. *I'm not ready...* she thought to herself. Over and over again, she heard the countdown that hadn't happened yet, and a knot in her stomach made her tranquility turn rapidly to unease. This was the loudest silence she had ever experienced. Between the radio static, the explosion of fire beneath her, and the countdown... over and over again, the countdown... Zara couldn't hear her own thoughts. Her body began to shake, and her breaths quickened as she lay on the damp grass in the quiet night. Fifteen meters from home on a neighborhood lawn in Houston, Zara drifted into a deep sleep.

Ever since Zara was eight years old, her dream had been to go to another planet. Every year on Halloween, her friends would navigate a colorful selection of Disney princess outfits and show them off to each other. Zara would sneak off and slip into her astronaut costume, which she asked her mother to custom resize each year. She would sit for hours, staring at herself in the mirror in solitude, with the background noise of prissy princesses in the other room escaping her attention. Through the thick astronaut helmet, she could see a silhouette in the mirror and would imagine a world far different than any she had experienced. At one point a childish dream, she was now on her way to being not only one of the first women to ever travel into space, but among the first people entirely to be sent to Mars.

"Zara!" Alarms sounded violently, and Zara could hear her sister crying out frantically from an unknown location on the spaceship. "Zara!" The voice drew near, but all Zara saw was blackness. Zara searched desperately for her sister, but she was nowhere in sight. Suddenly she saw her sister's blonde hair whip across the window outside of the spaceship and float away into the vast darkness. In a panic, Zara pressed the emergency window release but forgot to follow the safety measures and secure her oxygen. She couldn't breathe. Something nudged violently at her arm, but on the verge of becoming unconscious, she ignored it. Suddenly, her body was cold and wet.

Confused and terrified, Zara jolted into a sitting position. Only now, there was an unexplained stillness around her and an immediate transformation to all of her surroundings. Except one. Zidia hovered over her with an empty bucket.

"I'm sorry. You were having one of those dreams again. I tried to wake you peacefully, but you just kept shaking and were starting to break a sweat," Zidia said, twirling the bucket in her hands as she spoke.

Zara sat up and blinked at her sister in confusion. She looked around and saw the sun gleaming off the amethyst titanium vinyl wrap of a neighbor's Nissan Altima. The vibrancy of the color and the familiarity of the vehicle helped orient her back to reality. She grumbled tiredly and rubbed at her eyes.

"Today's the day, and given that you slept on freshly rained on grass," Zidia bickered, "I'd say you should shower."

"Might as well have added some soap to the bucket," Zara smugly replied. "You could have saved me the trouble."

Zara walked sluggishly to the house, and her sister followed. While ashamed to be living with her younger sister at twenty-nine years old in order to make ends meet, Zara was thankful that twenty-six-year-old Zidia had offered to help and manage her home while she set out to complete NASA's mission and her own lifelong dream. Zidia really didn't mind. To her, her sister was all she had to live for, and she was used to living in her shadow. Zidia looked up to her sister, seeing her as beautiful, intelligent, and determined. She envied her sister's shiny brown hair and how it smoothly waved all the way down her back. Her own blonde pixie cut paled in comparison. She was thankful that she had her sister's same bright blue eyes, but when she admired them in a mirror, it was like she was looking at Zara's shadow instead of her own reflection. Since Zidia moved into Zara's house, she avoided mirrors, worried their reflections would one day be indistinguishable despite their marked differences in appearance.

"I can't find my toothbrush! Where did you put it?" Zara yelled out in frustration from the bathroom. Zidia shook her head in disbelief. For how brilliant her sister was, she sure was a ditz.

"Did you check the shower? You were in quite the hurry yesterday. You probably tried to multi-task again," Zidia sarcastically jabbed. Zara stayed silent, but Zidia heard her sister rummage through her belongings in the other room, stop, turn the water on, and scrub away at her teeth. Zidia sighed and fell lazily onto the couch, turned the TV on, and flipped directly to the local news channel.

"Today's the day of NASA's unprecedented launch, sending five astronauts to Mars," the news reporter informed in monotone. "Eight hours to launch time, and still, the public has not been informed of the risks NASA is taking with this mission." Zidia swung her feet from the end of the couch to the floor and leaned forward anxiously.

"Yes, this is all theoretical, John. While we have been able to gather footage of the terrain of Mars from our satellites, the route to Mars is a blueprint so far, and it won't be long before that blueprint becomes a reality. The public's fear of the unknown is unnecessary and will ultimately be a roadblock to the possibilities we can achieve as human beings," a NASA representative communicated to the news reporter. The TV went black, and upon looking at her limp hand, Zidia realized she was no longer holding the remote.

"You shouldn't watch this stuff," Zara scoffed, handing the remote back to her sister.

Zara pulled her hair out of the towel on top of her head and continued to dry it off. Zidia watched in amazement as Zara's hair formed perfect waves and fell beautifully to her waistline. She was speechless, both at Zara's beauty and carelessness. She turned the TV back on but flipped to the HGTV channel in silence. She knew from experience that there was no talking Zara out of going, especially since she was at the head of the mission.

Mid-day came too quickly for both girls, and Zidia couldn't stop crying. There were just too many uncertainties about this mission. Zara hugged her sister reassuringly and told her to close her eyes. Normally Zidia would be distrusting, thinking her sister was trying to pull a practical joke on her, but hearing Zara's calm yet demanding tone prompted her to comply. Zara grabbed her sister's hand and set a small object on her palm. She folded her sister's hand into a fist with the object enclosed within.

"You can talk to me while I'm gone, Zidia," Zara whispered softly. Zidia opened her eyes and slowly lifted her fingers, revealing a communication device completely foreign to her. "The signal won't be strong, and the responses will be delayed," Zara continued, "but you will be with me every step of the way." After showing her sister how to operate the device, Zara inertly grabbed her backpack and exited the house. She had two more stops to make before going to headquarters.

The drive to her parents' house was a blur. She could hear the wind smack against the half-open windows and had the radio on but was inattentive to the songs. The sound of the gravel beneath her tires came to a screeching halt as she came to the end of the driveway and pulled up to an open garage. Her father pulled off an eye shield and set a power tool on his work bench. He silently embraced his daughter.

"I... uh... I didn't think the time would come so soon," her father stuttered nervously, "but I am so proud of you." Zara wiped a tear that was beginning to form from her eye and pulled away from him.

"I'll be fine," Zara assured him. "Where is mom?" The two of them entered the house. Zara walked into the living room and sat on the reclining chair adjacent to her mother's wheelchair. She reached out and took her mother's hand in her own.

"I know you're feeling uneasy about this, Mom." Zara made no effort to wipe the tears that were beginning to form this time. "But I'm ready for this. I am more than ready. I'm going to travel further than anyone has, and..." Her words cut off, as her throat began to swell, and tears blurred her vision.

Her mother tightened her grip on Zara's hand, and she nodded as she stared solemnly into the distance. "It's okay, Zara." Her mother cleared her throat before continuing, "I know I've always told you it's not, but only because I worry about you. I love you more than words can say. Go. Go live your dream."

Zara hugged her mother gently and kissed her forehead. She stood up straight, took a deep breath, and headed back through the garage to her car. She sat in the car without moving for a while, neglecting to even turn it on. The sun beamed directly on her, and the unbearable heat somehow felt comforting in the moment. After collecting herself, she continued on. Her next stop on the way to headquarters would not be easy but was necessary.

Three years ago, Zara had started dating a guy that she had known since elementary school. He was never the caring or romantic type, but he somehow managed to sweep her off her feet with wit, financial assistance, and above all, blackmail. Dimitri knew that Zara had a potentially life-threatening genetic condition inherited by her mother, something that would immediately disqualify her from her NASA position if it became public knowledge. She didn't mean for such a douchey kid to find out about something so personal to her, but during a lunch visit that her mother attended when Zara was in third grade, Dimitri found her medical tag dropped in the hallway and read every detail prior to returning it. He held this knowledge over her until she had no choice but to accept him as a suitor. She constantly tells herself that he is not so bad, but she feels in the pit of her soul that something is missing. After three years of dating, she has grown to care about him, but this care strays far from the feeling of love that she so helplessly has desired.

After three knocks on the door and two pushes of the doorbell, Zara gave up and turned back toward her car. "Would you wait just a damn minute?" The front door swung open harshly, and Zara whipped around to see Dimitri's half-shaven face with shaving cream still covering the other side. "Jesus, Zar," Dimitri coldly called out, "come in so I can say goodbye."

Zara walked past him dismissively and sat on the couch. Her stomach filled with butterflies, and she began to feel nauseous. She wished she could just get this over with, but it had to be carefully planned out if she were to continue on to NASA headquarters. Dimitri shuffled past the living room, back into the bathroom, and slammed the door shut. Zara heard the click of the lock. She looked impatiently at her watch. Four more hours until launch and only one until she had to be at headquarters. She needed to make this quick, but she knew that there was no way she could hurry Dimitri, so she tried to relax and focus on her thoughts and breathing until he finished shaving.

After about twenty minutes, Dimitri came out and sat on the couch with Zara. Zara leaned her head half-heartedly on his shoulder. "I'll miss you," she lied through her teeth, "and I'm sorry that I'm leaving for a bit." She placed the same type of communication device she had given to Zidia on his lap and briefly explained how it works. Her voice was filled with pain and exhaustion.

Dimitri scoffed and looked away from her. "Have you given any thought to what I asked of you?" he inquired.

"I have, yes," Zara responded. "I'll move in with you when I get back." Again, she lied through her teeth, but she knew it was the only way he'd let her go through with the space mission.

"Alright. Well fucking go," Dimitri snapped. "I got shit to do today, and as you can see, I'm already running behind." Zara kissed him quickly on his chapped lips and darted obediently out the door, thankful for being dismissed after such a short interaction with him. This time she didn't linger. As quickly as she could, Zara started the car and flew out of the driveway and down the freeway toward headquarters.

Now that Zara was on her way to work, she felt a heaviness lifted from her shoulders, as if she were already losing gravity. She could finally enjoy her travels, and she turned the radio dial, letting herself become immersed in a joyful and calming tune. She rested her arm on the ledge of the open car window and felt the light breeze graze against it. Driving through farm territory on the way to NASA headquarters, Zara admired the bright green grass and the beautiful horses enclosed in their fences. She wrinkled her nose at the distinct smell of fertilizer. She took everything in as if she were experiencing it for the first time, committing every detail to memory. Home had never felt so foreign.

Zara pulled up to the gated entryway and entered a five-digit code into a metal box. The gates slowly opened, and she drove through to a surprisingly empty parking lot. There were cars scattered about, but she had imagined much more for the day of the launch. She hurried through the front door and checked in with security. Upon entering the spaceship control room, she realized that for some reason, the empty parking lot did not accurately reflect the number of bodies in the room. She guessed that there were about one hundred and fifty NASA representatives, all deeply immersed in their work. Some of them were focused on satellite screens, others on forms and filing. Some of them were discussing matters in large groups. Others were deep in thought, tuning out their surroundings. Zara felt overwhelmed by the amount of people in the adequately sized control room and scanned the room for the other astronauts assigned to the mission. It didn't take long for her to spot Sadie and Marquette.

Sadie, an enthusiastic twenty-eight-year-old with pale white skin, blonde hair tied back with a bow, and a current outfit choice of a red skirt and sparkled black flats looked more like she belonged at a cheerleading competition than a NASA control room. She swore over and over again to Zara that one of these days, one of those handsome scientists nose deep in their work would look up and fall in love with her. Zara could tell this is not the conversation that they would be having today, as closing in on Sadie and Marquette, she could see that Sadie's hair was frizzy, her posture looked like that of an elderly woman leaning on any object in sight for support, and the nail of her pointer finger was being shredded between her teeth.

"Rough day so far?" Zara inquired. She handed Sadie a coffee that she had picked up for herself along the way. "You need this more than I do."

Sadie took the coffee from Zara but looked as if her hands were too weak to hold it. Instead of drinking it, Sadie began to trace the caution symbol on the lid with her finger. She seemed fixated in thought.

Marquette, a slightly heavyset thirty-one-year-old woman with deep brown skin, square glasses, and glowing white teeth set her hand gently on Zara's shoulder. "We are calling the mission off," said Marquette. Zara's jaw dropped in disbelief. Marquette continued, "They've been analyzing the numbers all day, and something just isn't adding up with the coordinates. There isn't enough room for error, given our limited resources."

"We're going," Zara firmly replied. "Suit up." She walked away furious and hurried to the other side of the room to discuss with Charlie, the lead engineer. "I'm going on this mission," Zara asserted to Charlie. She startled him, and Charlie turned around wide-eyed.

"I agree," Charlie chuckled, "but not today, Zara." Charlie returned his eyes to a computer screen in front of him and clicked a few buttons on a keyboard. He guided Zara in front of the monitor. "Do you see those two red dots? There is only supposed to be one."

Zara looked at Charlie with bitter suspicion. "We're cancelling this mission because there is an extra red dot on a screen?"

"The dot is representative of the intended coordinates. We can't be sure which of the two locations the spaceship will end up at, given a glitch in what has been programmed into the navigation system. There's no room for error, Zara. There won't be enough supplies on the ship if you end up in the wrong zone."

"I know what the red dots resemble, Charlie. I've worked here longer than you," Zara jabbed. "We'll be fine." Zara quickly turned away and flagged down the administrator. She walked hurriedly alongside him and anxiously began to plead her case. "Sir, with all due respect..."

He cut her off. "Suit up."

Zara smiled victoriously and hurried to grab her suit. She twisted her long hair into a tight bun on the top of her head as she hurried out of the control room. After putting on her space suit, preparing her oxygen tank, and completing her pre-departure checklist, she returned to the control room.

Sadie and Marquette were now joined by two other astronauts, Jerome and Xavier. Jerome was a slim thirty-five-year-old man with a receding hairline. He had fallen for Sadie at first sight a year ago, but he had never quite been the attention that she was seeking. In contrast, Xavier was a twenty-nine-year-old man with toned muscles and a smile that could make an entire room full of people stop what they are doing and stare. Given that most of the NASA representatives had been working with him for years, they were habituated to his visual charm and paid him no special attention.

"You don't look so nervous," Zara remarked, nudging Xavier with her elbow. Xavier just smiled at her and embraced her in a hug. Despite every female at NASA initially pining for Xavier, Zara had never been interested in him in that way. He was like the brother she never had. She thought this might be due to him possessing traits which remind her of her father. He was hard-working, preferred hands-on tasks, and always put others before himself. He also would tell corny jokes that seemed to make everyone else laugh, while she would simply roll her eyes.

The other three astronauts all looked pale despite their varying skin tones and did not have the slightest hint of amusement in their expression. The administrator stood on a chair and held a hand in the air, stopping all chatter in the control room. "As you all know," his voice echoed through the room, "there was a flaw in our navigation system, and it will not be corrected in time for the launch." While this news was familiar to everyone, most of the NASA representatives in the room looked as if they were suddenly in shock. "We will continue as planned, as the chances of the glitch in our system leading the spaceship to a location that far off are miniscule. One hour to take off. Please take the necessary preparations." The administrator stepped down from the chair, and several representatives raced to his side with further questions.

Zara turned to her crew. "You guys going to be okay?"

"Not everyone is like you, Zara," Marquette answered coldly. "I have a husband and two little kids at home. I'm not leaving an ass of a boyfriend. Unlike you, I have a lot to lose here." Marquette collided shoulders with Zara as she hurried past her.

Xavier set his hand on Zara's shoulder, but she dismissively shook it off. Marquette may have been right about this being an escape for her from Dimitri, but she knew nothing about what she had to lose. She needed to come back for her parents, and above all, for Zidia.

The next thirty minutes went by slowly, and the control room continued to be contaminated with angst and distress. This was not how Zara imagined her lifelong dream would unfold, but she was still more than ready for take-off. Entering the spaceship was surreal. While she had of course been on it several times before, it felt so much different now. All five astronauts sat down and began to prepare the interior controls. There was high chatter and sufficient communication between Xavier, Jerome, and Sadie, but Marquette and Zara stayed silent.

"We're not leaving until you two figure your shit out," Xavier unexpectedly announced. Sadie and Jerome nodded in agreement. "This mission is going to require all of us to communicate. Can we do that?" Xavier sternly continued.

"Yes!" Marquette and Zara exclaimed in unison. Marquette promptly apologized to Zara, and they began to work together to set the controls.

"Fifteen minutes to take off," a voice announced through their headsets. Zara mindlessly continued with her preparations while she began to daydream about what it would be like when they arrived on Mars.

"A year is a long time to be away from my kids," Marquette quietly complained.

"How old are they?" Sadie asked softly.

"Four and six," Marquette replied as she tugged on her seatbelts and secured them.

Conversation died out for the remainder of the time prior to departure. Even Zara started having cold feet about the trip. Zidia had not ever been alone for so long. Zara silently wondered what she was up to right now, assuming she was either watching the news about the launch or actively avoiding it. She hoped that while she was away, her sister would find romance and start planning to carry out her own dreams. Zara suddenly felt like a terrible sister, as she realized in the midst of these thoughts that she had never inquired what her sister's dreams are and didn't have the slightest clue what she was passionate about.

"All passengers prepared for launch?" a voice interrupted.

Upon receiving a thumbs up from the four other astronauts, Zara replied on the radio, "Affirmative." The spaceship began to make a loud rumbling noise. Zara took a deep breath and let her mind go blank.

"Launching in three... two..." Xavier playfully mouthed the numbers that sounded through their headsets. "One."

The rumbling sound grew louder, and the spaceship launched crisply through the air. The other NASA representatives watched in wonder from the control room. The NASA administrator circled a date on a wall calendar over ten years out.

"What happens then?" an engineer questioned.

"Our next mission," the administrator replied as he straightened his jacket. He walked out of the control room, which was rapidly filling with indecipherable chatter.

2

# Frozen in Time

The unexpected. It is exciting and scary all at once and sometimes leads to a letdown. Zara imagined that the travel time to Mars would be filled with adventure, beauty, and inspiration, but as she sat silently, staring at a blinking light on the control panel, she began to acknowledge that boredom was profound and inevitable. The other astronauts felt no more enthused. Sadie stared intensely at a hangnail. Marquette ran her thumb over a photograph of her, her husband, and her children that she brought with to ease her troubled mind about the growing distance between them. The men were fast asleep. Jerome's hand was limply dangling over the side of his reclined chair and lightly touching Sadie's knee. Too restless and alert to sleep deeply, Jerome drifted in and out of consciousness. Each time he awakened, he discretely brushed his finger against Sadie's skin, admiring its smoothness. Xavier was turned away from the four others, with only his head emerging from the thin blanket encapsulating him.

Zara matched the blinking of her eyelids with the slow blinking light until her eyelids stayed closed. In a deep sleep, she looked around and could see straight out for miles in all directions across the flat plane of red sand. She instinctively knelt and scooped a handful of sand, squeezing it shut into her fist and letting the dry sand seep through her fingers. She had been here before. She had dreamed this before. She stood quickly and began running to her left, knowing the dangers of running to her right all too well. A thin wind whistled across her body as she ran as fast and as far as possible. As far as possible was not very far at all.

Something sharp pierced her leg, and Zara crashed hard onto the ground beneath her. She instinctively put her hand on the part of her leg that was hurting but was baffled to discover the skin was not broken at all. The pain however intensified, and Zara couldn't move. She looked around with clouded eyes as tears were increasingly blurring her vision. She expected to see at least some sort of figure or silhouette but saw nothing. Out of nowhere, Zara heard a screeching sound and looked up to see an unfamiliar large-winged bird circling above her head. The screech grew closer and closer as the bird drew nearer.

Zara gasped heavily, and her eyes shot open. The other astronauts were at her side, even the men who had been peacefully asleep just moments ago. Zara looked at them with concern and confusion.

"What was that?" Marquette demanded.

"Huh?" Zara slid her hand over the part of her leg that had been injured, relieved to no longer be in pain.

"You sounded like a bird being tortured!" Jerome exclaimed.

"That was the loudest sound I've ever heard a human being make," Sadie added.

"Or heard anything make," Xavier chimed in.

Zara was startled by this information. "What sound did I make?"

Xavier put his hand on Zara's shoulder. "No one could or should repeat the sound you just made."

"I don't understand." Zara looked to Xavier for elaboration.

"Zara, you scared us all half to death! You woke me and Jerome up instantly. Your sound overpowered all the sounds from the engine and monitors. My ears are still ringing from it. It was like nothing any of us have ever heard before, and if we weren't onboard a spaceship, I probably would have rushed you to the emergency room. It wasn't even just the sound, Zar. Your face was cringing and changing color, and you were clenching your leg as if something were happening to it. None of us knew what to do, and it took us a minute to get you to wake up."

Zara shook her head in disbelief. "I had a bad dream is all," she reassured them. All four astronauts looked at her inquisitively. Zara asked for some space, and the team reluctantly respected her wishes. Everyone returned to their prior posts. Zara reached her hand into a bag and felt through several objects until she found her notebook and pencils. Though she kept a calm face to keep the others from worrying, she felt heavily uneased by the dream. She opened to the first clean page of her notebook and began to draw. Drawing had always been an escape for her and had also helped her to navigate her bad dreams. Seeing things on paper helped her feel that they were detached from her, as if she were pulling it from her mind and moving it to a new location, willing it to unburden her and not allowing it to exist in both places.

Hours passed, and Zara was finally finishing the drawing. She did not skip a fraction of detail in any of her drawings. She shaded them as if they were three dimensional and ready to evacuate the page. She reached back into her bag and swapped the notebook and pencils for a calendar. She looked longingly at the arrival date, which was still roughly six months out, and drew an "X" over the six days that had passed so far. She sighed heavily. For once, her mind was uncluttered. All she could think in that moment was that the trip was going to be long and tiresome.

Zara gazed around the room and found that Xavier and Jerome had fallen back asleep. Sadie was asleep now too. Zara felt uncomfortable when her eyes met Marquette's, as she realized Marquette had been staring at her, who knows for how long. Zara widened her eyes at Marquette, tilted her head forward, and raised her eyebrows, as if to silently inquire about this. Marquette did not pick up on the not-so-subtle hint and simply continued to stare.

"Can I help you?" Zara pressed impatiently.

"No," Marquette replied. She shook her head, rolled her eyes, and then disengaged eye contact. Before Zara could question her further, Marquette inserted an earplug in each of her ears, making sure to overexaggerate the gesture to make it obvious that she did not desire to further their communication, or better yet, lack thereof. She rolled onto her side and joined the others in sleep. Zara felt restless and had no plans to do the same. She decided to keep busy until the others awakened.

Zara began to go through the daily checklist, check the controls of the spaceship, and organize the food and clothing. Trying to drag out the task, Zara organized every food package by type, initially sorting them into proteins, vegetables, fruits, grains, and dairy. When the task was completed sooner than she imagined, she changed her mind and organized all the food packages alphabetically. After a couple of hours, Zara grew bored of the busy work and sat back down, reaching into her bag for something else to fill the time. She withdrew a portable DVD player and inserted the film *Gladiator* starring Russell Crowe. Something about this movie inspired her. Perhaps the sand on the floor of the Colosseum reminded her of the sand on the planet she was ready to encounter. Perhaps the persistence of Maximus reminded her of her own persistence through her faulty genetic potential and towards her dreams of traveling through space. Perhaps the strength of the Gladiators reminded her of the strength that not only she possessed, but also those closest to her.

As her mind wandered away from the images on the screen and she began to think about her sister, Zara noticed a faint and intermittent buzzing noise. With curiosity, she removed the portable DVD player from her lap and set it down gently beside her. After removing her headset, the buzzing noise sounded a little bit louder, but she couldn't pinpoint its location. She ran her fingers lightly across the controls, thinking something may be wrong with the wiring. As she bent down to check another panel, she realized the sound was coming from her bag. Realizing in that instant what was buzzing, Zara clasped the bag handles and yanked it onto her lap, already beginning to search through it before setting it down. Excited to finally hear from her sister, Zara clicked a button on the comm, anxiously awaiting the sound of Zidia's voice. She was taken aback when that wasn't the voice that came through the small speaker.

"Hello? Is this thing even fucking on? I've been trying you for days!" a flustered and annoyed voice crackled through the device.

"Oh... hi," Zara responded, struggling to cover up her lack of enthusiasm.

"Hi? Is that all you have to say to me? I think I deserve a little more of a response, don't you? Did you fuck anything up yet?"

Zara pressed the comm to her lips. She couldn't bring herself to respond. She hadn't planned to speak to Dimitri so soon after departing. She thought she'd have more time to think of what to say to him. Hesitant and scared, Zara decided not to respond at all. She couldn't help but wonder why Zidia had not been the first to try to reach her. Zara pressed a few buttons on the comm and listened to an intermittent beeping noise for ten minutes, hopeful that her sister would notice the notification and respond on the other end. She finally grew impatient and turned the comm to its rest mode. Reclining her chair and assuming the fetal position, Zara felt helpless and alone. As if Xavier had a sixth sense, he opened his eyes sleepily and looked toward Zara. His brows furrowed, and his gaze met hers. She quickly broke eye contact and buried her head against her knees. Within seconds, Xavier lay beside her and brushed his fingers through her hair. Zara felt comforted by his touch, and for the first time in a while, she slept soundly and blankly with not a single invasive dream interrupting her serenity.

The next few months dragged on slowly, and while the team was supportive of each other at heart, a heavy silence enveloped the spaceship and was seeming to last an eternity. Zara tried every day to reach Zidia, to no avail. Marquette no longer spoke a word of her family, and the hollow space they once filled for her became desolate and dark. Her chest physically ached with remorse for having left them, and her once heavy-set stature made her current emaciated appearance unrecognizable. Sadie no longer prided herself on her appearance and spent most of her days asleep in oversized clothes Jerome had lent to her when she guiltily admitted to having brought only skirts and form-fitting tops. Jerome draped a thin blanket over Sadie every day when she dozed off. Regardless that she had never returned his affection, he couldn't help but look after her. Xavier kept his distance from Zara, knowing it was better off that way when she was deep in thought. These days, not a second passed when Zara was not deep in thought.

Zara began to sleep comm in hand each night, desperately hoping for her sister to contact her. Her worry was beginning to spiral out of control, and negative thoughts circled torturously in her mind. *What if something happened to her? What if she is dead? She would never take this long to respond to me. What if she resents me for leaving?* Zara picked up the comm and pressed a few buttons, only to receive a failure tone indicating lack of signal. Just as she went to set the comm down, dispirited, it began to buzz against her fingertips. Zara lost herself in thought once again. *Am I hallucinating? Will it be Zidia, or Dimitri trying to contact me?* Initially feeling eager, she now hesitantly pressed a button on the comm.

"Zar?" a quiet and shaky voice asked. Zara suddenly saw her sister sitting across from her in the spaceship, and the four other astronauts disappeared.

"Zidi..." Zara gasped for air and couldn't bring herself to speak through her swollen throat and tears. She blinked her eyes rapidly, shifting her gaze back and forth between Zidia's face that she continued to hallucinate just an arm's length away and the comm she had set on her lap.

"Zara," Zidia's voice grew softer and fainter. "I've been trying to reach you, but this damn thing hasn't been working. Is there any truth to what I've been seeing on the news?"

"I miss you," Zara whispered back, speaking only to the hallucination.

"Zara, answer me!" Zidia softly pleaded. "Is there something wrong with the..."

Zara continued to gaze at her sister and grew confused, as her sister's lips pursed together without completing the sentence. Having witnessed this interaction, the four other astronauts grew concerned, both for Zara's present state of consciousness and the thoughts that infiltrated their minds regarding Zidia's incomplete warning. Zara furrowed her brows as she saw a hand waving in front of her face, blocking her sister from view. She slowly turned her head, and as if a blurry camera were being focused, Xavier came back into view. Zara glanced back to where her sister had been, only to find an empty chair.

"Why didn't she tell me she misses me?" Zara inquired to no one in particular. "Does she resent me for leaving?"

She scratched her head in confusion, and Xavier gently guided her with a hand on each of her shoulders to lie her down on her back. "Come back to me, Zara," Xavier said, with a tone more indicative of a gentle command than a request. Zara looked into his eyes and awaited clarification. "When your sister was reaching out to you on the comm, she mentioned new information she had seen on the news and asked you if there is truth to it. It sounded like she was warning us. Do you think this has to do with the glitch in the radar system that we found out about before departing?" Zara closed her eyes. "Zara!" Xavier exclaimed impatiently.

"I'm with you. I'm just thinking."

"Well think faster, because we've been out here three months, and if that's what she was referring to, we are running out of time to figure this out and change our trajectory."

Zara didn't feel pressed for time. She felt frozen in it. She needed something to propel her forward, and what better way to make strides toward a future goal than letting go of the past? Disregarding complaints from the four other astronauts about her dismissive attitude and behavior, Zara picked the comm back up and pressed a few buttons. The complaints from her counterparts ceased, as the team grew relieved and thankful that Zara was making an attempt to get ahold of Zidia again and find out more information about what was being reported back at home. To their dismay, a man's voice came through the comm.

"Hey, Dimitri," Zara clearly enunciated with newfound confidence. The team listened in, eagerly anticipating that she would bring up the topic of the news reports to Dimitri.

"Zara, are you a fucking idiot?"

*That line would normally make me wince,* Zara thought to herself. "No," she replied smugly.

"What's with the fucking attitude? How could you spend months not getting in touch with me and then have the audacity to..."

Zara pressed a button on the comm and cut him off. "It's my turn to talk." Dimitri's shock at Zara's forcefulness and bravery led him to be uncharacteristically silent. "I don't need you anymore, Dimitri," Zara started. "I never needed you. I just needed to shut you up about my condition long enough for me to get into space, and now you can do all the talking you want, and it won't matter. I'm three months out, and now achieving my dream is inevitable. You won't ever hold me back again." Zara spoke to Dimitri as if the others couldn't hear a word. None of them knew about her condition, and they were waiting even more eagerly now for clarification on this than they had been regarding Zidia's warning. Zara continued, "You can consider this my resignation from our relationship." Before Dimitri could reply, Zara clicked a button, temporarily disabling the comm.

Jerome opened his mouth to speak, but instead of words coming out, his jaw dropped, his eyes grew wide, and he reached out for Marquette's arm to gain balance. The other astronauts similarly reached out for the closest object or person to become stable. The spaceship jolted back and forth, emitted ear-piercing noises, and shook violently. The astronauts relentlessly resisted the jolts of the spaceship, as well as their own fear and imbalance. Zara helped Sadie get to her seat and secure the seatbelt before getting to her own chair. Jerome helped Xavier and Marquette get to their seats before taking his. Silence no longer existed amongst the team. Everyone shouted to each other words that could not be heard over the low-pitch rumbling and high-pitch squeals of the spaceship. Visible from each of the chairs was a circular window, nearly a meter long in diameter. Everyone glued their eyes to the window attentively from their seats. Bright flashes and streaks of color sped in and out of view. It was not long before the spaceship stabilized again.

Zara lifted her hand, silently signaling the others to stay seated. She hesitantly unbuckled her own seatbelt and secured the fasteners on her space suit. She stood up, feeling dizzy and disoriented as she looked out the window. "We're here!" she exclaimed.

"What? How is that possible?" Marquette demanded.

"We have only been traveling three months," Sadie reiterated.

Zara looked out the window with the same confusion the others were verbally expressing, but she knew what Mars looked like, at least in pictures and satellite views. "Prepare for landing," Zara commanded.

Zara sat back down by the control panel and re-fastened her seatbelt. The team did their safety checks, secured their space suits and oxygen tanks, and began manipulating the controls of the spaceship for landing. Zara took a deep breath. In a matter of minutes, her dream would come to fruition.

3

# A WARPED PERSPECTIVE

THE SECOND MY FOOT touched the sand, I knew it was all wrong. I shot a glance back towards the others, hoping their presence would mitigate my fears. It did not. The team anxiously awaited my signal. I looked around at a desert-like terrain and could not see much more than three meters out in any direction. A thick smog enveloped our surroundings.

"Zara?" Sadie quietly requested my attention, but when I turned around, she was speechless.

"Where are we?" Jerome spoke the words she couldn't say.

"I... I don't know." The whole team looked at me for guidance, and instead of providing it to them, I replayed the last thirty minutes in my mind over and over again, each time hoping I was currently hallucinating the outcome. I couldn't help but think that this was my fault. If I hadn't been so damn preoccupied with standing up to Dimitri and had just focused on our mission, we would have still been on our way to Mars and not... *No*, I thought to myself. *This can't be happening.*

Marquette interrupted my thoughts. "I thought you were leading this mission," she scoffed, "some leader."

I paid her jab no attention, as through the smog, I began to see the faint outline of a tree. I stared in awe. I couldn't help but chuckle, and my chuckle quickly turned to uncontrollable laughter.

"What's so funny?" Xavier inquired.

I withdrew my drawing pad from my satchel, flipped through a few pages, and handed it to him. I was laughing so hard that tears welled up in my eyes. It's likely those tears began to form more as a result of fear than amusement. As he looked intensely at the drawing, my laughter faded, and I looked at him helplessly, longing for him to ease my fears.

"I don't get it. What am I looking at?" he asked.

I pointed ahead. Xavier squinted in the direction of the tree, and his eyes widened. He handed the drawing pad to the others. They took turns looking at it with expressions of amazement and terror before handing it back to me. There was no question I had drawn a tree of a species foreign to Earth. I drew it from a dream, and here it was, haunting my reality. Suddenly I felt dizzy and disoriented.

"I don't feel so..." Before I could finish my sentence, my knees collapsed, and I couldn't resist closing my eyes. I'm not sure how many moments passed before they re-opened.

When I came to, I was lying on my back on a bed of sand. There were seven silhouettes surrounding me, four of which seemed recognizable. As I blinked repeatedly, they came into focus. Sadie, Marquette, Jerome, and Xavier were no longer wearing their space suits and did not have their oxygen tanks. I quickly looked down at my attire to see that mine too had been removed. I scanned three unfamiliar faces in confusion and terror. They did not look like my own. Their skin was tanned and wrinkled, their eyebrows were much thicker, and all three of them were bald. One had more feminine characteristics with a slimmer stature, longer eyelashes, and reddened cheeks. All three were wearing black fabric wraps around their torso and what appeared to be russet cargo pants. I tried to propel myself up into a sitting position, but the feminine looking one placed a hand on my shoulder and told me to take it easy. She explained that they already have enough clatofor and that over-exposure led to me passing out. I looked to my crew for further clarification.

"They call oxygen 'clatofor'," Jerome informed me.

"Where are we?" I asked to no one in particular.

"Suvia," a native responded. "As Kalari mentioned, you will need to take it easy getting up. But you do need to hurry. We have informed your crew that we must get you quickly to our base before the others obtain sight of you. My name is Tavion. I am sorry I cannot tell any of you much more yet, but please trust me, it is in your best interest to follow." Tavion extended his first two fingers, signaling the others to move forward. Kalari and the other native followed Tavion without hesitation. I slowly adjusted myself upright to do the same, noticing in the process that the gravitational force seemed oddly identical to that of Earth. Sadie, Xavier, and Jerome followed behind me. After pacing forward several meters, I glanced back for a head count and noticed that Marquette was trailing behind. No, staying behind.

"Please go check on her," I whispered to Sadie, knowing I would only aggravate Marquette if I walked back in her direction. Sadie jogged toward Marquette and was back beside me just seconds later.

"She wants to stay with the ship," Sadie informed me. Despite our orders to stick together as a unit on this mission, I couldn't help but find relief in her absence. I shrugged my shoulders and playfully nudged Sadie with my elbow. She looked at me sternly and shook her head. "Nothing about this is right, Zar."

My humor faded. "I know."

Following Tavion with suspicion, I took note of every detail. I silently wished I could draw the curvature of Tavion's face, the outline of Kalari's hand, and the bizarre cloud formation overhead. The clouds were a faded grey strewn out across a light orange sky, which blended into blood red at the horizon. Each cloud stretched in a uniform shape far across the sky. I was still convinced this was all a hallucination that I would snap out of any minute now.

"I need you to do something for me," I whispered to Xavier. Kalari glanced back at me. Xavier and I kept our eyes straight ahead and our mouths shut until she reverted her attention back to Tavion. Xavier looked at me inquisitively. "Please wake me up," I pleaded.

Xavier put his hand on my back affectionately. "I have been begging the others to do the same for myself. None of us can get a grip on this. A couple hours ago, none of this was known to exist. Who knows what happens next or where they are leading us..." Xavier trailed off on a pessimistic note. Minutes went by with no conversation before he added, as if continuing without pause, "But I am here for you."

I refused to let the tears welling up in my eyes fall past my lashes. I didn't want Xavier to know how scared and helpless

I was feeling. I didn't want anyone to know. I quickened my pace to move away from Xavier until I was side by side with the unknown native. It took me a moment to conjure up the words I wanted to say to him. *Him?* I wondered, unsure if he should be referred to as a man. I visually scanned the native and reaffirmed that they definitely looked more masculine than Kalari. *But that is by Earth's standards*, I reminded myself.

"What is your name?" I finally mustered up the courage to speak to them, but they did not respond nor look in my direction.

Kalari overheard. "That's Miravi. Don't worry about him. He's more worried about your presence here than you all are. He's what you would call on your planet 'superstitious'. He believes that your presence will bring us nothing but harm." She looked back at Sadie, scanned her outfit condescendingly, and added, "I'd say at least some of you are incapable."

"We didn't come here to fight," I retorted.

"Then what did you come here for?" Kalari asked.

We didn't want to come here, I wanted to reply. I chose not to tell her this, as the explanation in my mind wasn't suitable. How could I tell her we selfishly wanted to land on another planet simply to claim it as a discovery and accomplishment? How could I explain that we were hoping for and expecting it to be uninhabited? *No*, I thought to myself, *I better keep my mouth shut.*

"We came here to meet you." I spoke the words without thinking, and Kalari looked at me skeptically.

"How did you know about us?"

*Great*, I thought to myself, *now I don't have any explanation, suitable or not.*

"We knew about you from a device we have on Earth," Jerome chimed in, noticing my hesitation. "It's called a telescope."

Kalari looked baffled. "Tell me more about this device."

"It allows you to see other planets," Sadie informed her. "We noticed movement and some Earth-like features on yours and wanted to make contact, but we had no way to do so other than to come here."

Tavion lifted his arm into the air, with his forearm at a ninety-degree angle from his bicep, and he made a fist. We followed Kalari and Miravi's lead by halting. Dead silence ensued. We stood there on edge for what felt like ten minutes. All of a sudden, a blast of air terminated the silence, and an incredible gust of wind to the right of me knocked me off of my feet. My knees collapsed, and I fell to the ground, landing in a crawling position. The sand in the air formed a cloud, and the cloud intruded my lungs, making it hard to breathe. I coughed violently and could hear some of the others doing the same. When I looked up, Tavion was standing in what looked like a boxer's fighting stance, but he had a small sharp object protruding from one of his fists. The gust of wind came back with equal force, but this time, it was to my left and blowing in the opposite direction. I waited on my hands and knees for it to pass and then quickly rose to my feet.

When I got to my feet and swiped my hands hard across my pants to remove a residual layer of dust, I slowly looked up, and my eyes met a pair of eyes four times the size of mine. A creature stood in front of us panting. Its mouth hung open, exposing sharp teeth and a black tongue. Its long brown fur spiked out in multiple directions. Its height exceeded mine by four. I had never fought anything back on Earth. I had never used a weapon. I had never felt as helpless as I did now, looking into the eyes of a creature that could take one step and squish me like an ant. This feeling was short-lived, as no more than a few seconds after the creature stilled in a stand-off with Tavion, the sharp object that had been protruding from Tavion's fist cut rapidly through the air and punctured the creature's neck. Tavion protectively extended both of his arms with open hands and took two steps backward, causing us to move further back with him. The creature's fall was loud and shook the ground. Tavion walked quickly up to the creature, scanned our surroundings, and then knelt to withdraw the sharp object from the creature's neck. He wiped both sides of the blade on his pants and inserted it into a casing. He then withdrew a longer blade from a pocket and firmly pierced it into the creature's stomach. He dragged the blade slowly, with veins in his head bulging, demonstrating the difficulty of the task. After about fifteen minutes, he had sliced a large square of flesh from the creature's stomach and removed the layer of skin and fur.

"Sklovak!" His tone was demanding. Kalari opened a large bag she had been carrying and held it out in front of him, allowing him to place the chunk of flesh and the pelt inside of it. She closed the bag and slung it over her shoulder. Tavion motioned us forward.

"Kliskon?" Kalari softly spoke.

"Lestikon." Tavion replied.

The two of them continued to speak only to each other, in a language that my crew and I did not understand. I took note of our surroundings as we walked on, noticing more trees and plants that were nonexistent on Earth. I noticed that the clouds were now darkening, and the sky was becoming a more vibrant orange. Bright lights in the sky were emerging, and I wondered what they were. I opened my mouth to ask but stopped myself to listen to their foreign words.

"Tiskon lest klast klestinon." Miravi had joined in on their conversation. Sadie, Jerome, and Xavier seemed to share my feeling of exclusion based on their silence.

"Este planeta es terrible," I said to Xavier half-heartedly. If they were going to exclude us, I wanted to exclude them.

"No tienes idea," Miravi replied, speaking directly to me for the first time.

"You speak Spanish too?" I gasped. "How do you all know our languages?"

"We've been watching you too," Miravi informed me.

*Too?* I questioned to myself, before recalling our fib.

"We watch videos every day, chart patterns, and teach our young," Miravi continued.

"Why?" I asked.

"To be better," Tavion replied briskly.

"You want to be better than us?"

"No," Kalari cut in. "We want to be better than the others on Suvia."

I was speechless. *Who are the others?* I thought. *What are the others?* The entire group walked in silence the rest of the way until we arrived at what looked like a tall fence made of tree branches. It looked like there was no way to get through it. The smell of smoke in the air and the thin cloud rising above the fence brought a familiarity that instantly felt calming to me. A bonfire. My mind flashed back to when I used to have bonfires with Zidia in our backyard, and I suddenly felt achingly homesick.

"This way," Tavion urged. I didn't realize I was lagging behind. I jogged ahead to the others, and we all followed a path downhill that led to a large boulder.

"Sklovak," Tavion said to Miravi. I remembered him using the same word prior to Kalari's assistance earlier. I assumed this must be some translation of asking for help, as Miravi joined Tavion in pushing the boulder. When the boulder was pushed aside, an underground pathway was exposed. Xavier began to enter. Tavion quickly threw an open hand at Xavier's chest.

"No!" Tavion commanded angrily.

"They don't know." Kalari calmed him. She turned to Xavier. "You must never walk ahead of a leader unless you have obtained permission. That's true for us and the others."

"I apologize," Xavier replied.

*I apologize?* I looked at Xavier inquisitively. I had never heard him speak so formally. He must have been really shaken up. Granted, Tavion was 193 centimeters, in comparison to Xavier's 173.

Tavion proceeded to lead us through a narrow underground tunnel, just wide enough for two people to walk side by side, and only a few centimeters taller than Tavion's head. The tunnel was dimly lit by lanterns along the cave wall.

"How you holding up?" I whispered to Sadie and Jerome.

"I remember the way back to the spaceship," Jerome spoke, as if he had been waiting to say the words for days. "Let's turn around now and go home." He looked desperately at Sadie.

"I don't think that's a good idea," Sadie insisted, looking nervously at Tavion.

"How can we think to turn back now?" I added. "We'd have no way to ever contact them again. Anyways, do we even know how to get back?" I said the words before processing their meaning. *If we weren't sure what happened to cause our arrival on this planet, how could we reverse it to get back to Earth? Miravi had told us they have been watching us. Do they know the way?* I was lost in thought once more.

At the end of the tunnel, we encountered another boulder. Tavion and Miravi pushed this boulder forward and then to the side in unison. Suddenly my vision of this planet was drastically altered. Bright green grass, vibrant fruit trees, light tan tents, and tan-skinned natives to the planet were instantly exposed. Foreign chatter filled the air, along with laughter and more smoke than we had been able to see above the outer fence.

"You must not look directly into an Oranian man's eyes," Tavion firmly stated, making eye contact with me and Sadie. He turned to Xavier and Jerome. "You must stand and track the environment whenever in the presence of an Oranian woman."

"Oranian?" Jerome questioned.

"It is a name by which we refer to ourselves in the Klaysta tribe," Tavion clarified.

"That's where I draw the line," I protested. "I am a strong woman. I can track the environment for myself, and I will be damned if I act shameful in the presence of a man."

Tavion walked towards me and planted his feet on the ground, with his shoes nearly touching mine. I wanted to reach out and touch one of his muscles to confirm they were real. His veins were dark and bulgy, creating visible patterns along his arms. His arms had a constant curvature that I started to mindlessly trace with my eyes. I suddenly noticed my crew and a few of the natives staring, and I self-consciously straightened my shoulders, not nearly matching the intimidating stature in front of me.

"Yes?" I tried not to stutter and purposefully looked into Tavion's eyes to defy his attempts to minimize me based on my gender. For the first time, I noticed that the whites of his eyes were tainted with a light red.

"I don't know exactly how things are on your planet," Tavion's voice boomed, and more natives drew closer attentively, both in awe of our presence and intrigued by the interaction, "but here on ours, you either fit in or you're escorted out. The latter option will not be pleasant for you."

"I'll see myself out," I snapped, beginning to turn back toward the tunnel we entered through. I felt like an idiot when I realized the boulder had been returned to its prior position. I looked at Xavier and Jerome and nodded my head toward the boulder. Jerome looked down at his feet, and Xavier shook his head no. "Ugh..." I groaned. "I will not act shameful around a man," I stated boldly as I walked back toward Tavion. An image of Dimitri flashed in my mind. I was done being shameful.

Tavion drew closer to me and spoke more quietly, and if I wasn't mistaken, with a slight seductiveness in his tone. "Here, a man is a protector," he informed me. "His purpose is to serve his own kind and take care of his family. He does not consider his woman to be less valuable of a being, but differently valuable. She's responsible for nurture and growth of the community. She's a protector of the home when the man leaves to hunt. She's the strategy behind the kill." I looked at Tavion's chest, which was level with my face, and I silently reminded myself to breathe. I didn't dare look into his eyes. My heart was racing. *Strategy behind the kill?* I questioned to myself. *Who says something like that?* I couldn't tell if his words were seducing death or seducing me. He put his hand on the back of my neck, as if responding to my thought. "Look into my eyes," he commanded.

I put my hand on his and suddenly felt like I belonged here, in this community, on this planet, abiding by strange rules, and surrendering to a man's power. "Look into my eyes," Tavion repeated.

I shook my head and looked down at the ground. Tavion removed his hand from my neck and used it to lift my chin. "You misunderstand. You must hold your head high and demonstrate the same level of power as any man here, but you must do it with respect and without challenge to theirs."

"I hate to interrupt," Sadie spoke nervously, "but I really need a restroom." Startled by the sound of her voice, my eyes jolted in Sadie's direction, and I breathed deeply. It had felt like Tavion and I were alone for a few moments, and I was quickly reminded that we were surrounded by a community of beings. Tavion did not seem to have forgotten.

"This way." Kalari motioned for me and the others to follow her, and I glanced at Tavion who was clearly staying put.

"We part for now," Tavion stated. "Kalari will show you where you can settle in."

"Are we really going to spend a night here?" I overheard Jerome ask Xavier.

"Unless you have a better idea," Xavier replied. I could hear the exhaustion in their voices, and it made me realize how fatigued I was feeling.

"You will be requested to help with chores in the morning," Kalari spoke to all of us. "No one is allowed into our community without providing a contribution to it." I listened, but my eyes and mind wandered. So many natives were staring at us as we walked along the dirt path behind Kalari. We passed by many tents and campfires. The smell of cooked meat began to make me salivate.

"Will we eat?" I asked.

"Families here share food with each other individually," Kalari explained. "You two will need to learn to hunt," she informed Jerome and Xavier. "You can join Tavion tomorrow. He will teach you. For tonight, you can all join my family: Me, Tavion, and our two young."

I couldn't decipher my bitterness upon learning that Tavion and Kalari were together. *Am I jealous?* I thought to myself judgmentally. *How could I be jealous that a man I just met on a foreign planet has a family?* I drowned out the noise around me with my own thoughts until we reached an exceedingly small tent.

"Look lady, the four of us are not going to fit in there," I scoffed.

Kalari looked at me and leaned closer to Xavier. "Is she always this defensive?"

Xavier nodded. "She's very headstrong."

"Headstrong?" Kalari asked.

"Determined and stubborn," he clarified.

"Ah, she'll do well here," Kalari chuckled. I couldn't tell if she was being sarcastic.

"Still have to pee," Sadie reminded us.

"We don't have... What are they called..." Kalari scratched her head and furrowed her eyebrows.

"Toilets?" Jerome asked.

"Yes, thank you," Kalari continued. "We don't have toilets." She nodded her head at a large tree nearby. "You can relieve yourself behind any tree like that if it is distant enough from the nearest tent. Do not relieve yourself near a bush or fruit tree." Sadie hurried and concealed herself behind the tree. I waited impatiently. When Sadie returned, Kalari requested us to follow her into the tent. I followed behind her, annoyed and skeptic, mumbling snide comments under my breath regarding the size of the tent.

Kalari chuckled at my comments and pointed to a dirt staircase, leading underground beneath the tent. We started in single file down the stairs. When my foot touched the dirt floor, I looked around. The room was well lit by the same yellow lanterns that had aligned the wall in the cave we walked through earlier. There was a wooden table with wooden chairs, as well as a few sleeping pouches hung up on the wall by a protruding object. "You will sleep here," Kalari stated.

Despite the disappointment of sleeping in a pouch on the hard floor of an underground room, the area looked homey, and I was happy that I would be in close proximity to my crew overnight. I looked at Xavier and nodded in approval.

"Will you be joining us for food?" Kalari asked.

"I'm starving. Count me in," Jerome quickly replied.

I hesitated. "What will we be eating?"

"Velteis." Kalari turned toward the stairs and began to walk up. "Tavion killed it earlier."

An image of the large beast Tavion slaughtered made me shiver. "Beggars can't be choosers," I mumbled sarcastically, following the others up the stairs. When I exited the tent, I walked into Jerome, who was staring upward intensely. "Sorry..." I began to apologize for my collision but was caught off guard when I followed his gaze and looked into the black night sky. Seven large, bright, moon-like circles illuminated the night, and I quickly became overcome with unease.

"This way," Kalari urged.

4

# DISCONNECTED

M ARQUETTE OPENED HER EYES wearily to a still darkness. She closed them and rolled over sluggishly to put her arm around her husband. Her arm fell over the side of the small bed, and she jolted awake. Sitting up, she couldn't see a thing. She patted around at her surroundings in an attempt to turn on a light. Suddenly, reality set in that she was still on board the spaceship, and she hit a button on the control panel to her left, effectively illuminating the whole compartment. Memories flooded back to her. Quick flashes of light. Jerome grabbing her arm. Loud and abrupt noises. An unexpected landing. *What time is it?* she thought to herself.

Unbeknownst to Marquette, she had not slept through the night. Unbeknownst to Marquette, her crew had not slept at all yet. Hunger pangs influenced her to think selfishly, not wasting time on a single thought about the others and not worrying about preserving their food supply. She opened a couple packages of peanut butter, a package of green beans, and three packages of dried strawberries. She scarfed the food down quickly and then finished her meal with two packages of corn. After appeasing her stomach, she sat down on a bed and thought for a minute. *How long was I out?* she thought. *Did the crew just leave me here?* She longed to go home and see her family. The thought of returning to Earth motivated her to formulate a plan to find the others. Afterall, she couldn't man the spaceship alone and had no clue how to route them back after their mishap.

Marquette threw four packages of green beans, four packages of peanut butter, and three packages of granola into a bag, along with two water bottles, a flashlight, and a thin blanket. As she was doing a few final checks for needed items and securing the spaceship, she caught sight of a dull gold object on the control panel. The comm. *Zara must have left this behind in a hurry to evacuate*, Marquette pondered. She added it to the supplies in her bag.

Walking out of the spaceship, Marquette anticipated daylight but was alarmed to see seven bright lights contrasting with pitch blackness instead. She contemplated postponing her search for the others but decided against it, in part for fear of their safety, and in part for the eagerness of getting them back on board the spaceship to permit her to return home to her family. She set her bag on the ground and searched blindly for her flashlight. She tied her bag tight and slung it over her shoulder. When she clicked the button on her flashlight, she looked out in all directions but could only see so far, and every spot looked the same. Sand and darkness. The illumination in the sky was a vast improvement from nighttime on Earth, but Earth had streetlamps and building lights. Suvia was devoid of those luxuries.

Marquette took only a few steps before realizing she was taking a huge risk leaving the spaceship at night. She would likely not be able to return to it if she desired or needed, as it would be impossible to find again in the dark. *Will I be able to find my way back tomorrow?* she wondered. She debated whether she should leave a food trail that she could follow back with a flashlight but chuckled at the idea and regarded herself as a fool for thinking of it. She would quickly run out of food and have no trail left to follow, in addition to possibly attracting animals if there were any on this planet and depleting her supply of sustenance. She shook her head and slowly progressed forward into the night.

Meanwhile, the Oranian's grouped themselves by family around campfires, with Tavion and Kalari inviting Zara, Jerome, Xavier, and Sadie to join them and their two young. Zara couldn't keep her eyes off Tavion. She couldn't put her finger on it, but there was something mysterious about him. Sadie had never paid special attention to Jerome but was beginning to lean on him both figuratively and literally. She had spoken quietly to him throughout the night about her worries and rested her head on his shoulder when they sat down on a tree trunk next to the fire. Xavier was not saying much, but he was taking it all in and constantly glancing at Zara to make sure she was getting through this. With each glance, his eyes met hers. He could tell she was dazed and distracted, and he couldn't blame her. He was feeling the same way. He knew she cared deeply about him and that the bonds of their friendship were tied tighter than any foreign planet could unravel. She just had a different way of showing it. He smiled at Zara and felt comfort in his confidence that she would be alright. He felt confident that the whole team would be alright, although his thoughts drifted to Marquette, and he shivered at the thought of having left her behind.

"Should we send a search party for Marquette?" He spoke his thoughts to Zara, who was still lost in thought about Tavion. "Zara," he commanded her attention, after a while of no reply.

"Huh?" She slowly turned her head toward him.

"I want a couple of us to go look for Marquette," he insisted.

"No way," Zara snapped. "None of us know the terrain. Are you trying to get us killed?"

"I'm trying to keep us together, Zar, something that we should have been more careful to do in the first place," he urged, while accepting a chunk of meat off a wooden tray Kalari held out to him.

"She chose to stay, Xavier." Zara had no interest in discussing the matter further, but Xavier pressed on.

"Fine, I'll just go look for her."

"Absolutely not." Zara's tone grew harsh. "If she wants to get herself killed, fine. I will not let you make the same mistake. She's probably safer than we are right now, on board our secure ship, just waiting for us to eventually return... which we will."

"This isn't debatable, Zara. Right after this meal, I'm going to go look for her." Xavier took a bite out of the meat, and his eyes opened wide in shock. It was unlike anything they had on Earth. More flavorful than a gourmet meal by fivefold, a thin, warm, salty fluid ran down his throat with each bite. He terminated the conversation by constantly refilling his mouth with more of the meat.

Zara reluctantly took a bite. Astounded by the burst of flavor, she joined the others in silently devouring the helping given to her and then requested more, nearly immediately wishing she could take back that request.

"Kleistivok!" Tavion's voice boomed. He was so suddenly displeased with Zara's request for another helping that he instinctively responded to her in his native tongue. "This is a selfish act, and here we do not take a step in any direction without thinking of the impact that will have on our family."

"I just figured I wasn't taking from anyone," Zara replied. She felt ashamed but skeptical as she looked around and saw that everyone around the fire had an equivalent portion of the meat.

"Our leftovers go to other families," Tavion explained more warmly. "Some are ill. Some were unable to hunt successfully. Some do not have enough to provide for their whole family."

"Kalari said each person fairly contributes," Zara retorted, again with almost immediate regret.

"You will hunt tomorrow," Tavion snapped, "and you will not stop hunting until you have enough meat to feed every child, every elder who is too old to acquire their own food, and every member of this community who is ill. Understood?"

Kalari knew better than to question Tavion but was caught off guard by his demand. "Oranian women do not hunt," she countered.

"This woman is not Oranian!" Tavion slammed his hand on a wooden plate, which only contained a few scraps of meat and the deep auburn liquid that seeped out of it. "She will hunt, and she will hunt all day, into the night if that's what it takes."

"I have no problem doing my part," Zara softly replied. "May I be excused? I'd like to get some rest before the long day of work ahead of me."

Tavion grunted and consumed his last bite of the Velteis before acknowledging her request. "I will wake you in the morning."

"Looking forward to it," Zara mumbled as she walked away.

Xavier was the first to break the silence that ensued after Zara walked away. "I don't mean to cross a line here by saying this..."

"Then say nothing at all," Tavion barked.

Xavier continued as if he hadn't heard Tavion's remark, "But can you please not be so harsh with Zara? She has been through a lot, and we are all shaken up to be here, in a place we didn't know existed until earlier today and had no intention of coming to." In speaking from the heart, he slipped information he did not mean to.

Kalari rose to her feet and looked down at Xavier with disgust. "What did you just say?"

"I asked him to ease up," Xavier replied confidently.

"After that."

"I said we are all shaken up to be here."

Kalari shook her head. "You said you didn't know we existed and that you had no intention to be here."

"That too."

"So, your friends lied about viewing us from Earth. What is your purpose here?" Kalari was fuming.

"We have none." Xavier was brutally honest. "We wanted to get to a presumably unoccupied planet called Mars."

"To occupy it?" Kalari asked curiously.

"To claim it as an achievement," Xavier corrected. "To be the first humans to set foot on it."

"Is this a game to you? Coming to other planets for your own selfish desires..."

It was clear that Kalari was not finished with her accusations and judgments, but Xavier interjected. "We intended to come to one other planet, and we intended to do it selflessly to give the people on our planet hope that we are more than what we have been confined to and that we can surpass limits in a way that was once thought to be impossible." He didn't realize it, but he was speaking for himself. The others had their own reasons for trying to be one of the first astronauts on Mars.

"I don't want them here," Kalari spoke to Tavion, without looking directly at him.

"They need protection," he uttered.

"Then let someone else protect them." She walked away and ducked under the flap of a nearby tent.

"What's going to happen to us," Sadie asked with tears welling up in her eyes.

"She'll come around," Tavion insisted. "We will offer you protection until you leave to return to Earth."

Jerome looked at Tavion and Kalari's children, sitting on the other side of the fire next to Tavion. "Do they speak?"

"Their English is not so good yet. They must learn hunting and defense before we dive deeper into languages," Tavion explained. "Tell our Earth friends hi," he playfully teased. He smirked for the first time since the crew had arrived.

"Hi," they said in unison. Jerome silently tried to gauge their age based on their height and vocal tone and guessed that they were the Earth equivalent of six and eight years old.

"I need to get them to bed." Tavion stood. "Do you know the way back to your tent?"

Jerome nodded. He was the best with direction. Tavion departed with his children into the same tent Kalari had entered. Sadie warmed her hands over the fire.

"Shall we?" Jerome asked.

"Can we sit here a moment longer?" Sadie asked. "After a long and stressful day, it is so peaceful."

"Just for a minute," Xavier agreed. "I do want to get to bed soon though... Oh, wait... What about Marquette?"

"Better to search for her in the morning when we can see our way more effectively," Jerome stated. "I will come with you tomorrow to look for her."

After a few minutes, Jerome led the way back to their designated tent, and they all descended the stairs. Zara was fast asleep in a sleeping pouch already laid out on the ground. Xavier grabbed a sleeping pouch that was hung up on the cave wall and laid it down beside hers. Sadie and Jerome followed suit. It was not long before Sadie and Jerome fell asleep. Xavier lay on his back, staring up at the cave ceiling. He couldn't stop worrying about the others, wondering if Zara would be successful at hunting, wondering if they would be able to find Marquette, and wondering if he would be able to offer his team the protection that they deserved. His eyes finally closed.

While the others began to rest, Marquette was still amid a desert-like terrain searching for them. She shined her flashlight in every direction, but each step and each direction looked no different from the next. She felt she had been walking for hours and at this point was losing hope. Just as she was ready to sit down on the ground to rest, which she had already done countless times, she shined the flashlight to her right and noticed a pile of stacked tree branches that rose higher than her head. A dark silhouette was traveling quickly along the top branch. Before Marquette could make out what it was and think to depart, it jumped off the branch and landed beside her. Marquette blinked rapidly, sure that she was hallucinating, but the image of the man in front of her did not change or vanish. She wrapped her arms tightly around him and began to sob into his shoulder. She was far too relieved to see her husband to question how he had ended up there. "Our children?" she asked. The man stayed silent in their embrace.

5

# A Familiar Stranger

MARQUETTE COULDN'T BRING HERSELF to let go, but she was unnerved by the silence that followed her question. "Damon?" His silence continued. Marquette ran her hands along her husband's back, admiring the familiar curvature as she pulled away. Her confusion and worries persisted, but she began to relax her posture and adjust her tone with a newfound calmness. "Where are Elijah and Emilee?" she asked again.

"Come with me. I have a surprise for you," he responded. His voice sounded a little off and slightly higher in pitch than normal, but Marquette was too happy to see him and too preoccupied with the whereabouts of her children to pay mind to it.

"Are the kids here too?" Marquette asked.

He looked at Marquette inquisitively before responding. "The kids have missed you all day," he replied.

"I've missed them too." Marquette wiped her eyes of the tears that were beginning to well up again. "Can we go see them?"

"Yes, come with me," he urged, holding out his hand.

Marquette followed him around the perimeter of the stacked tree branches. It was so dark that she almost tripped a few times not being able to see her way, and each time, her husband tugged at her arm urgently. It seemed like they had been walking a while before they came to a halt. He looked like he wanted to tell her something but was speechless. He pointed at the top branch.

"Honey, what are we doing? I'm tired. I want to see the kids," Marquette pleaded. He shook his head and made climbing motions with his hands. "I hope you don't think I'm climbing these trees..." Marquette glared at him with frustration. He began to climb and looked down at her after a few strides toward the top branch. "Absolutely not," she reiterated. He continued to climb until he reached the top and sat on top of the highest branch looking down at her. Marquette raised her voice. "Damon! Come back down here, please!" It was no use. Desperate for answers and to make sure her children were okay, she began to climb. The wooden branches felt scratchy and were cool to the touch. Her feet ached with each movement, after already experiencing a long night of walking. "I can't do this," Marquette cried when she got about halfway to the top branch. She felt alarmed by how much distance there already seemed to be between her and the ground.

"Come on," he urged.

Marquette put her forehead against the branch, feeling drained and defeated. "I can't," she repeated.

"Be brave," Damon called down.

She lifted her head back up, tiredly shook it, sighed, and continued toward the top. When she reached Damon, she sat next to him to catch her breath. "I haven't seen you in months, and you haven't even given me a kiss," she stated with a winded voice. She chuckled playfully but felt genuinely annoyed at his reaction to seeing her after such a long time apart. It wasn't like him. Normally, coming home from one day of work was enough reason for him to wrap his arms tightly around her and become overcome with romantic and passionate gestures. "I deserve a kiss after you put me through that." Her voice became quiet with self-doubt as she began to wonder if he lost his attraction to her during the time away. Damon looked down at his hands as if contemplating something, and after an uncomfortable pause, he reached one hand out to her face and brought his lips to hers. His kiss felt different than she remembered. His lips tasted different. She pulled away and squinted at him.

"Let's go," he said, pointing to what looked roughly like a staircase made of tree branches. It led straight down to the ground on the other side. Marquette was relieved to see she wouldn't have to climb down. She hadn't even thought about that factor on her way up. Marquette grew suspicious of Damon's peculiarity. *This is my husband,* she silently reminded herself, slowly regaining her trust in him. She followed him down. Upon her shoes touching the grass on the other side, she looked around and was more confused than ever. It was just as dark on this side. Squinting, she could make out trees all around her, as if they were in some sort of forest. There were no other beings present, no other sounds... just an eerie silence.

"Come on," Damon said, holding out his hand again.

Marquette wanted to trust him but grew fearful. "Where are you taking me?"

Damon stared at her blankly. He proceeded to make an odd clicking noise with his tongue, and his face seemed to start darkening by a couple shades. Marquette took a step backwards. Damon looked off into the distance, still with a dazed look in his eyes. If Marquette were not mistaken, she could swear she saw the outer corner of his eyes begin to shift upwards, giving his eyes an inhuman-like slant. His brown iris disappeared, leaving behind only a large black pupil with hardly any of the sclera displayed. She watched in terror, too paralyzed with fear to move, as the muscle tone in his arms seemed to be vanishing. He seemed to be shrinking in height. His skin turned pitch black.

Marquette snapped out of it and began running. She ran faster than she knew she could and had no idea where she was going. Several protruding tree branches scraped her arms and legs as she fearfully bolted through the dark and foreign landscape. She began to hear more clicking noises from behind her and didn't dare look back.

Continuing forward, Marquette's mind eventually began to clear enough for her to observe her surroundings. Though the forest had originally looked pitch black to her, she now observed a greater amount of visibility from the illumination of the bright lights in the sky. She noticed vines webbed around each tree. She toyed with the idea of trying to break one of the vines free to use as a weapon, but she decided against it. She worried she would not have enough time and would give away her location with the noise of the breakage. She weaved through the trees as quickly as possible and could not seem to find any unobstructed path. She could hardly breathe. She struggled to keep her eyes simultaneously ahead of her and below her, worried she might trip as she had done on the other side of the wall.

*The wall!* Marquette became hopeful that if she ran in one direction while weaving through the trees, she would eventually reach another part of the wall of branches and could climb back over it. She continued on but became more deliberate about not making any turns or traveling diagonally. It felt like it was taking forever to reach it. *How long have I been running?* she wondered. It had been nearly thirty minutes. She slowed her pace and looked over her shoulder, praying she had lost him. Jolted with terror at the sight of him not too far behind, she quickly picked up her pace again.

*I don't know how much longer I can do this*, Marquette thought to herself, quickly sinking into a state of utter helplessness. She was used to exercising, which was a prerequisite to the space mission, but she kept herself at a manageable jog during cardio, and it was one thing to jog on a treadmill and another to run for your life through trees and foreign terrain. *How can I have been running this long and not reached the wall?* she contemplated with exhaustion. Though a part of her felt like each stride would be her last and that she could collapse any minute from fatigue, she knew she could continue on, especially if her life was on the line. Her adrenaline gave her brief bursts of energy every time she felt that her energy was almost entirely depleted. Capable of continuing to run or not, it was not long before she couldn't proceed any further. She abruptly stopped. Physically, she could have kept running, at least for a little while longer, but something ahead prohibited a continued attempt to escape. The clicking sounds tremendously multiplied. Closing in on her from each direction between the trees were hundreds and hundreds of Damons.

## 6

# WHO AM I?

I YAWNED AND OPENED my eyes with the expectation of seeing the familiar layout of the spaceship. "I just had the weirdest dream," I started saying aloud, but when my eyes did open, I became speechless. I silently took in my surroundings and recalled the events that unfolded the day prior. Light seeped through a slit in the tent opening at the top of the staircase and created a sliver of illumination against the cave wall. Sadie and Xavier were beginning to toss and turn but still hadn't gotten up yet. Jerome must have left. His sleeping pouch was hung back up on the wall. I scratched my head. "Wasn't I supposed to get a wake-up call?"

Xavier mumbled indecipherably, sat up, and rubbed at his eyes. "What time is it?" he asked me.

"We're on a foreign planet and you're worried about what time it is," I scoffed. Xavier tilted his head and glared at me. I could tell he was trying to suppress a smile. "How can you be smiling at a time like this?" I furrowed my brows and crossed my arms, but I could tell he picked up on my sarcasm exceeding my annoyance. I stood up, rolled my sleeping pouch up tightly, and tossed it at him. He caught it and playfully tossed it back. I sighed and hung it up. "I don't suppose they have a shower here."

"You want to shower before your long day of hunting?" Xavier reminded me of the arrangement I agreed to with Tavion.

"Hence, why I asked about the wake-up call. Also, don't forget..." I squatted down next to him, flipped my hair to the side, and poked his chest with my pointer finger. "You're coming hunting too."

He groaned and lay back down. I stood back up and started up the cave stairs while tying my hair up with a band that had been around my wrist. When I got to the top of the stairs, I spread the flaps of the tent open and exited, ducking my head on my way out.

Right as I stepped out, I inhaled the most amazing smell. Some type of food. I was sure of it, and my stomach started making noises in response. No one was near the tent, but in the distance, I could hear kids speaking a foreign language and adults speaking a combination of their native language and English. I could just barely make out Tavion's silhouette a few tents away, around the same campfire area we had eaten dinner at the day before. The sky was breathtaking. It was a light orange with purple and pink clouds faded into one another. There was a cool breeze, but the air felt warm against my skin each time the breeze passed. I closed my eyes and took a deep breath. When I opened my eyes, Tavion was walking towards me. It felt like my connection to the environment had signaled him in some way. I'm sure any realistic being would call me delusional for thinking that. I walked towards him to meet in the middle.

"I understand how overwhelming it must be for you to be here..." Tavion started as he approached.

"Oh, do you?" I retorted.

Tavion's face tightened at my reply. "Do you always talk over people?"

"I just don't think you could possibly understand how it feels to suddenly be thrown into an environment, who knows how far from home," my voice cracked with angst, "that you had no idea existed!" Tavion softened his expression towards me. I couldn't tell if he was expressing empathy or pity. He stayed silent for a moment. When he opened his mouth to speak, my anxiety heightened, and I started to ramble uncontrollably. "I mean, don't get me wrong, this is amazing! It is unbelievable that there are others out there that we didn't know about, but how could you even begin to understand being stranded in a place so astronomically far from home without any idea how or when you're getting back? How could you begin to imagine expecting to end up on one planet, feeling like the spaceship you are on is unstable, wondering in that moment if you'll even make it out alive, and then making it out alive but being so out of place and so far from home that you're not even sure you wouldn't have preferred the alternative?" I would have continued, but Tavion put his hand over my mouth, which in hindsight was probably for the best.

"As I was saying…" Tavion tried to suppress a smile, and in that moment, he reminded me of Xavier. "I understand how overwhelming it must be for you to be here, so I let you sleep in through the first round of hunting. Jerome seemed alert when I went down to your sleeping quarters, so he tagged along and had breakfast with us."

"About that, I was wondering…"

This time, he cut me off. "No, you will not be joining anyone for breakfast. You will be hunting for your own, and as we discussed, everyone else's meals too."

I was embarrassed by his accusation, despite his prediction of what I had planned to say being spot on. *I have to lie*, I thought to myself, not wanting to give him the upper hand. "Actually, if you'd be so kind as to not cut me off…" I silently praised myself on my degree of sarcasm and mockery. "I was wondering how soon I can begin hunting."

"Right now," he replied.

"Awesome, then I'll go back to my tent and wake Xavier and get ready to… wait what?" He placed the same object in my hand that he had used to kill the Velteis the day prior.

"Right now," he repeated, this time putting emphasis on the word "now".

"Ah… okay. How do I use this thing?" I examined the object in my hand. I hadn't been able to get a good look at it when he had used it the day before, but I did recall it having a blade. The object in my hand looked identical to a hockey puck in size, shape, and color, and as I flipped it around in my hand, there was no blade to be found. "Is this a joke?" I held it up in the air and looked at Tavion impatiently.

"No, and I'd be careful twirling it around like that." He took a step back. I lowered the object and held it flat with an open hand. Tavion came closer and grabbed it from me. "Squeeze here," he demonstrated, "and a blade comes out." As promised, a sharp blade that I must have overlooked quickly extended out of a slit in the object. "Squeeze it again, and the blade will retract." He showed me. "Squeeze here with the blade withdrawn," he continued without actually squeezing it this time, "and the weapon will fly out of your hands in the direction you are aiming the blade."

"Seems easy enough." He handed it back to me, and I toyed with withdrawing and retracting the blade.

"If you have good aim."

"I don't understand though." I looked at the weapon skeptically. "It's so small. How did it take down a creature that's so big?"

Tavion laughed. "Creature?"

"Yeah..." I tried to find a different word to help him understand. "How did it take down such a big beast?"

"The weapon contains poison that the blade comes into contact with each time it is retracted. The poison kills on impact. This is why you must be more careful with it. It's not a toy."

"Understood."

"What do you call those living beings you all go to gawk at in zoos?"

"Ah... animals?"

"Velteis is an animal."

"Whatever you say," I replied. I turned to walk away, and Tavion grabbed my arm.

"Whoa." I couldn't contain my reaction. His hand felt like sandpaper.

"Where are you going?" he asked.

"To wake Xavier and teach him how to use these," I replied.

"You're not done learning to hunt yet."

"Seems pretty easy to me. Just withdraw the blade and aim."

"Under pressure, that may not be so easy. Knocked to your knees, that may not be so easy..." I didn't appreciate his reminder that I was knocked down by the Velteis we encountered while he stood strong. "And this isn't going to be your only weapon. Several animals here are immune to poison and are in fact poisonous themselves. If I let you go out there with just this, you're... what do you call it on your planet... oh yeah, screwed."

I was speechless. I watched as he turned and walked away. It felt like forever standing there waiting for him to return. When he did, he was carrying three much larger weapons. "Can I ask you something?" I asked hesitantly.

"Hmm?"

"I left my satchel in my tent. Can you please come with me so I can show you something?" I requested. He nodded. "I can carry one of those weapons," I offered.

"No thanks," he grimaced. "I learned my lesson about handing you weapons prior to giving you an explanation for how to use them."

I couldn't argue that. I shrugged, and we walked together to my tent. When we descended the stairs, Xavier was awake, but his sleeping pouch was hung back up on the wall, and he was sitting at the wooden table eating food that looked foreign to me.

"Where'd you get that?" Tavion and I asked in unison. We looked at each other in shock at our synchronized inquiry. I started to think that perhaps I wasn't crazy to feel we had some sort of weird connection.

"Wow, you two must have been spending a lot of time together," Xavier teased. "Kalari brought me some food. She brought you some too, Zar." He pushed a plate to the other end of the table. Tavion threw his forearm out In front of me to block me from moving toward the table.

"I'm not too hungry." I looked up at Tavion, avoiding eye contact to the best of my ability but seeking his approval of my submission.

"You may eat before we hunt." He softened his stance and brought his arm back to rest at his side.

"Thank you." I was surprised he let up, but I realized then that I really wasn't hungry. I had lost my appetite with the anxiety welling up about what I wanted to ask Tavion. I walked to the corner of the cave and grabbed my satchel, which was on the floor leaning against the cave wall. I pulled out my sketchpad and brought it over to Tavion. Tavion removed the weapons he had been carrying and leaned them up against the wall. He leaned over to look at my sketchpad with full attention.

"I drew these pictures," I said, beginning to flip slowly through the pages, "but they're not just pictures, are they?" My hands were shaking. I held the sketchpad out to Tavion, and he gently took it from me. He started flipping through them himself. When he got to the picture of the bird, I put my pointer finger on it. "I know what sound it makes," I whispered. I started feeling distant from myself, as if I were reliving the dream. The room blurred. Next thing I knew, Tavion was holding me in his arms. I must have fainted. He set me down on the wooden chair at the table, across from Xavier.

"Have you seen these things?" Tavion asked, still paging through. There had to have been at least a hundred drawings in my sketchpad, all inspired by the subjects and scenery of my dreams. I wondered in that moment if they all were real and if they all were present on Suvia.

"I've dreamed those things." I felt nauseous, and the smell of the food in front of me was not helping. I lifted my knees to my chest, resting the heels of my feet on the edge of the chair. I wrapped my arms around my legs and buried my face between my knees and my chest. I heard the plate of food shift to the other end of the table, and the smell became less pungent. I looked up to see who had shifted it and to know who to thank for their sensitivity. Tavion had shifted the plate. I didn't thank him. I put my head back down.

"I need to see your leg." Tavion knelt down to the left of me and looked into my eyes. I had only known him for a day, but nonetheless, this seemed very uncharacteristic of him to me.

"Excuse me?" I was frightened by his gentle command. "Why do you need to see it?" I asked.

"Because depending on what mark is on it, if any, we need to get you somewhere fast." I had no idea what he meant, and yet, I felt like I understood. I lifted the leg of my pants and dropped my foot to the ground, extending my right leg out. "How did you know which leg," he asked.

"This is the one that got injured in my dream." I couldn't believe this was happening. Xavier was silent during this exchange and had stopped eating since the moment I handed Tavion my sketchpad. He looked at both of us with confusion and shock as Tavion inspected my lower leg.

Tavion withdrew something that looked like a flashlight from one of his pants pockets and shined a green light at my leg. He left it on for about a minute, pointing it at a spot on the side of my calf. Then he switched it off, pulled my pant leg back down, and lay down on his back on the cave floor. "Am I marked?" I asked.

"Yes," he replied. I waited. He didn't say anything more.

"Do we need to go somewhere?" I asked.

"I don't know where to go," he spoke softly.

I couldn't even tell if I was looking at the same being as yesterday. He seemed so fragile, lying there on the ground.

I rested my elbow on the table and rested my chin on my fist, looking toward Xavier. "Where is Sadie?" I asked, as if that were the main concern.

"She went to look for Jerome," he replied.

"I don't know where to go," Tavion whispered. He paused before speaking again. "And I can't protect you," he firmly added, rising to his feet. Something inside of him seemed to snap. "You and your friends need to leave. Now."

"What do you mean?" I asked.

"I need to see your leg," he demanded of Xavier.

"No, dude. What the fuck?" Xavier stood up too.

"What did you all come here for?" Tavion's voice was booming, and he was pacing frantically. I was taken aback that he was even capable of losing his composure to this extent. He seemed so in control of himself and others up until now.

"We told you!" I exclaimed.

"You told me wrong!" he barked.

"What did you see on my leg?" I cried, beginning to become frantic myself.

"You really don't know?"

I pulled the leg of my pants up again and held my hand out, silently requesting the flashlight or whatever the device was that emitted the green light. Tavion reluctantly handed it to me. I turned the light on, sat on the cave floor, and leaned to the side to get a better look as I shined the light on my calf. Appearing like a white ink tattoo was a shape that looked like a crescent moon with a sharp spear cutting diagonally through the middle of it. I had never seen it before, not even in a dream.

"What does this mean?" I asked.

"It means you're from Suvia."

# 7

# FOREIGN AND FAMILIAR

"TELL ME AGAIN WHAT the mark means." Zara paced back and forth and asked the same question that she had been asking for the past hour.

"I've told you." Tavion sat down on one of the wooden chairs and pulled something that looked like paper out of a side pocket on his pants. He pulled out something that Zara assumed was a writing utensil despite its odd shape. By this point, Sadie and Jerome had returned to the underground cave and were filled in on what was happening. Their shock was evident by their prolonged silence. Xavier joined them in sitting on the floor along the wall of the cave, each one of them listening but not knowing what to do with the information they were absorbing.

Tavion began to draw something recognizable to Zara, albeit only recently. "What are they?" Zara asked, familiar with the sight of them but possessing no words to describe them.

"What do you see in the sky at night on Earth?" Tavion asked.

"The moon," Zara replied, already having made the connection to the Earth equivalent.

"Right..." Tavion hesitated. "I have never seen it, but I have heard those on Earth describe it. It's a bright white light in the sky if I am not mistaken, correct?"

"You could say that," Zara replied. "That's how it appears to us from Earth."

"I believe this to be similar," Tavion insisted.

"I guess. We only have one."

"Does it mean anything to you?" he asked.

"No, not really. It means there is something else out there I guess."

"Sadie…" Tavion turned in his seat to face her. "Can I please see your leg?"

Sadie looked at Zara, and Zara nodded to encourage her to comply with Tavion's request. Sadie rose to her feet and sat down on a chair next to him. She straightened out her skirt, gently tugging the bottom of it down, and extended her leg onto Tavion's lap. Tavion pulled the green light out of his pocket and examined the side of her calf. Nothing showed. He threw his head back discouraged. After a moment, he returned to the drawing.

"We have seven moons on Suvia," Tavion explained, "and each has a link to a different tribe."

Zara interjected. "If I am from Suvia, which tribe am I a part of?" There was a playfulness in her voice as she entertained the idea of actually being from Suvia. She couldn't bring herself to believe that there was any truth to it. There were too many memories and connections she had to Earth for that to be true. She shook her head as she recalled watching home videos with her mother, even the video of her mother delivering her. She did not have a shred of doubt that Tavion was confused, and she wished now more than ever to return to Earth where she did belong.

"Please, let me finish." Tavion pointed to the drawing. "There are seven moons. While each looks the same at night from down here, we have a device that allows us to take a closer look as you do with your…"

"Telescope?"

"Yes," he continued, "and each has a soft glow around it of different color: blue, green, yellow, pink, red, orange, and purple. While they do each have a name, I feel you'll remember them best by color since those are familiar words to you."

"I don't know how long we will be here," Zara firmly replied, "but if you know our language, I feel it best that we learn yours as well."

"So be it." Tavion backtracked, "Listun, Kleit, Klaysta, Tul, Vultra, Eyla, and Tuvon."

Zara nodded attentively. "Continue."

"When each of us are born on Suvia, we are marked by a bird..."

"In a dream?" Zara interrupted.

Tavion winced. "In real life."

"I was marked in a dream," Zara assured him.

"No, in a dream, you were recalling being marked. We all have those dreams on Suvia, tortured by a repressed memory."

"I was an adult in the dream when I was marked," Zara countered.

"Did you actually see the bird marking you?" Zara confirmed Tavion's conclusion with a long silence. "As I was saying," he continued, "we are each marked based on the tribe we are born into. We think it has something to do with the light emitted from each moon having different activation types based on location at birth. The color of the marking on our calf coincides with the color of one of the seven moons. My tribe's is yellow, Klaysta." Tavion shined the green light on his own leg, revealing the same shape that Zara had on her leg but outlined in yellow instead of white. Zara sat down anxiously and furrowed her brows in confusion. She inaudibly mouthed words and slowly counted to seven with her fingers. "What are you doing?" Tavion inquired.

"You didn't mention white. You said the glow around each moon has a distinct color of blue, green, yellow, pink, red, orange, and purple," she spoke slowly, second guessing herself on whether she recalled the correct colors.

"I've never seen that mark outlined in white." Tavion rose to his feet and began pacing as Zara had been just moments ago. "Each color coincides with a moon, in addition to an ability that is unique to the tribe. Ours, yellow, coincides with the ability of our tribe and only our tribe to locate and observe beings on other planets, in other galaxies, and wherever they may be."

"Miravi said you've watched us on videos," Zara interjected.

"Look around you," Tavion retorted. He continued to pace and began making overexaggerated gestures with his hands and arms. "You really think we have videos? We see you when we close our eyes. We see you in our dreams. But not just you, many, many others who look drastically different, have different possessions, immerse themselves in different lifestyles, speak different languages..."

"So maybe my ability is to see Suvia, being that I keep having these dreams."

"Unlikely!" Tavion boomed. "Being from Suvia, it would serve you no purpose to have visions of Suvia."

"But I am from Earth!" Zara slammed her hand down on the table.

Tavion shook his head. "People from Earth are not marked!"

Jerome stood up and walked over to Tavion hastily. "Check my calf," he firmly requested. "Perhaps we are missing something. Perhaps Zara isn't the only one from Earth with that marking. Perhaps it is normal for people on Earth to have that marking and Sadie is the one outside of the norm."

Tavion sat back down and reluctantly shined the light on Jerome's calf, realizing in that moment that there was something about Zara that made her seem different than the others who arrived with her. He looked at Zara with wonder in his eyes, while shining the light on Jerome's calf.

"See, I have it too, no biggie," Jerome declared.

"What?" Tavion was taken aback and quickly turned his head to look at Jerome's leg.

"Oh... Wait... That's a birth mark." Jerome pulled his pants leg down, shrugged his shoulders, and walked back toward where he had been sitting.

"That wasn't funny," Tavion remarked.

"I thought it was kind of funny," Xavier chimed in.

"Tavion, please tell us about the other tribes." Zara brought everyone's attention back to the matter at hand. "Maybe knowing about the other tribes will help me piece together what part I might have in all of this." Still skeptical that she had a part in it at all, Zara felt more and more persuaded by the recollection of her recurrent dreams.

"Purple," Tavion continued, "is the farthest tribe from us in terms of location. Their unique ability is rapid and efficient climbing. Likely not coincidental, they live in a mountainous region. It is rare that they come into contact with any of the other tribes, and it is rare that any of the other tribes try to come into contact with them. Blue is the next farthest from us. They have the ability to camouflage completely, matching their skin to the color of their surroundings."

"Surely they can't do so completely," Sadie stopped him. "What about their clothing?"

"That tribe does not wear clothes. They go without to aid in their survival and maximize the opportunity of that trait. They frequently carry pelts for warmth but burn or drop them when needed." Sadie blushed. Tavion continued without skipping a beat, "Red is about as distant from us as blue. The red tribe has the ability to paralyze people and animals as they approach, although the effects wear off quickly, and they consequently need to be fairly close to make that attribute useful."

"Tavion?" Kalari ducked under the tent opening and started down the stairs. "You haven't gone hunting yet?"

"Not now, Kalari," he responded. "Come down here. We have a lot to figure out."

Kalari walked back up the couple of stairs she had descended and exited the tent, returning just moments later with the two little ones. The three of them walked down to join the others. Tavion picked up the youngest and sat him on his lap. "Liviton," he said, squeezing the little one's shoulders and speaking quietly into his ear.

"Hi," the little one spoke gently. Zara, Xavier, Sadie, and Jerome all waved, for a moment feeling a greater sense of universality, as if looking into the eyes of a child on Earth.

"What are we doing?" the little one asked. "I want to hunt!"

"Yeah, you'll get there," Tavion replied, while lifting him off his lap and setting him down on his feet. He playfully ran to Kalari, who was now sitting cross-legged on top of one of the sleeping pouches. He leaped into the air, outstretched his limbs, and wrapped himself around her when he fell into her lap. His sibling was sitting on the sleeping pouch next to their mother.

"I am telling them of the tribes," Tavion said to Kalari, leaving out the anomaly of Zara.

"Elista Kleit?" Kalari inquired. Her expression grew stern, and she pursed her lips.

"No," Tavion replied, "I haven't gotten to that yet." He paused and had a far-off look in his eyes before resuming where he had left off. "The orange tribe has the ability to breathe under water indefinitely. We have somewhat of an alliance with them, as we have been making trades with them through several generations now. They provide us with fish and underwater plants which have medicinal qualities, and we provide them with meat and weapons."

"There are fish here?" Sadie gasped. "I love fish! What about sushi? Do you guys have..." Jerome put his hand over Sadie's mouth, drowning out the sound of her continued mumbles. "Hey!" She shoved him offendedly.

"Well, this is not the time to be inquiring about their diet!" Jerome exclaimed.

"Pink?" Zara put her hand on top of Tavion's, urging him to continue. She did not make eye contact with him. She was beginning to become accustomed to not looking directly into his eyes. However, she did notice a scowl from Kalari out of the corner of her eye and quickly pulled her hand back. *I guess jealousy is a thing here too*, she smugly mused.

"Those in the pink tribe..." Tavion looked around, as if telling a tall tale to a room of clueless children, although the children in the room seemed bored while Zara and her colleagues leaned forward with angst. "Those in the pink tribe are capable of bringing the dead back to life." He paused for a moment with a contemplative expression. "Although... their lack of efficiency in doing so leads them not to waste that talent on any outside of their own kind."

"Lack of efficiency?" Jerome asked.

"Bringing the dead back to life?" Sadie began to hyperventilate.

"How?" Zara asked, extending her hand once again to gently place it on Tavion's. This time she paid no mind to Kalari. Zara slightly jumped at the sound of Xavier clearing his throat. She hadn't realized she was so on edge. She took a deep breath but continued to lean forward attentively.

Tavion didn't carry on with an immediate explanation. Instead, he looked at the top of Zara's hand, still resting on his. Her skin looked so pale, so smooth... His mind went blank, and his eyelids became heavy. Something about her made him feel at peace, despite a war he had been battling inside of his mind ever since he saw that she had been marked in an unfamiliar fashion.

"Tavion?" Kalari spoke with a pleading tone. She had never seen the calmness he was exhibiting in him before, and she was beginning to feel enraged at the sight of Zara's continued contact with him. Tavion briefly glanced at Kalari, shook his head defiantly, and closed his eyes. He didn't want to come back from this tranquility. For the first time since his birth, he had nothing on his mind.

"Tell me how beings are brought back to life." Zara looked at Tavion's eyelids intensely while she waited for his response, unsure of the rules for eye contact if his eyes were not exposed. To Tavion, her voice seemed to echo, as if he were unwillingly falling asleep after a long day, slipping into a trance where sounds begin to intensify. His eyes remained closed as he started to explain.

"When one dies in the pink tribe, it is true that they can bring them back to life," he spoke slowly and quietly, "but it takes time, patience, vulnerability..." He trailed off.

"That seems like a sensical price to pay to bring a loved one back," Zara responded.

Tavion shook his head. "They must sit with the deceased body every day, from daylight to nightfall, for..." He seemed at a loss for a word to describe the length of time.

"Years?" Zara asked, feeling like she already knew the answer.

"They watch their young grow at a glance and miss so many years with them. They leave themselves open to attack. They waste so much of their life..." Tavion couldn't bring himself to keep talking about it.

Zara followed Tavion's lead in closing her eyes, and in doing so, it felt to her like they were the only two in the room. "I can understand why they wouldn't make that sacrifice for anyone outside of their own."

"I can't understand why they would make that sacrifice for their own." Tavion's voice finally returned to its normal volume and intensity. His eyes and Zara's opened at the same time, and they seemed to immediately stare through each other, as if their eyes were each a portal to the other's universe.

"I think you can." Zara felt chills run down her spine. She didn't think he could understand. She knew he could. For a moment, it felt as if his feelings, his motives, his values, and his priorities were her own. She had never felt so close to anyone in her life.

Xavier raised his hand. "Green?"

Tavion sighed and nervously fidgeted with his hands. "Green."

8

# KLEIT

THE WIND RUSTLED THROUGH the trees, making thin branches dance enthusiastically. Small critters scurried through the grass. Under the cover of the trees, very little light seeped in. It smelled as if it had rained not long ago, but the grass was not wet to the touch. Despite movement, everything felt still. Despite nothing being weighed down, everything felt heavy. Her eyelids felt heavy. Her body felt glued to the ground. Her breaths sounded calm and even. Her heartbeat was slow and steady. Despite having full control, Marquette felt paralyzed. She lay on the forest floor in the same spot she had fainted, staring at the leaves of the branch high above her. She hadn't the faintest idea how many hours she had been lying there.

A familiar clicking noise sounded, bringing a swift end to the stillness. Marquette rolled to her knees. She crawled forward in a panic while trying to bring herself to her feet, but she fell clumsily in a state of insurmountable fear.

"Marquette?" a voice called out to her.

"Zara?" Marquette scrambled to her feet, successfully this time.

"Hey," Xavier said, walking out with Zara from behind a tree.

"It's time to go," Sadie said, walking up to Marquette from the other direction.

"Where's Jerome?" Marquette asked, comforted by the sight of her colleagues.

"He's waiting for us," Zara replied.

Marquette looked around anxiously. She hadn't seen Damon since she fainted. *It must have been a hallucination*, she thought wearily to herself. "Let's get out of here!" Marquette exclaimed.

The four of them walked together through the forest.

"The green tribe, Kleit, is the reason you are here with our tribe," Tavion explained to Zara and her colleagues. "Not only do they have malintent, but their unique ability makes them incredibly dangerous in carrying out their intentions. We brought you in without hesitation to protect you from them, and in the long run, to protect ourselves from you. Now that I see you are marked with an unknown ability," he said, holding his hand out and motioning to Zara, "I realize I either made a fatal mistake or a miraculous decision. Only time will tell."

"What makes this Kleit group so dangerous," Jerome inquired.

"Well for starters, they can fully shape-shift."

"Like into an animal?" Sadie asked.

"An animal, a human, a tree... They can appear as anything they desire but only within the realm of the memories of an outsider."

"What does that mean?" Xavier came closer and sat on the floor by Tavion and Zara, who were occupying two of the chairs.

"It means they can look identical to anything or anyone you have seen before."

"How is that dangerous?" Sadie asked.

"They can manipulate you into doing what they ask of you by portraying a loved one," Tavion responded. "They can trick you into believing you are in a different environment by portraying objects or scenery you have seen previously. They can make you feel safe as they are about to trap, torture, or kill you."

"Torture?" Sadie began to hyperventilate again.

"Kill?" Jerome asked.

"Surely they don't all have malintent," Zara added skeptically.

"They do," Tavion assured them.

"Their only weaknesses are flaws in trying to replicate voices and mannerisms identically to their origin, trying to replicate details which are limited in one's memory, only being able to repeat words that have been said before by the person being replicated, and only being able to hold that form for thirty minutes at a time before beginning to shape-shift back into their true form."

As Marquette walked through the forest with Zara, Xavier, and Sadie, she was continuously startled by noises behind her.

"Is something wrong?" Sadie checked in with her.

"No, I guess not," Marquette replied. "I'm just really happy to see the three of you and get out of this place. Where are we going? Back to the spaceship?"

Zara stopped walking for a moment, seeming to be lost in thought. "Yes." She finally responded and resumed walking.

"I don't know if I remember how to get back," Marquette informed them. "There weren't exactly landmarks along the way to help me retrace my steps."

"No worries," Xavier replied.

"It was the weirdest thing guys," Marquette chuckled anxiously, "I swear I saw my husband. How silly of me to think there is any way he could possibly be on this planet with us. I guess I just really miss him. The mind sees what it wants to I suppose. I followed him into this forest, and he began to transform into something else. Next thing I knew, I saw hundreds of him. I must be dehydrated," she said, removing her bag from her shoulders to grab a water bottle.

"Yeah," Sadie said in agreement, placing her hand on Marquette's shoulder.

They walked on a while longer and eventually arrived at a defined line where forest grass turned to desert sand. "I don't think this was here before..." Marquette scratched her head in confusion. She had never seen anything like this. It was like standing on the border of two worlds. If she looked out straight ahead, she could see miles of red sand, darkened by a mostly black night sky. If she looked over her shoulder, she could see thick redwood trees and rich green grass, just like she used to see at the National Park she visited each year with her grandma as a child. The comfort of this memory empowered her to walk on.

"You pulled us in so urgently when we arrived," Zara recalled. "Did we arrive close to their tribe?"

Tavion opened his mouth to respond, but Kalari replied before he could get a word out, "Yes, you were very close to their tribe. If we hadn't brought you here, you may have faced severe consequences."

"What about Marquette?" Sadie cried. "She stayed with the spaceship which means she's still near that tribe!"

"The transportation device you came in appeared to be very secure," Tavion responded hesitantly.

"How would you know?" Zara asked. "When did you inspect the spaceship?"

"While you were out from receiving too much clatofor, your colleagues gave us a tour of it."

"You did what?" Zara snapped at Sadie, Jerome, and Xavier, taking turns to glare at each of them individually. "You had no idea who these individuals were or whether they could cause us harm, and you thought, yeah, let's go ahead and welcome them to our quarters? Nonetheless, you left me there unconscious while you did so?"

"They seemed nice," Sadie quietly replied, "and we didn't know how long it would be until you came to, but we knew you'd be okay."

"I can't believe this!" Zara threw both her hands over her face and slid her fingers down her cheeks in an overexaggerated expression of her stress.

"Can we get back to the matter at hand?" Jerome asked.

"Fine," Zara replied, "and if Marquette has left our secure spaceship?"

"Then she's screwed and so may be the rest of us," Kalari coldly replied. She rose to her feet, picked up her youngest, and ascended the stairs.

"Can I get an answer from you?" Zara barked at Tavion, fuming in response to Kalari's rude remark.

"I think Kalari said it all," he sighed.

It was not long before Marquette, Zara, Xavier, and Sadie arrived at the spaceship. It was a little troublesome to find it, as each time Marquette failed to retrace her steps accurately, her colleagues seemed equally uncertain of where to go. Several times, she noted that she wished Jerome were there, as he was the best of them when it came to directions. This comment was received each time with nods of agreement, but Marquette grew increasingly annoyed that she seemed to be the only one with much to say about anything.

"Here we are," Sadie said, looking at the spaceship. "I have to pee!" she suddenly exclaimed.

"Same!" Zara and Xavier said in unison.

"Okay... That was weird. I think you three have been spending too much time together," Marquette nervously sneered.

"Definitely," Xavier replied. "Be right back." He disappeared behind the spaceship. Zara and Sadie followed not too far behind him.

"Ah... You're not going to take turns, I see. Well, there goes personal boundaries on the job," Marquette pronounced judgmentally.

"Did you say something, Marquette?" Zara asked as she returned.

"Not a thing."

"Are we just going to stand here all day?" Zara asked.

"If I had a quarter for the number of times you've been up in my business about standing around, I'd be rich. Can you mind your own for once?" Marquette could not stand Zara sometimes. "You do what you want. You know the access code. I'm going to stand here and wait for the others."

"Access code..." Zara said to herself, continuing to stand in place. After a moment, she walked forward to the spaceship, lifted the lid on a metal box, and entered an eight-digit code.

"*Access granted*," a robotic voice welcomed her.

She proceeded into the spaceship while Marquette continued to wait outside for Sadie and Xavier.

"So, you mean to tell me, you left Marquette at the spaceship, just banking on her staying in it until we returned a full day later?" Zara exclaimed.

"Pretty much." Tavion had no explanation to defend himself.

"Well let's get moving! We need to make sure she's still there!" Zara rose quickly to her feet and moved her arm in a circular motion, urging everyone to follow.

"We still don't know what you are," Tavion responded hesitantly, still seated.

"What I am?" Zara cocked her head to the side with irritation.

"Being around you could put me, my family, and my community at risk." Tavion's voice boomed throughout the cave, as did the echo from his fist slamming down on the wood table.

"And being around you could do all the same for us, but as you said before, Marquette being off that spaceship right now could pose a risk for us all. Let's conquer this problem together and then we can go our separate ways, remain together, or who the hell cares. Can we go now?" Zara didn't let the feeling of her desperation seep into her tone, although her words demonstrated hints of it.

"I'm coming with you. I think I remember the way." Jerome got up and began to follow.

"Count me in too, Zar," Xavier said.

"Same," Sadie replied.

The three of them began to ascend the stairs when Tavion stood up and grabbed his elder child who had somehow fallen and remained asleep during the heated discussion. "Don't make me regret this," Tavion pleaded to Zara.

"You seem to fear me now," Zara stated, not bothering to look behind her for a reaction from him.

"You've given me a lot to fear," he replied as he ducked beneath the flaps of the tent. "Please give me one moment."

He carried his elder child to Kalari, set him on the grass beside his sibling, and rested a palm on the opposite side of each child's face.

"Ah… Hello? Are you guys coming?" Marquette grew impatient.

"Yes, sorry," Sadie said, coming back around to the front of the spaceship.

"What were you two doing back there, fornicating?" Marquette jeered. "Never mind," she quickly added, "I don't want to know."

"Sorry," Xavier said, coming back around to join them.

"Yeah, yeah, enough with the apologies. Let's just go in. I'm tired beyond belief." Marquette ushered them into the spaceship.

Upon entering the spaceship, Marquette gasped. "What are you doing?" She stood over Zara who had taken the metal board off the control panel and yanked several wires out.

"Inspections," Zara stated informatively.

"Look, can we just go to sleep? It has been a long day, and I don't have the energy to fight you on this, but I am dying to return home, and I think those wires might be an essential component in achieving that goal, so can you please stop touching things?" Marquette demanded.

"Marquette, I'm sorry. I'll stay out of your way." Zara tucked the wires back in and replaced the cover of the control panel. The only other time Marquette had heard Zara say she'd stay out of her way was when they had a NASA employee luncheon, and Zara was making fun of her for practically knocking her over to get to the dessert table. She couldn't help but hear her words now in the same condescending tone she remembered.

"Whatever, I'm going to bed," Marquette muttered, reclining one of the chairs.

"Okay," Zara replied. Zara sat on the chair next to Marquette and watched as her body seemed to relax and her breathing seemed to slow. She gently brushed her fingers through Marquette's hair. After a while, she looked to Xavier and Sadie and cocked her head to the side, gesturing for the three of them to exit the spaceship. On the way out, they began communicating with each other only through the quiet clicking of their tongues.

"We can't go yet," declared Tavion.

"What's the hold up?" asked Jerome.

"We need to bring hunting equipment," Tavion replied.

"You've got to be kidding me," Xavier cut in. "You're still prioritizing hunting when all of us, especially Marquette, could be in danger?"

"We will be in more danger if we aren't prepared. On Suvia, if you are not hunting, you are hunted," Tavion insisted.

"So, we don't need to take the time to bag the meat and pelt?" Sadie asked.

"Of course we do! If we are killing an animal, we will not do so wastefully," Tavion scoffed.

Zara threw her head back impatiently. "Jerome, you've been taught how to use the weapons, correct?"

"Yes," he confirmed.

"Jerome will teach me along the way, and we will get a head start. I already know how to use the hockey puck."

"The hockey puck?" Tavion looked at Zara scornfully.

"Well, you haven't given me a name for it," Zara remarked.

"We need to forget about what Suvians call these weapons for now and refer to them by words that are easy for you to remember and quick to say. Sometimes, you only get one shot with them, and it is a matter of life or death. It is imperative you can choose and utilize the correct weapon quickly and efficiently."

"On second thought, can I stay here?" Sadie asked. "I don't feel so hot."

"I'll protect you, Sadie," Jerome assured her, throwing an arm around her shoulders.

"Alright," Zara announced, "Jerome, Sadie, and I will get a head start."

Tavion handed them one of each type of weapon, as well as a bag for meat and pelt collection. As Jerome, Sadie, and Zara departed, he proceeded to teach Xavier how to use the weapons.

Each time she tried to turn, the ropes pulled tighter. Marquette panicked when she finally opened her eyes to her outstretched limbs secured to each post of the chair. "This isn't funny!" she yelled, looking around for her colleagues. They were nowhere in sight. "Hey! Get me out of here! Do you hear me?" she continued. "I swear, Zara, if it was you that did this, you should know I'm an expert when it comes to revenge!"

"It wasn't Zara," Xavier said, walking back into the spaceship.

"It was you?" Marquette asked.

Xavier nodded. "I only want to protect you."

"To protect me from what?" she asked calmly. She trusted Xavier. If he said he was trying to protect her, then she was sure without a shred of doubt that his intentions were in the right place. She had only ever heard him assuring Zara that he would protect her. She felt special knowing he had it in mind to protect her as well.

"A lot," he said.

"What did you guys see while we were apart that has you so rattled that you'd feel the need to tie me up to protect me? And why is it that I am the only one tied up?" She looked around, double checking that was the case.

"I'll get Zara," he replied, beginning to walk away.

"No!" Marquette cried. Zara was the last person she wanted to see while restrained. "I want you to explain this to me."

"You have to stay here," he assured her. "I can't explain right now. Trust me."

"I trust you," she replied, "but..." Xavier walked out of the spaceship before she could finish. She wished she could wipe the tear that was trailing along her cheek. She wished someone would stay to comfort her. Having only slept for a short time in the last couple of days, these thoughts did not last long. They faded away as her mind became inactive. Despite the restraints, she slipped into a peaceful slumber.

"Can we take a break?" asked Sadie. "I feel like we've been walking forever."

"It hasn't been that long." Jerome looked at Sadie, trying to assess if she was serious. She sat down on a boulder and genuinely looked drained.

"Whatever," Zara resigned. "Taking a break will at least give the others time to catch up." She looked around at an unobstructed view of red sand in each direction. "Well, this couldn't get any more interesting," she jabbed sarcastically. "We will have so much food for tonight with all the animals we've slain." She shook the empty sack.

"Did you guys feel that?" Sadie asked.

"Feel what?" Zara replied.

"It felt like the ground just shook." Sadie stood up nervously.

"I didn't feel anything." Jerome looked around at the ground suspiciously.

"I swear it." Sadie took a couple cautious steps backward.

Before she could alert the others that the boulder she had been sitting on was shifting, it rapidly slid through the sand and knocked her off her feet. She shrieked. Jerome grabbed Sadie's elbow and yanked her back up. The three of them took off running. When they looked back to see If It was following them, they noticed Xavier and Tavion coming into view. Tavion was laughing as they approached.

"I forgot to tell you about those," Tavion noted while trying to suppress further laughter.

"What the hell was that thing?" Zara snapped.

"Eh... You'd probably call it a ground rock rhino, since you like to refer to things by what they remind you of on Earth. That was a baby one. It just wanted to play."

"Play? Sadie was knocked down by it in the blink of an eye."

"Those are relatively harmless," Tavion assured her, moving forward to walk ahead of everyone. "Oh no..." He stopped in his tracks. They were coming up on the spaceship, and squinting his eyes, he noticed the entrance door was wide open with three Kleit guarding it.

9

# Double Deceit

M Y HEAD WAS WHIRLING, rightfully so I suppose. I couldn't decide whether to look backward at the... ground rock rhino... or forward at the spaceship. I could just barely make out three silhouettes in front of the entrance. They appeared as Tavion had described the Kleit. They were incredibly slim, and disproportionately long arms hung loosely at their sides. They looked rather short. *Is there truly much to be afraid of?* I wondered. I couldn't understand how their ability to shapeshift would be so useful against those who know and expect their deceit. The others had stopped in their tracks. I wondered if I should be doing the same, but my curiosity outweighed my nerves. I continued walking toward the spaceship. I did look back a few times. I couldn't help it. *Ground rock rhino?* I wondered if it actually looked like a rhinoceros. The boulder wasn't sharp or pointy like a horn. It really just looked like a boulder. I couldn't wrap my head around it. I was so lost in thought about it that I didn't see it coming when I face-planted into Tavion's chest.

"I asked you several times to stay put for a moment while we figure this out," he scorned me.

"What for?" I asked. "They don't look too harmful to me. There are only three of them, and they're not even presenting in another form right now."

"How do you know there are only three?" Tavion asked me.

*Touché*, I thought to myself, but I couldn't give him the upper hand. "There is nothing but desert a long way out in any direction. What would they be shapeshifting as? Sand?" I spoke the words confidently but started to ponder whether they could in fact shapeshift into sand. Tavion's silence had me wondering if he were assessing the same possibility.

"Well? What's the plan?" Xavier asked to no one in particular.

"To talk to them," I answered. I took a few steps forward, and once again, Tavion stepped out in front of me.

"You cannot talk to them," Tavion corrected me. "They do not speak English."

"You said they do if they shapeshift."

"Only repeat phrases," he replied.

"In context?" I inquired.

"It's hard to say." From the look on Tavion's face, it was clear he was stumped.

"Seems like there's a lot you don't know about them." I tapped his chest and walked around him.

"Zara!" He grabbed my arm. This was the first time he had spoken my name. Something about it sent chills through my spine. There was urgency in the way he grabbed my arm, but also gentleness. Something about it felt intimate. I was pulled out of my web of thoughts about it when he waved his free hand in front of my face to get my attention.

"Yeah?" I felt like I barely choked the word out.

"Please don't do this. We should go back to Klaysta and come up with a plan." Tavion's eyes seemed to be speaking to me louder than his words. *Oh shoot*, I thought to myself, suddenly recalling that I wasn't supposed to be looking directly at his eyes. That was hard for me to get used to. Nonetheless, he seemed to be looking at me as if I might die any moment. *Would I if I proceeded?*

"I have a plan," I insisted.

"Care to share it with the rest of us?" Jerome urged as I walked on.

Sadie ran to my side. "What's the plan?" she whispered to me.

"To ditch the plan," I replied.

I don't know what came over me then, but I began to run. I started suddenly and ran as quickly as I was able. I didn't look behind me. I was sure Tavion was chasing after me. Let him. I needed to at least try to get there without the others. I had no idea what I intended to say when I got there. I had no idea how I would keep myself safe. I just knew this was something I needed to do on my own. I could feel it. It was a mix of protectiveness, empowerment, curiosity, and adrenaline. I pushed myself to run faster. I was running out of breath by the time I arrived in front of the spaceship.

"How the hell did you get ahead of me?" I asked Tavion as I approached the entrance. The Kleit must have gone inside of it, as Tavion was the only being between me and the door. *Wait a minute. Is this him or one of them? Only one way to find out I suppose.* "You know, I sense a lot of chemistry between us," I said to him flirtatiously.

"Zara, it takes time, patience, vulnerability," he responded.

"Chemistry or bringing the dead back to life?" I asked.

"Yes," he playfully muttered.

I simply stared at him. *If he were a Kleit, they clearly could respond in context despite their limited vocabulary. If he weren't a Kleit, did he actually feel something happening between us? Had he ever said yes to me? I only recalled him ever saying no. Could a Kleit recall a detail that I had forgotten in a conversation with someone? How does this memory thing work?* My mind was a mess, but that was fairly typical when I conversed with Tavion. *But was it Tavion standing in front of me?* I wondered.

"Get away from it!" Tavion yelled from behind me.

Well, I knew I hadn't heard him say that before. Before I could react, two long limbs which seemed to continue to increase in length wrapped around my body. My instinct was to resist, but my struggles were unsuccessful, and I really didn't try that hard. I still had the same feeling that this was a curiosity I needed to explore on my own. When the Kleit realized I wasn't resisting, it put me down. I followed it willingly into the spaceship, and the door closed behind us.

Upon entering the spaceship, the first thing I heard was Marquette sobbing. Her arms and legs were tied to a chair. I looked around and saw wires taken out of the control panel, food scattered about as if carelessly tossed, and a bag upside down on the floor not too far from where Marquette was seated. Light reflected off a small gold object peeking out from underneath the bag. *The comm. Damn it*, I thought to myself, *I'll have to distract them*. There were three Kleit standing around me and observing me. I was glad to see there weren't more of them we didn't know about awaiting me in the spaceship.

"Ugh, I really hate a mess," I spoke aloud. "You guys! Really?" I started picking up the packages of food as I spoke.

"Zara?" Marquette gasped.

"Yepp, just gonna clean this mess and then I'll get right to ya Marqui Marq." I couldn't help but find joy in seeing her restrained. She responded to me with a pleading, yet resentful glare. I paid no attention to it. I needed to distract, not to be distracted. Lucky for me, there was a package of food close to the bag on the floor. As I grabbed the food with one hand, I grabbed the comm with the other and quickly slipped it into the pocket of my pants. I stood up with several food packages and went to place them back into the storage compartment. Distraction was an understatement. Even a distorted face was capable of displaying an expression of confusion, as was apparent from each of theirs.

"Alright," I said as I placed the last food package, "which one of you is going to talk to me? And as who?" My tone was intentionally smug.

Before my eyes, one of them began to transform. Its arms began to shorten and slightly expand in thickness. Its eyes became a beautiful sky blue, and the outer corner of its eyes shifted downwards from an original upward slant. Its jawline became fuller. Beautiful blonde hair grew out several centimeters. Before it was even fully transformed, I knew it was Zidia. *They could pick anyone from my memory*, I thought to myself, *but they have thus far chosen Tavion and Zidia.*

I interrupted Marquette's whimpering to ask her a question. "Who have they shown you?" She continued to sob and did not reply. "Who have they shown you?" I demanded, with so much urgency that my voice cracked.

"Damon!" she cried.

"Who else?" I demanded unsympathetically.

"You, Xavier, and Sadie." She was hysteric.

"Not Jerome?" I asked.

"N... No!" She could barely get the word out.

*Why not Jerome?* I asked myself silently. *Why not Jerome?* I searched my brain for answers and found none before Zidia began talking to me. *Not Zidia*, I reminded myself.

"I've been waiting for you," announced the Kleit disguised as my sister.

"Why?" I asked. Despite knowing in advance about their ability, watching them transform was a wonder. I looked at the soft glow of my sister's face, the contoured makeup bringing out her cheekbones, the paleness of her skin, and the off-white of her teeth.

"I need your help," it responded. I continued to analyze the uncanny resemblance. Despite this being looking identical to my sister, I reminded myself that they were worlds apart, both literally and figuratively.

"What can I do to help you?" I asked. "Clever transformation by the way. Being my sister will give you access to a much broader vocabulary than being Tavion would," I added.

"I know," they responded. They did not accurately reproduce my sister's voice, but knowing I was not deceived by their image to begin with, I don't think working on the voice was at the top of their priority list. "I have a problem," they informed me.

"Go on." I felt like they were beating around the bush. *Are they trying to stall me?* I wondered. I deliberated checking on my friends outside to ensure this wasn't a premeditated diversion by the Kleit.

The Kleit resembling my sister paused for a while with a blank stare. The other two Kleit stood relatively motionless, not making any noise. "I need you to get something for me," my sister's double finally requested.

"What do you need me to get?" I was growing impatient.

"A weapon," they responded. Marquette let out a terrified yelp, but I continued the conversation without pause.

"What kind of weapon? What would you use it for?" I humored them.

"Something sharp. Bring me a lot of them. A better world." They gave up on full sentences. It was becoming clear to me that the restriction on their vocabulary highly limits their communication skills.

"Are my friends in danger if I bring you these weapons?" I asked.

They seemed to be searching for a usable response. "They already are."

"What can I do to get you to leave them alone?" I asked.

"Return home," they responded quickly, as if they had already been planning to say that to me upon our encounter.

"Done deal!" *I get to go home, and I get to save good people on this planet? Count me in!* I thought to myself. "I just need to figure out how to restore those wires," I said, pointing to the ones that had been removed from the control panel, "and figure out how to navigate there, and then we'll be on our way out of your hair!" One of the other Kleit began making clicking noises with its tongue. "So that's how you typically communicate," I noted.

"I don't think you correctly understood," another Kleit stated mid-transformation. I was horrified to see Dimitri's face not far from mine, even knowing it was not Dimitri.

"Come back here!" the Kleit disguised as Dimitri demanded.

"This is not home for me," I informed them. "I am from Earth."

"You have been wrong all along," announced the Kleit disguised as Dimitri. "You belong here."

"Where exactly is here?" I asked.

"With us," the Kleit disguised as my sister replied. Two hands reached out to grab mine. The hands were soft like Zidia's. The fingernails were even painted a sky blue, like Zidia's often were. I had to remind myself not to let them catch me off guard with their impersonations.

"I want to go home to the real Zidia." My curiosity began to fade. I didn't want to explore this further. My protective instinct faded along with it. I suddenly felt the need for protection. My confidence plummeted. If there was any adrenaline left, it was out of fear for my own safety and not knowing what events would transpire.

"It's me, Zidia," the Kleit disguised as her assured me.

"Cut the bullshit." I shook my head in annoyance. "Show me who you really are." If I were going to be afraid, I wanted it to be of reality, not an illusion.

"I need to talk to you," the Kleit responded.

"You can clearly understand me either way. Help me understand you." The Kleit opened their mouth to respond, but I put my hand over their lips, still resembling the lips of my sister. "Help me understand the real you," I clarified.

"You'd have to come see," the Kleit responded, gently removing my hand from its face.

Their interaction and tone felt so genuine. I began to realize that my reason for asking that they transform back to their true selves was that this was beginning to feel too real. There were brief moments where I felt my sister was standing in front of me. I wanted to trust her. I wanted to come with her. I didn't feel like I was home, but I felt like a piece of home was here. As I studied the faces of Zidia and Dimitri, I was swiftly encapsulated in darkness.

I felt the fabric slip over my face. I attempted to gasp for air as they tightened it around my neck to prevent me from escaping, but I quickly realized the struggle was making me feel even more breathless. I felt all six of their hands lift me off the ground in one swift motion until I was being held horizontally and entirely at their mercy.

"No!" I heard Marquette scream in horror. I heard a loud noise, as if something were chucked at a wall. "Please, no," Marquette continued to plead, her voice becoming clouded with tears. It was an odd sensation hearing Marquette's anguished cries, feeling six hands along my elevated body, and sensing that something bad was about to happen, but only seeing darkness. Something about the darkness was calming, like nothing bad could possibly happen if I weren't able to see it. I closed my eyes and could tell no difference. I could hear the steady exhale of my breath, despite the noise of what I imagined to be Marquette struggling. I felt like I could hear my heartbeat amplified, though my calmness persisted. The calmer I felt, the more in control I felt. The more in control I felt, the more it crossed my mind that I could try to escape. The more the thought of escaping crossed my mind, the more I didn't desire to escape. I was calm, and escaping would just bring me back to being carried away by adrenaline and fear.

I imagined myself in Breckenridge, floating on my back in Mohawk lake, as I did one Summer vacation in my teens. My sister had egged me on to jump in after our mother warned us how cold the water would be. The second my skin touched the water, I felt the urge to scream out how cold it was and retreat, but I didn't. I wanted my sister to continue to see me as brave, calm, and collected. I always put on a show for her, trying my best to be perfect in her eyes. She had always been perfect in mine. Instead of retreating, I yelled out to her that the water felt perfect. I tried to hide the discomfort in my expression as I backstroked further toward the center of the lake. Then I floated there for what felt like an hour, staring up at the sky. I examined the white clouds that looked like stretched out cotton balls, making up stories in my mind of what each cloud looked like and where it was off to. I recall one that looked like a dog with its mouth open, as well as the cloud next to it that looked like a dog bone. I watched as the dog slowly followed it across the sky, constantly longing for it and persisting in its turtle chase but never quite getting to complete its goal and savor the taste of victory. As the clouds continued to drift on by, my mind eventually went blank. Everything was just peaceful and still.

That was how I felt now. I felt that everything was still. All of a sudden, the bag around my face was loosened and yanked off, and Marquette was frantically screaming words at me that I couldn't quite yet register. She looked like she was in a wrestler's prep stance, crouched down with her knees bent at almost a ninety-degree angle and her arms out in front of her. I looked around and saw all three Kleit lying motionless on the floor. One of them had an arm extended toward me, as if they had either just let go of my ankle or were about to grab onto it. *Did they drop me? Of course, I couldn't see before, but wouldn't I have noticed a fall?* What initially felt like coming back to reality in slow motion quickly sped back up.

"We have to go. Now!" Marquette yelled while stuffing food from the storage compartment into a bag. *Leave it to her to worry about food at a time like this.* As I stood up, the Kleit began to shift and try to upright themselves as well. The adrenaline was back, and the serenity was left in the dust. I yanked the sleeve of Marquette's shirt on my way to the spaceship door, pulling her away from the food that she was still shoveling into the bag. I quickly input the code to exit and stumbled out onto the desert terrain. Marquette tripped on the way out and landed at Tavion's feet. I whipped my head around to watch the door shut and to watch all three Kleit disappear behind it.

10

# A Connection Within and Among

Zara helped Marquette to her feet. "What the hell are those things?" Marquette exclaimed.

"Kleit," Sadie responded, with an irrationally bubbly tone.

"Huh?" Marquette rubbed her wrists where the ropes had visibly left indentations.

"We'll explain back at Klaysta headquarters!" Zara snapped. "We need to get away from here, now!"

"Do you have a way to get back faster?" Zara asked Tavion.

"On foot is the only way," Tavion replied.

"Can you all run?" Zara quickly inquired.

"No, my ankles are killing me." Marquette crouched down to rub at where the ropes had been restraining her ankles.

A decision was made for them when the entrance of the spaceship began to open back up. Zara was the first to run, with the others trailing not too far behind.

"Where are we going?" Marquette yelled out. She was beginning to fall behind, although she was trying her hardest to keep up.

"Klaysta's enclosed community!" Xavier replied.

"What?" Marquette shouted back at him.

"Just keep running!" Xavier responded. "We will explain later!"

Marquette groaned and slowed for a split second, but adrenaline hastened her movements when she looked behind her and saw the Kleit gaining on them.

"Not now..." Zara noticed from the corner of her eye that a boulder was shifting. "Tavion!" she yelled.

"I see it!" he responded. "Just keep running!"

"I'm not going to make it," Sadie cried out to Jerome.

"You will. You can do this!" he assured her. She shook her head and continued to run, but tears of frustration were running down her face as she pushed herself to keep going.

"Zara, do you know how to use this?" Tavion asked, touching a weapon strapped to his back while continuing to run forward.

"Yes," Zara responded.

"You're about to need it!" he yelled. He quickly removed it from his body and threw it at her, hoping she would catch it, but it landed on the ground to her right. She didn't slow her speed at all, but instead, she crashed to the ground and slid to it on her knees. She quickly rose to her feet with the weapon and scanned her perimeter, letting the others pass her. Looking around, she noticed the Kleit were now out of view, although that didn't mean much since they could be presenting in a different form.

Before she could position the long weapon into the horizontal position she needed to, an animal much larger than the Velteis leaped into the air in her direction.

"Xavier!" Tavion demanded his attention and threw a duplicate weapon at him. He caught it, whipped around, and shot a sword-like blade at the creature.

"Look out!" Xavier called out to Zara. Zara ran forward, the large animal crashing hard to the ground behind her and sending a massive cloud of sand into the air.

"Are you okay, Zar?" Sadie called out while coughing.

"Thanks to Xavier." Zara hunched over and joined the others in a violent coughing fit.

"What the hell is that thing?" Marquette asked, removing her glasses and wiping them on the inside of her shirt.

"A Seltivor," Tavion answered, walking over to it. It was lying on its side, with four long thick furry tan legs limply outstretched. Tavion climbed onto one of its front legs and walked up it as if it were a ramp, until he reached the shoulder. He withdrew the blade from its neck. "Nice shot, Xavier," he laughed.

Xavier waved it off while crouching down with his hands on his knees, still trying to catch his breath. Tavion stabbed the sword-like weapon back into the creature at the shoulder and used his full body weight to drag the weapon across the length of the animal, down to its stomach, and back across.

"How are we going to carry that back?" Zara inquired.

"In pieces," Tavion laughed.

"How can you be laughing?" Sadie asked.

"He's desensitized to all this," Zara responded for him. "He does this every day."

"How do you survive here, man?" Jerome asked.

"How indeed." Tavion shook his head with a mixed expression of humor and disgust.

"How close are we to where we are going?" asked Marquette.

Zara put her hands on her hips and looked at Jerome. "It's about a fifteen-minute walk?" Jerome guessed. He looked to Tavion for reassurance.

Tavion nodded as he sliced the thick raw flesh into squares. Zara looked out at the creature, trying to commit every detail to memory and debating drawing it upon their return. Its nose was the first thing to catch her eye. It looked like a fifteen-centimeter-long jigsaw blade, with the jagged edge on the top. Its large, pointed teeth were sharp and asymmetrical, with roughly eight on top and eight on the bottom. Its legs were cylindrical and as thick as the base of a bottle tree. Its fur was a beautiful light tan color. Zara gracefully ran her fingers through its coarse short fur while walking around to the other side of the animal and proceeding to explore its other features. Its ear was sharply pointed and slightly angled back toward its body.

"Can I come up there?" Zara yelled to Tavion.

"Yes, come up the way I did. Be careful," he instructed. Zara returned to the other side of the animal. Her eyes widened at the size of the creature's stomach. "Give me your hand," Tavion requested as he reached out to her.

Zara placed her hand in Tavion's, and he hoisted her up onto the leg. "I see how you got your muscles." Zara poked his arm with her pointer finger. His subsequent glare led to her prompt apology. Zara walked carefully up the creature's leg as Tavion had, until she reached its shoulder, careful to step over the gap where the flesh had been removed and onto the creature's neck. She gagged at the smell and sight of the creature's carcass, and her gag was quickly followed by uncontrollable dry heaving. She leaned over, thinking she might throw up. She reached out her arm with an open hand, mindlessly trying to find something quick to grab to stabilize her. Nothing was there, and she was losing her balance. Tavion noticed as she began to lose her footing and came quickly to her side, helping her into a sitting position on the creature's neck.

"Close your eyes," Tavion commanded. Zara did as she was told. Tavion then wrapped his hand over the top of hers and guided her hand back and forth slowly along the creature's fur. "We can make you a nice fur coat," he joked. Zara opened her eyes and glared at him. He put his free hand over her eyes, signaling for her to close them again. "I will be serious," he said, with no longer a trace of humor or lightheartedness in his tone. "Just continue to feel the fur." Zara continued to move her hand back and forth slowly along the creature's fur, even when Tavion withdrew his hand from hers. Everyone on the ground was quiet, both silently gawking at the creature and pondering what Zara and Tavion were still doing on top of it. "Differently," Tavion urged, "explore it."

"Huh?" Zara went to open her eyes, but Tavion covered them once more. He placed his hand back over hers, and instead of guiding her in the back-and-forth motions she had been doing, he held her palm in place with his hand and used his fingers to guide hers in back-and-forth motions along the creature's fur. He scrunched her fingers back toward her palm and then let them re-extend. He repeated this motion a few times before removing his hand once more and letting her continue to pet the creature on her own. She appeared like a cat kneading a blanket.

"Describe it to me," Tavion commanded.

Zara cleared her throat. "It feels coarse when moving my hand back and forth across it lengthwise, but when I do this," she continued to brush through its fur with her fingers, "it is extremely soft."

"The smell... it..." Tavion paused searching for the English word, "nauseated you."

"Yes." Zara's nose wrinkled as she recalled the horrid smell and began to notice it again.

"Only focus on the feeling of the fur," Tavion redirected her. "Continue to describe it to me."

"It's tan," she started.

"No!" he demanded. "The feeling."

"It's warm," she corrected.

"Yes, continue," he pressed on.

"Really warm... and it feels... a little oily... like if I hadn't washed my hair for a while."

"How does it smell?" he asked.

Zara leaned over with her eyes still closed to smell the creature's fur. "It smells like a tree!" She opened her eyes, surprised by the unexpected scent. "Kind of like a pine tree," she added.

"Very good," Tavion replied. "They spend a lot of their time in forest regions."

"What do you smell in the air now?" Tavion asked.

Zara took a deep breath in. "Trees!" Tavion stared out into the distance. "How did you do that?" Zara asked.

"Do what?"

"How did you change how I perceived the smell of this animal?"

"I didn't," Tavion responded. "You did. How do you see the animal?"

"It's beautiful," Zara replied.

"Even with a chunk missing?" Tavion asked. If Zara weren't mistaken, she could swear she saw a mournful expression on his face as he glanced back at the large pit across the length of the animal where its flesh and fur used to be. She looked at the empty pit in its body and took a deep breath.

"Yes." She closed her eyes, trying to remember what it looked like prior to the slaughter. "It is beautiful."

"As is everything here," Tavion noted.

"What about the Kleit?" Zara asked.

"I may have misunderstood what the English word 'everything' means." Tavion displayed a half smile.

"I guess I just don't understand how you can see something that is trying to kill you as beautiful." Zara looked at Tavion for clarification.

"There are two reasons in life that beings do what they do," Tavion explained. "The first is to survive, and the second is to use their action as a means to achieve a positive feeling." Zara looked more confused than before. "How can I say this differently?" Tavion asked rhetorically. "What is an action that you do that someone else might not be understanding of?"

Zara hesitated. "I mean... I brush my teeth in the shower... My sister has always judged me for that one."

"You have a sister?" Tavion smiled.

"Yes, back at home... er... on Earth," Zara corrected herself, remembering that Tavion believes her to be from Suvia, although she was still in disbelief.

"What is a shower?" Tavion asked.

"It's what we use to clean our bodies," Zara replied. She mentally noted that Suvians seem to have a firm grasp on the English language but get stuck when it comes to names of objects and devices that they don't use on Suvia.

"Okay, so you clean your body and your teeth at the same time? How is that odd?" Tavion asked. "Either way, you are cleaning parts of your body."

"That's a good point," Zara reflected.

"But what is your reason for doing it?"

"I guess to save time," Zara thought out loud to herself.

"What do you need the extra time for?" Tavion asked.

"To work and spend time with family." Zara brushed her hand along the animal again, feeling the coarseness of the fur.

"So, you brush your teeth in the shower in the long run to survive, because it gets you to work faster, and you need work to live. You also brush your teeth in the shower as a means to achieve a positive feeling, because it gives you more time with your sister, which feels good to you. Do I understand correctly?"

Zara zoned out contemplatively. "Yeah, I guess you do."

"The Kleit are not inherently bad," Tavion reiterated. "They have reasons for their actions that mean something to them. They are trying desperately to fulfill a need, whatever that need may be."

"I understand." Zara stood up and reached out her hand to help Tavion up. He waved it off and stood without assistance.

"Finally!" Xavier yelled when Tavion and Zara rose to their feet. "What the hell are you guys doing up there? Marquette has been groaning this whole time, Jerome has a headache..."

"We're coming!" Zara cut him off.

"About damn time," Marquette whined.

The group proceeded to return to Klaysta headquarters with chopped up Seltivor in tow, divided amongst three meat and pelt bags. When they arrived, Marquette was filled in about Klaysta, the other tribes, and the way of life for Klaysta on Suvia. Jerome, Sadie, and Xavier went to the underground sleeping quarters to rest. Marquette offered to help Kalari cook, hoping that participating in the making of the food would lead her to be the first to eat it. Zara requested to speak with Tavion privately.

Walking into Tavion's sleeping quarters with him, Zara felt nauseous. She couldn't pinpoint if the nausea was residual from earlier or newly developed from her nerves. She looked around the underground cave and noticed it was far less empty than the cave she and her crew had been sleeping in.

"Would you like anything to drink?" Tavion asked her.

"Yes, please." She barely let him finish the sentence, as her stomach continued to churn. He handed her a cup filled with liquid, and she drank it without inquiring what it was. It tasted sweet and slightly thick, almost like a smoothie.

"It's a type of fruit here. It is mostly liquid when you crack open the shell, and the thicker part of the fruit is thinned by hand and added to the liquid," he answered her unasked question. Zara just nodded and continued to drink. "More?" Tavion pointed to a bucket that likely contained twelve liters of the liquid.

"No, thank you." Zara looked around the room. There were five beds, as well as a long table carved out of wood and eight chairs tucked underneath it. Zara admired the woodwork. It reminded her of her father's work. She slid her hand along the curvy design of the chairs. There were drawings along the cave wall that appeared to be drawn by Tavion's children. Zara was captivated by a drawing of a Seltivor. *It truly is beautiful,* she thought to herself.

"Have your kids seen one?" Zara asked, pointing at the drawing.

Tavion shook his head. "I have only described it to them."

"Uncanny resemblance," Zara complimented.

"I'll tell them you said so," Tavion replied. "What is it you wanted to speak with me about?"

Zara ran her fingers gently along the cave wall, realizing based on the indentations that the drawings were carved into it. She walked the perimeter of the room and then sat on one of the beds. "Why are there five beds in here, and why is it that my friends and I have none?" Zara furrowed her eyebrows and looked at Tavion with an accusatory glare in her eyes.

"We didn't expect guests," Tavion answered honestly. "This bed is mine," he said, motioning to the one she was seated on. Zara brushed her hand along the blanket, realizing it was made from the pelt of an animal she had not seen before. "This one is Kalari's," Tavion continued, "two beds are for our children, and one is for a guest."

"Why do you and Kalari sleep on different beds?" Zara asked.

"That's just the way it is." Tavion paused for criticism, knowing that on Earth, partners typically share a bed.

"Does every man and woman on Suvia sleep in a different bed?" Zara inquired.

"To my knowledge, we are the only tribe with beds at all." Tavion sat down on Kalari's bed. "The others do not know about beds as far as I know. We made them after observing those on Earth use them."

"Well do others in this tribe..."

"Yes," Tavion interjected, "all men and women here sleep apart. Is this what you came here to talk about?" Tavion shot Zara an expression indicative of his annoyance.

"No, I'm sorry." Zara shifted nervously. "I've been trying to figure out what happened on board the spaceship." She proceeded to explain everything that happened from her perspective. After she finished explaining, Tavion took a moment to process the information.

After a long pause, he spoke. "So, you are confused as to why you felt so calm?"

"No..." Zara stood up and sat next to Tavion at the foot of Kalari's bed. She dangled one leg off the bed and tucked her other foot under her thigh. "I am confused as to how I suddenly ended up on the floor. I didn't feel like I was falling at any moment, and the Kleit all seemed to be momentarily still while Marquette and I evacuated."

"What did you feel?" Tavion asked.

"I just felt calm the whole time, and lost in thought, and before I knew it, I went from being held up by three pairs of hands to lying on the floor in confusion."

"Hmm..."

Zara continued, "It was as if I blacked out for a moment."

"Blacked out?"

"Just lost all awareness," she clarified.

"What did the Kleit look like when they were on the floor with you?" Tavion asked.

"I guess..." She paused as she tried to recall. "They were in their true form, arms outstretched toward me, as if they were either trying to grab me or had just let me go. They appeared to be momentarily stunned by something."

"Was anyone else present other than you, Marquette, and the three of them?"

"I don't think so." Zara closed her eyes as she tried to retrieve more details.

"Perhaps a member of the Vultra tribe was present and paralyzed them," Tavion stated.

"I forgot that they could do that," Zara replied, "but no, I am sure they were not present. I would have seen them. There is not really a place to hide onboard."

"Perhaps you were simply too lost in thought to notice the fall then," Tavion suggested.

"Perhaps," Zara agreed.

"Do you want to sleep here tonight?" Tavion asked, motioning to the guest bed.

"No thanks," Zara replied. "It would only cause tension between me and my friends if I separate from them for better sleeping accommodations."

"Understandable," Tavion replied. "You hungry?"

"Starving." Zara smiled.

Zara walked up the stairs and out of the tent, with Tavion trailing behind her. She was surprised to see far more beings in the Klaysta community than expected and to see beings that looked nothing like any others she had seen before. They were all scattered around at different campfires, feasting on the Seltivor.

"Who are they?" Zara asked, pointing at the unknown beings.

"Members of the Eyla tribe," Tavion responded, walking up to one of them to greet them.

Zara visually explored their features. They appeared to have scales on their skin like a fish but have arms like a human. Their fingers were webbed together. Their head had three elongated triangular prisms at the top, stretching out from their forehead to the back of their head. Their eyes glowed a fluorescent blue. They appeared to be wearing body jewels that draped over each shoulder, looped around their stomach, and winded down their legs. They were not wearing any clothing, and their skin color was a pale blue. Shades of blue, purple, pink, and red reflected from their scales. Zara was mesmerized. She looked down and realized their feet were uncovered. Their feet were thick and webbed, with the webbed part being twice as wide as their heel. The member of the Eyla tribe made a few sounds that to Zara sounded like nails on a chalkboard. Tavion spoke quietly to them.

"It's a pleasure to meet you," the being said, reaching out a hand to Zara. Their voice was highly unpleasant, crackly, and high-pitched.

It took Zara a moment to react, still astonished by the sight of them. "I am pleased to meet you too," she replied, shaking their hand. Their hand felt cold and slimy, and it was odd to shake their hand when the fingers were webbed together. She was initially shocked that they shared this greeting custom but presumed Tavion must have told them that it is custom on Earth so they would greet her in a way that she was comfortable with.

"We have a surplus of food from the Seltivor, so we invited them to join us," Tavion informed Zara. "It's a celebration of good fortune."

"Does this mean I can have more than one serving?" Zara asked. Tavion and the Eyla both laughed and guided Zara to the campfire.

# 11

# A Gut Feeling

THE EYLA THREW ITS fist into the air and shot an aggressive gaze at each of the Klaysta around the campfire that Zara and the others from Earth were not excluded from. Before Zara knew it, the Eyla had both webbed hands sprawled out over each of her knees and was leaning in toward her. She could see in its eyes, now only fifteen centimeters from her own, that the aggressiveness was gone. Fear had emerged in its absence.

Zara wanted to respond. She wanted to ask questions. How could she though? The Eyla seemed to be in the process of learning English. Most of their verbal communication throughout the night had been with members of the Klaysta tribe, through a mixture of English, their own native tongue, and the language native to the Klaysta. Amongst the varying communication styles, Zara couldn't keep up. She wasn't alone. Jerome, Sadie, and Xavier all had different expressions of confusion throughout the night. Marquette seemed to be disinterested and disengaged as she plowed through the dinner leftovers. To her, the Seltivor tasted like a sweet and salty chicken, with a lightly salted broth seeping out of each bite.

The Eyla was currently communicating solely through visual expressions, catering to the language barrier of Zara and the others from Earth. From what Zara gathered, the Eyla was informing them that there is a cave somewhere on Suvia that should be avoided, and yet is filled with alluring wonders. There are drawings on the walls, she put together, as the Eyla made the motion of carving a picture along an imagined vertical surface. There are traps along the floor, she interpreted, as the Eyla mimed stepping a foot down carefully and experiencing what looked like an electric shock.

Everyone around the campfire was on the edge of their seat, thrilled by the visual story being told. Klaysta and Eyla from other campfire groups had migrated over to observe the Eyla's story as well. The Eyla telling the story crossed both arms into an "X" formation with closed fists and threw its head back passionately. Then the Eyla relaxed its arms at its side, dropped its head forward, slowly walked backward toward the log of a tree that was being occupied by Tavion and Kalari, and sat down in between them. The Eyla threw its arms over Tavion and Kalari's shoulders and let out a scratchy chuckle.

"Where is this cave?" Zara asked Tavion. Everyone froze and looked to Tavion and the Eyla who had told the story for clarification.

"It doesn't exist," Tavion responded, without hesitation.

"What do you mean?" Sadie asked.

"It's what you would call a tall tale." Tavion stood, as most of the beings around the campfire began to disperse and turn in for the night. Their interest diminished as a result of the new information.

"So, nothing the Eyla showed us was real?" Jerome asked.

"The message of the story was real." Tavion turned to a few of the Eyla and wished them a good night, as well as safe travels back to their tribe. He picked up a bucket of water next to the fire and lifted it, preparing to put the fire out, but Zara put her hand on his wrist and gently pushed down on it. He set the bucket back down, and the fire remained lit.

"You can't tell me none of that was real." Zara shook her head in disbelief.

Marquette rolled her eyes. "Real or fake, I don't give a damn. I'm tired, and my feet are sore. I'm going to bed. Can someone show me the way?" She looked around expectantly, waiting for someone to fill her in on the sleeping arrangements.

"I'll accompany you. I'm getting tired myself," Jerome said. The two of them walked away from the campfire.

"Why are you always so close with him?" Kalari demanded an answer from Zara. She seemed to finally have snapped at the sight of Zara touching Tavion's wrist.

Zara opened her mouth to respond, but Tavion held up his hand toward Zara and commanded Kalari to return to their sleeping quarters. Kalari glared at him resentfully. "Kostuul," he said in a demanding tone.

"No!" Kalari cried out, not wanting to leave. She was embarrassed beyond words to be dismissed in front of Zara. Tavion took a step toward her. She quickly wiped away a tear of frustration and retreated to her sleeping quarters.

"What would you have done if she didn't listen?" Zara asked, after noticing the fear in Kalari's eyes.

"Oranian women always listen," Tavion asserted confidently.

"Then what will you do if I don't?" Zara coldly inquired.

"We will see when the time comes." Tavion lifted the bucket of water, this time pouring it quickly over the fire, leaving Zara no time to protest.

"If you do anything to hurt Zara, you'll be answering to me," Xavier announced. He straightened his posture in an attempt to appear more threatening. Sadie couldn't contain her smirk. Xavier noticed and felt slightly disheartened but continued to uphold his posture anyway.

"You two should go to bed," Zara requested, looking at Xavier and Sadie warmly. "I'll catch up with you in a bit." Xavier looked at Tavion and Zara hesitantly, not sure if he should leave them alone. "Go on," Zara urged. Xavier rolled his eyes and set off for the tent with Sadie.

"Goodnight, Zara." Tavion started to walk away, but Zara followed right behind him. "Is there no personal space on your planet?" Tavion halted and turned towards her, not making any attempt to hide his frustration with her.

"I just need you to tell me more about the cave that the Eyla was telling us of." Zara looked at him apologetically.

"Look, I know it was a fascinating story, but it isn't real. I don't know what else you want me to tell you."

"I can feel in the center of my gut that it is real."

Tavion shook his head, "Well, here on Suvia, we don't say to trust your gut. Goodnight." He turned away.

"If you won't talk to me about it, then tell me how I can get to the Eyla who told us of it." Zara raised her voice assertively.

"You're being ridiculous." Tavion shook his head, still facing away from her.

"Not only do I have a gut feeling that there is truth to the story, but I also have a gut feeling that I was sent here from Earth to help you... that we were sent here from Earth to help you," Zara expressed, holding an open hand out in the direction of the tent where Sadie, Jerome, Xavier, and Marquette were. "I can't help you if you don't trust me."

"Which one of us is distrusting?" Tavion asked. "I told you there is nothing more to the story, and it is you who does not trust me."

Zara paused in thought. "Fair enough, goodnight."

"Goodnight."

They both went their separate ways, but Zara could not let go of the notion that the cave did exist and that there was a lot more to it. If Tavion wouldn't help her, she'd find the answers herself.

When Tavion arrived in his underground sleeping quarters, his young were fast asleep, but Kalari was sitting up at the foot of her bed waiting for him. "What was that out there?" Kalari wouldn't look at him.

"What do you mean?" Tavion removed a bag with weapons and gear that had been strapped around his back and chest. He set it on the floor beside his bed, lay down, and covered himself with a pelt. He stared up at the ceiling.

"I mean, why would you send me away? Why wouldn't you send her away? You don't even know her!"

"She wasn't the one making unfounded accusations. If she were, I would have asked her to leave." Tavion pulled a string that hung above his head along the cave wall. The lights went out in response, leaving the underground cave pitch black. Kalari closed her eyes, and a single tear seeped through her sealed eyelids. She lay down and rolled onto her side, facing away from Tavion's bed.

"Goodnight," Kalari whispered. Silence ensued.

When Zara descended the stairs to join her colleagues in their sleeping quarters, everyone was still awake. Marquette was yelling loudly at Jerome, infuriated that he was refusing to return to the spaceship with her to try to return home. Sadie was yelling at Marquette for insinuating that the rest of the crew should be left stranded on Suvia. Xavier was pacing back and forth anxiously, trying to decide whether to chime in. No one acknowledged Zara's presence. She silently walked past everyone, grabbed a bag that she had set against the wall earlier that day, and returned up the stairs. When she exited the tent, she opened the bag to examine its contents, some of which she had packed up earlier, and some of which Marquette had managed to grab before their escape from the Kleit. Zara was happy to see a blanket she could use. She pulled it out and laid it flat along the ground beside the tent. She sat down and sighed. "What a nightmare," she spoke aloud to herself. She was feeling unbearably alone.

Zara reached back into the bag and pulled out the comm. She held it against her chest near her heart and began to tear up. She hadn't even attempted to reach her sister since she arrived on Suvia. She longed to hear Zidia's voice but had no idea what she would say to her. She wondered how she could possibly describe what had happened over the course of the last couple days, and she pondered whether she should tell her sister any of it at all. She set the comm down on the blanket in front of her and stared at it. She looked at it almost expectantly, as if her sister would try to contact her any moment. After an interval of silence and introspection, she picked it back up.

Zara breathed in and out, in alternation with each intermittent beep of the comm. The sound of the beeping was simultaneously calming and anxiety-provoking. Zara bit her lip and picked at the skin around her fingernails. When she realized she was doing it, she stopped, recalling how many times her sister nagged her about it being a bad habit.

"Hello?" Dimitri's voice came through the comm.

"Hey." Zara stared solemnly at a far away tent, lost in thought.

"What's going on?" Dimitri asked skeptically. Something sounded different about his voice, as if there were a hint of worry in it.

"I just needed someone to talk to I guess," Zara responded flatly. There was a long enough pause for Zara to ask Dimitri if he was still there.

"I'm here," he confirmed. "I guess I'm just confused as to why you lashed out at me and now are crawling back."

Zara opened her mouth to argue that she wasn't crawling but stopped herself. She thought more deliberately about what she wanted to say. "I guess... I really wanted to talk to my sister," Zara confided as she ran her fingers through her hair, feeling overwhelmed, "but I can't burden her with this. I can't talk to any of my colleagues, because they're preoccupied..." She paused and looked over her shoulder at the opening of the tent, still hearing yelling from the underground area below. "I can't talk to anyone right now," she continued, "except you."

"Zar, you're scaring me," Dimitri replied. "What is it?"

"We didn't make it to Mars." Tears streamed down Zara's face as she grieved the loss of her plan, the loss of being in control, and above all, the loss of hope to return to her family.

"So, they've been lying to us?" Dimitri questioned.

"Huh?" Zara wiped her tears on her sleeve.

"Zara, the mission is still being discussed on the news. NASA has reported that they changed the mission, and that you and the others are to inhabit Mars for eight more years."

"What?" Zara gasped.

"They indicated that it will be a ten-year plan in total."

Zara began to hyperventilate and couldn't help but begin to ramble. "I need you to do something for me. Dimitri, I need you to grab a pen and paper. I need you to write a phone number down. I need you to contact someone right now. You're going to have to write down every detail of the conversation and contact me immediately after. Do you understand? Did you say ten-year plan with eight more years to go? I don't... I don't understand..." Zara closed her eyes, praying that she would wake up and this would all just have been a dream.

"Zara, explain to me where you are and what's happening."

"Please just get the pen and paper," she responded. Her voice was slightly muffled as she burrowed her face into the blanket beneath her.

"Will you tell me after?" Dimitri demanded.

"Yes. Yes. Are you ready for the number?" Zara asked.

"Yeah, what is it?"

"1-800-777-6272. When someone picks up, ask for Nolan, the NASA administrator. He won't speak to anyone who dials NASA's phone line until they provide a six-digit employee code. Write down mine. It's 877246. Immediately after presenting him with that code, present him with the emergency code 8120-398. Let him know we did not make it to Mars. We went through some sort of wormhole in space and ended up on a planet no one knows exists." Zara tugged at her hair and sobbed. She waited for Dimitri to confirm his understanding, but he was silent. "Hello?" She waited for a response. After about ten seconds, the comm began to beep. Zara put it into rest mode. *He couldn't have said ten years*, Zara thought to herself. *And what of the news channels lying? Or do they think we really did end up on Mars? Ten years? Are they even trying to get us home?* Zara curled up into a ball on the blanket outside and drifted off to sleep.

When Zara woke the next morning, Tavion was standing over her. She blinked her eyes a few times in confusion. "I already told you, I have a spare bed if your sleeping arrangements are inadequate," he chuckled. Zara sat up and stretched. Her body was sore from sleeping only on a thin blanket on the ground.

"I'm okay," she muttered. "The sleeping arrangements are fine. I just had a bad night." The conversation with Dimitri played back word for word in her mind.

Tavion shifted with discomfort in response to the emotions Zara was displaying. "Ehrm... Do you want to talk about it?"

"No." Zara stood up and began to roll up the blanket.

Tavion's shoulders relaxed. "I was thinking we could go hunting this morning, just the two of us. There is something I want to show you."

"Sure." Zara put the blanket back into the bag and threw the strap over her shoulder. "Let me go put this away." She presented herself calmly, but she was one piece of bad news away from having a meltdown. She tried desperately to clear her mind by focusing on the environment around her. She paid special attention to the cracks along the walls and the stones embedded in the stairs as she walked down into the sleeping quarters.

"I'm so sorry about last night, Zar," Sadie greeted her. "I saw you come in, but I was just so angry with Marquette. I couldn't think of anything else. When I woke up and you weren't with us, I realized I should have asked how you were. Where did you end up last night?"

"I just..." Zara motioned to the top of the stairs but decided not to tell Sadie she had slept outside. She had no reason to make Sadie feel bad or guilty. "It doesn't matter. I understand. You were upset, and it sounded like you had reason to be."

"Thanks, Zar. I'm dying to return home. Will you help me try to figure out how soon?"

*Yeah, sure, in ten years.* Zara physically shook her head trying to rid herself of that idea.

"You won't?" Sadie asked, noticing Zara's gesture.

"No, I will, Sadie. I'm just under a lot of pressure right now. I'm gonna need you to hang tight." Sadie nodded her head in agreement.

"You ready?" Tavion peeked his head through the tent flaps at the top of the stairs.

"Yeah, let's go," Zara responded tiredly. "We'll be back soon," she informed Sadie.

"Okay." Sadie sat down at the table, folded her arms over on top of the wood, and lay her head down.

"Where are the others?" Zara didn't think to ask about Marquette, Jerome, and Xavier's whereabouts until she noticed how alone Sadie looked sitting at the table.

"They went on a walk, I guess. I didn't want to go."

Zara looked at Tavion. He shook his head no and mouthed "just us".

"I'll see you in a bit, Sadie." Zara wrapped her arm around Sadie's shoulder and pressed her cheek against Sadie's, hugging her affectionately from behind.

"Thanks, Zar." Sadie sighed and lay her head back down.

"I grabbed the weapons," Tavion said, handing one off to Zara.

"Thanks," she spoke solemnly. "Let's go."

As Tavion and Zara walked along, the only thing she had on her mind was her conversation with Dimitri from the night before. *We've been gone for two years*? she silently questioned to herself. It had only been three days since they arrived on Suvia. It made sense, she supposed, that the wormhole would impact how much time had gone by, but she could not comprehend the exact science of it. *Zidia must think I haven't even tried to contact her in the last two years*, Zara thought to herself. *How does the comm even work from Suvia?*

"Everything okay?" Tavion asked.

Zara laughed. "Not at all."

He seemed to know that what she needed most was silence. They walked along without speaking a word to each other until they reached a grassy area with lots of trees. The bark of the trees was light tan in color. The branches were outstretched far, and the leaves were bright orange. Tavion held his palm toward Zara, signaling her to stop as he scanned the area. Zara withdrew her weapon and aimed it forward expectantly.

"Come," he said, as he cautiously moved forward.

"I haven't been here before." Zara looked around analyzing the surroundings. "I haven't dreamed it either." The sky was a blended mix of orange and purple. The clouds were grey, and the purple from the sky seemed to reflect off the bottom of them. The grass looked slightly browned, as if it were desperate for a little bit of water.

"What animals should I be looking out for?" Zara asked.

"None," Tavion replied.

"None?"

"Most animals avoid this part of the terrain. The Kleit have put traps here too many times. The animals have learned."

"Well, if we are not hunting, what are we doing here?" Zara lowered her weapon.

"Stay on guard with that," Tavion urged. Zara quickly lifted her weapon back up and looked at him for further explanation. "Kleit could be nearby," he warned.

"Where are we going?" Zara asked.

"I wanted to show you something, remember?"

"Yes, but what?"

"Just wait." He rolled his eyes. Zara noticed and figured her mannerisms must be rubbing off on him. They walked on through the trees.

"We are sure these trees aren't Kleit, right?" Zara looked around cautiously, aiming her weapon in each direction as she scanned the environment.

"We can never be sure," Tavion responded.

"Well, that's cool," Zara nervously responded. She stopped for a moment. "I hear something."

"Water?" Tavion asked.

"Yes... It sounds like a waterfall."

"There is a fountain near here," Tavion confirmed her senses.

"Oh, you're taking me to see a fountain! Uhm... Thank you?" Zara lowered the weapon for a moment and scratched her head in confusion.

Tavion walked up to Zara, put his hand underneath the base of the weapon she was holding, and lifted it back up. "Do not lower it!" he firmly stated. "I am not taking you to see a fountain. I truthfully forgot it was even here." Just as he said that, they came into a clearing with a large, roughly circular field of bright green grass and a fountain dead center in the middle of it.

The fountain took up a sizable portion of the clearing. The base of it was gorgeous. A slanted octagonal foundation held up three pillars, which supported another octagonal platform. Atop that platform was a statue of what looked like a Kleit practicing some form of meditation or ritual. One foot rested on the platform. The foot connected to a slim leg, underneath an elongated torso and a vertical-oval-shaped head. Zara stared at the head, not knowing how to react to the statue's absence of a face. The other leg on the statue was bent, with the foot resting vertically along the midsection of the standing leg. The Kleit's hands were together, as if engaged in prayer, with its elbows extending outward at a forty-five-degree angle. Its head was held high, and Zara was certain that if it had a face, it would be staring expressionless into the distance. Zara traced the stream of water from the fountain from the bottom up with her eyes. When she realized the source, she was intrigued. There was a tipped stone bucket next to the Kleit's foot on the higher octagonal platform that was producing an ongoing stream of water.

"How does it keep going?" Zara asked aloud rhetorically. She approached the fountain slowly and reached her hand up to try to touch the bucket, but it was just out of reach. Being closer to the fountain, she could see fine detail carved into the stone. It was mostly just swirled patterns, but when she looked down at the base, some lettering caught her eye. She knelt down to get a better look.

"S.. I.. L.. V.. I.. A.." she read aloud. "Does it stand for something?"

"I think it's a name," Tavion responded. He paused for a moment and looked up at the trees with furrowed eyebrows. "There is an old saying... or I guess you might refer to it as a riddle or a poem. I believe it originated from the Kleit. My mother used to recite it to me to warn me of them."

"Your mother? How did it go?" Zara asked, looking up at him with the most genuine interest.

Tavion opened his mouth but closed it hesitantly. "It will sound odd in English."

"Well, tell it to me in your language first," Zara encouraged.

"Okay." He cleared his throat. "Destik ik alamon. Cort esta ik. Destik ik alamon. Nistul huuva sik. Leest Kleit loovon, dutra, eesta, vik. Letista vula Silvia, cort esta ik."

"That's beautiful," Zara responded.

"Only because you don't know what it means." Tavion shook his head and rolled his eyes.

"Okay, so tell me."

"It doesn't really have an exact translation..." Tavion scratched his head. "It is something along the lines of, 'Beware of the night devil. Run from the night. Beware of the night devil. It feeds on death. The Kleit have control, strength, happiness, and unity. Protected by Silvia, run from the night.'"

"Protected by Silvia?" Zara asked curiously. She brushed her fingers along the letters carved into the stone. "Who or what does Silvia protect?"

"I believe Silvia protects the Kleit," Tavion answered, "if Silvia is even a real being."

"If the Kleit are so happy and already have control, why would they need to be malicious?" Zara inquired.

"This poem is generations old. Maybe they do not anymore," Tavion reasoned.

"I guess." Zara stood up.

"We need to keep moving," Tavion urged.

"Lead the way." Zara let Tavion walk ahead of her and followed closely behind, still holding up her weapon on high alert.

As Tavion led them through the trees, he reached up repeatedly to snap off low branches and allow them more room to walk through. Zara thought about making conversation as they walked along, but there was something so tranquil about the silence. Occasionally during the walk, she would hear something small scurry through the trees. She didn't ask Tavion what it was, despite it making her jump a little bit the first time she heard it.

The trees seemed to be changing color with the sunset, gradually changing from a bright orange color to a dull copper. Zara admired the change but was beginning to feel eerie vibes as the cool air and the darkening forest alerted her to how late it was getting. She silently debated with herself whether it was time to break the silence. She still chose not to.

"Don't worry, we are almost there." Tavion looked back at Zara and noticed a wide-eyed expression on her face. "I'm sorry if I startled you," he added.

"No, it's just that I was thinking to ask." Zara let out a small breathy laugh at their continued synchronization.

"You can probably lower the weapon," Tavion informed her. "If we haven't been attacked yet, it is likely we won't be."

"Just to be safe," she responded, continuing to hold it in a ready position.

"You're learning," Tavion commended.

"So it seems," Zara replied with a slow nod of her head, her eyebrows raised, and an angled glance at Tavion. Something about her body language distracted him. He neglected to watch where he was going, and a low branch scratched against his head.

"Ow... Watch your step," he warned, rubbing a droplet of blood off the newfound scrape on his head. The blood was so dark. It was almost black.

"Are you talking to me or yourself?" Zara asked sarcastically.

"Ha," Tavion chuckled, squinting his eyes at her.

They walked a while longer in a silence that was only broken by snapped tree branches and a light breeze sifting through the leaves. "This is it," Tavion finally announced.

Zara looked around, only to see similar surroundings to what they had seen most of the day. "This is what?"

"This is what you asked me to show you," Tavion responded sullenly.

Zara froze and tilted her head in confusion. When it finally registered, her excitement caused her body to move faster than her mind. She walked quickly ahead of Tavion and cleared the branches ahead of her by pushing them away from her body and off to each side with her hands. Her jaw dropped. Ahead of her was a massive cave. Unlike the underground tunnel leading to the Klaysta community, this cave's entrance was not blocked by anything, nor could it be. It had to be five times as tall as her and proportionally wide.

"Wow," Zara said, walking forward.

"Hold on." Tavion grabbed Zara's hand and pulled her back towards him. She kept her head turned toward the cave, wide-eyed with wonder and excitement. "There is a reason I didn't want to tell you about this place, and there is a reason that most beings on Suvia believe it to be a myth." Zara looked back at him speechless. "It's not safe to go inside," Tavion declared.

"Oh no. No. No!" Zara shook her head in frustration. "You can't tell me you brought me all the way here and won't let me go inside. I'm going inside," Zara asserted.

"I didn't say you can't go inside. I said the inside is not safe," he clarified, "but we are both going in."

"Wait... You're not worried?" Zara asked skeptically. His lack of worry caused hers to spiral. She placed her hand on her stomach, as she began to feel nauseous.

"Of course, I am worried!" Tavion exclaimed. "But I know you would have searched for this either with or without me, and I will be less worried about your safety if I am here with you."

"You only just met me. Why are you so worried about what happens to me?" Zara knelt down at the base of a tree and brushed her fingers through her hair anxiously.

"Call it a gut feeling," Tavion responded.

"I thought you don't have those on Suvia." Zara looked up at Tavion with a slight harshness in her eyes. She felt like he was mocking her.

"Call it a connection." He knelt down next to her, and her gaze softened.

"I'm getting another gut feeling," Zara said, turning her head towards him.

"What's that?" Tavion inquired.

"That it's time to go in." Zara rose to her feet and held out a hand.

Not reaching for her hand, Tavion stood as well and nodded in affirmation.

They both slowly walked toward the entrance of the cave. "Have you gone in here before?" Zara asked hesitantly.

"Once," Tavion nodded.

"And?" Zara prompted.

Tavion cleared his throat and tilted his head, seeming to be anguished by a sudden emotion. "I didn't get very far," he informed her. He held out his forearm, displaying a thick scar.

"What happened?" Zara asked, stopping in her tracks for a moment.

"There are traps inside. I left after encountering one, so I am not sure what others are in there."

"Tell me of the one you encountered." Zara turned toward him. They were only about a meter from the entrance of the cave.

"There isn't much to tell," Tavion replied. "I apparently stepped in the wrong place, or maybe crossed a motion sensor, triggering a blade to shoot out of the cave wall and through my arm."

"Through your arm?" Zara asked.

Tavion twisted his arm to show her a second scar where the blade had caused a perforating wound. "Through my arm," he repeated. Zara was silent and still. "Still want to go in?" Tavion asked, pulling a flashlight from one of his pockets and turning it on.

"Yes," Zara spoke hesitantly.

Together, they entered the cave.

12

# THE CAVE

AN OVERWHELMING DARKNESS WAS all around me. I was cold. I was wet. I was alone. I was bleeding. When I had entered the cave with Tavion, he promised he wouldn't leave my side. As I put pressure on the wound on my shoulder, I closed my eyes and cringed at the memory of his words, wishing he was able to keep that promise. There was no point in sulking over what could have been. I had to move forward, but with every step, a new threat came my way.

I looked down at the circular bruise on my leg which looked about equivalent to the circumference of a baseball. I chuckled hopelessly. That bruise was the least of my worries. I couldn't stop thinking that this cave could be the end for me. I might not ever make it out. I might not ever see my family. I might not ever be reconnected with Tavion. If I wanted to get out of this, I had to think more optimistically, but that was hard to do when I had already encountered seven traps and been scathed by two.

I took a deep breath and scanned the cave floor, walls, and ceiling. Most of the cave floor had embedded rocks and a rough, uneven surface, but parts of it looked smooth, as if they had been sanded down. The walls were far apart in this area of the cave, while in other areas, the cave broke off into various narrow pathways. The ceiling looked similar in texture to the rough part of the cave floor but had an arched curvature. I didn't see anything to fear, but that didn't say much. Everything looked more or less the same up until this point. And yet... I looked at the blood still dripping along my shoulder and sighed helplessly.

I didn't know if I could progress, but I knew I couldn't stay still. I cautiously lifted one foot off the ground and stepped down just a few centimeters forward. Nothing happened. That didn't bring me any relief. If anything, it made me more anxious. I did the same with my other foot. Still nothing. My shoulder was stinging, and my eyes were slightly clouded by tears of pain. I continued to move my feet, little by little, quickly looking around the room with each movement. After about ten small steps, I decided to take a slightly larger step. Still, nothing happened.

I ended up making it to the center of the room. If there was any part of the room that I would have expected to be most dangerous, this was it. I was out in the open. Each wall and pathway were approximately equidistant from me. There was nothing between me and the walls to block potential projectiles.

I had a feeling that the next step would have a negative outcome. I crouched down and put pressure on the cave floor with my hands. Nothing came of it. Remaining crouched down, I put my foot out in front of me and leaned my body weight into it. A sharp blade shot quickly from the cave wall to my right, flew over my head, and seemed to disappear into the wall to my left. Startled, my breathing intensified, and I felt like I was repeatedly gasping for air.

After taking a few minutes to calm myself, I looked at the wall the blade had gone through. The slit it disappeared into must have been microscopic, because examining it visually, I could not observe any gaps in the structure. This trap was a repeat. I cringed at the memory of the blade that shot out of the cave wall and grazed my shoulder. My blood seemed to finally be clotting, as I noticed none of it was dripping down my arm anymore.

Thinking there may be safety in staying low, I continued to stay crouched down as I moved forward. I became hopeful as I approached the edge of the room where it branched off into other pathways. I looked at each pathway, wondering which to take. They all looked way too similar to make any sort of informed decision. I chose the one that was furthest to the right. I made my way to it slowly, still in the crouched position. Almost there. I just needed to move my feet a few more times. With the next step, a sharp spike went through my foot. Before I could process the extent of the pain, the sight of it caused me to faint.

When I came to, I was lying on the cold cave floor, with my foot still planted where it had been impaled. My body felt so sore all over. I lifted myself up with my elbows and forearms, enough to see my injured foot. The spike was no longer protruding through my foot. It must have retracted back into the floor. I couldn't see the hole in my foot, only blood. Scared that I would eventually see it and pass out again, I tried to rip the fabric of my shirt to use part of it as a bandage. I didn't have the strength. Determined to cover the injury, I looked at the rocks embedded in the cave floor. Some of them were sharply sticking out. I took my shirt off and ran it along a sharp rock until it separated the threading. I ripped off a piece of the shirt, starting to pull from the tear I created. After removing a large chunk of the fabric to use as a bandage, I put the torn shirt back on and carefully secured the part I ripped off around my foot.

"Agh," I cried out in agony. My cry echoed through the cave. My foot hurt so badly. I knew I would no longer be able to put pressure on it. I carefully lifted myself up into a standing position, not touching my injured foot to the ground. I limped to the wall on the righthand side of the entrance to the narrow pathway, praying I would not set another trap off in the process. When I first entered the cave, all I wanted to do was explore it. Now, all I wanted to do was escape it.

I wasn't looking to search new areas of the cave at this point. I was looking for any exit I could find. I had gone through too many branched off hallways of the cave to know how to get back the way I came. Also, despite knowing what traps there were between the entrance and here, I did not desire to relive them. I prayed, probably foolishly, that if I kept moving forward, the traps would diminish.

I thought for a moment about what to do. I felt like I would lose balance if I didn't hold the cave wall for support. Before I could come to a conclusion about the best plan of action, I heard a noise come from behind me. Two circular saw blades were moving quickly along the floor of the cave in my direction. Though I noticed quickly and hopped on my uninjured foot to get out of the way, one of the blades nicked the back of my right ankle, on the same side as my injured foot. I grabbed the wall on the other side of the entrance to the narrow pathway and lifted my leg to inspect the damage.

I didn't know if it was the adrenaline, the small size of the cut, or the overshadowing pain of my foot, but I didn't really feel it. I did feel something though. I noticed my ankle was quickly beginning to swell up. I started to feel incredibly nauseous, and just a few moments after getting scratched by the blade, I leaned over and began to vomit. Once I started, I couldn't stop. My mouth tasted of acidity, and the cave started to reek of a mix of vomit and mildew.

I crouched down along the cave wall feeling weak and helpless, continuing to vomit until there was nothing left in me for my body to reject, at which point I started dry heaving. I looked at the back of my ankle. It was changing color from pale tan to a brownish red. I put the back of my hand to my forehead and noticed my body temperature increasing. I didn't know if I was poisoned, sick, or experiencing a reaction to intense stress, but I knew for sure that something was not right.

I needed to get out of the cave, and I needed to get out quick. I was becoming more certain by the minute that if I stayed put, I would die. My thoughts became frantic, and I could no longer incorporate logic into planning my exit strategy. I bolted. I bolted on one foot. I got surprisingly far without encountering any traps and began to wonder if the trick to navigating the cave was speed. I began to wonder if perhaps I could out-hop the traps. Water splashed up at me from puddles along the floor of the cave. The smell of vomit and mildew traveled with me. I was feeling extremely fatigued, but I relentlessly kept moving forward.

My eyes widened when I saw a hint of light at the end of the pathway, still fairly far from my current position. *Could that be an exit?* I hopped faster than I thought I could, as a newfound hope sparked my motivation. The closer I got, the more certain I was that it was indeed an exit. A smile spread across my face. I felt insane for having the capacity to smile with a hole in my foot, a massive bruise, and a bloodied shoulder. I closed my eyelids over my watery eyes and leaned my head back, thinking only of how thankful I would be to exit the cave. When I opened them again, I pursed my lips and cried hysterically. There was no light. There was no exit. I was so sure it had been an exit. How could I have seen something so clearly, only for it to vanish?

"Zara," Tavion's voice boomed through the cave. He sounded close.

"Tavion? Where are you?" I called back. I got no response. I looked in each direction. There were only three directions I could go. I was at a T-shaped fork in the cave. I could turn left, right, or go back the way I came. When I got separated from Tavion, it was due to a boulder that crashed down from the ceiling separating the only path we had to each other. Turning back would not help me find him. But where should I go then? "Tavion?" I called out again.

"Zara, I'm over here!" he yelled. It sounded like his voice was coming from the left pathway. The pathway was narrow and dark. I had to feel my way through it.

"Tavion, keep talking to me," I begged. There was no response.

I felt something slimy along the walls and almost gagged as it enveloped my hands. Suddenly, it was getting hard to breathe. I could hardly feel where I was going, as the slime prohibited me from running my fingers along the wall as a guide. Before I knew it, the entire front of my body was covered in slime as well. I hit something hard beyond the slime. *It must be a dead end*, I thought to myself. Now I really couldn't breathe. Slime was covering my entire body in the front, including my mouth and nose. I pulled the back of my shirt, which was still free of slime, and wiped it across my mouth. I gasped for air. The air was filled with some sort of chemical. I still couldn't breathe. A loud crash sounded behind me, causing me to jump. I reached my hand out behind me and felt a large blockade. I was trapped.

I turned forward and felt around in a panic. I felt nothing but slime. I crouched down and continued to feel for the walls. *Bingo*. I went to touch the wall ahead of me, anticipating more slime, but my hand fell forward onto the floor of the cave. I lifted my hand straight up from where it had fallen onto the floor and felt an extremely low ceiling. This was another pathway, but I would have to blindly crawl through it, not knowing what was on the other side. I stood back up and used the clean side of the back of my shirt to wipe my eyes. I crouched down again and looked through the crawl space. Crawling through this would be like crawling through a vent. I could see a little bit of light on the other side but couldn't tell what it was leading to. It didn't matter. It was my only option.

I entered the crawlspace. As I moved forward, my injured foot kept making contact with the cave floor, and my shoulder kept making contact with the cave wall. I repeatedly stopped, as the pain became unbearable. I was beginning to feel claustrophobic. I willed myself to move forward. The pain intensified. I pushed myself to take just a few more strides. It felt like knives were piercing my wounds. I could see that the crawlspace did not extend much further. It felt like I was being crushed. I began to quicken my pace.

The walls were moving in. I was being crushed. I began to hyperventilate but still moved as quickly as I could. So close to the exit of the crawlspace, I realized I could no longer move. For a moment, I accepted that this is how I was going to die. Just in time, an idea came to me. I quickly slid my hands under my body and rapidly moved them up and down my chest and stomach. Then, I wrapped my arms across my stomach beneath me and spread slime to my sides. I wiggled around, trying to get the slime to spread to other parts of my body. I extended my arms in front of me and was able to latch my hands around the wall of the exit. I pulled myself forward. My torso was out. The crawlspace was still shrinking. I pushed off the ground with my knee and got one leg out. The crawlspace shrank further. Just as I pulled my injured foot out of the crawlspace, it fully sealed, as if it had never been there to begin with. I stopped to catch my breath and realized I could actually breathe now. I fell onto my back and stared up at the ceiling, not bothering to look around the room I just entered.

"Is she okay?" I heard a nasally voice ask.

"She doesn't look okay," another nasally voice answered.

"I think she got caught in the pit," a new voice chimed in.

"Ooh, not another one. This is the fifth victim this week!" the first voice exclaimed.

I blinked a few times and saw small creatures floating above me. They looked no bigger than a cell phone, and they had four tiny wings attached to their backs that were rapidly fluttering to keep them in the air. They had big round noses, round heads, and pointy ears. They looked like little colorful elves with wings. They all had green eyes but different colored skin. One was blue. Another was orange. The third was yellow.

"Helloooo?" the orange one said to me. I looked up at it and blinked in confusion.

"Don't talk to her. She could be dangerous," the blue one cautioned.

"She doesn't look very dangerous." The yellow one flew down, strained itself to lift my pinky, and let my pinky fall back onto the floor.

"She's injured." The orange one poked at my foot.

"Okay, that's enough!" I yelled.

"Zara? Zara is that you?" I heard Tavion's voice. "Zara, are you in here?"

"Oh boy, the big guy is crying for help again." The orange one pointed behind him with his thumb and shook his head, seeming to be annoyed.

"Tavion? Yes, I'm here!" I exclaimed. "And so are... these things?"

"Hey! Watch it lady!" the blue one scolded me.

"Yeah! Who you callin' a thing?" The yellow one crossed its arms, offended.

"What things?" Tavion called out. "Come help me."

"These.... Uh... What are you?" I asked the floating elves.

"We're lucinegens!" the orange one proudly stated.

"No, we're not, Larry. We're lucinations," the yellow one clarified.

"Hallucinations." The blue one rolled his eyes.

"You're not real?" I asked.

"What? Of course, I am real," Tavion responded. "I'm stuck! I need your help."

I ignored Tavion. "Why am I hallucinating?" I asked.

"You're not!" Tavion exclaimed. "I really am here!"

"You went into the hallucination room. It smells like chemicals in there," the blue one responded.

I tightened my eyelids hard and then reopened them. "How do I stop hallucinating?" I asked.

"What? You're tired of us already?" the yellow one asked. "Hmph!" He snapped his fingers and disappeared.

"You're not tired of me though? Are you?" The orange one flew down by my face and pouted. I swatted at him. He disappeared too.

"You don't have to worry. I'll do the honors," the blue one stated with harsh sarcasm.

"Thanks," I said once they all had vanished.

"Thanks for what? Are you okay?" Tavion reminded me of his presence in the room.

*Wait, am I still hallucinating?* I thought to myself. I stood up and looked around the room. "Tavion!" I ran to a metal net that was suspended from the ceiling with Tavion trapped inside of it. He was curled into an unimaginable position for his size. His dark blood was dripping off the metal and onto the floor. Visible spikes were all along the inside of the net.

"I need your help." Tavion breathed heavily.

"How long have you been in there?" I questioned as I quickly inspected the net.

"Since we got separated," he informed me. That had to have been at least an hour ago.

I looked at the pool of dark red on the cave floor. "You've lost a lot of blood."

"Yes. When I first got trapped by this, I tried to get out. The more I struggled, the more I got stabbed. I can't move without getting injured further."

I stared up at the net, hoping some clue would come to me for how to release him. The net was connected to the cave ceiling by a thick metal ball. It didn't look like there would be any hope of getting that to budge. I traced each part of the metal with my eyes. It was a highly secure, expertly constructed contraption. Whoever made this did not intend for anyone to ever escape it. I bit my lip. My eyes squinted at the pain in my foot and shoulder. I was having trouble focusing on anything but the pain.

"Zara, does it look like there is any way for me to get out of this? If not, leave me here. We are right by the exit to the cave."

The absurdity of his request helped me return quickly to the matter at hand. "No, what are you crazy? I can't leave you in there! You would die!" I shouted.

He looked at me out of the corner of his eye, not moving his head, trying desperately to avoid getting stabbed by more spikes. "You're injured!" he exclaimed. "It's only going to get worse and put you in more danger to stay. The only reason I came here is to protect you! If there isn't a way to help me, just go."

"There is a way!" I yelled.

"How?"

"I don't know," I cried. "I don't... Wait a minute... One, two, three, gap, four, five, gap, six, seven, eight, gap, nine, ten, gap... There is a pattern of gaps in the spikes! If you can slide your limbs into those gaps, you can gain control without getting stabbed."

"Guide me!" Tavion looked at me again out of the corner of his eye.

"Okay." I limped over to the net and crouched underneath it to get a better view of where his arm was. "You need to lift your right elbow straight up. Keep your arm at the same angle it is at now. Slide your elbow to the right three centimeters and set it down slowly. If this works as planned, your arm should fit right into the gap between the spikes, and you won't get stabbed."

Tavion did as I instructed and let out a sigh of relief. "Keep going."

"Okay, next, you need to lift your right foot, and pull it back about five centimeters. Keep your knee bent. Don't let your leg touch the net."

He lifted his foot, and the net began to sway back and forth. *Crap.* I hadn't thought about his position being an essential component of balancing the net. Worried he would get stabbed as the net moved back and forth, I put my hand around one of the metal wires to stop it from moving.

"Ow!" I yelled out. I pulled my hand back and looked at it. I was bleeding, but the injury wasn't deep.

"Thank you!" Tavion exclaimed. "But please do not do that again!"

"Wasn't planning on it," I said smugly. "How good are you with balance and strength?" I had an idea.

"Just tell me what I have to do." He looked at me with a hint of worry in his expression.

"Flip onto your right arm and your right foot and hold yourself in that position. Don't let the rest of your body touch the net."

"I think we're shooting for the stars, Zara." Tavion relaxed his body a little, as if he were about to give up.

"I shot for Mars, and it led me to you!" I exclaimed. "You can do this!" Tavion took a deep breath and quickly flipped himself up, touching only his right foot and his right elbow to the net. "Yes!" I hopped up and down with joy. "I don't know how long you can stay like that, but you need to look around and try to find a way out! I think I have given you all the help I can from over here."

Tavion looked around at the top of the net from the inside. "There's a screw!" he exclaimed. He reached up quickly with his left hand, untwisted what was holding the net together, and the net came collapsing down onto the floor, Tavion falling on top of it. He yelled out in pain as he landed with his back face down on the spikes.

"Tavion!" I ran to him. He closed his eyes. "Tavion, are you okay?" He grumbled something I couldn't understand. "We have to go!" I pleaded.

"Can you carry me?" he asked.

"Glad to see you still have your sense of humor." I smiled, and a tear of joy leaked from one of my eyes. "You're going to have to accept my help this time." I held out my hand. He grabbed it, and with both of our strength, he was able to get off the spikes with minimal injury. Tavion had blood dripping down all over his body. "Are you going to be okay?" I asked.

"We're going to be okay." He wrapped his hand gently around my injured shoulder, brushing his thumb along my skin to the side of my wound. "Let's go," he said. "The exit is this way."

"Wait!" I exclaimed. Wrapped up in releasing Tavion from the trap, I had neglected to look around the room we were in. The cave walls were covered in pictographs. There were carved pictures of kids playing, families hunting, the Kleit mid-shapeshift... and there was an odd picture of what looked like a dark cloud with a face on it. My foot was in severe pain. I looked up at Tavion. "After we heal, we need to come back here," I asserted. He looked at me with undeniable disappointment.

13

# THE RIDE AND FALL

W HEN ZARA AND TAVION returned to the Klaysta community, it was the middle of the night. There was a heavy fog in the air that blocked the light from the moons and darkened their surroundings. What looked like a safe haven earlier in the day now looked eerie. There was a cold breeze, giving Zara goosebumps and adding to the effect.

"Wow..." Zara watched every step she was taking as she and Tavion walked toward the tents. "Something feels off."

"I feel it too," Tavion replied.

"When will daylight come?" Zara asked.

"It'll be a while," Tavion replied. "As soon as it does, you and I are going to reconnect with the Eyla tribe to get medicine and heal our wounds."

"Will they come here?" Zara asked.

Tavion sighed. "No. We will go there. I don't want anyone here knowing what happened. Please say nothing of the cave to your friends."

Zara glanced at her shoulder and foot. "I can barely walk. How will I explain that to them?"

"You'll come sleep in the guest bed in my tent. We'll be gone before they wake. You can't be sleeping on the ground with those injuries anyway."

"What about Kalari and your children?"

"They'll be asleep by now, and they aren't the earliest of risers."

"This doesn't feel right." Zara looked at Tavion with a shameful expression.

"It'll all be fixed tomorrow, Zara. You just have to trust me."

Zara nodded. The two of them continued walking toward Tavion's tent, stopping a few times for Zara to rest her foot.

When they made it to the entrance of the tent, Zara turned toward Tavion. "What if my colleagues wonder where I was all night? What if they're worried about me?"

"I will go speak with them before we meet with the Eyla and let them know I am taking you hunting."

"And explain your injuries?"

"I will cover them." Tavion motioned for Zara to enter the tent.

She ducked her head under and began to descend the stairs. She took each step slowly, as it was pitch black. She had to feel her way, brushing her fingers along the wall to her right and using her good foot as a guide. On the fifth step, she tripped. In a quick effort to balance herself and avoid falling forward, she flailed her arms. Her left arm hit Tavion's chest.

He held his breath, trying not to wake Kalari and his kids as agonizing pain overcame him. Zara had hit him in a spot where he had been injured. Tavion grabbed Zara's arm and pulled her back toward him. She regained her balance.

"Whew," Tavion whispered. Worried she would fall again trying to get down the ten remaining stairs, he lifted her in his arms and carried her the rest of the way. He quietly grunted, as his pain intensified from holding her up and sustaining the extra weight down the stairs. Beside the guest bed, he set Zara down to stand while he pulled back the pelt for her. He then picked her back up and laid her down on the bed.

"ALTERI!" a small voice yelled.

Zara jumped out of the bed, fell onto the floor, and slid herself backwards on her bottom until her back was against the cave wall. Thinking fast, Tavion grabbed the pelt from his bed and wrapped it around his body. There was a soft clicking sound, and light came on in the cave.

"Tavion?" Kalari rubbed her eyes.

"Yes. I'm here," he replied, quickly moving in front of her to block Zara from her view. "Turn the light off. Go back to sleep."

"Why did Avio yell?" Kalari asked. "Avio, is everything okay?"

Tavion looked at Avio, a friend of his children who he recognized, and vigorously nodded, hoping Avio would understand his gesture and respond to Kalari that all was fine.

Avio squinted in confusion. "Mmm… I'm good," Avio said, lying back down to sleep.

"Why are you back so late?" Kalari turned her attention back to Tavion, her eyelids drooping with exhaustion.

"Time escaped me on a walk back from visiting the Eyla," Tavion replied without hesitation. "Let's rest." He brushed his hand along her skin, and she closed her eyes in response. Before her eyes could open again, Tavion took advantage of the moment by leaning over and turning out the light. He walked over to the guest bed and draped the pelt back over Avio. Then he approached Zara, still frightened against the cave wall, and lifted her in his arms once more. This time, he carried her to his own bed and gently laid her down.

Zara wanted to protest and ask Tavion where he would sleep, but she said nothing in fear of waking Kalari. Her question was answered anyway only a moment later when Tavion lay down beside her and draped the pelt over both of them. Zara didn't know how to react. She felt like she should be upset with this sleeping arrangement but also felt a deep sense of comfort as he wrapped his arm around her. She buried her face in his chest. He smelled like bamboo and wildlife. His chest was smooth, unlike his rough hands. Tavion shifted the pelt slightly to ensure Zara's head was fully hidden, in case Kalari should wake up. Warmed by the soft pelt and comforted by Tavion's smooth skin against her cheek, Zara fell asleep quickly. Tavion stayed up for hours.

Morning came quickly, especially for Tavion and Zara, who needed to evacuate Klaysta headquarters unnoticed. Tavion nudged Zara gently.

"Hmm?" Zara sleepily inquired.

"Shhh, we need to get up," Tavion whispered. He nudged her again.

Zara's eyes opened slowly at first but proceeded to shoot open quickly when she registered that she was still lying in bed with Tavion. She sat up and looked around the room anxiously. Everyone else was still asleep.

"You go up first, and then I will follow," Tavion instructed.

Zara nodded. She slowly lifted the pelt, gently put her feet on the floor one at a time, and walked as quietly as she could to the staircase. She was thankful the stairs were made of stone and dirt instead of something more creaky like wood. With four more steps for Zara to take, Kalari sat up in bed.

"Zara?" Kalari paid no attention to Tavion, who was filled with worry in the bed next to hers.

"Oh, hey." Zara waved nervously.

"What are you doing here?" Kalari proceeded to interrogate.

"Oh... I... was going to come down here and ask what the hunting plans are for today, but I saw that everyone was asleep and decided I'll come back later. Please don't let me disturb you." Zara turned back toward the exit, hoping she was in the clear.

"Well, I'm up now, and it appears Tavion is too. You might as well ask him since you're here," Kalari urged in a harsh tone, slightly annoyed by Zara's presence.

"Uhm... Well, I'm really tired, so if we won't be hunting for a while, I think I'll just go back to bed," Zara spat out anxiously.

"Suit yourself." Kalari waved her off as if she were shooing a fly and lay back down with her eyes closed. Zara departed from the tent.

"I'm going to go talk to her," Tavion said to Kalari. "It is best we get an early start on hunting."

"Why is she still hunting?" Kalari asked with her eyes still closed. "I thought that was a one-day thing as punishment."

"It was, but it turns out she is good at it. We can use the extra help." Tavion stood up and stared at Kalari for a moment, fearful that she would open her eyes and see his injuries. He debated taking the pelt with him to cover himself but worried that would cause more suspicion. He slowly grabbed weapons and a meat and pelt collection bag and walked up the stairs. Unbeknownst to him, Kalari quietly sat up in bed. At the sight of scrapes and cuts all over his back, her eyes widened, and she quickly covered her mouth with her hands to refrain from audibly gasping.

When Tavion exited the cave, Zara was waiting for him outside. Zara was looking up at the sky amazed. It looked so different this early in the morning. Instead of the usual shades of orange with hints of purple, red, and pink, it was now an equal mix of blue and purple with dark blue clouds. The blue in the sky almost looked like a sea green. Zara began to feel like she was out at sea, as the image seemed to merge with her, glistening in the reflection of her eyes and moving a river of quiet thoughts through her mind.

"No time to linger," Tavion said, wrapping his arm around Zara's shoulder and guiding her forward. He was careful to avoid contact with her injury.

"How long will it take us to get to the Eyla?" Zara asked quietly, so as not to wake anyone in the Klaysta community.

"About half a day, walking," Tavion informed her.

"Half a day?" Zara furrowed her eyebrows, and the corner of her lips pulled down with a look of disgust and exhaustion.

"I said half a day, walking," Tavion clarified. "We will not be walking."

"Then how will we get there?" Zara asked.

"We will discuss it when we get out of here," Tavion responded. He heard someone yawning and coming up the stairs of a tent nearby. Tavion jogged forward, motioning for Zara to keep up. It took both of them to move the boulder that blocked off the exit tunnel to get out of the Klaysta community. Their injuries made it difficult for them to complete this task. When they exited the tunnel and replaced the second boulder, they were able to speak more freely.

"We didn't tell my friends where I will be!" Zara turned back anxiously.

"I thought it over, and we can't risk it," Tavion responded.

"But..."

"It will be fine, Zara. Let's go," Tavion harshly commanded.

"Not if you're going to talk to me like that," Zara said, crossing her arms. The two of them looked at each other impatiently.

"Do you want to heal your injuries or not?" Tavion pressed. They smirked at each other and shook their heads in unison, both well aware by now of their shared stubbornness.

"So, how are we getting to the Eyla?" Zara asked.

"The same way they got to us. We will travel on the backs of the ground rock rhinos." Tavion smirked.

"Very funny," Zara responded. "How are we actually getting there?"

Tavion looked at Zara smugly and made a low whistling noise. This noise was followed by vibration in the ground, accompanied by a low rumbling noise which quickly got louder and louder. A boulder was coming right at them. Zara went to limp quickly out of the way, but Tavion grabbed her by the sleeve of her shirt to keep her next to him. Appealing to Tavion's confidence, the boulder skidded to a clean stop in front of them.

"Well, we can't both fit on one," Zara stated breathily, trying to conceal her state of utter shock.

The ground began to vibrate again, and this time Zara jumped at the sound of the rumble and the sight of a second boulder which moved towards her much quicker than the first one. It skidded to a stop alongside the other one.

Tavion looked at Zara's shoulder. "Whatever you do, do not fall off of it. You're already badly injured."

Zara thought of a sarcastic reply but simply nodded, acknowledging his request for her to be careful. "How do we do this?" Zara asked.

"Sit on the ground straddling the boulder between your legs. Keep your legs fully extended." He demonstrated.

"Okay..." Zara copied him, but she couldn't see how they were going to travel this way. They would certainly be further injured if they rapidly skidded along the ground on their bottom.

"Now, on the count of three," Tavion instructed, "you and I are both going to knock on the boulder twice with our knuckles. You are going to hold on to it tight, like this." He leaned his body against the boulder, wrapped his arms around it, tucked his elbows in, and interlocked his fingers."

"Will this hurt?" Zara asked.

"No, not if you do as I have just instructed. We will do it together. Are you ready?" Zara nodded hesitantly. "One..." Tavion started, "two... three!" In unison, Zara and Tavion both knocked twice on the top of the boulder with their knuckles. Zara didn't need to consciously follow Tavion's instruction. They were both quickly lifted from the ground, their legs falling into a ninety-degree sitting position, and their arms wrapping tightly around the boulder instinctively. Tavion was not exaggerating when he described these beings as ground rock rhinos. As they emerged above the ground, sand rained from their back, and their full bodies became exposed. They looked wide, thick, and muscular, though their bodies appeared to be made up of some sort of rock formation. Like rhinos, their legs looked short in proportion to the bulk of their body. Unlike rhinos, their head looked somewhat flat, making them a convenient ride. From Zara and Tavion's perspective, it was as if they were straddling a chair, with a boulder attached to the seat to hold onto for support. It wasn't the most comfortable ride by any means, but it would do.

"I will guide mine, and yours will follow," Tavion called out to Zara.

She nodded. She couldn't display any emotion other than bewilderment. Tavion slapped the side of the boulder, and the ground rock rhino took off galloping. The one underneath Zara followed suit. As they ran, it appeared as if they were caught in a sandstorm, with sand constantly being kicked up into the air. Zara coughed violently. She looked at Tavion with pink and watery eyes. He appeared to be used to it, as he stared out into the open desert terrain seemingly unaffected.

"How long until we get there?" Zara yelled out between coughs. As she held on for dear life and watched her surroundings speed by in a blur, she presumed that it couldn't possibly take too long to get there.

"Not too long. We will be there before you know it!" Tavion confirmed.

Zara watched as shades of brown, green, yellow, and orange zoomed past to her left and right. The environment was changing as they moved along from a dull brown desert to what seemed to be woodsy areas bursting with color. They were moving too fast for Zara to be sure of what she was seeing. All she knew was they were traveling across many types of environments. The wind rushing past Zara's face felt liberating to her, and it felt like they were slowing down. She slowly separated her fingers from their intertwined position, leaned back until she was sitting with upright posture, and held her arms straight out with open hands. She tightened her legs on either side of the creature's head to keep her in place while the creature continued to move forward at a lesser speed. She took a deep breath and closed her eyes. In this moment, she decided that she wouldn't rather be anywhere else. Of course, the moment was short-lived.

Tavion whistled loudly in a high pitch, much unlike the low-pitch quiet whistle he had used to summon the creatures. Startled by the noise and the resulting consequence, Zara's eyes shot open. The creatures came to an abrupt halt, and before Zara could grab back onto the boulder in front of her, she went flying straight forward off the creature's head and into the air. Almost landing headfirst, she managed to land on her shoulder blades and tumble a few times until she stopped in a crouching position facing away from the creatures. Tavion put both hands on his face, dragging his fingertips from his forehead to his cheekbones. He shook his head in disbelief at Zara's recklessness.

Zara didn't have to look at Tavion to gauge his reaction. "Can you spare me the lecture? I almost died." She looked down at the ground, still facing away from him.

"I'll postpone the lecture," he compromised.

"Fair enough," Zara settled.

Tavion made the low whistling noise once more, and the ground rock rhinos slowly merged back into the ground until all but the boulder on their head was underneath it. Zara watched, mesmerized by the sight of it.

"We have arrived," Tavion announced.

"Good grief, I should hope so after my near-death experience," Zara snapped.

"Good grief?" Tavion asked as the two of them began to walk forward.

"It's an expres-," Zara stopped in her tracks and looked up in amazement, "-sion." A gigantic waterfall was straight ahead of them, leading into the clearest pool of water Zara had ever seen. The bottom of the water was filled with bright and colorful rocks. The rocks were several shades of pink, blue, yellow, orange, and purple. Bright green plants were emerging between some of the rocks. Each plant looked the same. They had several layers of leaves stacked vertically, attached to a single stem. Each layer almost looked like a green spider with its legs dancing in the water, as four thin leaves stuck out on either side of the stem.

Zara walked forward toward the water, but a blue scaley creature stepped out in front of her, making eye contact with piercing fluorescent blue eyes. "We meet again, Zara," a familiar scratchy voice called out, followed by a scratchy high-pitched chuckle. Zara nodded mechanically and tried to walk past the Eyla to get closer to the water. "Mustn't touch darling," the Eyla warned, with no attempt to physically stop her.

Zara couldn't help herself. She was so intrigued by the water. She loved water, and this water in particular was breathtaking. She continued to approach it.

"She does speak English, right?" the Eyla asked Tavion.

Tavion nodded and mouthed, "She's stubborn."

The Eyla cocked its head, unsuccessful at comprehending Tavion's unspoken words.

"I said don't touch!" The Eyla went to prevent Zara from making contact with the water. It was too late. Zara put just one finger into the water, and as if the water was a giant vacuum, it sucked her in. Her arms flailed and her mouth opened as she sank to the bottom. The second her back made contact with the rocks, her limbs seemed to move only with the slight motion of the water.

# 14

# Relax and Recruit

"**W**E HAVE TO SAVE her!" Tavion exclaimed, putting a hand on each shoulder of the Eyla. Tavion contemplated jumping in after her, but he knew he would suffer the same fate as Zara if he did. He looked over the glossy water at Zara and cringed at the sight of her pale body on the bed of rocks. "Do something!" he urged.

"There is nothing that can be done." The Eyla frowned. "Now, her life is in the hands of the plants. It is what you came here for, no?"

"I didn't come here for her to die!" Tavion shouted at the Eyla.

"You came here for her to heal," the Eyla spoke calmly, "and heal she may."

"May?" Tavion couldn't take his eyes off of Zara. If he were not mistaken, he could swear her skin was starting to look blue. "Look at her! She's dying!" Tavion pleaded. "What happens if you jump in?"

"If I jump in, she has no chance to survive," the Eyla responded. "Let me explain to you how the plants work. They have a mind of their own. Excuse me if I lose my words. You know my English is not well."

Tavion paced back and forth, infuriated and overwhelmed by anxiety as the Eyla proceeded to explain. Part of him wasn't listening. Part of him felt like he was drowning at the bottom of the water with Zara, though he looked at her from above the surface.

The Eyla cleared its throat, not reducing any scratchiness in its voice. "You see, the plants will offer themselves freely if I jump in. I can harvest. I can bring them to someone in need. The plants will offer themselves to those who they see fit, should they enter the waters uninvited." The Eyla stopped its informative speech to gesture toward Zara. It then continued, "If I should enter while an uninvited girl is at the bottom, one of two things are likely to occur. The plants may be in the middle of healing, and I may interrupt at a time that is imperative to her survival, causing distraction and consequently the loss of her life. Alternatively, the plants may misinterpret my entrance as a sign that this girl is a threat and is not worth saving. Either way, I enter, the girl dies."

Tavion barely heard a word. "I'm going in!" he announced, taking off the gear strapped around his chest and back.

"Then you both will die." The Eyla shook its head. "Such a meaningless waste of life. Right now, alone, she stands a chance. With you, she dies."

Tavion couldn't help but wonder if the Eyla meant that more as a general statement or circumstantially. "I have to do something!" Tavion shouted.

"That is the problem with your tribe. Your downfall. You are always doing something. For once, sit still. For once, observe. For once, do nothing. For once, trust Silvia. For once..."

"What did you just say?" Tavion's eyes widened and the Eyla, for the first time since Zara got sucked in, had his full attention.

"Look." The Eyla pointed webbed fingers in Zara's direction.

Tavion looked back toward the pool of water, alarmed by what he was seeing. The plants were all stretched and fanned out over Zara's body. The hint of blue in her skin turned slowly to pale and then back to her normal complexion. The leaves of the plants weaved in and out of her clothing. A plant near her foot encapsulated her wound. Tavion was ceasing to doubt the Eyla's statement that the plants have a mind of their own. Tavion took a deep breath and watched with his mouth open in awe as the plants continued to navigate Zara's skin. All at once, the plants lifted into their upright positions. Zara's body floated to the top of the water. The second her mouth broke through the surface of the water, she gasped desperately for air.

"Zara!" Tavion cried.

"Don't help her out, you'll go in," the Eyla advised, placing a hand on Tavion's shoulder empathetically. Tavion nodded and stood his ground, looking at Zara with a hopeful expression.

Zara climbed out of the water and lay on her back on the grass beside it. She felt that all her energy had been expended. As soon as she lay down, Tavion rushed to her side.

"You're okay!" Tavion smiled.

"You're smiling," Zara acknowledged. "That doesn't happen too often."

"I'm just glad to see you will be okay," Tavion responded. "What were you thinking?" His smile quickly faded.

"I wasn't." Zara shook her head and closed her eyes. "I wasn't thinking at all."

"Now I owe you two lectures." Tavion furrowed his eyebrows, both angry and disappointed in Zara's careless behavior.

"I look forward to your lectures." Zara smiled. Zara lifted her shirt sleeve, still lying on her back. Her voice was weak. "Can you believe it?" she asked. She ran the fingers of her left hand along her right shoulder, no longer feeling any remnant of her injury.

"I've seen these plants in action. They have healed me many times," Tavion informed her, "but never the way they healed you."

"I guess I'm special," Zara replied softly. Her eyes closed. The sound of the waterfall soothed her as she rested.

"Something tells me you are," Tavion agreed.

"You need to heal also my friend, yeah?" the Eyla asked.

"Yes, preferably in a safer manner," Tavion replied, overexaggerating his eye contact with Zara.

"Good choice!" The Eyla let out its familiar scratchy chuckle and quickly dove into the water. It pulled a plant gently from the bottom and sprang back up to the surface. The Eyla climbed out of the pool of water with ease. "As usual, rub on the wound or mix with water and ingest." It paused to look at the pool of water beside them. "Please, not that water."

Tavion squinted at the Eyla, unappreciative of its dry humor. "Very funny. Yes, I know the drill."

"Is that all the business you have here today?" the Eyla asked.

"No", "Yes", Tavion and Zara responded in unison.

Zara sat up slowly and looked at Tavion inquisitively.

"Remember the large supply of weapons I delivered to you recently?" Tavion asked.

"How could I forget?" the Eyla asked rhetorically.

"I need a favor," Tavion spoke confidently.

"Consider it done." The Eyla nodded its head once, in agreement of the unexplained request.

"Before I tell you of the favor, I have a question," Tavion stated. Something the Eyla had said was eating at him.

"Ask me anything," the Eyla urged.

"You said," Tavion paused to recall the Eyla's exact words, "for once, trust Silvia. What did you mean by that? Who is Silvia?"

"Your friend." The Eyla looked at Tavion confused, as if Tavion should have already known that.

"You are mistaken," Tavion replied. "Her name is Zara."

"That's what I thought," the Eyla nodded, "but the water speaks to me. It whispers to my soul. It told me a different story. The second the plants touched her, the water whispered Silvia."

"Perhaps it was indicating some sort of protector?" Tavion inquired.

"No, I am certain it was calling her by name, and the water never lies," the Eyla chuckled.

Tavion turned to Zara. "Are you hiding something from me?"

"Of course not! I am certain the Eyla is mistaken!" Zara replied, emphasizing her certainty over his.

"Of all the names..." Tavion got chills down his spine as he recalled the riddle he had learned from his mother.

"The favor?" the Eyla reminded him.

"Yes," Tavion replied, still fixated on the peculiarity of the previous conversation. "I need volunteers from your community to accompany us to the cave."

"The cave?" the Eyla asked.

"Yes, the Kleit cave," Tavion replied.

"You know as well as I, that cave does not exist." The Eyla looked truly baffled.

"It does," Zara chimed in. "It is how we obtained our injuries." The Eyla looked stunned and was entirely speechless.

"We are going to need your help," Tavion reiterated.

"If it is true this cave exists, I need to see it for myself. I suppose you have your first volunteer," the Eyla spoke.

"Outstanding," Tavion replied, "but we will need many more."

"Walk with me," the Eyla requested.

Zara stood up and stretched. Her body felt somehow tense and rejuvenated all at once. She and Tavion followed the Eyla. As they walked, Zara took in the new surroundings. The environment looked like something straight out of a fairy tale. The grass was bright green, and there were pools of water all over the place, some of them connected to each other by streams, and most of them being filled by waterfalls from cliffs on higher land. The sun reflected off the water and made the vibrant rocks at the bottom even more vibrant. There were wooden bridges all over the place, crossing over streams and pools of water. The railings of the wooden bridges were carved out into elaborate designs. There were pink and orange flowers blooming all over the grass.

"This is stunning," Zara said aloud to herself. She spun slowly in a circle, trying to take it all in.

"Stunning?" the Eyla asked.

"Beautiful. Gorgeous!" Zara spoke loudly, grinning from ear to ear as her voice echoed.

"Ah, thank you, Silvia," the Eyla responded.

"It's Zara." Tavion frowned.

"It's fine," Zara chimed in. "I'm getting really hungry."

"Here, we eat fish," the Eyla informed her. "You are welcome to as much as you'd like while we negotiate our terms."

"Negotiate our terms?" Zara asked.

"I heard that's a common English phrase, no?"

"Who'd you hear that from?" Tavion inquired.

"Your son," the Eyla laughed.

"Really?" Tavion laughed along with him. "My young are learning too quickly."

"It's a common phrase in movies maybe." Zara shook her head at their naivety. They both looked at her with straight faces and then laughed in unison again. Zara couldn't help but laugh with them, especially at the ridiculous sounds the Eyla made while laughing. Its laugh sounded like a creaky door at certain moments.

"This is the one time I won't ask how long until we get there. I could be happy right here forever." Zara smiled.

"Ooh, you will be disappointed in a moment then." The Eyla smirked.

They were coming up on what looked like a giant bright green Weeping Willow tree, with its leaves bunched together and extending all the way down to the grass. The Eyla looked as if it were going to walk straight into the leaves.

"Where are we go-," Zara began to ask as she watched the Eyla walk straight through them and disappear to the other side. Zara pursed her lips, looked right and left out of the corner of her eyes, and took an exaggerated step through the leaves, as if she were breaking and entering and anticipated getting caught. Tavion walked forward unenthused, having been there before.

"Whoa!" Zara scanned the environment. Everything was different. They must have entered some kind of cave, and everything was brown. The walls were brown, the ceiling was brown, and the floor as well. It all looked like the color of dirt, as if a chunk was carved out of the ground and they stepped inside it. Five Eyla were in a line and seemed to be doing some sort of performance ritual. Zara watched as one of them twirled a large stick in its hands, threw it behind its back, caught it, and twirled it to another Eyla. The next Eyla twirled it, threw it into the air, spun itself around, caught it, and then twirled it to the third Eyla. They continued on as such until the last Eyla similarly twirled it in a unique way and then passed it back to the fourth Eyla in line.

There were several pools of water, and Eyla were relaxing in each of them. Some of them had their elbows propping their torso out of the water. Some of them were dipping their entire body into the water. Steam filled the room, and

Zara could feel the warmth of it entering the pores of her skin. Small and large fish swam in the water with the Eyla, surrounding several of them. Zara was taken aback when one of the Eyla submerged itself into the water and came back up holding a fish by its tail fin. The Eyla held the fish there for a few moments, as if posing for a photo. Zara was disturbed as the Eyla dropped the fish into its mouth and swallowed it whole.

Zara turned toward the Eyla standing beside her and Tavion. "Suddenly, I am not hungry anymore," she said, making it clear from her scrunched facial expression that she was repulsed by the idea of eating a live fish straight out of the water.

"I was planning to cook a fish for you," the Eyla warmly informed her.

"Then I'm starving." Zara forcefully half smiled, but she couldn't get the image out of her head. Her stomach growled, and she began to feel hunger pangs, but she also felt a little bit queasy.

Just when Zara thought she had seen it all, an Eyla from one pool dived into the water and shot up from the bottom of a different pool. It was propelled up with such force that it flew into the air. In the split second prior to falling back into the water, the Eyla opened its mouth and caught a fish that an Eyla from the first pool had thrown to it. It swallowed the fish before flipping in the air and diving head-first into the water. Zara was wide-eyed and instinctively began clapping. The Eyla reminded her of when her mother used to take her to the zoo as a child and she would see the dolphins do tricks for food. She suddenly stopped clapping and put her hands behind her back coyly when she noticed several Eyla giving her odd looks.

"What are those fish doing?" Zara asked, pointing to a pool of fish swarming a different Eyla. She was both curious, and eager to take the attention off herself.

"Those ones there?" the Eyla asked.

"Yes."

"They are nibbling at Amala's skin. It helps us and the fish."

"How?" Zara asked.

"For us, it cleanses the skin and feels good... like..." The Eyla threw a hand over its face ashamed. "This is why I do not try to speak your language often; I forget all the words."

"Like a massage?" Zara asked.

"Yes! That's the one!" The Eyla regained confidence. "How could you tell what I wanted to say?"

"Well, we have something on Earth that this reminds me of. It is called a spa. At the spa, people get massages. We also have fish massages where I come from."

"Ah, I see. I thank you for helping me learn." The Eyla smiled, revealing what looked like three sets of gums with no teeth.

"Anytime." Zara smiled at the Eyla, hoping it would not be discouraged from continuing to speak English. "Tell me about what that does for the fish," Zara requested, gesturing back to them as they continued to nibble away at Amala's skin.

"Ah, it is a source of nutrients for them, helping them to grow and helping us to have large fish to eat."

"So, in the long run, it is for your benefit and not the fish," Zara concluded.

"The fish live happy lives until their time comes!" The Eyla squinted at Zara, slightly offended by her accusation.

"I'm sure they do," Zara mumbled sarcastically. "They live to please."

"That's enough talk of fish!" Tavion asserted, swiping his hand through the air diagonally in a gesture for them to end the conversation. "Tell your tribe, I have an announcement."

"Deeeest slee dost," the Eyla spoke quickly, admittedly frightened by Tavion when he presented urgent matters. Its voice shocked Zara, as it sounded far less scratchy and high pitched when speaking its native tongue.

Every Eyla turned their head attentively. Those that were in the middle of eating put their fish back in the water reluctantly. Those that were distracted by the fish nibbling at their skin swiped their hand quickly through the water to get the fish to disperse. They gave their full attention to Tavion, at the request of the Eyla who spoke on Tavion's behalf.

Tavion's voice surged through the room as he announced his need for volunteers. One of the Eyla spoke up to ask what they'd be volunteering for. Clearly, they were not as blindly trusting as the other Eyla, who had agreed to Tavion's request without any knowledge of what the request might be.

"You would be volunteering to accompany me and my new friend, Zara, to the Kleit cave." The Eyla all simply stared. A long silence followed. One of the Eyla let out a small chuckle. Another followed suit. Suddenly, the whole room of them broke out in laughter.

"Quiet!" Tavion yelled in frustration. It took only a moment for the room to go silent once more. "Now, someone tell me what this laughter is about!"

No one wanted to speak up, but one of the Eyla in the far back of the room did anyway. "We all know the cave is a myth, Tavion," it said, with a tone that begged him not to waste any more of their time.

Tavion turned his back to the Eyla, and several of them let out audible gasps at the sight of his injuries. There were murmurs throughout the room in a language foreign to Zara. "I am going to ask again. Who will volunteer?" Tavion asked, swinging his fist up and then back down aggressively.

An Eyla turned around, put both of its hands on the ground, and lifted itself out of the water. "I with you, friend," the Eyla replied with slightly broken English. Several others got out of the water to show respect and make the same commitment. In total, twenty-three more Eyla volunteered.

"We will leave here at the start of the new day," Tavion informed them. There was a mix of nodding, bowing heads, and empty gazes. A moment later, they all returned to their relaxation.

"You can rest here tonight," the Eyla informed Zara and Tavion. "We do not have beds, but the grass is warm and comfortable."

"I can sleep anywhere," Zara replied, "but my friends are going to be worried about me."

"We will be back with them in a day or two. It will be fine," Tavion encouraged.

"Okay," Zara spoke hesitantly. "Can we eat?"

"Of course," the Eyla guiding them responded. It turned to another Eyla in the water and made a request that was incomprehensible to Zara. Complying with the request, the other Eyla collected ten large fish from the water and handed them over.

"Let's go. We need to cook these before we lose sunlight," the Eyla urged.

The three of them exited the cave, separating the leaves of the Weeping Willow tree as they walked out. The Eyla gestured for Zara and Tavion to continue to follow it.

"You haven't told me your name," Zara told the Eyla.

"We don't have names." The Eyla shrugged.

"Hmm... Well, is there something I can call you by? What name would you want if you could choose one?"

The Eyla had never pondered that question. "I suppose something natural, like this," the Eyla responded, gesturing to the land.

"What about Current?" Zara suggested.

"Current?" the Eyla asked.

"Yes, it refers to the movement of water." Zara smiled and searched the Eyla's expression for a hint of its approval.

The Eyla thought for a moment. "I like it."

"Then Current it shall be," Zara confirmed.

"Current..." The Eyla repeated, examining the way the word sounded. "I am Current."

Current guided Tavion and Zara across four bridges and up to a cliff where there were several boulders along the ground. The sun was reflecting perfectly off one of them. Current detached a jewel from the string of body jewels draped around its stomach and used it to filet the fish. It put the fish bones in its mouth and swallowed.

"Ow..." Zara reacted.

"It's the best part of the fish!" Current exclaimed.

"How did you know I would want it removed?" Zara asked.

"Tavion whispered it to me while we were walking," Current disclosed with honesty.

"Thank you," Zara mouthed to Tavion. Tavion nodded.

Current laid the fish out on the boulder and let them cook one at a time in the sunlight. They had perfect timing. By the time Current laid the last fish on the rock, the sun was starting to go down. When it finished cooking, Current asked them if the area they were at seemed okay for a place to sleep. Zara stared straight out at the edge of the cliff with the sudden thought of falling off of it in the middle of the night. Surely the drop would kill her if she didn't land in the water below.

"Maybe we will walk back down and sleep by the water," Zara suggested, looking to Tavion for approval.

"I like that idea," Tavion agreed.

"Okay, I will see you when the sun comes up," Current said, bidding them farewell.

Zara and Tavion stayed at the top of the cliff while they ate the fish Current had cooked for them. Zara anticipated that it would taste bland, but it was actually quite tasty. It was a little bit salty and broke apart easily. Zara still couldn't get the image out of her mind of how the Eyla ate the fish. She shivered at the thought and set the fish she was eating down on the rock in front of her.

"Where do the Eyla sleep?" Zara asked Tavion. She licked the salty taste off of her lips while waiting for his response.

"They sleep in the water," Tavion told her.

"It must be nice. I wish I could have their lifestyle." Zara thought of how freeing it must feel to constantly swim in such a beautiful environment with not a hint of threat in the vicinity.

"I think that too," Tavion replied. "I like it here."

"It looks magical." Zara closed her eyes and smiled, recalling what it looked like down below the cliff.

"It's beautiful," Tavion replied, looking at Zara. She opened her eyes, and he quickly looked away.

"I can't eat anymore." Zara nudged the remainder of the fish away from her.

"Bedtime?" Tavion asked.

"Yes," Zara agreed. The two of them packed up the rest of the fish and started heading back down the way they came up.

"I feel I should apologize," Tavion spoke to Zara while walking. "I shouldn't have assumed you would be okay sleeping next to me last night."

"No, you shouldn't have," Zara looked at Tavion angrily, "but I didn't mind it." She blushed and looked away embarrassed.

"It is the first time I have ever slept right next to anyone," Tavion confided, "but I didn't mind it either." He smiled.

The two of them walked silently the rest of the way. When they got to the grass at the bottom, they each lay down about an arm's length away from one another.

"Goodnight." Zara closed her eyes.

"Goodnight," Tavion whispered. He visually traced the outline of her long brown hair, which was sprawled out on the grass, and listened to the sounds of the calming waterfall beside them. He continued on to trace the outline of her body. His eyes closed before he could circle back to the starting point.

15

# THE PLACE WHERE IT ALL BEGAN

I WOKE TO THAT horrible feeling that everyone is staring, opened my eyes, and they were. All twenty-four Eyla who volunteered were standing over me expectantly. I suddenly felt immensely fearful of letting them down. Although, perhaps it wasn't me they wanted something from. I rolled over and looked at Tavion who was still asleep.

"Silvia?" a voice I hadn't heard before asked.

"Zara," I corrected.

"Oh."

I watched as the Eyla who spoke what it believed to be my name walked to the back of the crowd disappointedly. *Great, I thought to myself, I've already let them down.* I turned to wake Tavion, but before I could, one of the Eyla yelled his name in a three-syllable screech. Startled, Tavion's eyes popped open, and he jumped to a crouching stance. For a moment, he looked like a wild creature to me. I wasn't sure I liked the sight of it, but I can't say I was surprised. He always seemed to be on edge.

"We are ready," one of the Eyla informed. Tavion blinked a few times, confused of the purpose of the rude awakening.

"Let's go! We are all eager to see the cave!" another Eyla demanded.

I couldn't understand why they were so eager. They had it all here. What reason could they possibly have to want to venture to a dangerous cave, especially after having seen Tavion's injuries? If not for the pictographs on the wall of the cave, I would never go back there again. *Maybe I should warn them of the traps*, I thought to myself. Then I recalled it was an Eyla who warned me. It was an Eyla who warned all of us.

And yet, here we all were, well aware of the risk but more than willing to take it. Even Tavion looked like he was coming around to the idea of further exploring the cave's mysteries. He strapped his gear around his body, stood tall, and seemed to have a brightness to his eyes I hadn't seen before.

"Zara, are you ready?" Tavion asked me, bringing me out of my mind and back to reality.

"Of course," I responded. "How are we getting there?"

"I suppose the Ground Rock Rhinos." Tavion sounded reluctant to use that mode of transportation.

"Will you tell me what they are actually called," I said, more as a demand than a request.

"I call them Gladiators," Tavion laughed.

"No you don't," I replied, somewhat annoyed and yet somewhat amused. "What do you really call them?"

"Gladiators." Tavion raised his eyebrows and nodded his head more convincingly.

"Why?" I inquired, thinking it odd that he calls them Gladiators when I had been watching the movie *Gladiator* on the spaceship.

"They ram the boulder atop their head into people, while the rest of them is underground. They always look like they are trying to pick fights," Tavion explained. "Plus, I simply like the way the word sounds."

"That makes sense," I replied. "They don't have another name?"

"None that I am aware of. What do you call them?" Tavion turned to ask Current.

"Oylas," Current responded.

"I like Gladiators better," Tavion and I said in unison. We laughed at our unexpected synchronization. I felt maybe I should start expecting synchronization between us with how often it had been occurring.

"Can we go now?" Current asked, unamused.

"Yes," Tavion replied, "but I worry there will not be enough Gladiators for us to travel on. We may need to double up."

"Ahhh..." I didn't like the sound of that. It was scary enough to ride on them in general, and my fear was currently heightened after flying off its head on my ride here. I couldn't imagine having much less space between my rear and the edge of its head. Presumably, I'd be sharing one with Tavion. I looked him up and down, suddenly terrified of his stature.

"Let's go out to the entrance," Tavion recommended. "They won't come in here."

We all walked to the entrance, and I did my best to replicate Tavion's low-pitched whistle to summon the Gladiators.

"What was that?" Tavion asked me.

"I was trying to summon a Gladiator." I shrank self-consciously.

Tavion looked at me like a parent looks at a child when the child is unsuccessful at completing a task but looks cute trying. He whistled, and the ground began to rumble. I felt my cheeks flood red with embarrassment.

Before I knew it, a Gladiator was in front of me and Tavion. Several members of the Eyla began to let out low-pitch whistles as well, each time having a Gladiator at their feet just moments later. I couldn't figure out what I did wrong when I whistled. I whistled quietly to myself, trying to replicate the sounds they were making. It sounded the same to me.

I felt inadequate next to the entire group. *What am I even doing here?* I thought to myself. I felt so outcasted next to Tavion and the Eyla that I wished I could be back with my colleagues from Earth. I especially missed Xavier. More than that, I missed being on Earth.

"You ready, Zar?" Tavion asked. I looked around, and all of the Eyla had already raised their Gladiators from the ground, sitting on each of them in pairs. *Wow, do I have the tendency to zone out,* I thought to myself. I shook my head, realizing that in processing my spaciness, I was zoning out again.

"Yes," I said aloud, my head still swarming with thoughts.

"Sit in front of me. It will help you feel safer," Tavion directed.

I appreciated him looking out for me. I sat in front of him and extended my legs straight out, with his legs extended straight out beside mine and his stomach against my back. I knocked twice on the boulder, feeling somewhat overconfident of the growing repertoire of knowledge I was acquiring regarding Suvian rituals.

The Gladiator beneath us rose up much quicker than I was expecting. I lost my balance as a result of being unprepared and unobservant. Luckily, Tavion noticed and extended both of his arms, locking me in place between them. *How many times am I going to need to rely on this man?* I thought to myself, annoyed by my newfound tendency to trip over my own two feet. On Earth, I had always felt powerful, stable, and athletic. Here, I felt less than mediocre in all domains.

"To the cave?" he prompted.

"To the cave." I somehow smiled with anticipation, despite knowing what dangers awaited us.

I must have zoned out again, because it seemed only seconds later that we had arrived. I barely noticed the Gladiators slowly retreating into the ground. All I could think about was the pictographs and whether I'd be able to make any meaning of them. The second my legs touched the ground, I sprang up and started running.

"Wai…" Tavion called out, his request fading out with the growing distance between us.

I couldn't wait. I had to see it again. I was so angry with myself for neglecting to bring my sketchpad. How else would I commit all those images to memory? I ran quickly through the bright orange trees. Too eager to watch for protruding branches, several of them scraped across my arms. I didn't bother checking to see what damage they were doing, and they hardly slowed me down. I ducked and weaved through the trees until I made it to the fountain clearing.

I looked up at the fountain with renewed curiosity and debated exploring it for a moment. The first time I had come here, I was on edge. I was distracted. I was worried a Kleit would pop out of the trees at any moment, or even shapeshift out of the form of a tree. Now… I don't know. Something had changed. Maybe seeing the pictographs of family on the wall of the Kleit's cave changed my perception of them. Maybe I was less worried, as this area was abandoned the last time that I explored it. Whatever the reason, I felt curiosity storming through my body and taking over where fear had once resided. I looked at the fountain, then in the direction of the cave, then back at the fountain, then back toward the cave. I couldn't decide what to do. I continued running. I ran through the remainder of the trees so quickly that when I found myself outside of them, I almost ran into the outside wall of the cave. I stopped myself and put my hand on the wall. The massive rock was warm to the touch.

Finally hesitant of my movements, I walked slowly up to the opening of the cave and entered cautiously. My body reacted quicker than I could upon entering the first room of the cave, the room where I had crawled out of a death trap to find Tavion stuck in one. I felt like I could still see him there, helpless. I felt my heart start racing. I felt beads of sweat formulating on my skin. I felt my body getting hot. I sat down on the floor of the cave and tugged at my hair, overwhelmed with emotion. The pictographs were a black blur on the distant wall ahead of me. Footsteps approached, and Tavion and the Eyla carefully filed themselves into the cave. Though they were right in front of me, they were a blur too.

"Zara, what are you doing? Are you hurt?" Tavion looked at me with concern.

"Huh?" I looked up at him and visually examined his body, standing tall and strong in front of me.

"I'm fine," I replied, rising to my feet. I glanced back at the middle of the room where he had been entrapped during our last visit to the cave, and I no longer visualized his agony. Tavion persisted in a look of deep worry. I cleared my throat. "Really, I'm fine."

I walked over to the wall covered in images and felt the presence of the Eyla and Tavion following right behind me. I didn't know where to start my analyzation of the wall. Left to right seemed appropriate, as did top to bottom, but the images weren't even in straight lines. They were scattered all over the wall, seemingly without rhyme or reason. Tavion stepped forward and stood next to me, scanning the wall with his eyes.

"There is a lot to take in here." I looked at Tavion, flustered. He nodded.

We both heard footsteps and turned our heads quickly, only to see two Eyla starting to walk around the room. "Hey, what are you nuts?" I yelled. "You saw our injuries. Are you trying to get some of your own?"

"Apologies," one of them said. They walked slowly back to the rest of the group.

I sighed. "Why do we need them here for this?" I asked Tavion, purposefully amplifying my voice to be overheard.

"Protection," Tavion responded.

"I don't think they offer a whole lot of that," I scoffed.

"They brought quite a bit of Tura," he informed me. "The healing plant," he added, in reaction to my blank expression.

"Well, that will do some good," I admitted. I glanced back, and several of the Eyla were looking at me with disdain. "Clearly, I'm not here to make friends," I whispered to myself, somewhat shamefully. At home, I prided myself on being warm and inclusive. Sure, I often had an attitude, but I would never have told someone to their face that they were useless. I returned my attention to the wall, quickly leaving social circumstances behind me. I scratched my head, puzzled by the chaotic organization of the images. There must have been two hundred of them! I glanced behind me and got an idea.

"How were these drawn?" I asked Tavion.

"They were carved," Tavion responded.

"Yes, but with what?" I asked, running my fingers along one of the images.

"I don't know," Tavion responded. "It could have been any sharp tool I guess."

"Can I borrow a knife?" I requested.

"Are you going to change the images?" Tavion asked.

"No..." I replied in deep thought. I looked at the blank wall on the other side of the room. "I am going to replicate them." Tavion handed me a blade, and I walked to the other side of the cave with it. "Can you call out the images to me?" I spoke loudly to him.

"Call out the images?" Tavion asked.

"Yes, can you describe them to me?" I clarified. "Do your best to go in order from left to right and top to bottom. Try not to describe the same image twice, unless it is there twice."

"Ah... this one looks like... a weapon?" Tavion questioned.

"Okay, I'm going to need you to be a lot more specific than that." I walked back to the other side of the cave beside Tavion and looked at the image myself. The image he was referring to was indeed the leftmost image but not the highest image up on the wall. "Start up here," I traced my finger in the proper order of pictographs, "and after you finish that whole row, move to this one and do the same, okay?"

"Okay," Tavion responded, seemingly baffled by me taking charge.

I described the image he was trying to describe to me originally to give him an idea of the specificity I needed from him. "It has two parallel lines going from bottom right to top left. It is cylindrical with a sharp end. It seems to have some sort of handle at the base of it. The handle looks like a T-shaped sword handle." I looked at Tavion to assess his comprehension. "Can you do that?"

"Of course," he confirmed.

I felt bad patronizing him, but he had done it countless times to me in the last few days, so I decided not to dwell on it. I was happy to finally feel more useful than the others. Perhaps I was meant to be there. I returned to the opposite side of the cave and rested the point of the blade I was holding against the wall while I waited for Tavion's instruction.

"Start with the top left image," I reminded him.

"Draw an upside down 'V'", Tavion directed. I pushed the blade firmly into the wall and dragged it downward at a diagonal. The point of it bent to the side. I inspected it and realized it was now consequently useless. I chucked it at the ground in frustration.

"What happened?" Tavion called out to me.

"The blade broke." I shook my head and took a deep breath.

"Here, use this." Tavion held out a thicker blade. It looked a lot sturdier. *This should do the trick*, I thought to myself. Once more, I pushed the blade firmly into the wall and dragged it downward diagonally.

"You've got to be kidding me!" I yelled as I heard the tip of the blade snap off. "What the fuck did they use to carve into this?"

"Seriously? That one is no good either?" Tavion asked.

"Well, I'm not in the mood to joke. Yes, it's no good," I stated, kicking a rock away from me.

"Zara, we're going to blow through our weapons on this. Can't we do this another way?" Tavion asked.

"Hang on..." I walked over to the rock I kicked and picked it up. There was an incredibly sharp edge on it, almost as if it were designed to...

I put the sharp edge of the rock against the wall and dragged it down. It slid with ease through the cave wall. After drawing the first line, I lifted the rock back up and drew the second. I looked at the upside down 'V' and tried to decipher what it was. *A tent maybe?* After a moment, I realized that probably wasn't the whole drawing.

"Same image, next step?" I called out. No response. Tavion was walking alongside the cave wall, examining the images curiously.

"Draw six more upside down 'V's, all connected to each other, with a circle resting on the top point of each," an Eyla instructed.

I drew what the Eyla described. I turned to check if I had gotten it right, but before I fully spun around, I saw something bizarre out of the corner of my eye. A bright yellow glow illuminated the lines I carved.

"Ahhh... Tavion, you need to see this." I stood back, cautious but intrigued.

"What in the world?" Tavion had a similar reaction. I looked back, and the Eyla seemed mesmerized by the light.

"What do you think it means?" I asked Tavion.

"I think it means you should keep carving," Tavion replied.

Hesitantly, I re-approached the wall and asked for a description of the next image. An Eyla described the next image, specifically, as it had described the first. After drawing what loosely looked like a person planting something, that image also began to glow. We followed suit with drawing the images for hours on end. Tavion and the Eyla took turns instructing me of what to draw, although some of the Eyla did not participate, unable to keep up linguistically.

Into the night, I continued to carve images into the wall, until the entire wall was aglow. The yellow light emitted from the lines on the wall was enough to illuminate the whole room of the cave. I hardly stopped to analyze what the images might mean or represent, caring only about carving them into straight lines.

"Last one," Tavion announced, excited to be the one to describe it.

"I'm ready," I prompted.

"You're not going to believe this." Tavion paused. "I certainly don't."

"What is it?" I asked.

He was speechless. I walked over to where he was standing, looked down, and joined him in being at a loss for words. Spelled out in capital letters, the bottom right carving read S I L V I A.

16

# WRITTEN ON THE WALLS

"**S**ILVIA," ZARA READ ALOUD to herself, trying to make meaning of it.

She jumped at the sound of a rumbling noise coming from behind her. No, not behind her. All around her. She watched as vibrations caused the floor and walls of the cave to shake. Current crouched down into a fetal position, with the other Eyla following suit.

"What's happening?" Zara yelled to Tavion, wishing she could find comfort in changing her position. He shrugged and put his hand on the cave wall for stability. Loud crashing and thunderous sounds echoed through the cave. Suddenly the noise and vibrations stopped, and there was an eerie stillness. Trapped in an after effect, Zara could swear she felt the floor still moving.

"I think we should leave," Tavion urged.

"Yeah, probab..." Zara looked to the left of the still glowing wall of replicated pictographs. "Hold on, was that there before?" she asked, in reference to an unrecognizable pathway.

"No," one of the Eyla reported confidently. Zara and several of the Eyla looked at the Eyla who reported it to be a novelty with suspicion. "What? I have a good memory." The Eyla stepped backward self-consciously.

Zara walked forward toward the entrance of the pathway. As she got closer, she could see light coming through from the other side. "I'm going to walk through here," Zara asserted.

"Are you insane?" Tavion snapped. "Have you forgotten about the traps and what happened the first time we went exploring this cave?"

The Eyla looked back and forth between Tavion and Zara, as if they were on the edge of their seat watching a thriller.

"No, I haven't. I just have to..." Zara trailed off and took another step toward the pathway. "It's like I feel it calling me."

"Of course, it's calling to you! Traps lure you in. That's why they are called traps," Tavion reasoned.

"Yeah, but this is different. I'm not afraid."

Tavion threw his hands in the air in frustration. "You not being afraid doesn't mean there is nothing to be afraid of!"

Zara could swear she heard voices from the other side of the pathway literally calling out her name. "I have to," she reiterated. She shrugged at Tavion apologetically and walked slowly through the tunnel.

"Well? I brought you guys for protection. Let's go!" Tavion waved the Eyla onward, signaling them to follow Zara.

"I don't want to go through there," Current responded.

"You like Zara. She named you," Tavion said to Current, while walking past Current to catch up with Zara.

Current shrugged nervously. "Well yes, that is true." Current proceeded into the tunnel along with them. The other Eyla anxiously followed suit.

Zara felt like her movements were being watched by someone other than the Eyla and Tavion, but she attributed the feeling to the eeriness of walking through a dark and abandoned cave. As she drew nearer to the light on the other side, she saw more pictographs along the walls in the unexplored room. In this room, there were far more than two hundred. They covered the entire wall that wrapped circularly around the room, and they covered the floor as well. Zara looked around, bewildered and unbearably overwhelmed.

She turned to Tavion. "I don't think we will be sorting through all these images." Zara let out a breathy laugh, devoid of humor.

"No," Tavion agreed, "we won't."

Zara walked around the room slowly, looking at the images. "Some of these are repeated several times," she noted.

She decided to start by simply looking at one cluster of images on the bottom corner of the wall by the pathway. There were five images there that appeared to be roughly clumped together. One of the images looked like an adult member of the Kleit. One of the images looked like a tree. One of the images looked like Kleit children at play. Zara recognized similarities between the images in this room and the images in the room on the other end of the pathway. One of the images looked like the sky. The last image in the cluster looked like a Kleit engaged in some form of meditation, in a similar pose to what Zara had seen atop the fountain in the woods on the way to the cave.

*Simple minded creatures*, Zara thought to herself, noticing how repetitive her findings were. She looked around, and now that she was conscious of it in her inspection, almost all the images around the room looked overly simplistic; all but four clusters along the back wall.

She walked over to them. "These," she said to Tavion. "These are the images I need to interpret. They appear to tell a story."

"How will you know if you interpret them accurately?" Tavion inquired.

"I don't know. Maybe they'll glow," she replied sarcastically. "There are sixteen images here that stand out." Zara discussed her thought process aloud. "None of them are repeats..." She paused, taking quite some time to look around the room. "None of them are repeats of each other nor any of the other images around the room. That tells me they are more significant. They also appear to be drawn differently."

"What do you mean by 'drawn differently'?" Current asked.

"I don't know. I get the feeling they weren't drawn by the same being. The others look uniform. These are bold and more meticulous. They stand out." Zara slid her fingertips softly over the images and felt something between her skin and the lines carved into the wall, almost like static electricity.

"I'm going to read the first thing that comes to my mind for each image," Zara informed the others. She proceeded,

"Kleit eating together as a community, Kleit hunting together as a community, Kleit carrying children along on their backs, and several Kleit holding up an elongated object." She took a step to the right and proceeded to interpret the second cluster. "A large dark cloud with several Kleit underneath it, Kleit ushering their children into sheltered caves, and a similar cloud with hands coming down and wrapping around a child. The last image in this cluster appears to be a Kleit crouching down on the ground, holding the elongated object over its head, seemingly for cover, and the elongated object being taken by the cloud."

"What?" Tavion thought Zara must be losing it. He came over to check on her perception of the images. Sure enough, the images looked without a doubt like her descriptions.

Zara stepped to the right once more and stood in front of the third cluster of images. "A Kleit putting its hands over its face. A Kleit picking up a child." She stopped. "Hey Tavion, what is this?" She pointed to the third image.

Tavion came closer to analyze it. "I don't know," he admitted. "I've never seen it before."

It looked to Zara like a Kleit and a child encased in some sort of spherical contraption. The Kleit and the child were carved as if the viewer were seeing the backs of their bodies.

Zara continued, "The fourth image is just a circle." She scratched her head. "I don't understand."

She took one last step to the right to examine the fourth cluster of images. "A Kleit shapeshifting," she guessed, as half of the body looked like a Kleit and half looked like a human. "The child shapeshifting," she guessed, based on the same happening with a body a quarter of the size. "Some sort of weapon," she guessed, based on a sharp elongated object. "The last image looks like a community of Kleit."

"Okay, so what does it all mean?" Tavion asked.

"The hell if I know," Zara responded. "Let's take a look at the images in the other room once more and see if we find anything enlightening there."

Zara led the group back through the pathway into the other room. The room was well-lit by the images still aglow on the righthand wall of the cave. She scanned the wall of images again, finding nothing particularly stood out. That was, of course, excluding S I L V I A.

Zara walked up to the letters carved neatly into the wall in all capitals and read them aloud. "Silvia... Silvia... Silvia..." she repeated, hoping that if she repeated the word enough times, some meaning would simply come to her.

An unexpected and unfamiliar voice echoed through the cave. A series of clicking noises sounded, followed by an announcement in English. "Welcome, Silvia. All traps are now deactivated." Tavion drew a weapon in response and pointed it in all directions, uncertain of where the voice had come from.

"All traps are now deactivated?" Zara questioned. She looked around the room. She walked to the center of it, an area they had been avoiding due to the spiked net that Tavion had been caught in a couple of days ago.

"Zara!" Tavion exclaimed. "You're going to trust that they really have been deactivated? Get back here before you get yourself killed!"

"I do trust it," Zara replied, in a state of euthymia. She walked toward an unexplored tunnel, ignoring Tavion's objections. She entered the tunnel and walked into pitch blackness, continuing to proceed forward despite her inability to see her surroundings. She felt for the walls as she walked.

Tavion and the Eyla anxiously awaited her return to the room they were in. They stared at the entrance of the dark tunnel expectantly and began to worry when several minutes passed by and Zara did not come back out.

"You! Go find her!" Tavion demanded, pulling an Eyla toward him by the string of jewels wrapped around its body and then shoving the Eyla toward the tunnel.

"M... M... Me?" the Eyla stuttered.

"Yes, go!" Tavion raised his voice.

The Eyla looked back at the others of its community, and they collectively took a step backward, not wanting to be the one to take that Eyla's place.

"I... I... go... but... I'm scared." The Eyla informed them. The Eyla had never really been scared. There was never much reason to be scared in their community. Having learned some English from the Klaysta tribe, the Eyla knew that the word scared was an appropriate descriptor of how it was feeling, but the feeling itself was new. The Eyla wanted to crouch down into a fetal position again but was even more fearful of what Tavion might do if it didn't comply with his request. The Eyla walked toward the tunnel slowly. Beads of sweat developed on its skin. Its eyes were wide. Its webbed hands were shaking. Just as it approached the entrance of the tunnel, it let out a great sigh of relief.

"What are you doing? Go in!" Tavion yelled.

Zara walked out of the tunnel, back into the room they were in. She scolded and shamed Tavion. "You were going to make the Eyla go in there? Look at the fear in its eyes."

"His eyes," the Eyla corrected, its voice still shaking.

"His eyes." Zara put her hand on the Eyla's shoulder respectfully. "I apologize. It is difficult for me to tell apart your genders."

"We are all male," the Eyla replied.

Zara raised her eyebrows. "All male? How do you have kids?"

"We reproduce.... Ah.... Tavion?" The Eyla looked to Tavion for help explaining, despite feeling strong resentment toward Tavion in the moment.

"Asexually." Tavion shook his head with annoyance. "Can we go now?"

"Go where?" Zara asked.

"Home!" Tavion barked.

"No!" Zara reacted hastily. "I want to sleep here. It is getting late, but never mind that. There is so much more to explore, and from what I can tell, the traps really have been deactivated."

"Even if that is the case, which we cannot be sure, we don't know at what point they reactivate."

"Yes, but we know how to re-deactivate them," Zara countered playfully. "Please, can we stay?"

Most of the Eyla nodded in agreement, but one Eyla, continuing to be fear-stricken, cowered in silence. This was an adventure to the Eyla, and most of them were less than eager to return to the life they've always known and never strayed from. They were unsure when they might have the courage to stray again.

"Where will we sleep?" Tavion asked.

Zara jumped up and down with exhilaration. "Ah, right here is fine!"

There were several groans as Tavion and the Eyla looked down at the hard cave floor. Zara probably would have had the same reaction if she actually intended to sleep. She had no intention whatsoever of sleeping. While she walked through the dark tunnel just moments ago, she found herself deep in thought. She thought about how most of the pictographs did not seem violent or malicious. She thought about how most of them displayed family and lifestyle. She thought about how all of them seemed to represent the Kleit. She thought about how much she wanted to know the true meaning behind the sixteen images that stood out. Based on all considerations, she made a decision. She decided that after everyone was asleep, she would set out to find a Kleit and bring the Kleit back with her to help her interpret the images. She was sure she'd be back long before the others awakened if she could summon a Gladiator. She recalled her failed attempt at summoning one earlier but was sure she could do it now with her determination heightened.

Zara yawned and stretched her arms into the air in an overexaggerated gesture. "Wow, I am getting really tired now that we mentioned sleep. Well, goodnight." She lay down on the cave floor, curled her body into what looked like a comfortable position, and closed her eyes convincingly.

"She does know I didn't actually agree to this?" Tavion asked Current rhetorically as they both sat down on the cave floor and prepared to rest.

"I don't know where that girl's head is at," Current replied, "but I trust her down to my last scale."

Tavion shook his head and sighed. "She's something," he said. "Goodnight."

"Goodnight." Current smiled.

Everyone got into sleeping positions, and the room went silent. It took everything in Zara not to immediately spring to her feet. She waited patiently while she was internally drowning in impatience. After roughly an hour, Zara was confident everyone had fallen asleep. She lifted herself up slowly and looked around the room just to make sure. She struggled not to laugh when she saw that one of the Eyla had their arms wrapped around Tavion's stomach. She quietly departed from the cave.

The night was dark, with thick clouds covering the light from the seven moons. Zara walked slowly, watching each step to avoid noisily snapping any twigs beneath her feet. As she walked into the woods and weaved between the trees, she could swear she heard scurrying through the bushes and leaves. When she made it to the clearing and stood in front of the fountain, she squinted up at the top of it, having slight difficulty seeing the statue of the Kleit meditating in the darkness. As her eyes adjusted, she smiled, realizing she did not need to go any further. Beside the statue of the Kleit, there was a statue of a beast that had not been there previously. Simultaneous to Zara's reaction, the beast began to transform, shapeshifting into the true form of a Kleit. The Kleit made clicking noises at Zara.

"I don't understand." Zara shook her head and shrugged apologetically.

The Kleit proceeded to shapeshift again. Zara watched as it morphed. Wavy brown hair grew out of its head. Its arms shortened and widened. Pink lips emerged on its face, and its skin color morphed from black to a soft tan. Its eyes changed from black to hazel. Its body fell into a sitting position, and a wheelchair emerged beneath it.

"I knew you'd come," it spoke, in a voice similar to her mother's.

"I need your help." Zara stared into its eyes, fully trusting its intentions. Fully trusting its intentions, not because it took the image of her mother, but because she saw its story written on the walls. A story of happiness. A story of community. A story of love. A story of life. Zara walked back towards the cave, and the Kleit followed closely behind, shapeshifting back into its true form after a few strides forward.

17

# A Visitor Gone too Soon

WHEN ZARA RETURNED TO the cave with the Kleit, everyone was still asleep as expected. Zara motioned for the Kleit to follow her into the cave. The Kleit walked in with no hesitation and looked around the room. When it made eye contact with Zara's replicated images on the right-hand wall of the cave, it fixated on them. It began to shapeshift and quickly took the form of Zara's dad.

"No, no, no," Zara whispered harshly, "you can't talk just yet."

The Kleit stayed in the form of her dad but remained silent. Zara was unphased by the familiar face. She motioned for the Kleit to continue forward, leading it into the tunnel and through to the other room. They stood among the countless pictographs.

"Okay," Zara continued to whisper, "we can talk here, but quietly. Do you know how to talk quietly?"

The Kleit nodded. "You should not have done that," it whispered.

"Should not have done what?" Zara asked, genuinely confused by the reprimand.

"The wall." The Kleit pointed her dad's chubby finger toward the tunnel.

Zara realized the Kleit typically chose who to shapeshift into primarily as a means of communication. Nonetheless, it was still odd to hear things she has heard her family say before coming out of a clone's mouth in a different context.

"Why shouldn't I have done that?" Zara asked the Kleit.

"It's dangerous," the Kleit responded.

"None of this looks dangerous." Zara looked at the images skeptically.

The Kleit began to clarify, "It's dangerous to know..." It quickly shapeshifted into her mother to continue, "who you are."

"That's cool," Zara complimented. "I didn't know you can do that." Zara thought for a moment about the Kleit's words, not knowing what to make of them. "It's dangerous to know who I am?" Zara questioned. The Kleit nodded. "But I already know who I am." Zara chuckled nervously, wondering if the Kleit could truly know anything about her that she didn't already know herself.

"Then you know," the Kleit continued to speak as her mother, "that you are..." It shapeshifted. "Silvia," it finished its thought in the form of Tavion.

"Please shapeshift back before he sees you!" Zara whispered anxiously. She realized right after the words came out that it wouldn't matter what form the Kleit was taking. Either way, she had a lot of explaining to do if anyone should wake up. The Kleit seemed aware of that too, as it paid her comment no mind and continued to present itself in Tavion's image.

Zara relaxed and addressed the Kleit's statement. "Why do people keep saying that? I'm not Silvia. I'm Zara." Her tone contained more than a hint of annoyance. She just wanted to get to the point. She yearned to address the reason she brought the Kleit to the cave in the first place.

"Fine, then it's who you were," the Kleit spoke in staccato. It struggled to piece together the proper words as a result of being limited by Zara's memories of her conversations with Tavion.

"Maybe you think I'm someone I'm not," Zara responded with a tone of resignation. She just wanted the conversation to be over so she could ask about the pictographs.

"No," the Kleit responded reassuringly.

Zara decided to redirect. She pointed to the pictographs. "Can you tell me what these images mean?" The Kleit quickly shook his head no. "Do you know what they mean?" Zara rephrased.

The Kleit shapeshifted back into its true form, stared at Zara for a moment with large black eyes, and then closed them. With its eyes closed, the Kleit nodded.

"I need you to explain them to me," Zara pleaded.

The Kleit shook its head no again, this time more vigorously. It proceeded to walk out of the tunnel. Zara tried to grab the Kleit by the arm as it walked away. Its arm felt like Jell-O, and it stretched when she pulled it. By involuntary impulse, Zara let go.

The Kleit walked quickly through the tunnel with full intent of leaving and not coming back. Its intent was to protect Zara, but it realized that she was too headstrong and would proceed on her current path with or without its help. Just as the Kleit got to the other end of the tunnel, Tavion startled it by blocking the entryway to the other room. Tavion stood tall with his chest puffed out and looked at the Kleit with a piercing glare. The Kleit reached its hands out in fear, with the intent to signal that it meant no harm. Tavion saw its hands come toward him and instinctively drew his weapon.

"Tavion, no!" Zara yelled.

It was too late. Tavion's blade slid straight through the Kleit's torso. Tavion withdrew the blade, and the Kleit fell to its knees. Zara ran to the Kleit. Tavion backed away. Based on Zara's reaction, Tavion knew he had done something unforgivable.

"No, no, no. I need your help!" Zara knelt down to be level with the Kleit, and tears poured from her eyes.

The Kleit closed its eyes. Using the only strength it had left, it shapeshifted one last time, taking the form of Dimitri. It looked at Zara apologetically with Dimitri's eyes and softly replied, "I was never going to help you anyway." It wrapped its hand, also resembling Dimitri's, around Zara's and looked at her with an expression of love and longing. As it shapeshifted back into its true form, it gradually morphed into what looked like a goo and slid into a pool of black on the cave floor. Zara, originally shedding tears for the loss of a pictograph interpreter, shed one more tear for the loss of life that just took place before her eyes. She looked up at Tavion with contempt and stormed out of the cave.

18

# PROTECTION AND DANGER ARE NOT SO FAR APART

I COULD NO LONGER stand the sight of him. My voice was hoarse from yelling, my eyes felt heavy from crying, and my cheeks felt hot with rage. Part of me knew he acted on impulse, but that's kind of the reason it felt impossible to forgive him. If he had just waited for a moment... If he had just let me speak on behalf of the Kleit or let the Kleit transform and explain itself, then an innocent life-form wouldn't have been taken today.

My thoughts leaked into my words. "How could you steal an innocent life?" I yelled, my voice cracking noticeably.

"Innocent?" Tavion barked. "You've hunted innocent lives with me!"

"For food!" I raised my voice even louder.

"So, it is okay to take a life if it sustains your own, but otherwise it is not?" he asked me. I paused. I didn't know what to say. He continued, "I thought taking the Kleit's life was sustaining my own! I thought he was going to harm us, Zara. Don't you get that?"

He had a point of course, but not one strong enough to persuade me to drop the argument. I refused to back down on this, still haunted by the image of the blade puncturing through the Kleit's body.

"You could have waited two seconds to hear him out." I emphasized two seconds, knowing Tavion would come up with some bullshit response about how he needed to get rid of the "threat" in a timely manner.

Sure enough, Tavion still countered, "Zara, how could I have known he wasn't planning to kill me in one second?"

I looked Tavion up and down. He was built beyond belief with defined muscles and bulgy veins. "I think it would take more than two seconds!" I yelled.

This conversation was pointless. No matter what I said, he had a witty comeback. No matter what he said, I didn't feel any better. If anything, with each word he released, I felt worse.

"I'm done, Tavion." I shook my head and wiped a tear from my eye. "I'm going to return to the Klaysta community, inform my colleagues of what has happened, and return with them to the ship to try to figure out a way home."

"The Kleit are guarding it," Tavion reminded me.

"If it is the Kleit who are guarding it, they will let me leave!" I assured him, with tears in my eyes.

Tavion shifted his demeanor and looked at me with a softer gaze. "Please stay," he spoke quietly. "You don't have to talk to me. You don't have to look at me. Please, can we just spend another day here so you can go back to trying to determine what the images mean. I know it is important to you."

I had honestly forgotten all about the pictographs, but having it come back to mind, my curiosity did reawaken. I thought for a minute about how to proceed. His change in demeanor had little to no effect on me, but his words were in fact persuasive.

"In honor of the Kleit, I will stay to learn the story they have written on the walls," I decided.

"Thank you," Tavion replied.

"Save your gratitude. I'm not doing it for you." I walked past him angrily.

"Thank you anyway," I heard him say from behind me as I re-entered the cave.

The second I walked back into the cave, the Eyla all scattered. I don't think they could have made it any more obvious that they had been listening in. I didn't care. I was angry. I was tired. I hadn't slept at all. I lay down on the cave floor and shut my eyes. Only a moment passed before sleep overcame me.

I meant to sleep only for a few hours, but when I woke up, it was clear by the darkness outside that I had slept all day. *So much for deciphering the pictographs*, I thought to myself. I looked around the room, and all the Eyla appeared to be fast asleep. Tavion wasn't among them.

I stood up tiredly and went to look outside for him. I called out his name outside of the cave. There was no response. I went back in to look for him, thinking maybe he decided to explore the cave. I walked through the first tunnel leading to the room with the other pictographs and found him there staring intently at the sixteen undeciphered images. He heard me come in behind him and turned around.

He opened his mouth to speak a couple of times, but no words came out. He seemed to shift his body nervously. *Yeah, that's right, tread carefully*, I thought to myself, finding pleasure in his discomfort. I didn't really have any desire to speak with him. I was only curious of his whereabouts. Now that I confirmed his location, all I wanted to do was separate myself from him. As much as he was trying to forcefully pull words from his larynx, I was trying to suppress words in mine. I turned around, whipping my hair in an overdramatic gesture, and began to walk away. Apparently he found the right words, because they stopped me in my tracks.

"Zara, I told you before that I don't believe the Kleit to be inherently bad. I'm sorry I didn't let that belief show through in my actions today." Tavion looked down at the ground shamefully, which was very much unlike him. "It cost a life," he continued, "a life that we can never get back, and I understand that now."

I continued to face away from him. I hadn't prepared for him to apologize, and I definitely hadn't prepared to hear the sound of mourning in his voice. I had suppressed my words to such an extent that they felt glued to my larynx now.

"Zara, I don't know if you can ever forgive me. I don't know if I can ever forgive myself. I don't think either of us desire to talk about it. So, how about we only talk about this?" Tavion pointed at the images on the wall.

I turned around and agreed to move past our tension, for the purpose of working collaboratively to decipher the pictographs. There was clearly still physical tension between us, as we stood several arm lengths apart. We avoided eye contact or even a head turn in one another's direction.

"Three of the images in the first cluster seem to be regular components of lifestyle," I noted. "A family eating together, a family hunting together, a family holding each other..."

"Yes," Tavion agreed.

"But what is this?" I asked, pointing to the image of several Kleit holding an elongated object high in the air.

"Hmm..." Tavion brushed his fingers along his chin speculatively. "It looks like they are holding up a prized possession."

"It does, doesn't it?" I exclaimed. I had been thinking it kind of seemed as if they were holding up a trophy. Tavion's words provided me with greater confidence in my interpretation. "Do you think it is perhaps a metaphor?" I asked. "Like the trophy is life?"

"Trophy?" Tavion asked.

"Yes, like a prized possession that you get for accomplishing something special."

Tavion shrugged. "I perceive the Kleit to be more literal."

I nodded. If it were to be taken literally, then the Kleit have a trophy somewhere. But for what? *What warrants a trophy on Suvia?* I wondered.

"And here we have the same object." I pointed to the trophy being held over a Kleit's head in the fourth image of the next set.

"Being taken by a cloud?" Tavion asked, seeming to think the image to be foolish.

I thought it to be foolish too, but again I thought that the images could be metaphorical. Perhaps the Kleit lost their most prized possession to an act of nature. I looked at the first image in the cluster, hoping it would hold further clues. The same dark cloud as in the fourth image was looming over several Kleit. This image seemed to be confirming my suspicion of a natural disaster having taken place. The next image was of Kleit ushering their children into caves. That also fit my interpretation. And the third, the cloud wrapping hands around a child. Perhaps the natural disaster took the child's life. It all made sense to me. I shared my interpretation with Tavion.

"A natural disaster?" Tavion asked. "Yes, that would make sense."

"Do you have those here on Suvia?" I asked.

"We do," Tavion responded, "although it seems to have more to do with the moons than the clouds. I am not sure if you have noticed, but they slightly shift each night. When they are too close together, we get what for you is similar to an earthquake."

"Strange," I replied. It was all I could say as I got lost deeper in my own thought process. If they only had one type of natural disaster and it only corresponded to the position of the moons, then maybe the images were metaphorical for something else. I wondered to myself if I should rule out that they were not metaphorical at all. After all, I had already seen so many things on Suvia that defied what I have learned to be possible on Earth.

I moved on to the next image. "In this image, a Kleit is covering its face with its hands," I described aloud.

"Perhaps in fear?" Tavion suggested.

"Perhaps in fear," I agreed. "And then the Kleit picks up a child," I continued.

"Perhaps for protection," Tavion offered.

"Yeah, maybe," I concurred with hesitation. "It does appear this spherical contraption in the next image, whatever it might be, has not harmed the child, as the child is present again in this image." I pointed to the Image of the child shapeshifting in the fourth cluster. This congruence led me to believe more confidently that the Kleit did not mean the child any harm.

I returned my attention to the third cluster of images to analyze the last one. "It's just a circle. How can I decipher the meaning of a circle? Could it be a moon?" Out of the corner of my eye, I saw Tavion shake his head no.

"Anyone on Suvia who is trying to represent a moon would draw all seven of them as a reference," he assured me.

"Could it represent Suvia?" I asked.

"Maybe." Tavion took a closer look. "It's not Suvia," he confirmed.

"How do you know?" I asked.

"Look closely," he directed.

I took a few steps forward and leaned in, seeing letters carved into the wall, unimaginably small in size. The image was literally labeled as Earth. Written in English, I wondered if it was either meant for a Klaysta to see, or more alarmingly, if it were meant for the eyes of someone from Earth. The thought slipped into my mind that these images were specifically meant for me to find, but I shook the thought quickly, thinking I must be losing my sanity to imagine something so absurd.

I decided that the images seemed to be telling a linear story, so I internalized the next set prior to speaking my thoughts on them. Both the adult Kleit and the child shapeshift, there is a stand-alone weapon, and then a whole community of Kleit. Metaphorically, their shapeshifting could be a weapon in and of itself. Literally, perhaps they shapeshifted, and then a weapon was used to help the community reunite. Or perhaps I had the whole thing wrong. *Ugh. This feels hopeless*, I thought to myself. *How will I ever know the truth behind the images with certainty?*

"What's wrong?" Tavion asked, noticing my posture changing with my frustration.

"It just feels pointless to interpret these images when we may never have confirmation of the interpretations," I replied. I tugged at my hair, reiterating my irritation.

Tavion nodded. "It's hard to not have the answers," he responded.

"We might have had the answers if you hadn't killed my interpreter," I coldly asserted.

"We might have," Tavion quietly agreed. "How long will you be angry with me?"

"I don't know that I ever won't be," I answered with honesty. I folded my arms and looked away from him, but I could feel his piercing eyes aimed at me.

What occurred next happened much faster than I could react. If I had been allotted the time to react, I'm certain I would have protested. But by the time I could protest, I no longer desired to. Tavion's arms wrapped firmly around my body, and not a split second after my body was turned towards his, his lips connected with mine. His lips were warm, as was his breath each time his lips separated from mine for air. Our lips seemed to fit together perfectly and move in unfathomable unison. My body felt safe locked into his arms.

He walked forward as he continued to press his lips against mine until I was wedged between him and the wall behind me. He explored my back sensually with his hands.

He separated his lips from mine, suddenly cautious of my reaction. "Should I stop?" he asked.

I shook my head no and reconnected my lips with his. I knew this was wrong. I knew he had Kalari. But I couldn't stop. Our bodies seemed to move in such perfect synchronization that I wouldn't have doubted we were being pulled together by a force much more powerful than us. I felt no sense of control and complete desire to give in to the temptation. I wondered briefly what must be going through his mind. To me, it seemed he had complete control and knew exactly what he was doing. *Could this be a manipulative tactic to get me to forgive him, or could it be that the urges he is feeling are beyond his power as well?* The thought didn't linger, and my thoughts faded altogether as his lips moved from my lips to my neck. He pulled me closer. I didn't know our bodies could be as tightly held together as they were in this moment. I felt him become erect. It didn't occur to me to question whether he had the same parts as a human, but as he pressed against me, it felt probable that he did.

Tavion removed his shirt, then mine. He seemed unfamiliar with a bra. I reached my arms behind my back and unhooked it. Before I knew it, we were on the cave floor. Our bodies merged and moved gracefully together. Each time I opened my eyes, the room was a blur, but Tavion was completely in focus. I looked lustfully at his muscular body, seeing it in full for the first time. Hours must have passed. It certainly felt like it.

Tavion held me in his arms, both of us lying on the cave floor long after our passion subsided. He gently pressed his lips against my forehead. I pulled myself closer affectionately. He chuckled.

"Did you plan for this to happen?" I asked.

"Never in a million years could I have planned for this," Tavion responded.

I was on the fence of whether to believe him or not. I looked into his eyes and decided that his expression appeared to be genuine. Relaxed in each other's arms, we both jumped at the sight of a silhouette near the other end of the tunnel leading to the room.

"Go back!" Tavion demanded, believing he was communicating with an Eyla. "Zara and I will be back in that room in a moment." The silhouette came closer defiantly. "Did you hear me? I said go back!" Tavion repeated loudly.

As the individual entering the room came into view, Tavion and I both fell silent. I sat up and slid myself to the back wall of the room in fear. Tavion tried to get to his feet but was too slow to react. A blade came at me quickly and pierced my lower abdomen. I lifted my eyes slowly, first seeing blood seep out of my stomach, then seeing a tan hand with clean fingernails upon the blade that penetrated my skin. My eyes continued to drift upward until they met Kalari's, and then everything faded to black.

19

# Left Alone, She Finds Herself

WHEN ZARA AWAKENED, SHE was lying on the grass staring up at the sky. She instinctively tried to sit up to figure out where she was, but at the slightest tightening of her abdomen as she tried to lift herself, she fell back down in agony. She recalled getting stabbed by Kalari and gently felt her stomach for the wound. She groaned in pain but felt nothing but a thin scar in its place.

"Try to avoid moving," Tavion said, coming to her side and kneeling on the grass. "Here, drink this."

Tavion handed her a wooden cup. Zara reached out her hand to grab it from him, but he pulled it back and set it on the grass. He slid a hand under her back and helped guide her into a sitting position. Then he held the edge of the cup to her mouth and waited for her lips to part to slowly tip it back. Zara didn't know what fluid she was drinking, but she didn't care. The second the liquid touched her throat, she realized how thirsty she was and guzzled it down.

"We need to talk, Zara," Tavion spoke reluctantly.

"Can it wait? I don't feel well. Where are we?" Zara rested a hand on her lower abdomen over her scar and stared up at the sky, feeling too weak to even turn her head.

"We are in the Eyla community," Tavion replied. "I brought you here to heal. You were near death."

"Where is Kalari," Zara asked. There was a sorrow in her tone that demonstrated she felt no resentment toward Kalari, only shame toward her own actions.

"Kalari went home to the Klaysta community. I plan to accompany her shortly." Tavion looked down regretfully.

"What was she even doing at the cave?" Zara questioned.

"She followed me," Tavion replied. "I didn't know she had seen the markings on my back. She followed us all the way from the Klaysta community."

Zara took a moment to absorb the information. "So, you are leaving? What about me?" Zara asked. She didn't particularly want to be around Tavion and Kalari right now, but she felt the growing need to reconnect with her colleagues from Earth. She also wanted so badly to get to her comm and call Zidia.

As if responding to her thoughts, Tavion informed her that her colleagues were on their way, being guided to the Eyla community by Miravi. He assured her that all of her possessions would be in tow.

"So that's it," Zara said, her throat swelling up with sadness. "You're just going to go, and the Eyla will take care of us from here."

"I think it is the right thing to do," Tavion replied. "You need their resources for your injuries, and I need to make things right with Kalari."

Zara recognized that Tavion was never hers to begin with, yet she still felt a great sense of loss emerging. She strained herself to look at Tavion's face and couldn't see even a hint of the hurt she was feeling in his expression. She presumed he was pained more by his betrayal of Kalari than his abandonment toward her. Rightfully so. She looked away.

"You don't need me," Tavion assured her.

Without making any effort to console her, he rose to his feet and began his departure from the Eyla community. Zara continued to look away. She couldn't bear to watch him leave. It pained her even more to know that he was leaving now, while she was at her weakest moment. He was leaving now, after they had connected so intimately. Based on his words, Zara tried to immediately release the hope that he would ever return to her... a hope that was somehow so deeply rooted inside her after only a matter of days knowing of his existence.

A familiar face approached and stood over Zara, assessing whether she was okay. Zara looked up at Current warmly, feeling gratitude for his presence. He looked down at her with a toothless smile.

"You seem to be doing a lot better," Current evaluated aloud. "It will take a couple more days until full recovery, but rest assured, you will fully recover," he stated confidently.

"Thank you, Current," Zara spoke softly. "Can you do me a favor?"

"Anything!" Current replied. "That is why Tavion left you with me. He knew I would be fully at your service."

Zara cringed when he mentioned Tavion leaving. She closed her eyes and reopened them, as if to reset her mind. "Can you please help me to my feet?" Zara requested.

"I don't think that's a good idea, Zara," Current noted. "Your wound could re-open."

"Let it," Zara responded. She figured nothing could be worse than the internal wound that was piercing through her heart like a thousand knives.

"Zara, I can't." Current shook his head with a look of sadness.

"You said you were at my service. Did you not?" Zara asked. She rolled her eyes and began to try to get up herself. She groaned loudly and clutched her abdomen.

"No!" Current anxiously grabbed her arms. "I will help you. Just relax." Zara loosened her muscles and allowed Current to do most of the work in guiding her to her feet.

Once Zara was standing up, she wrapped her arm around Current's shoulder, and together they walked toward the cave with the pools. Zara felt so vulnerable out in the open. She requested to be hidden. Current felt the cave would be a great recovery area for her regardless and saw no reason not to comply with her request.

"When will my friends be here?" she asked Current as they walked slowly toward the cave.

"I am here," Current replied.

Zara smiled and turned her head slightly to look up at him. "You know what I mean." She nudged his arm lightheartedly.

"They should be here sometime today. Just rest," Current encouraged.

When they entered the cave, Zara was met with a surplus of stares from all of the Eyla. She hadn't thought about the fact that they all must know what happened. No doubt, they had come running to see what had occurred after she was stabbed by Kalari. No doubt, they were aware that she was under their protection now instead of the Klaysta community. She felt so scrutinized that physically and mentally, she shut down. She pushed Current away from her, not wanting to be touched any longer. She wanted to be alone… as alone as she could be in a room full of Eyla. Current kept his hands loosely at her sides until she was in a sitting position at the edge of a pool.

An unfamiliar Eyla came up to Zara and sat down next to her, swinging its legs over the edge of the pool. Current walked away. The Eyla sitting next to Zara sensed that she didn't desire his company, so he tried to make his presence unnoticeable. He sat there with her for about half an hour, not saying a word.

After a while, he broke the silence, only to inform Zara that this was a pool she could swim in, unlike the one outside with the plants. After providing Zara with that knowledge, he slid into the pool, dove down into what looked like a dark tunnel at the bottom, and flew into the air over a different pool, landing far away from Zara in a disconnected body of water.

Zara was now alone at the pool he had been accompanying her at. She looked around. None of the Eyla were looking in her direction any longer. She slid herself into the pool and willfully sank to the bottom. Under the water, she fell into a state of complete relaxation, tightly holding her breath and somehow not feeling the need to breathe. She simply sat there at the bottom of the water for a minute, feeling the slow motion of her hands and arms swaying and the tension in her body releasing.

Still submerged, her eyes shot open, and it felt like she had teleported to a different place in time. In what seemed like a slow-motion transition, a blast dispersed the water particles and sent them falling to a puddle on a tiled floor. All the scenery around her changed. She was in the living room of a house. Her vision seemed to tunnel, with only one segment of the room coming into focus at a time.

The house had a brick fireplace with pictures along the mantel. The living room was spotless, with only a few pieces of mail on the glass coffee table. The walls were white. Zara turned around to see a tan couch with the NASA administrator sitting on top of it, staring at a photograph in a golden frame. She circled the couch until her viewpoint allowed her to see beyond the back of the NASA administrator's head to the photograph. The photo was of her. If that weren't odd enough, she began to hear his voice. Zara looked around the room. No one else was present. He was talking to himself. Zara focused on his words. She could barely make them out. She tried harder to focus. His voice was almost audible, but still not quite. She let go of all other thoughts and only listened for his voice. Finally, she could hear him. She backed away slowly with a look of terror in her eyes as she realized, unmistakably, that he was talking to himself about Suvia. Zara continued to back up until her back hit the wall of a kitchen counter in the next room. She blinked a few times, realizing it was not a kitchen counter she had bumped into at all, but rather the inside wall of the pool in the Eyla cave. She shot up to the surface and gasped for air.

The Eyla all looked at Zara with concern. There must have been fifty pairs of eyes on her. Zara pulled herself up out of the pool despite the immense pain it caused her and stumbled her way out of the cave to be alone. When she exited, she sat down immediately against the outside cave wall, still hidden by the leaves of the Weeping Willow tree.

Zara tried to piece together what had happened. She had zoned out before, but this hadn't felt like zoning out. It had felt as if she were truly there, in the home with the NASA administrator. She wondered why she would see him looking at her picture and talking to himself about Suvia, even if it were all in her imagination. She thought back to when he had authorized the departure of her and her colleagues despite the possibility of them ending up at a different location than Mars. She began to wonder if he had planned the whole thing but couldn't fathom what motivation he would have to do that, or how he would even know of Suvia's existence. She laughed at herself for taking what she had seen so seriously. Clearly, she had hallucinated it. Clearly, she was dehydrated. But it had felt so unbelievably real. Zara's thoughts paused as two hands reached through the leaves and separated them to walk through.

"Xavier!" Zara exclaimed.

She couldn't be happier to see him. More than that, she was happy just to see someone else from Earth, after having spent several days apart from her colleagues. Finally, there was something on Suvia that gave her a sense of normalcy.

"How are you, Zar?" Xavier sat down beside her. "I was so worried about you. We had no idea where you went! None of the Klaysta were able to provide us with any information. Please don't ever leave without telling me where you're going again. At least, not until we are back on Earth, okay?" He looked at Zara with genuine fear in his eyes.

"I'm sorry," Zara replied, leaning her head on his shoulder.

"What has happened since you've been gone?" Xavier asked.

Zara shook her head. "I wouldn't even know where to begin."

"You could begin with the day you left the Klaysta community," Xavier suggested.

"That day alone would take so much time to explain," Zara replied.

"Well lucky for you," Xavier replied, leaning back, stretching his arms, and crossing them behind his head, "I've got nothing but time."

Zara chuckled, but instead of telling him of the events that had unraveled in the last few days, she shook her head again and curled up next to him like a child finding comfort next to a parent. She closed her eyes and fell asleep as Xavier brushed his fingers through her hair.

While she slept, Zara dreamed that she was back in the presence of the NASA administrator. Only, in the dream it was a Kleit disguised as the NASA administrator. He knelt down to talk to a little girl, who was a Kleit child in disguise as a human. The disguises looked transparent, and Zara could see right through their tan skin to the black skin of the Kleit. The Kleit told the child that she was going to be safe now, adding that she would one day return to Suvia and emerge a hero, but not until she was ready. The child looked up at the Kleit with an expression of confusion but trusting eyes. She nodded to him. The Kleit then spun the child around and pushed her gently away from him. "Until we meet again, Silvia," he stated warmly.

Zara awakened heavily breathing and in a cold sweat. She looked around. She was still between the external wall of the Eyla cave and the leaves of the Weeping Willow tree. It was dark out with no light at all seeping through the leaves. Xavier was still by her side. She relaxed but thought back to the dream. Suddenly, she felt sure she understood the sixteen images in the Kleit cave. A Kleit removed a child of its kind from Suvia to protect it. *Now the question is what was the child being protected from?* Zara wondered if it could be possible that she truly was Silvia. She had always thought that she seemed different than the others on Earth, and she had always imagined it her destiny to travel to space.

As she connected the dots, she wondered too if she had been experiencing Suvian powers. She had the marking on her calf. The Kleit in the spaceship had seemingly become paralyzed with no one around to paralyze them. She had seen something so clearly that was happening on Earth. Her mind started to flood with childhood memories, photo albums of her as just a baby, and home videos of her mom in labor. *How could the two sets of thoughts exist together? Could I have somehow lived two lives?* she wondered. She felt like her head was going to explode and recognized the onset of a massive migraine. Feeling once again like a helpless child, she curled back up next to Xavier and tried to fall back asleep. She stayed awake for hours with her eyes closed, unable to will her thoughts to shut off. Nevertheless, after some time, she was out in a dreamless sleep.

Zara awakened the next day in confusion, still lying in the grass between the Eyla cave and the leaves of the Willow tree. Xavier was no longer next to her. She could hear Eyla chatting in their native language from within the cave. She stood up slowly, still in pain but noticing it subsiding. As she stood up, Xavier re-entered through the leaves.

"Oh, good. You're awake," Xavier noted. "I woke up not too long ago and left to get some water from the pond outside. Luckily, one of the Eyla caught me in time and rerouted me to water that is safe to drink. That could have been bad." He chuckled lightheartedly. "Let's go to the top of the cliff," he suggested. "Marquette, Sadie, and Jerome are all hanging out up there. I told them to give you some space, but they are all eager to see you. They're getting impatient."

"Sure," Zara replied. "Can we hang out here alone for a moment though first?"

"Yeah, why, what's up?" Xavier asked. He sat down and motioned for her to sit down next to him.

Zara crossed her arms and rubbed at them anxiously. "You're not going to believe what I have to say," she mumbled.

"Try me," Xavier responded warmly.

"I uh... I..." Zara couldn't get the words out.

"Zara, you know you can tell me anything," Xavier encouraged. "What is it?"

Zara looked fearfully into Xavier's eyes. She was fearful not only of how he might react, but also that saying the words aloud might make them feel more real. She bit the corner of her bottom lip, wanting so badly to confide in him, but wanting equally as badly to crawl into a hole and be alone.

"Zara, just spit it out," Xavier gently demanded.

"I think I'm from Suvia!" Zara loudly announced, breathing heavily after getting the words out.

Xavier visually examined the leaves of the Weeping Willow tree, admiring how loosely they hung in the air. He paid no mind to Zara, and he didn't speak a word in response to what she had said. She looked at him expectantly.

"Xavier, did you hear me?"

Xavier looked at Zara as if he felt sorry for her. "You think you're from Suvia?"

"I mean, all the signs point to it! Tavion told me I was from Suvia, the Kleit told me I was from Suvia, the Eyla and the Kleit believe me to be known as Silvia, and I'm fairly sure I've experienced Suvian powers!"

"Suvian powers," Xavier reflected. "Like the powers Tavion told us about?"

"Yes, exactly!" Zara smiled, happy that Xavier seemed to be on the same page.

Xavier shook his head. "Zara, you're not from Suvia. That's crazy."

Zara's smile faded. "I thought you might understand, but I get it. Even to me it sounds crazy."

As Xavier watched Zara's confidence fall at his doing, he shifted his demeanor. "Tell me what powers you experienced," he said, putting his hand on hers. He wanted her to know he meant well. Zara could tell he still didn't believe her but continued on anyway.

"Remember when I went into the spaceship with the Kleit?" Zara asked.

"How could I forget?" Xavier nodded.

Zara went on to explain how she believes she had paralyzed the Kleit that day, and how several days later, she had a vision of the NASA administrator on Earth. She did her best to summarize her experience in the cave, purposefully leaving out her intimacy with Tavion. As she discussed the NASA administrator, she went into detail about her theory that he was somehow connected to the Kleit and that the Kleit had sent her to Earth to protect her. In her dream, he had actually been a Kleit, but she knew that theory would be way too far-fetched to maintain Xavier's attention.

"When would they have sent you to Earth?" Xavier asked, trying to help lead Zara to the clues that counteract her theory.

"That's the hard part," Zara admitted. "My mom has shown me videos my dad took of her in labor."

"Could it have been your sister?" Xavier humored her theory.

"No, my dad definitely took the videos. Zidia can't hold a camera straight to save her life," Zara chuckled. "Besides, she wasn't born yet."

Xavier rolled his eyes. "I meant in the video being born."

"Oh..." Zara laughed at her misinterpretation. "No, because there is a separate one of her being born, and hers was an at-home birth compared to my hospital birth, so there's definitely no chance that they were clips of the same delivery."

Xavier threw his hands in the air and shrugged, as if to say case closed, but the case was certainly not closed for Zara. She continued to ponder the timeline. If there was a video of her being born on Earth, perhaps she was Suvian in a previous lifetime. She shook her head and laughed at her own thought process. After seeing things on Suvia that she previously thought to be impossible, she would take anything as a possibility. She had no idea how to tease apart what could happen from what couldn't anymore.

"I think the only way to learn the truth is to get into contact with the NASA administrator," Zara said, shrugging her shoulders. Now, the case was closed for her.

"And how do you plan to do that?" Xavier asked.

Zara raised her eyebrows and leaned in toward Xavier. "Who brought the bag with my comm?"

20

# A Large Request

WHEN ZARA AND XAVIER reached the top of the cliff, Sadie was hysteric. She ran to Zara with pink teary eyes and hugged her tightly. Zara returned her hug but was surprised to see that she had been such a mess over her absence.

"Please don't ever leave again. You told me you would be right back. That was almost a week ago!" Sadie kept her arms wrapped around Zara longer than Zara would have liked.

"It's fine, Sadie," Zara soothed, "I'm here now."

Sadie let go and sniffled. "I was just so worried about you," she said as she wiped her nose with her arm.

"I'm happy to see how much you care about me," Zara responded, genuinely appreciative of Sadie's concern.

Marquette chimed in, "Well, someone had to worry. You know damn well it wasn't going to be me."

"Well, I've missed you, Marquette," Zara teased.

Jerome was the last to get reacquainted. He came up to Zara and gave her a much shorter hug than Sadie had, respectfully joining in with expression of gratitude for her return. While Zara was thrilled to be reunited with all of them, she couldn't wait to get her hands on the comm.

The bag of their belongings was on the ground next to Marquette. Zara walked over and reached into it, ignoring the dirty look Marquette gave her. She rummaged through blankets, water bottles, packages of food, and flashlights. The comm was nowhere in sight.

"Where is it?" Zara demanded of Marquette.

"Where is what?" Marquette asked with a harsh tone.

"You know very well what," Zara replied. "Hand it over."

"Are you looking for your comm?" Sadie asked.

"Yes." Zara turned towards Sadie, caught off guard that she had chimed in.

"I was hanging on to it for you," Sadie informed her. She reached into her pocket and held it out in her hand. "It seemed too important to carelessly be tossed in with everything else in that backpack. Plus, there are water bottles in there. I worried they would spill and lead it to short circuit."

Zara nodded. Sadie's explanation was understandable. She turned to Marquette to apologize, but Marquette held up her hand dismissively. Zara truly felt ashamed of her accusation. She grabbed the comm from Sadie and walked away from her colleagues. She walked all the way back down through winding paths and bridges until she returned to the lower ground. She decided to re-enter through the leaves of the Weeping Willow tree and sit with her back against the Eyla cave wall, finding comfort and peace in the secluded area.

As quickly as she sat down, she was pressing the required buttons to connect with Zidia. She waited eagerly to hear Zidia's voice on the other end. Shockingly, Zidia answered right away.

"Zara!" Zidia exclaimed. "I've been trying you for so long!"

"Zidia," Zara cried. "It's so good to hear your voice. How are you?"

"I'm good," Zidia replied. "I just miss you so much."

"Same," Zara responded, wiping a tear from her eye. "As much as I'm dying to catch up with you and hear what you have been up to, I'm reaching out because I need your help."

"You need my help?" Zidia asked. "How could I be of help from here?"

"I need you to put me in contact with the NASA administrator," Zara informed her sister. There was a long pause on the other end of the comm. "Zidia, did you hear me?" Zara asked.

"Yeah, I heard you," Zidia confirmed. "It's just that... well... what you asked isn't going to be an easy thing to do."

"I understand that," Zara responded, "but I will walk you through how to get the comm to him."

"No, Zara..." Zidia paused again. "It isn't going to be an easy thing to do because it was reported on the news recently that the NASA administrator is dead."

Zara didn't know how to react. That was the last thing she expected to hear, and her heart dropped as she realized that her questions about herself and about Suvia might never be answered.

"How did he die?" Zara asked, feeling like she had a lump in her throat.

"He was murdered," Zidia responded.

"When?" Zara gasped.

"Twenty-three years ago," Zidia replied.

"Twenty-three years ago?" Zara asked. "How long have I been gone?" She began to shake in a panic.

"Relax," Zidia directed. "You've only been gone two years. The man you knew to be the NASA administrator was not in fact the NASA administrator."

"Then who was he?" Zara asked. She had been with NASA for seven years. Had someone been impersonating the NASA administrator, she found it hard to believe that it wouldn't have been caught in that amount of time.

"They still don't know!" Zidia exclaimed. "Whoever it is, they're now on the run for fraud. If they are found, they are to be charged with a felony."

"Wow." Zara was baffled by the news. "Well, I need you to find him."

Zidia laughed. There was a brief silence before she responded to Zara. "Oh, you're serious..."

"Yes," Zara replied with no humor in her voice.

"Zara, that's insane. The cops can't even find him. How would I?"

"We're going to find him together," Zara assured her.

"Easy for you to say. You're not here," Zidia responded.

"My voice is all you need. I'll be your courage. I'll be your direction. We will find him together," Zara reiterated.

"Okay," Zidia agreed reluctantly. "Where do I start?"

Zara thought hard about where the man she knew to be the NASA administrator might be hiding. She searched her memories for every interaction she had with him, every word that came out of his mouth, and every word that was said to him by others in her presence. He had mentioned that when he wasn't working, he often went golfing. He had told her that he has a wife and kids. Zara wondered how she could know if anything he mentioned of his personal life was true. She thought to herself that if she were to kill someone and then impersonate them, she would make shit up left and right out of fear of unintentionally leaving clues if she told any component of the truth.

Zara switched her angle. She wondered if perhaps the clues weren't in things that he said, but rather in things that he did. She thought about how he constantly straightened his jacket. She thought about how meticulous he was. She thought about the way he held a pen when he went to write things down. Zara suddenly let out a breathy gasp.

"What is it?" Zidia asked, still waiting for her sister's guidance.

"The NASA administrator really is a Kleit... but how?" Zara was now speaking aloud to herself instead of responding to Zidia. She thought about how the NASA administrator would always write words in clusters. When she asked him about it once, he had mentioned that it helps him organize his thoughts and that it almost paints a picture of a story on a page, so that you can simply look at it and recognize its significance. She thought back to the sixteen images on the Kleit cave wall. That's how she would have described those. She shook her head.

Zara wondered if this was all a hallucination, because it seemed far too bizarre to even be a possibility. But then again, if a human could end up on Suvia, why should she doubt that a Kleit could end up on Earth. She prayed her theory that the Kleit were good and moral creatures was accurate. Otherwise, she feared what the NASA administrator might be up to, especially now after having its identity compromised.

"What is a Kleit?" Zidia asked, starting to become impatient.

"Huh? Never mind that," Zara replied. Zara wondered where a Kleit might hide on Earth. She knew they liked caves. Zara knew of several caves near the NASA launch site, but all the ones she was familiar with were highly publicized and accessible through paid tours. She knew the NASA administrator wouldn't set foot in one of those right now. Luckily, Zidia enjoyed exploring.

"Zidia, have you explored any abandoned caves near Houston?" Zara asked.

"Yeah, a couple," Zidia responded. "What makes you think someone like that would hide out in a cave?"

"Just a hunch," Zara replied.

"How does this communication device work all the way from Mars by the way?" Zidia asked.

"I'm still trying to figure that out myself," Zara answered, deliberately not correcting her sister in reference to her whereabouts. "Tell me about those caves," Zara urged.

"Well, one of them is pretty easy to find. It's actually pretty close to our house. It has..."

Zara cut her sister off. "Tell me about the other one."

"Ah... okay. The other one is quite the hike to get to. It's way more relaxing because it is pretty well-hidden, and I've never seen anyone else there when I..." Zidia stopped herself this time, realizing why her sister was asking for the description and realizing she had just described the perfect hide-out for a fugitive. "I'm on my way there now," Zidia assured Zara.

Zara could hear the jingle of Zidia's keys through the comm as she got ready to leave the house. "You got this, Zidia," Zara encouraged. "When you get to the NASA administrator, proceed with caution and don't get too close to him. Tell him it is me that wants to speak with him, and toss him the comm. Once it is in his hands, you need to leave."

"But then I won't get the comm back," Zidia protested.

Zara thought for a moment. She too was concerned at losing the potential to communicate with her sister. "Dimitri has one too!" Zara exclaimed. "Go to him first, and get hold of his comm."

"Zara, you and I both know Dimitri won't willingly hand over his only method of contact with you," Zidia replied.

"He's spoken to me only a couple times since I departed. I am sure he won't know the difference. Just ask him for it," Zara directed.

"Okay," Zidia replied, confident that it would be a hopeless endeavor, but nonetheless, agreeing to it to appease her sister. "I'll get back in touch with you when I arrive at the cave," Zidia told her sister.

"Okay, but if anything goes wrong, tell me immediately," Zara demanded.

"Yeah, yeah. You can stop holding my hand now," Zidia teased.

Zara put the comm to her lips and put it into rest mode. "Never," she said to herself.

21

# THE SEARCH BEGINS

Z IDIA DEPARTED FROM THE house in a hurry, knowing that her sister was relying on her. It occurred to her that she had not asked Zara why she needed to be put in contact with the NASA administrator in the first place. However, she figured if it was relevant to the mission, it should be highly prioritized. She prayed for the mission to be successful and hoped that it would run its course faster than expected, believing that the chances of Zara coming home sooner would be heightened by the unexpected turn of events with the NASA administrator.

Zidia set off for Dimitri's house first, following her sister's instructions to go to him for the comm. She felt the breeze flood in through her car windows as she drove sixteen kilometers over the speed limit. The rush of the wind and the other cars passing by were the only sounds she heard, as she decided she wasn't in the mood to listen to the radio. She was so anxious to carry out Zara's request. It was unlike Zara to ask for help, and now she was asking for help from another planet in outer space. Zidia felt that there was so much pressure for her to get this right.

Zidia realized when she was nearing Dimitri's house that she should have called ahead to make sure he would be home. She was relieved when she pulled up and saw his silver Pontiac in the driveway. She walked up to his front door and lifted her hand to knock. The door opened before her fist made contact with it.

Zidia jumped back, startled. "You scared me!" Zidia exclaimed to Dimitri.

"You scared me. What are you doing on my front porch?" Dimitri asked.

"Zara asked me to come," Zidia replied.

"Is that right? She doesn't fucking call me, but she sends her sister to check up on me. Real cool," Dimitri said, shaking his head discontentedly.

"No, it's not like that," Zidia tried to explain.

"Whatever, I'm late for an appointment. Later Zidia," Dimitri said as he walked past her.

Zidia followed him toward his car. "Zara needs help locating and getting in contact with the NASA administrator," Zidia informed him. "Will you help me?"

Dimitri stopped in his tracks, seeming to think for a moment about it. It almost looked as if he was tempted to say yes but held back by something.

"No," Dimitri replied curtly. He opened the door of his Pontiac and got into the driver's seat. "Sorry, Zidia. I'm in a hurry. I can't help you." He shut his car door and rolled down the two front windows.

"Well then at least give me your comm," Zidia requested.

"My what?" Dimitri asked as he buckled his seatbelt.

"Your comm, the device Zara gave you to communicate with her."

"No way!" Dimitri snapped. "Listen to what you just said. She gave it to me to communicate with her. If she wanted to talk to you, she would have given you the device instead."

Zidia rolled her eyes at his stupidity. "She gave me one too, asshole. How do you think I learned she needs to contact the NASA administrator?"

"Well, then you have one. You're all set," Dimitri commented as he shifted his car into reverse.

"No, I'm not all set." Zidia quickly walked to the passenger side of his car. She got in as the car was already slowly rolling backward down the driveway.

"What are you doing? Are you crazy?" Dimitri yelled, slamming on the breaks. "Get out!"

"Not until you give me the comm," Zidia asserted.

"I'm not giving you the comm. Now get out of my car," Dimitri demanded. Zidia shook her head no. Dimitri put the car in park, unbuckled his seatbelt, leaned over Zidia's lap, and opened the passenger side car door. "Get out!" he yelled again.

"I need the second comm, Dimitri. I need to give it to the NASA administrator to put him in contact with Zara."

"You'd be giving my comm to the NASA administrator?" he asked.

"Yes," Zidia confirmed.

"Here, take it." Dimitri reached into his pocket, pulled it out, and handed it to her.

Zidia was surprised he gave in. "Thank you." She took it from him skeptically.

"Can I go now?" Dimitri asked, running his fingers through his hair in frustration.

"Yeah." Zidia got out of the car, thanked him, and shut the door behind her. She watched as he drove away. She looked down at the comm in her hand. She pulled hers out of her pocket. They looked identical. She decided she should test it just to be sure it was functional. She pressed a few buttons.

"Hello?" Zara's voice came through. "Are you already at the cave?"

"No," Zidia replied, "I am just testing Dimitri's comm."

"Oh okay," Zara responded.

"Have you been crying?" Zidia asked, noticing that Zara's voice sounded shaky.

"No, I'm fine," Zara assured her. "Get back in touch with me when you're at the cave."

Before Zidia could ask any further questions, the comm beeped, signaling Zara's disconnect. Zidia was sure her sister was crying, but she knew she had no time to waste, and even if she did, she was sure her sister would be unresponsive until she completed the task Zara had asked of her.

Zidia got into her car and departed from Dimitri's driveway. Getting to the caves would take another fifteen minutes driving, plus a thirty minute hike on foot. As Zidia drew nearer to the caves, she began to develop goosebumps and felt chills along her spine. She had never met the NASA administrator, or anyone important for that matter. She had also never met a fugitive on the run for impersonation of someone important. She started to talk herself out of going at all, but the looming threat of Zara being stranded on Mars or Zara's mission going awry was enough motivation for her to stay on course.

When she got to the base of the hike, she parked her car and took a deep breath, looking up at the hill she needed to climb and the trees she needed to navigate through. "Here goes nothing," she said to herself. She commenced the climb.

The trees were gorgeous shades of orange and red, but Zidia hardly stopped to acknowledge their beauty. The hill was at a steep slant, so Zidia used the thin trunks of the trees for stability and to pull herself up. She also occasionally took breaks to rest against them. When she finally got to the entrance of the cave, she stood in front of it and pulled out both comms. On one of them, she contacted Zara.

"Hey, I'm here," Zidia informed her.

"Do you see him?" Zara asked anxiously.

"No, not yet. I figured I would reach out to you before looking around," Zidia replied.

"Thank you," Zara responded. "I would have worried if you waited too long to reach back out to me."

"I know." Zidia smiled. Little did Zara know, Zidia reached out more as a result of her own worries.

Zidia looked around, walking toward the cave entrance cautiously.

"Hello?" Zidia called out. There was no response.

"If he is in hiding from the cops, maybe it would help if you announce that you aren't one," Zara suggested.

"Ooh, good point," Zidia replied. "Hello?... I'm not a cop," Zidia called out.

"Because that doesn't sound suspicious," Zara remarked sarcastically.

"What... You told me to!" Zidia replied.

"Announce that you're in contact with me," Zara instructed.

"No thanks. You'll probably just yell at me for doing it incorrectly." Zidia rolled her eyes. She never felt like she was up to par with her sister's expectations.

"Ugh... Zidia... Just do it. I'll stay quiet. I promise," Zara assured her.

Zidia scrunched her face up in annoyance. "I have my sister Zara here with me. She wants to talk to you."

"Zidia!" Zara's voice came through loudly.

"What? I said what you wanted me to, and you promised you would stay quiet!"

"Yeah, but you just announced that you're with me. You are not with me. You have to be more specific," Zara directed.

"Fine," Zidia replied.

"And announce me as Silvia, not Zara," Zara requested.

"Silvia? Who the hell is..."

"Just do it!" Zara snapped.

Zidia was beginning to feel like she was on a wild goose chase, and her sister kept making this adventure feel more and more bizarre.

"I'm currently in contact with... Silvia..." Zidia called out. "She wants to speak with you. If you are here, please come out."

"Perfect," Zara praised.

"Right..." Zidia didn't even know what she was talking about anymore. "Who is Silvia?"

"I'll explain later," Zara responded. "Is he there?"

"I don't think so..." Zidia replied hesitantly. "Should I go in the cave and check?"

There was a brief silence. "No, just go home. Thank you for trying."

Zidia felt like she had failed her sister. She stayed there a few moments longer just to be sure the NASA administrator wasn't present. She leaned to each side, trying to get a better view of the area around the cave without going any closer to it. Everything was silent, and there was no one in sight. She turned to head back down the hill, but she halted at the sound of an unfamiliar voice.

"Did you say Silvia?" The NASA administrator walked toward her slowly. He seemed just as fearful of Zidia as she was of him.

"Yeah," Zidia said to him. "I did. I am talking to her through this communication device." She held it up to show him.

"I gave her those devices," he informed her.

"They're pretty impressive. They work at quite the distance," Zidia complimented. The NASA administrator just stared at her, with no verbalized response. "Zara, my sister... She wants to speak with you."

The NASA administrator nodded. Zidia threw the comm and the NASA administrator caught it, clasping it between his hands. Zidia hastily departed as Zara had previously instructed.

## 22

# WHO ARE YOU TO ME?

**"Y**OU REFERRED TO YOURSELF as Silvia?" the NASA administrator asked through the comm.

"Sure, let's skip the greeting," Zara scoffed. "Yes, I did refer to myself as Silvia."

"So, you know who you are," the NASA administrator noted aloud. "What else do you know?"

"Not a lot," Zara admitted, "but there is a lot I am speculating."

"Such as?" the NASA administrator pressed.

"Such as you potentially being a Kleit, such as you having taken me to Earth to protect me, such as me being from Suvia..."

"By now, I am sure you know I sent you to Suvia on purpose," the NASA administrator stated.

"For what reason?" Zara asked.

"I am not sure you are ready for the answer to that question yet," the NASA administrator replied.

"Are you a Kleit?" Zara inquired.

There was a long pause before the NASA administrator answered her. "No, I am human."

"But you are connected to the Kleit," Zara said, more as an accusation than a question.

"There is a time that I was," the NASA administrator responded truthfully. "Now I am only connected to you."

"Connected to me how?" Zara asked.

"It's a long story," the NASA administrator informed her. "A thirty-three-year-long story," he added.

"Around the time you killed the real NASA administrator?" Zara bluntly inquired.

"About a decade prior to that, yes," the NASA administrator willingly confessed.

"Well, I've got time," Zara replied.

"Are you safe?" the NASA administrator asked, with genuine concern.

"Yes," Zara confirmed. "I am with the Eyla."

# 23

# Thirty-three Years Prior

"**P**RIVELION, MY BOY! You did it!" Privelion's Grandpa exclaimed pridefully. "After all these years!"

"Yes." Privelion had a glow in his eyes as he examined his creation.

To anyone who knew him, he became unrecognizable. He had shapeshifted into a man twice his size, a man that he himself had imagined. Finally, he could possess the ability of the Kleit to shapeshift, without the limitations of being dependent on the memories of others. It was better than Privelion had imagined. He expected no more and no less than what the Kleit had to offer, and yet he exceeded their abilities by a long shot. It was time to put the second trial to the test.

"I'll be back, Grandpa," Privelion announced as he draped a pelt over his shoulders. It was a chilly night on Suvia. Privelion's grandpa did not need to ask him where he was off to. He was well aware and incredibly honored to have such a determined scientist in his lineage.

Privelion had always been a scientist at heart, wondering of the mysteries of the world long before he learned how to manipulate them. Nonetheless, his true journey began when as just a boy, he had a vision of a Chemist on Earth. He watched as a man mixed a series of chemicals, the reaction of which resulted in a contained explosion. Privelion was mesmerized by the explosion and imagined implementing it on a much wider scale. However, as he grew older and learned of the different roles on Suvia, his interest in the explosion declined. He became more interested in how to utilize chemicals as a means to expand his abilities and potential. Born with the ability to see all beings, Privelion wanted to acquire other abilities. To his knowledge, no being on Suvia had ever been gifted with more than one. The fire from his vision was now in his eyes as he set out to be the first of a kind.

Privelion carried his creation carefully as he walked along. Though he was eager to put the second ability to the test, he enjoyed the feeling of holding something so powerful in his hands. Plus, the fluorescent purple coloring of the liquid intrigued him. Traveling on foot the whole way, it took him quite some time to arrive in the vicinity of the Vultra tribe.

Upon his arrival, he opened the top of the container which held his creation within. He dipped his hand into the liquid and spread it over his skin like a lotion. He undressed and covered his entire body in it. He stared up at the fifth moon which had a soft red glow around it, barely visible to the Suvian eye. He waited.

After about half an hour, he put his clothes back on. He looked around for something to test his ability on. The night was still. He was the only one around. Unfamiliar with the territory and afraid of what creatures he might encounter in the night, Privelion headed back to the Klaysta community. He was sure he could find a being to test his new ability on when he got closer to home.

Privelion didn't feel any different. He began to doubt that the second trial of his creation had any success at all. He walked along in deep thought, so lost in his perception of failure that he made it home without searching for a creature to utilize as a test subject. When he walked into the cave, his grandpa was still awake awaiting his return.

"You're back!" his grandpa exclaimed. "Did it work?"

"I don't know," Privelion shamefully replied. He walked over to his bed to lie down and stared up at the ceiling.

"How can you not know?" his grandpa enthusiastically inquired.

"I didn't test it out, Grandpa," Privelion replied, rolling onto his side and closing his eyes.

"You've got to!" his grandpa eagerly encouraged. "Why, test it out now!"

"I can't test it out now, Grandpa. I have no being to test it on. Go to sleep." Privelion shook his head in frustration.

"I'm right here," his grandpa stated softly. "I'm right here," he raised his voice confidently. "Test it on me!"

"I'm not going to test it on you." Privelion sat up, wide-eyed at his grandpa's request.

His grandpa walked toward him, nodding his head and making eye contact, in assurance that he was a willing test subject. Privelion tucked his bottom lip in and furrowed his brows in contemplation. On one hand, he did want to know if his endeavors had been successful. On the other hand, he feared the possibility that he would learn he had failed. He also did not like the idea of using his grandpa as a test subject. His grandpa continued to walk toward him.

"Do it!" His grandpa egged him on. "I'm right here…"

"Do it!" His grandpa repeated in an angry tone, trying to rile him up.

His grandpa took another step. "I said do it!"

Privelion rapidly extended his arm and faced his palm toward his grandpa. Without another thought, he fixated his mind and energy on his desired ability. In the blink of an eye, his grandpa's body went limp, causing him to fall backwards toward the floor. On the way down, his head slammed harshly into the corner of a table.

Privelion jumped out of bed and ran to his grandpa's side. His grandpa was all he had left on Suvia. He searched for a pulse just in time to feel his grandpa's final heartbeat. He put his head on his grandpa's chest and yelled so loudly that every light in the Klaysta community turned on.

By the time members of the community had come to check on Privelion, he was gone and had taken his grandpa with him. After weeks of them not returning, the memory of Privelion and his grandfather were upheld by the Klaysta tribe only through rumors. After more time had passed, the rumors subsided, and Privelion and his grandpa were long forgotten.

By the time Privelion showed his face again, the face he showed was not his. He spent days and months on end mastering his new abilities. He found that not only was he not limited in what or who he could shapeshift into, but that there was also no time limitation on how long he could remain in a different form. Using that to his advantage, he shapeshifted into a storm cloud and began to watch over the tribes from above, becoming more and more power hungry by the day. He planned to continue to watch until he found a weakness. He started with the Kleit.

Privelion didn't know it at the time, but there was one being on Suvia who exceeded his potential, and she was right under his nose. Her name was Silvia. Just a small child, no one paid much attention to Silvia outside of the Kleit who fathered her. Her mother had died in a hunting accident. The Kleit who fathered her was called Leto. Silvia and Leto did everything together, except hunt, a task Leto considered far too dangerous for her to be present for. Leto would tell Silvia stories at night and teach her new skills during the day. Knowing only of her ability to shapeshift, Leto sensed there was something special about Silvia. One day, he found out for sure.

Silvia missed her father when he went out hunting and one day snuck away from the Kleit community to search for him. She walked along on her own for quite some time until she found herself face to face with a Seltivor. Leto had eyes on the Seltivor for a while, planning to strike it down at the right moment. He felt the life sucked out of him when he noticed Silvia walking up to it fearlessly. He slowly walked toward her, determined to carefully grab her and pull her out of harm's way. Before he could get to her, the Seltivor lunged forward. Just then, something incredible happened. The Seltivor seemed to nonsensically immobilize mid-air and fall to the ground several meters short of Silvia.

"What happened?" asked another Kleit hunting with Leto.

Leto quickly covered up his theory. "I think the Seltivor was already on his deathbed." Leto quickly ran up to the Seltivor, climbed it, and put a blade through its neck. "Just to make sure!" he loudly exclaimed, wanting the other Kleit to believe the animal would have died with or without his blade. "Are you okay?" he asked Silvia.

Silvia smiled up at him as if nothing had happened other than her finding him. He hugged her tightly. It was in that moment that Privelion saw the Kleit's weakness: love. So focused on finding a weakness, Privelion failed to notice Silvia's strength. Privelion found the unconditional display of love detestable. He considered it to be a weakness and a lie. Afterall, he had once claimed unconditional love for his grandfather, only to realize the dependency of it and the loss of it broke him into nothingness, and only to realize his grandfather could be murdered at his hand. He decided then that the love the Kleit shared for one another would be held against them until they agreed to combine forces with him and aid him in his task to grow even more powerful. He strived to use that power to take over every planet and reign over every being in existence.

Though he had found a weakness, Privelion continued to watch over the Kleit for more to use against them. In doing so, he noticed that every night before they turned in, the Kleit would run their hand across an object that was positioned atop a pedestal in the center of the community. Though Privelion could not figure out the significance of the object, he swore to himself he would get his hands on it.

It occurred to Privelion that perhaps he was taking unnecessary measures. He wondered if simply asking the leader of the Kleit to join forces with him or persuading the Kleit with empty threats would be sufficient. Accurately perceiving Leto to be their leader based on his observations, Privelion desired a conversation with him. He waited until all the Kleit were asleep to initiate contact. When the night grew silent, Privelion shapeshifted out of the form of a storm cloud and into the form of a Klaysta.

He slowly approached Leto while he slept, doing his best not to startle him. He reached a hand outward and gently set it on Leto's shoulder, rocking it back and forth ever so slightly to bring him to a conscious state. When Leto opened his eyes, he looked around frantically.

"Silvia?" Leto whispered loudly.

"She's right there." Privelion pointed to the small girl lying in her bed.

Leto stared up at Privelion with his jaw hung open and nodded once in an unspoken agreement to communicate with him. Privelion nodded his head toward the exit of the cave. Leto quietly got out of bed and followed Privelion outside into the dark night.

"She's cute," Privelion stated in reference to Silvia.

"What do you want? Have we met before?" Leto asked. "I'm sure I'd remember you."

"We haven't had the pleasure," Privelion replied with glowing eyes.

"That brings me back to the first question," Leto spoke curtly. "What do you want?

"Your compliance," Privelion responded.

"And what might I be complying with?" Leto inquired.

Privelion told Leto the entire story, leaving out the memory of killing his grandfather that he couldn't bring to words. He told Leto of his history with science, his fascination with chemicals, his successful development of three Suvian abilities, and his desire for so much more. He hoped that sharing his background and ambitions might lead Leto toward a genuine empathy for him that might bond them together in the common task he so desperately craved. Instead, Leto looked at Privelion as if he were a patient who just broke out of an insane asylum.

"No," Leto simply stated. Privelion was instantly infuriated to have his life's work and well thought out request be rejected with one word. As Leto walked away from him, he decided to say just one word in response.

"Silvia," Privelion spoke quietly but harshly with wide eyes.

Leto turned around. "If you even think about coming near her, you'll regret it," he cautioned. He stared at Privelion menacingly before returning to the cave.

That night, Leto was unable to fall asleep. He returned to his bed to lie down but spent most of the night staring at Silvia, trying to determine the best means of protection for her. When morning came around, Leto, and all the Kleit for that matter could hardly tell. A dark storm cloud enveloped the Kleit's territory, causing day and night to seemingly merge into one. When Leto exited the cave and saw it, he knew what he had to do.

He went back into the cave to wake Silvia. "Silvia, sweetheart, wake up." He nudged her. Silvia's eyes opened slowly. "Silvia, we must go now. Hurry up," he urged. He glanced outside frantically.

Silvia did as she was told. She got out of bed and grabbed her father's hand as he guided her out of the cave. What she saw outside was complete chaos. The grass and several of the trees were on fire. There was a heavy wind, with rain drizzle to accompany it. There were children crying and moms trying to usher them into their respective caves. There were fathers drawing their weapons. The storm cloud came down to the ground as if forming a tornado and pulled three Kleit children up to the sky. A Kleit ran to the object on the pedestal in the center of the community. He grabbed it in a frenzy but panicked when he saw the storm cloud headed back toward the ground in his direction. He held the object over his head for protection. The storm cloud rapidly swallowed it, bringing it up to the sky as it had with the Kleit children. The children did not come back down, nor did the object. They were nowhere in sight.

Silvia listened to all the Kleit go from speaking coherently to making strange clicking noises that she didn't understand. She opened her mouth, and she too was making clicking noises that hardly made sense to her. Leto realized that he was experiencing the same problem. Leto held on tightly to Silvia's hand, and the two of them ran. They ran faster than anyone could possibly imagine, and seemingly breaking the realm of possibility, they eventually outran the storm cloud.

After a while of running, Silvia and Leto arrived at the Kleit sanctuary, entering a massive cave filled with traps that were well-known to them. Leto made clicking noises at Silvia repeatedly. She shrugged, not understanding that form of communication. Leto looked at her helplessly. His eyes lit up when an idea came to him. He walked carefully in the areas he knew to be safe, leading Silvia to do the same. When he got to the righthand wall of the cave, Leto knocked on it at a very specific tempo for seven seconds. The wall, made of what looked like solid rock, crumbled to sand on the cave floor. Silvia and Leto walked through a tunnel leading to a different room. The room they walked into was full of pictographs all over the floor and walls. Leto grabbed a rock that had fallen from the makeup of the cave wall and guided Silvia to the back wall of the room.

Finding one of the only unmarked spaces left on the wall, Leto marked it meticulously with an image of himself and Silvia shapeshifting. Silvia understood. She quickly shapeshifted into the form of a Klaysta tribe member. Leto did the same. In their new forms, they were able to communicate somewhat more effectively, but only as effective as the memories of their interactions with the Klaysta allowed.

"We need to go," Leto informed Silvia.

"How?" she asked.

Leto drew a story on the wall. It was a story he was confident Silvia would not misinterpret. Silvia watched as he drew sixteen images in four distinct clusters. When he finished, Leto looked at her for approval. Silvia nodded in agreement, trusting her father whole-heartedly.

Leto took a deep breath. "Let's go," he softly directed. Leto guided Silvia out of the cave. On the way out, he sealed the wall of the hidden room back together by knocking on the left side of the wall differently than he had knocked the first time. He grabbed hold of Silvia's hand once more and guided her out into the night. They walked for a little bit and halted at a clearing with a fountain and statue in the center of it.

Leto let go of Silvia's hand. He walked up to the base of the fountain, crouched down, and knocked on it, as he had the cave wall. Part of the stone slid down, revealing a hidden compartment. Leto reached in and grabbed four objects and then resealed the hidden compartment. In his hand were three communication devices that he himself had created. Though he hadn't tested them at the range he would need them to operate at, he was confident that they would be more than effective. Unlike Privelion, Leto never had a moment of self-doubt when it came to his own scientific abilities. While Privelion toyed with chemicals, Leto had been experimenting with technology. The communication devices were far from his first creations, and his technological devices had never failed him. Not once.

The fourth object in Leto's hands was a device smaller than the comms. This device had also been thought up and created by Leto himself. Silvia had never seen any of the items in her father's hands. She leaned forward attentively, trying to peek at what he was holding.

"Come with me," Leto instructed, still in the form of a Klaysta.

Silvia followed Leto. They walked through and past the trees, into the desert. Once they got far into the desert with open land in every direction, Leto put the three communication devices in his pockets and set the fourth device on the ground. He motioned for Silvia to back up. She took a few steps back. He motioned her back further. She took a few more steps. Further. She continued to walk backwards. Leto held up his hand, signaling her to stop and stay put. He pressed a button on the device and ran as fast as he could toward Silvia.

Silvia watched in awe as a device the size of a bottle cap transformed into a ginormous spherical contraption. Silvia looked up at her father, smiled, and shook her head, wonderous of when he had snuck away to create the device. She was with him all the time and had never seen it before.

"Get in," Leto instructed, nodding toward the contraption that now towered above them in height.

Silvia entered the contraption with a smile from ear to ear. As soon as she did, she shapeshifted back into her natural form as a Kleit and relaxed in her seat. She was so excited for the thrill of what might happen next. She didn't have an ounce of fear, mimicking the fearlessness of her father. Leto got in and sat next to her. Seeing that she had shapeshifted back into her true form as a Kleit, Leto did the same. He held her hand and hit three buttons on a control panel. To anyone's eyes on Suvia, the contraption would have instantly vanished. But no one was there to see. Two years later, which to Leto and Silvia felt only like minutes, they arrived in an empty field on Earth.

# 24

# Thirty-One Years Prior

Leto ran frantically with Silvia's hand in his. He knew their thirty minutes was near up and needed to find a private space for them to renew their form. Silvia tried to run at the same pace, but she couldn't stop herself from slowing down to absorb her surroundings. Everything was new. There were grey interconnected paths that appeared to be endless. The sky was so vastly blue. The trees were dispersed, with tall, windowed structures in between them.

"Silvia, come this way," Leto instructed, tugging at her hand.

Silvia pulled her focus back to her father and ran with him into a dimly lit alleyway. Leto and Silvia simultaneously began to morph, with Leto's transition taking longer as a result of his size. As quickly as they could, they shapeshifted back to their disguises. Silvia's black skin morphed into ivory. Leto's black skin morphed into tan. Silvia's hair was long, blonde, and wavy. Leto's was black and slicked back, resting at his shoulders. Having chosen their disguises based on real people they had just passed by on the street, they peeked around the corner and waited for them to be completely out of sight. Once they were, they still waited longer for the fear that those people might return or that someone who had seen them walk by might call out the peculiarity of seeing them pass by again.

"How many times will we have to do this?" Silvia asked her father as they waited.

"Shapeshift?" Leto asked. Silvia nodded. "Hopefully not too much longer." Leto knelt down and kissed her forehead.

Leto looked off into the distance and saw a woman with a baby carriage outside the alleyway. The baby was crying loudly, with the sounds of its distress carrying all the way across the street to him and Silvia. Leto watched as the woman lifted the child out of the carriage and soothed it by rocking it side to side. He looked at Silvia with a sadness to his gaze.

Silvia looked up at her father curious of his expression toward her. She looked at the baby, and then back up at her father. Silvia was blissfully unaware of her father's intentions.

A couple of tears dropped down from Leto's disguised eyes. "Shapeshift back," Leto instructed.

Silvia complied, shapeshifting back into her true form. She didn't understand why her father asked this of her, but nevertheless, she trusted him.

"Now, I'm going to help you shapeshift into something new," he informed her. "But you're going to have to stay in that form," he added, closing his eyelids tightly as more tears squeezed out from between them.

Silvia quickly shapeshifted back to the human form, with a desperate urge to get further information from her father. "For how long?" she asked.

"Forever," Leto responded.

"Will I still be me?" Silvia asked.

"I don't think so," Leto answered honestly.

Silvia began to join her father in shedding tears. They were grieving the loss of all that Silvia was and might never be again. Silvia wrapped her arms tightly around Leto's disguised form as she shapeshifted into her Kleit form for what she understood would be the last time.

"Close your eyes," Leto gently commanded.

Silvia shut her eyes tightly. Continuing to cry, Leto grabbed on firmly to Silvia and willed her to shapeshift into the baby. He used all his strength to help her shapeshift, in comparison to the partial strength that allowed for a temporary thirty-minute transformation. He knew that the full use of his ability would lead to a permanent transformation. He mourned the loss of Silvia as he watched her form as a Kleit vanish for good into the body of a child that could not yet speak or function independently. He looked at her helpless new identity, believing her form as a baby to be permanent.

As days turned to months, and months turned to a year, Leto went through a surplus of transformations. To Leto's surprise, so did Silvia. Her body grew over time, and when a year rolled around, she was able to crawl and take a few steps at a time on her own. Leto was happy to see that he had not sentenced her to an indefinite life as a human baby but had instead sentenced her to life as a human. A human that could grow. A human that could love. A human that could live. He was relieved to see that there would be more hope for her than he had initially imagined.

Realizing that he was now a liability for her, Leto decided that it was time to act in her best interest, despite the difficult decisions he would need to make in the process. It broke his heart not to be able to explain what was happening to Silvia, but her brain was now that of a human baby, and explaining complex situations to a baby would most definitely be a hopeless waste of time.

After using a restroom stall inside a building to shapeshift into his temporary disguise, he carried Silvia out in his arms and stopped the first human he saw for questioning. "I can't care for her anymore," Leto said as he approached the stranger.

An elderly woman looked into Leto's eyes with a warmth Leto had never seen. "Are you trying to hand this girl off to a stranger?" the old lady asked him.

Leto thought for a moment. He really wasn't sure what his intentions were. His only wish was that Silvia would be relocated to a safe space for now and would one day reunite with him when the timing was right. He wished to reunite when he had the means to protect her. He thought longer. He wondered if perhaps a more long-term separation would be necessary, allowing Silvia time to develop the means to protect herself.

"Well, no," Leto finally responded. The old lady looked at him as if she already knew his intentions. She reached out and gently wrapped Silvia's tiny hand in her own. Leto looked down to see wrinkled and aged skin against soft and new skin. It was an unfamiliar sight to him.

"What does she need?" the old lady asked Leto.

"A safe home," Leto replied. He looked at the old lady expectantly.

"She's beautiful." The old lady smiled. "I would take her in myself if that were legal."

Leto just continued to look at her, not understanding what she had meant by "legal".

"Look, here's what you need to do," the old lady instructed. She proceeded to provide Leto with directions to an adoption agency and explained the steps he would need to take upon arrival. He thanked the lady and walked away, but the information she had provided him with went over his head, and he walked away feeling less certain of his plan than he had prior to speaking with her.

Though he had no idea what an adoption agency was, he walked in the direction that the old lady had guided him towards. After following every step of her directions, he arrived in front of a tall, windowed structure towering over him. On top of it were the letters ECDAH. Leto had no idea what the letters represented, but still feeling the warmth that the old lady had offered him, he walked into the structure with a sense of courage. Seeing a manmade structure this elegant and complex for the first time, Leto marveled at the large, bright, intricately designed light fixtures above him. Even Silvia smiled and cocked her head curiously at the sight of them. He looked down at the floor, seeing square tiles for the first time. About four and a half meters in front of him was a massive desk, with five humans seated behind it eagerly awaiting him to come closer.

When he approached the desk, one of the ladies greeted him with a smile. "What's your child's name?" she asked.

Leto ignored her question. "How does this place work?" he inquired.

"Well, we are an adoption agency," the lady explained gently. "We take in children, interview families, and try to provide the best match for the needs of the child. Then they go to their new home. We only process closed adoptions."

Leto looked at the lady with an expression of confusion. She apologized for being vague and proceeded to explain further. "You see, a closed adoption is where a parent no longer has contact with the child." Leto pulled Silvia closer to his chest and didn't speak a word. He gave the lady a brief look of terror. "How long have you been considering adoption?" she asked warmly.

Leto cleared his throat. "I'm not. I am looking for work," he improvised.

"Are you credentialed in social work or psychology?" the lady asked him skeptically. He had no idea what that meant, but he shook his head no. "I'm sorry," the lady responded, shrugging her shoulders.

"Thanks anyway," Leto replied. He proceeded to exit the building. As he was exiting, he noticed a seemingly happy young couple entering through a different set of double doors.

"Hey!" Leto called out before they went through the doorway. The woman had wavy brown hair halfway down her back. She was slim, gorgeous, and confined to a wheelchair. The man was average height and stocky.

The woman backed her wheelchair up and turned it toward Leto. "Are you talking to us?

"Yes." Leto jogged over to them, still holding Silvia in his arms. "Are you going in to adopt?

"Why, yes. That's the plan," the man answered.

"Please, please adopt from me. It can be a closed adoption," he assured them, assuming it to be what they wanted since they were ready to enter and adopt from this agency.

"Adopt from you?" The woman laughed. "Heavens no! We need legal documents to be signed. We need to be sure this child will belong to us. We need a history of her records."

"I can't care for her anymore." Leto's voice cracked, and he began to sob. He also became anxious, as he realized it had been a while since he last shapeshifted, and he feared he might morph into his true form any minute now. If he were going to convince this family to take Silvia in, he would need to do it quickly.

"Please take her." Leto held her toward them. "You'll never see me again. She doesn't have any records."

"I don't feel comfortable with this," the lady said, looking up at the man she was with.

The man reached out and grabbed Silvia from Leto's arms. Silvia smiled up at the man. "Does she have a name?" he asked.

Another tear fell from Leto's eye as he shook his head no. He felt responsible for the erasure of her identity and swore silently that he would never forgive himself for it.

"What should we name her?" The man directed his question to the woman in the wheelchair.

"You can't seriously be considering this!" the woman exclaimed.

The man pursed his lips. "We don't even know how long the adoption process might take. Evelyn Gates next door told us it took years for her to get custody of Sammy. Besides, after losing our little one last year to pneumonia, this little ray of sunshine could benefit us just as much as we could benefit her." He gently bounced Silvia up and down in his arms.

Leto nodded vigorously, encouraging their ongoing consideration.

"I just don't know. This doesn't feel right," the woman responded.

"This child is in danger, and you may be her only hope," Leto assured them. "The only way she will be safe is if you take her in and convince her every day of her life that she was born into your family."

"This is what we wanted," the man continued to consult with the woman in the wheelchair, "a closed adoption." The woman looked up at him speechless. "What should we name her?" he asked again.

The man handed the child over to her. The woman looked into the child's eyes and developed an instant affection for her. The woman let out a short breathy laugh. "Zara," she smiled.

"Thank you. We will care for her as if she were born to us, and we will not tell her of her origins. I promise we will respect your wishes with that," the man assured Leto. The man was thankful to be able to bring a child home with his wife without the waiting period most people are subjected to for adoptions.

The man and the woman proceeded to depart, and Leto watched as they left. He fell to his knees on the sidewalk they had been standing on. He felt as his body began to transform, but he couldn't will himself to move. Luckily, no one was around to see as a man turned into a black figure, shrank in height, and grew elongated arms. Realizing after a couple of minutes that he was still in front of a windowed structure and was at significant risk of exposure, Leto took off to find shelter and isolation.

25

# TWENTY-THREE YEARS PRIOR

I T TOOK LETO NEARLY a decade to devise a long-term plan for himself and Silvia. He decided it would be carried out in four overarching phases. Phase one of Leto's plan required him to find Silvia. Luckily, he had a starting point: Evelyn Gates and Sammy. Leto did not know how to find them quite yet, but he did learn how to find general information on Earth. Leto walked twelve blocks to the community library. He had been there before on numerous occasions to learn of Earth, as well as what humans perceived to be beyond Earth. It was through his visits to the library that he learned of an organization called NASA and began to envision a plan. The librarians knew him well now, or rather, knew his disguise well.

When Leto arrived at the library, he stopped at the desk to speak with one of the regular librarians. He told her of his dilemma, explaining that he was searching for someone and was unsure how to find them. The librarian warmly pointed him in the direction of something called a "phonebook". The term was entirely unfamiliar to him. Believing Leto to have some sort of learning delay based on prior conversations with him, the librarian walked him through a step-by-step procedure for how to look someone up and contact them based on the information in the phonebook. Leto nodded, acknowledging her instruction. She walked away, allowing him to look through the book of contact information on his own.

Leto traced his finger down the first page of "G" last names and quickly located the name "Evelyn Gates". The only problem is there were three people with that exact same name. Leto picked up the book and brought it to the librarian. He pointed to the three names and displayed an expression of confusion.

"Do you know anything else about this person?" the librarian asked him. Leto shook his head hopelessly and sighed. "You could give each of them a call or go to their address," the librarian suggested.

Leto knew that going to their homes would be of no use. He didn't have a clue what Evelyn Gates or Sammy looked like. He wondered if calling them might be a good option.

"Thank you," Leto nodded. "I'll call."

"There is a public phone right there on the wall." The librarian pointed.

Leto walked over to the phone and dialed the first number.

"Hello?" a woman with a soft voice greeted.

"Is Sammy there?" Leto asked.

"No. I think you have the wrong number," the lady informed him. He heard a click on the other end, followed by silence.

*Well, that was easy*, he thought to himself. It occurred to him when he thought back to his conversations that the limitation of language he and his tribe have experienced when in shapeshifted form had somehow disappeared. He wondered why this must be and decided something about the environment must be a contributing factor. Knowing that he was no longer limited, he planned to speak with a higher level of sophistication, hoping it would lead him more quickly to answers. He dialed the next number.

"Hello?" a man greeted this time.

"Hello sir, I am looking for Sammy. My kid says they know yours and would like to set up a time to play together!" Leto informed the man enthusiastically.

"Wrong home," the man snapped. The line went silent.

Leto put his head against the wall in frustration, worried that if this didn't work, he would never see Silvia again. One last time, he dialed ten numbers on the phone and waited as it rang.

"Hello?" a child answered.

"Hi!" Leto exclaimed, caught off guard by the small voice. "Are you Sammy?" Leto asked skeptically.

"Yes," the child responded. "Do you want to speak to my mom?"

"No!" Leto exclaimed instinctively.

"I'm actually calling because I'm friends with the family next door to you, and they aren't picking up their phones. I guess I am getting pretty worried," Leto fibbed.

"You mean Maria, Roy, and Esther?" the child asked excitedly.

"No." Leto closed his eyes tightly and shed a tear, worried this last option was a dud.

"Or do you mean Zara and her parents?" the child asked more glumly.

"Yes!" Leto's eyes lit up.

"Yeah, they're fine," the child responded, "but Zara never wants to hang out with me."

"I'm sorry to hear that, kid," Leto replied. Leto placed the phone back on the wall holder, ending the call abruptly. He now had the information he needed. Leto looked around the room suspiciously to see if anyone had eyes on him. They didn't. He quickly tore the page out of the phone book that had Evelyn Gates' address on it. He coughed as he did so to cover the sound of the ripping paper. Leto quickly folded the paper and put it in his pocket.

"Thank you!" Leto waved quickly to the librarian as he exited. As he set off walking toward his apartment, a luxury he was most thankful for, he began to plan phase two in his head. Over the course of several years, Leto decided that Earth was only a temporary solution to a long-term problem. He was determined to find a way for him and Silvia to eventually return to Suvia. Leto could only think of one organization on Earth that could get them there, and in his favor, he had read enough about that organization to know what steps would be necessary to ensure their successful return. Lost in thought the whole walk, Leto was amazed at how quickly he seemed to make it back to his apartment.

Initiating phase two, Leto shapeshifted into a tall, bulky, muscular, bald man. He was relieved that he no longer had to worry about finding a secluded place to shapeshift. He had learned how to rent an apartment on a month-to-month lease and had found a minimum wage job to pay for it.

The job he found required heavy labor, moving equipment around in a factory, but no one questioned his background, money was under the table, and no one judged his excessive use of the bathroom each day. This made it the perfect job for him. Nevertheless, phase two would require him to quit.

Leto walked out of his apartment, not bothering to lock the door behind him. It was more essential that he locked it if he were in it, as he worried someone might walk in while he was mid-transformation. He walked down a long hallway, hurried down the stairs, and exited through a door at the bottom of the staircase leading directly outside. Once outside, Leto pulled a map out of the back pocket of his jeans. He looked for a building on the map called "The Ocean Bar Café".

The café was three blocks from Leto's current location. He walked along confidently with a stiffness to his posture. There was a fury in his eyes. Phase two would be perhaps the most important phase of all. Leto felt the pressure, but there was not a doubt in his mind that he would be successful.

When he arrived in front of the café, Leto pressed his hands against the glass window to block out the sunlight and peek inside. His target was in there. Now all he had to do was wait patiently for him to come out. It was bound to happen eventually.

Eventually came about thirty minutes later. "Alright, it was good to see you guys again. Same time next week," a middle-aged man called out as he exited the café. He waved goodbye to his friends inside. Leto waited for the man to walk toward his car. While the man was distracted trying to find the right key on his chain to unlock the car, Leto quickly snuck toward the opposite side of the vehicle. As the man opened his driver side door, Leto simultaneously opened the door diagonal from the driver's side in the back. The man didn't notice. They both got into the car. The man did notice when he heard both doors shut at the same time, but by then it was already too late. Leto held a blade to the man's side and instructed him to drive. The man did as he was told. Leto directed him toward an alleyway and told him to park the car. The man again complied.

"What do you want from me?" the man asked.

"I want you never to show your face at work again," Leto answered. "If you do, your family will pay the price. I also want you to travel somewhere far from here and never look back."

"I have to go to work!" the man exclaimed. "I'm the lead administrator of the launch division at NASA. If I don't show, they'll come look for me. I'm needed there," the man rambled.

"No one will look for you," Leto assured the man.

Filled with adrenaline, the man tried to grab the knife from Leto's hand. Leto pulled back and the man's hand got sliced. The man persisted, throwing his fists wildly at Leto and reaching several times for the knife. Leto tried to push the man off of him to no avail. In one quick motion, Leto wrapped one hand around the man's neck and shoved the blade through it. Leto heard a gurgling noise, and the man quickly lost consciousness and began to bleed out. Leto quickly withdrew the blade and dropped it onto the center console. The blood spurted out of the man's neck, splattering the dashboard and the seats. After a few seconds, the blood flow slowed, and the remaining drops dripped slowly down the man's neck before seeping into the collar of his shirt. Leto looked down at himself, noticing he had somehow evaded getting the man's blood on his clothing, though his hand was covered in it. He instinctively wiped his hand on the man's shirt until the only blood remaining was a shadow of red stained on his skin.

Leto panicked. His intention had not been to kill the man. He quickly grabbed the man's identification badge from his pants, took one last look at him, and left the vehicle. Worried that someone might find the man's body in the alleyway, which would lead to the discrediting of Leto's impending identity shift, he opened the car door and dragged the man out onto the pavement. He rummaged quickly through the man's glove compartment and found cigars and a lighter. Knowing how to use a lighter from an advertisement he saw on television during his time on Earth, Leto lit it up and held it to the man's shirt until it caught fire. He waited to ensure the fire spread throughout the man's body.

Leto quickly glanced at the car with hints of fear and wonder in his expression. He approached the driver's side of the vehicle and examined the mess that was left behind, horrified at the sight of it and the careless missteps in his planning. He thought quickly about how to do away with the blood on the seats and dashboard. He looked around, ensuring there was no disrupt to his solitude. Without a second thought, he picked up the blade from the center console, shoved it firmly into the edge of the seat, and dragged it in a large square formation. After pulling out the blade, he re-inserted it at a slant into the top of the seat cushion and pried it from the metal frame.

After carving the passenger's seat of the car in the same fashion, Leto sliced a thin piece of clean fabric from it and scrubbed away rigorously at the dashboard. To his surprise, the fabric absorbed almost all of the blood, leaving faint traces of it that were even less noticeable than the stains on the skin of his hand. Before considering his task complete, Leto dragged the squares of seat cushion toward the man. While the man's body was still engulfed in flames, Leto grew concerned that the cushions beside the man were not immediately catching fire and used the lighter to hasten the process.

Leto hurriedly hopped into the driver's seat and began his transformation into the guy he had just killed. Just as he had sentenced Silvia to a new life, he chose to do the same for himself. Using all his strength to transform, he permanently assumed the identity of the NASA administrator. He latched the identification badge to the beltloop of his jeans, buckled the seatbelt across his torso, and put his hands on the steering wheel, ready to enact phase three of his four-step plan.

After pressing seven buttons on the dashboard, turning the wiper blades on and back off, and fiddling with the headlights, Leto finally moved the shifter and got the car into drive. It took him ten more minutes to figure out the foot pedals. Once he did, he slowly stepped on the gas pedal. When he made it to the edge of the alleyway, he slammed on the breaks. His head shot forward and then hit the back of the seat. He began to tremble, fearful of operating the vehicle but knowing it was a necessity to have one. He slowly exited the alleyway. While there were people around, no one seemed to glance in his direction or pay any mind to the smell of the NASA administrator's body being incinerated behind the car. Perhaps the fumes of gasoline mitigated the smell of burning flesh. He drove twelve kilometers under the speed limit to his apartment. After going through one red light and three stop signs without so much as pausing, he noticed a car in front of him making these periodic stops, which alerted him to his errors. He stopped at every remaining red light and stop sign until he reached his apartment complex.

He parked the car, recalling the initial position of the shifter, and got out. He held up his hand and observed it continuing to tremble. Leto only came back to the apartment for one reason. He ran up the staircase of his apartment and bolted through his unit door and into the bathroom. He stared at his reflection in the mirror. Looking back at him was a man likely in his lower forties with ashy brown hair, sky blue eyes, slight wrinkles on his forehead and cheeks, bags under his eyes, and a glaringly white smile. Leto had gone through more transformations than he could ever count, and this one did not startle him any more than the numerous other faces he had worn over the course of his lifetime. His only concern was recalling the panicked rush of having to run to transform every thirty minutes. He knew he would not feel comfortable or certain of this transformation in particular until he waited it out.

It took Leto two hours to gain confidence that his new disguise would not falter. Once he did, he left the apartment, got back into the car, and headed for NASA headquarters. He figured out how to turn the radio on and turned the volume up, nodding his head to the blasting sound of Little Red Corvette while cruising along in his newly acquired little red Volvo. When he stopped at a red light, a man pulled up next to him and looked at him with a penetrating glare. Leto noticed and turned the volume down.

When the light turned green, Leto took off quickly, embarrassed by the interaction. Upon arrival at NASA's facility, Leto held his badge up to a metal box, and two gates slowly opened as a result. He drove through the gates and stared up at a massive building. He knew that in order to pull this off, he would need to walk into the building like he was meant to be there. He got out of the car, stood up tall, and walked toward the nearest building entrance to him.

As Leto reached out to the door handle, the door opened, startling him and causing him to take a step backward. A man dressed in all blue was walking out, dragging a towering dumpster out with him.

"What are you doing over here, boss?" the man asked.

"I... uh... I got locked out," Leto answered, not knowing how to respond.

"But ya got your badge right there on your pants." The man pointed.

"Right," Leto nodded, trying to quickly think of another excuse, "but when I pulled on the door, it wouldn't open."

"You feelin okay, Chief?" the man asked, looking at the NASA administrator as if he needed to be escorted to the nearest mental institute.

"Feeling great. Why do you ask?" Leto responded.

"Because the doors you enter slide open..." The man looked at him skeptically.

"I'm just joking around with you," Leto covered. "I got bored over there. I came to say hi and see what goes on over on this side of the building."

"Oh." The man scratched his head. "You know, not a whole lot. It's quite the dump!" The man laughed and slapped his hand against the dumpster.

Leto didn't understand the joke but let out a forceful chuckle so as not to look any more suspicious. "You gonna head back to work?" the man asked, nodding his head to the left.

"Yes, of course. It was nice talking to you," Leto quickly replied.

Leto walked away rapidly, concerned that the man may be on to him. After lengthening the distance between them, Leto realized that it was foolish to worry. He knew that seeing was believing for people on Earth, and the man had been looking into the eyes of the NASA administrator. There is no way his identity would have been compromised that easily.

Walking up to the correct door, Leto held his badge to another metal box, which led to two glass doors sliding open. Security greeted him right away and quickly approved his entry. A beautiful Black woman sitting behind the front desk also greeted him.

"Good morning, Nolan." She smiled at him.

"Good morning," he nodded to her, acknowledging the name she had called him by and quickly trying to commit it to memory. "Hey, my daughter is really interested in our organization, and there is only so much information I can bore her with. We wouldn't happen to have anything to fuel her interest here, would we?" Leto asked.

"Of course, we do," the woman replied in a playful tone, clearly thinking Leto was joking around with her and already knew the answer. She reached down behind the desk and opened a cabinet. When she popped back up, she was holding several pamphlets and handed them to Leto.

Leto gently grabbed them from her hand and paused. "If it isn't too much to ask, could you give me a sizable number of these?"

"Anything for you," the woman responded. She popped her head back down again and came up with a handful of about thirty pamphlets.

"Thank you so much," Leto replied.

"No worries!" The woman waved off his appreciation. "Like I've told you over and over again, Rita's got your back!"

Leto was happy that the woman reminded him of her name without him prompting. It seemed she was awfully familiar with the real NASA administrator, and if anything would cause suspicion, it would be him inquiring her name.

"You're the best, Rita!" Leto exclaimed.

"So you've told me," Rita replied happily. Leto turned around to walk back out the door. "That all you came here for?" Rita asked.

"That's all for today," Leto responded, holding up the pamphlets in a gesture of farewell as he walked back through the double doors.

"Ooh, that man never fails to entertain me!" Rita laughed to herself as he walked away. She returned to her administrative duties.

Phase three wasn't over. Leto walked back out into the parking lot and returned to the red Volvo. There was a man leaning against the driver's side door. Leto's body tensed, as he feared the man was there to question him about the mutilated seats and faint traces of blood.

"Ah... hello," Leto greeted the man with unease.

"Hey, Nolan! Sorry to disturb you. I just wanted to inform you that you left the car running with the key in the ignition. I wasn't sure if you did that intentionally. Probably safe here, but I wouldn't go around doing that outside of these gates," the man advised.

"Thank you!" Leto let out an overexaggerated sigh of relief. The man misinterpreted it, thinking Leto must be thankful for his warning. In reality, Leto was thankful that the man wanted to protect him and not interrogate him.

"Looks like you are doing a bit of reupholstery?" the man asked.

"Reupholstery?" Leto asked, unfamiliar with the term.

"Yeah, I see you're changing up your seats," the man clarified.

Leto frowned. *Ah, here is the interrogation*, he thought to himself. He replied to the man curtly, still unsure of his intentions, "Yep. Started to. Off to get that finished up."

"Well hey, I'd love to see how it looks when it is complete. Take care, Nolan."

The man stepped aside so Leto could get into his car. Leto quickly got in and waved to the man politely as he drove away. *That was a close call*, he thought to himself. He passed back through the gates, using his badge once more to open them. Once he got past the gates, he parked along the shoulder of the road and pulled a folded piece of paper out of his pants pocket, reviewing the address of Evelyn Gates. He wasn't sure how to get to it. He decided he better return to the library and look up directions, as he had for NASA headquarters.

Upon his arrival at the library, Leto turned the key to his car and pulled it out, taking it with him this time as the man had suggested. When he walked through the library doors, he squinted at the librarians who paid him no attention at all. It took him a moment to realize they would not recognize him due to his drastically different appearance. He walked on to the computers and inputted Evelyn Gates' address into the system. He printed the directions as the librarians had taught him previously and headed to her residence.

When he got to Evelyn's address, it occurred to him that he should have asked Sammy which house Zara lived at. Although, perhaps it was best he did not, as he was trying to avoid raising suspicion at all costs. Leto parked the Volvo by the curb and waited. He hoped someone would come out of one of the houses to clue him in on which one he was looking for. Sure enough, after about an hour of patience, Sammy exited the house and walked next door excitedly toward the house on the right. Based on Sammy's expression, Leto gathered he was about to see a friend. Based on their earlier conversation, he was sure that friend wasn't Zara. Leto walked up to the house to the left of Sammy's and set two of the NASA pamphlets on the front porch. He rang the doorbell and quickly ran back to the car.

Leto watched from the car as a familiar face appeared in the doorway of that house. It was Zara's adoptive father. He looked down at the pamphlets curiously. He picked them up and looked through them, still standing in the doorway. Then he shrugged and brought them into the house. Leto had hoped that would go a little bit differently. He needed to ensure that the pamphlets made it into the hands of Silvia.

He tried again, this time implementing a more direct approach. He walked up to the door with five pamphlets, each one different than the next. He rang the doorbell and stood on the porch, waiting for someone to answer. Zara's adoptive father answered once again, this time face to face with the NASA administrator.

"Hello, sir," Leto greeted nervously. "I am the head of the launch division at NASA. I apologize for leaving after ringing the bell the first time. I ran to my car quickly to get more pamphlets."

The man looked at him flabbergasted. "Seriously? Did you say NASA? What are you doing here at my house?" The man seemed highly intrigued.

"I know there are a lot of kids in this neighborhood, and I am trying to get the young ones interested in what we do at NASA to fuel young brains," the NASA administrator lied through his teeth.

"That sounds great. I think that could certainly be an inspiration to the younger generation!" The man hesitated, "But I have two daughters. This kind of stuff would undoubtedly spark my interest far more than theirs. I am definitely going to give these pamphlets a look. Thank you for sharing this." The man raised up the pamphlets with gratitude and went to shut the door.

"Wait," Leto prompted. The man re-opened the door, curious as to what more the NASA administrator wanted. "You seem like a very nice man," Leto complimented. "I don't normally do this," he whispered, as if sharing top secret information, "but I could come in and talk to your girls about what NASA is. Hearing it from me is sure to spark their interest!"

"Ah, yeah, I suppose that would be alright." The man opened the door wider and motioned for the NASA administrator to enter.

Leto entered the house and looked around. The house was neat and tidy with not a shoe print on the hardwood floor, nor a speck of dust on the furniture. To Leto's right at the entryway was a brown dresser against a teal wall. Along the dresser were intricately designed metal picture frames, but Leto was far more interested in the pictures themselves. He picked up the first one he saw. It had the mom and dad and two beautiful little girls, one far outshining the other. He was sure that was his little girl who he had sentenced to this new life. It wasn't so new anymore.

The mom rolled her wheelchair into the room, and Leto quickly set the picture frame back down on the dresser. "Who was at the..." The woman halted as she looked Leto up and down.

"Honey, this is the lead administrator at NASA," the man said, with an unsureness in his voice.

Leto cleared his throat anxiously, "Yes, I'm Nolan, the lead administrator of the launch division." Leto reached his arm out to offer a handshake, but the woman did not reciprocate.

"Oh?" the woman asked. "What have you come to our home for?"

"I'm just trying to get the next generation interested in our programs. I thought I might share some top-secret information with your girls," Leto chuckled.

"No, thank you. We're not interested," the woman dismissed.

The man gave her a harsh look. "Hey now. Don't be rude. The man has already taken his shoes off." The man gave Leto a quick nod.

Leto took the hint and quickly stepped out of his shoes, folding his hands coyly.

"I'm sorry," the woman said genuinely. "Where are my manners? I'll go get the girls."

Leto could tell that her initial rudeness was out of protectiveness of her children. He had nothing but gratitude for her watchful behavior. As the woman wheeled off into another room, the man motioned for Leto to follow him into the living room and welcomed him to sit anywhere he would like. Like the entryway, the living room had teal walls and brown furniture. There was an enormous window covering the entire back wall of the house. Leto stood in front of it and looked out. There was a wooden structure in the backyard with two slides and a swing-set. Leto visualized the two girls sliding down from it, laughing hand in hand. Past the wooden structure, there were fruit trees with bright green leaves. The grass was an even lighter shade of green. Leto silently praised himself for his selection of adoptive parents for Silvia.

Leto walked over to a brown leather reclining chair. Just as he was about to sit down, the woman returned with her two daughters. Leto stopped himself from sitting and stared into the eyes of a beautiful eight-year-old girl with brown hair and bright blue eyes that he knew to be Silvia. Looking at her now, he was astonished at her beauty, which far exceeded even that of the beauty she possessed in her original form as a Kleit.

She looked up at him without any hint of recognition, seeming to be only curious of the presence of a strange man in her living room. Her five-year-old sister looked up at the man with more judgement than curiosity. Leto smiled at the girls.

"How do you do?" Leto reached out his hand. Silvia shook it. Leto could swear he felt an electric shock the moment her skin touched his.

"Who are you?" Silvia asked.

"And why are you here?" Zidia chimed in.

Their mother guided them to the couch to sit down. "Now, now, let us not be rude. This man has come to show you something."

"What are your names?" Leto asked the girls.

"I'm Zara," Silvia responded.

"I'm Zidia," the younger sister introduced herself, while crossing her arms impudently.

"I'm Let..." Leto cleared his throat, quickly realizing his mistake. "Let me get more comfortable." Leto laughed anxiously and shifted a pillow on the leather chair underneath his arm before continuing. "I'm Nolan," he corrected.

Leto explained to the girls of his status with NASA, of course leaving out the part about him stealing that status from a man who was now likely disintegrated into a pile of ash. He handed them each a pamphlet and walked them through the details of space travel, details of which he only recently learned of through books at the libraries and the pamphlets themselves. Silvia stared at Leto with beady eyes, while Zidia's interest declined and transitioned to a greater interest of what her finger could dig out of her nose.

Silvia turned toward her mother. "Can I go sometime?"

"To NASA?" her mother asked?

"No, to Mars!" Silvia pointed at one of the pamphlets and directed her mother's attention to a picture of the planet on the front page.

"I don't know, honey," her mother responded. "I think that's something that only adults will be allowed to do."

"Your mother is absolutely correct," Leto replied, "but, one day, you will be an adult." Leto successfully held back tears, remembering holding a human baby in his arms and seeing that same child now in front of him at eight years of age.

"And then I can go?" Silvia's face lit up.

"We'll talk about that when you're older," Silvia's father chuckled.

Her mother looked at her with worry in her eyes. Leto walked over and sat beside the mother of the two girls. He handed her a few more pamphlets. "It's just to get kids interested," he assured her. He put his hand gently on her back, seemingly to comfort her, but as he pulled his hand away, he pulled a medical tag off the back of her wheelchair and discretely slipped it into his back pocket. The woman, unaware of this action, smiled at him and dabbed at her watery eyes with her shirt.

"Would it be okay with you if I drop off a few fun things from NASA... say a couple times a year?" Leto asked Silvia directly. Silvia nodded enthusiastically. "Is that okay with you, Mom?" Leto asked the mother of the girls. Their mother nodded hesitantly. "Don't worry." Leto smiled at her. "She's not going anywhere..." *Yet*, he thought to himself.

"Well thank you, sir!" The father reached out his hand and shook Leto's. "I am shocked you even sparked the interest of one of my girls."

"Of course," Leto smiled. "I'll drop by from time to time, if that is okay, to see if that interest continues."

"You are welcome here anytime." The father walked toward the entryway and opened the front door, signaling that the conversation was over for the day.

Leto looked at Silvia one last time as he walked out. He tried to memorize every detail of her face, just in case it was the last time he would see it. He couldn't bear the thought. He shook his head as if physically shaking the thought away, thanked the family one more time for their hospitality, and walked out the door. With his exit, phase three was complete.

The next day, Leto set out to initiate phase four. Leto knew phase four would not be easy after he had shown his face to Silvia. For the first time since his permanent transition to a human body, he regretted his newfound inability to shapeshift. He drove to Silvia's house at four in the morning, pulled over alongside a curb on the street opposite her address, cracked his window open slightly, and leaned his seat back so he could not be as easily seen. He powered the car off and waited.

After two hours, the front door of the house across the street opened, as did the neighbor's front door. Silvia, Zidia, and Sammy all exited their houses. Silvia and Zidia were very talkative with one another, but Sammy didn't say a word to either of them as they waited at the curbside for their ride to school. Leto slightly lifted his seat to get a better look at Silvia. Her hair was twisted up into a messy bun, and the sunlight was reflecting off of her bright white sneakers. Her pink backpack looked even brighter against the dark black T-shirt she was wearing.

After only five short minutes, a standard yellow school bus pulled up, and all three kids got on it. A door slammed at the house on the other side of Sammy's, and a child came running, making it to the school bus just in the nick of time before it took off. Leto could see through the school bus windows that Zara and Zidia chose to sit together, and that Sammy and the other neighbor made no attempt to talk to them. He wondered if Zara and Zidia were outcasts for a reason that could be tied to Zara's origins.

Leto turned on his car and followed the school bus. When it arrived at the school, he parked his car and waited about twenty minutes while the children got off the bus, entered the school, and got settled into their classes. When he no longer saw kids flooding through the front door of the school, he decided it was safe to go in. He walked through an empty hall to a welcome desk. He could hear the voices and laughter of children coming from the branched off hallways with classrooms.

"How may I help you?" the lady at the welcome desk greeted Leto.

"I'm Let..." Leto stopped himself, irritated that he made the same mistake he had made the day before. A creature of habit, he cleared his throat and corrected his mistake with fluidity. "Let me introduce myself," he said, holding out his hand with a friendly smile. "I'm Nolan."

"The Nolan?" The lady stood up from her desk chair with her jaw dropped.

"Ah... I don't know," Leto replied, pulling his hand back and dropping it at his side.

"Nolan from the launch division at NASA?" the lady gasped.

"Yes, but how do you know that?" Leto took a step backward, genuinely frightened by the lady.

"My son is obsessed! With NASA... With you... I can't believe you're here at my work and my son's school. He goes here! Can I pull him out of class to meet you? What brings you here today?"

Leto couldn't seem to match the lady's energy and enthusiasm. Not only that, but he had also come in with the intention of keeping a low profile. He could tell that idea went out the window. "I actually don't have too much time," Leto politely rejected.

"Oh, but it would mean the world to him. Please?" the lady pressed.

Leto had no obligations toward this woman and yet couldn't bring himself to disappoint her. He figured it may benefit him anyway to be on her good side, as phase four would require her assistance and discretion. "Sure, I'll meet your son," Leto yielded.

"Oh, perfect!" The lady clapped her hands together excitedly.

She picked up a small sign from behind the desk and placed it on top of the desk for people to see. The sign read, **_Will be back in 5_**. Leto chuckled at the sight of it. He wasn't even from this planet, and he recognized the ambiguity. Five minutes? Five hours?

The lady stepped out from behind the desk and guided Leto down another a hallway toward her son's classroom. Leto looked into the classrooms they were passing anxiously, hoping he would not be seen by Silvia or Zidia. So far so good. They continued on until they arrived at the last classroom on the right at the end of the hallway.

"There's my boy. Right there," the lady whispered, pointing a wrinkled finger toward the classroom.

Instead of following the direction of her finger with his eyes, Leto backed up and stood beside the wall dividing her son's classroom from the next one over. "Listen, I don't want to distract the whole class," Leto whispered. "How about you go get your son and bring him back to the main hallway? I'll meet you over there." Leto turned to walk back to where they had come from.

"The other kids would love to meet you too, I'm sure!" the lady protested.

"I just want it to be a special moment for your son," Leto turned around to reply.

"I suppose you're right." The lady hunched her shoulders in disappointment. "A one-on-one greeting would be more special for him."

Leto nodded and quickly walked back to the main hallway before the lady had the opportunity to change her mind. He sat on a wooden bench along the wall while he waited for her to return with her son. While he waited, he got lost in thought about how he might execute the final step in his four-phase plan. He ultimately needed a way to track Zara from a distance. Perhaps he could get updates from a staff member at the school. *No*, he thought to himself, *a child*. A child would be oblivious to his motives, and he knew that human children could easily be persuaded by rewards.

"Oh... my... goodness..." An eight-year-old boy walked up to Leto and broke him out of his thought process. The boy had messy blonde hair, a skinny neck, a freckled face, and glasses. Leto immediately decided that this would not be the child to help implement his plan. He was far too much of an eyesore and would draw far too much attention to perform any task discretely. Furthermore, his voice was squeaky, and his striped shirt drastically clashed with his plaid shorts.

"Hi there, I'm..."

"I know who you are!" the boy exclaimed.

Leto was happy to not have to introduce himself again, lest he mess up the introduction a third time. "That's great, kid," Leto replied, hoping the child would end the conversation after the introduction.

He didn't. "Can you tell me about the next launch, Nolan?" the kid asked.

"Top secret," Leto replied apathetically.

"Well, can you tell me about some of the past ones?" the kid responded eagerly.

"I thought you were a major fan... Shouldn't you know these things already, kid?" Nolan asked.

"Well, what about what the control room looks like?"

Leto had not yet seen the control room. He wondered himself what it looked like and was determined to find out soon. "It has a lot of controls," Leto replied dryly.

The child's enthusiasm plummeted, and he stared at Leto expressionless.

"Isn't this so cool, Kyle?" his mom exclaimed obliviously. "Who knew you'd get to meet your idol!"

"Yeah... thanks, mom." The kid looked at the floor in dejection.

The lady placed a hand on each of the kid's shoulders and guided him back toward the hallway with classrooms. Leto watched the kid and his mother out of the corner of his eye as they walked away. Kyle looked back just before proceeding down the hallway and going out of view. Leto felt the child's utter disappointment in him through his empty gaze and wondered if his efforts would ultimately result in the same look from Silvia. He wanted nothing more out of life than her happiness and safety. A look like that from her would kill him.

The lady returned with a smile, blissfully unaware of her son's crushed spirits. "Alright, now, where were we?" she asked.

"I was going to tell you the reason I am here," Leto replied.

"Oh, yes! Certainly, it wasn't to see my son," the lady chuckled.

"I regret to inform you it was not," Leto confirmed. "I came here in hopes that I could inspire the kids with NASA pamphlets and information during their lunch hour."

"Oh, that would be wonderful!" the lady cried out. "And you have perfect timing! The lunch bell should be ringing..." A loud bell sounded throughout the school, and within only seconds, the main hallway was flooded with kids. "Oh, heavens! It's that time already! I need to get the kids to line up for lunch. Please write your name on this sticker and put it on. It's your visitor's pass. It was great to meet you, Nolan!" She scurried off quickly, ushering kids into a more organized fashion as she made her way toward the cafeteria.

Nolan was worried that Zara or Zidia might recognize him in the crowd, but he figured if he didn't act now, they'd be far more likely to recognize him in a lunchroom when everything has settled down. Nolan tugged at the shirt of a child who was quickly passing by him.

"What's your name?" Leto asked.

"Why?" the kid replied harshly.

"Do you like money?" Leto tried a different approach.

"Yeah..." The kid's interest seemed to increase at the word alone.

"Come with me," Leto gently instructed.

The child listened and followed him out of the school. Through the hustle of the lunch hour, no one noticed. Once they were outside, Leto guided the child toward his car.

"Get in," Leto gently commanded.

"No, I'm not going to get in your car," the child scoffed, "and you haven't shown me any money."

"You'll get the money if you complete a task for me," Leto replied.

"And the task is?"

"I can't tell you out here." Leto looked around to check for bystanders. "Would you feel better about getting in my car if I give you the key and you sit in the driver seat?"

The child thought for a moment and then nodded. Leto unlocked the door and then walked over to the passenger side, handing the key to the child on the way. The child opened the door but hesitated to get in at the sight of the damaged seats.

"Don't mind that," Leto said to the child. "Get in."

"Why is it like that?" the child asked.

"I'm getting new seats. Get in," Leto urged.

"Why did you only remove part of them?" the child pried further.

"So I'd still have something to lean against while driving. Would you just get in?" Leto requested, growing frustrated with the boy's questions.

The child squinted at Leto and then hopped into the driver's seat. "What's the task?" the child asked, closing the door behind him.

"Do you know who Silvia... I mean... Zara is?"

"Yes," the child confirmed. "She has a younger sister? Zidia?"

"Yes," Leto verified. "I need you to keep tabs on her."

"Keep tabs? Like spy on her?" the child asked.

"Yes," Leto replied, "and I need you to do it for many years."

"Why would I do that?" the child asked.

"Because by the time you turn thirty, you'll have been reimbursed for your time with one million dollars. I will pay you monthly, starting this month. If you ever decide to stop the task, you will no longer receive any money. If you tell anyone of this task, you will no longer be able to say the word money."

"Are you threatening me?" the child asked.

"Not yet," Leto responded genuinely.

The child squinted his eyes at Leto. "Okay, I'm in," the child replied, "but how am I supposed to spy on her outside of school?"

"Make friends with her, ask her to play outside of school, ask her to be your girlfriend... I don't care how you do it, but she must never find out that I asked this of you, and you cannot tell a single person about our arrangement. Deal?"

"Deal." The child agreed and shook Leto's hand.

"If you need a higher level of persuasion, you can use this." Leto handed the child the medical tag he had swiped from Zara's mother the day prior. He had done research on it at the library and knew just how to use it to his advantage. "Tell her you know about her mother's condition. Tell her you know it is genetic. Tell her you know that anyone who has that condition is disqualified from space travel."

"Why would she care about that? She's eight," the child countered.

"She has a newfound interest in traveling to Mars." Leto smiled, recalling his success of phase three. "I'll be in touch to pay you," Leto promised. The child opened the door of the car and handed the car key back to Leto. "One more thing, kid," Leto added.

"What's that?" the child inquired.

"You haven't told me your name," Leto noted.

"Dimitri."

## 26

## SILVIA, DAUGHTER OF LETO

WHEN ZARA GOT OFF the comm with Leto, she was unnerved. In one conversation, she had learned of Privelion and his plans to overtake all planets, her origins as a Kleit on Suvia, Dimitri's twenty-three-year deceit, the deceit of her adoptive parents, and the deceit of Leto in disguise as the NASA administrator. She put her hand over her heart, her chest physically aching at the realization she had been lied to all her life. She swore Xavier had a sixth sense when he entered through the branches of the Weeping Willow, sat down beside her, and said nothing.

Zara rested her left hand against her lips and looked away from Xavier, trying to hold back tears. "I'm not who I thought I was," she whispered.

Xavier closed his eyes and leaned his head back against the cave wall. "You're everything I always thought you were," he replied.

"How can you say that? You don't even know who I am. I didn't know who I was until today," Zara argued.

Xavier reached out and held Zara's right hand in his. He opened his eyes. "No matter what you think you found out about yourself, I know who you are. You are smart. You are beautiful. You are adventurous. You are brave. No matter what your past looks like, those components of your identity are written in stone," he assured her. Zara looked at him with pursed lips and nodded. "What do you need from me right now?" he asked.

Zara took a deep breath. "I need you to hear this before everyone else does..." She proceeded to share with him a highly condensed version of what she had learned from Leto.

Xavier didn't know whether to react with shock or to not react at all. He had a hard time believing any of the information she was sharing with him. He listened attentively to her every word and did nothing more than nod intermittently with a serious facial expression. When she was done sharing the story, he simply threw his arms around her and held her tightly. She rested her head against his chest, feeling a deep sense of a relief in having shared the burden of what she learned about herself with another human.

"So, what's next, Zara?" Xavier asked.

"I need to reconnect with the Kleit," Zara replied.

"Those things that tried to kill us?" Xavier exclaimed.

"The same," Zara confirmed. "But they won't try to kill me," she reassured him, "not once they learn who I am."

"I don't know about all this," Xavier cautioned.

"Nor do I," she whispered fearfully. She rose to her feet.

"Where are you going?" Xavier asked.

"To tell the others," Zara informed him. She parted the branches of the tree and walked out into the afternoon sunlight.

While Sadie and several of the Eyla greeted her as she walked past, she ignored them and kept moving. She wanted to get to a place where she could address everyone at once and not have to repeat a story a million times that made her cringe to tell just once. Once she made it to the top of a low cliff, she waited silently for those on lower ground to notice her presence. Her hair blew in a wind that picked up right after she made it to the cliff, almost as if it were meant for her.

"What are you doing up there?" Jerome called out.

Zara stayed silent, waiting for others to wonder the same. Sure enough, Eyla came pouring out of their cave in small clusters to gather at the base of the cliff. Marquette and Xavier joined Jerome and Sadie in staring up at Zara. Once a sizable crowd had formed and Zara believed most of the Eyla to be present, she prepared to tell her story once more.

"My name..." Zara started, "is Silvia." She spoke slowly and clearly. "I am the daughter of Leto, leader of the Kleit tribe," she said, emphasizing Leto's title as leader. "I am thankful for your hospitality and wish for our alliance to continue, but it has come to my attention that I have a home here on Suvia, and it is not here with you. I will be leaving first thing in the morning for the Kleit tribe to re-establish my status in their community."

Several of the Eyla gasped. Most of them were lost and didn't know enough English to comprehend Zara's disclosure. As Zara descended from the cliff, the Eyla conversed, and those who did understand conveyed the message to those who didn't. Jerome, Sadie, and Marquette were baffled.

"I always knew she wasn't one of us," Marquette jabbed, trying to hide her astonishment from the crew.

"That was a lie to get more beings here on your side, right?" Sadie asked hopefully when Zara approached them.

"I'm afraid not, Sadie," Zara replied. "I am truly from here."

"But you don't look like the Kleit!" Sadie countered.

"They shapeshift," Zara shrugged, "remember?"

"Well yes, but temporarily, right?" Jerome asked.

"They can make it permanent," Zara corrected. "My father sentenced me to life as a human for my protection."

"Sentenced you? You say that like to be human is to be punished," Sadie spoke softly.

"For me, it is," Zara said, setting her hand gently on Sadie's shoulder. "Don't get me wrong, I love my adoptive parents and my sister and all of you, but I didn't get to know who I truly am and where I came from until now. Not only that, now I'm split between two worlds." Zara wiped a tear beginning to form from her eye.

"How can you possibly know that any of this is true?" Xavier asked.

"Because it makes sense!" Zara exclaimed. "I don't look like any member of my family. Dimitri never seemed to care about me, yet he wanted to be in my life since elementary school, and Leto knew about Dimitri blackmailing me. He told him to. I've had dreams of things on Suvia as if I'd seen them before. I have a Suvian marking on my ankle. Beyond all that, I can just feel it. This is home."

The others were speechless. Even Marquette, who always seemed to have something to say, was silent. Zara kept walking, and they all followed her, as if expecting her to say more. She didn't. She couldn't think of anything more to say. She was still processing it all herself.

"Does Zidia know?" Xavier asked.

"Not yet," Zara replied. "Let's say our goodbyes to the Eyla and get some rest. We will travel to the Kleit tribe in the morning."

"I'm not going with you!" Marquette protested. "They tied me up and tried to kill me."

"Alright, stay here," Zara offered.

"Yuck, with these fish-head things? You can't be serious," Marquette quickly rejected.

"I'm not going to babysit you, Marquette," Zara said teasingly. Zara walked into the Eyla cave feeling slightly childish and giddy while also maintaining a sense of levelheadedness. She slowly lowered herself into one of the pools and swam around, playfully splashing her colleagues still standing outside of the water.

"What are you doing?" Xavier asked dryly.

"Swimming!" Zara shouted out happily. "Care to join?" She splashed the water at them again.

Xavier smirked and rolled his eyes. "Well, if you can't beat 'em, join 'em," he said to the others as he removed his shirt. He jumped into the pool splashing more water at Jerome, Sadie, and Marquette than Zara had. When he got in, he playfully splashed water at Zara, which initiated a lively aquatic war. Marquette had no interest in joining them, but the other pools did look relaxing to her. She went to the other side of the cave, slipped into a pool, and let out a loud sigh. An Eyla who was already deeply relaxed in the same pool turned his head toward her, and they engaged each other in scrutinizing eye contact.

Jerome and Sadie went outside to rest on the grass in the daylight. Jerome looked longingly at Sadie. It was rare for them to have a moment alone. Jerome sat down and patted the grass beside him. Sadie sat down and smiled at him.

"Have I ever told you how beautiful you are?" Jerome asked.

Sadie shook her head, flattered, but not very enthused by his compliment.

Jerome didn't know what to say next. He felt so nervous around Sadie, and yet, so comfortable at the same time. "I really like you," Jerome confessed.

Sadie nodded. "I know."

"So, uh, I don't really know where to go from there... and I'm sure you don't feel the same way but..." He stopped talking, as Sadie's lips connected with his. His eyes widened in shock and then closed as he kissed her back. He placed his hand gently on the back of her head and weaved his fingers through her hair as they passionately explored each other's mouth.

When Sadie pulled away, Jerome thought he blew it. "I know, I'm probably not the best at that." He looked at the grass, feeling disappointed and self-conscious.

"This is what makes you unattractive to me," Sadie replied, "all of your self-doubt and pity. Why can't you just compliment me with confidence, shut the hell up, and kiss me?"

"You're even more gorgeous when you're demanding," Jerome spoke confidently, heeding her advice. He leaned towards her and kissed her again, this time without a shred of self-doubt. He didn't want to stop kissing her, but again she pulled away. "Did I say you could stop?" he asked.

"Whoa, now. Don't get ahead of yourself," Sadie teased. Sadie thought for a moment. "You know, you are quite a bit older than me."

"Is that going to be a problem?" Jerome asked.

"Nope!" she exclaimed, as she rested her head on his thigh. "I prefer older men."

Jerome ran his fingers through her hair until she fell asleep. For a moment, it felt to Jerome like the two of them were not on Earth or Suvia, but in their own little bubble of bliss. His brows furrowed with worry, as he realized he now had more to lose than ever. Nevertheless, the adrenaline moving through him and the residual taste of her kiss made any fear that came to his mind subside.

Nighttime came quickly, and Zara and her colleagues from Earth went to bed early, aware that they would have a long day ahead of them. Zara slept next to Xavier on the grass, comforted as always by his presence. Jerome slept with his arm around Sadie, and their legs intertwined. Marquette slept holding on to a piece of fish that was cooked up earlier in the day. Current tossed and turned at the thought of Zara leaving and reunifying with the Kleit. The other Eyla relaxed and slept soundly, less affected by Zara's news. Zara dreamed of herself shapeshifting into a Kleit. What would have most definitely been a nightmare in the past was now one of the most pleasant dreams she ever had. What felt foreign in the past, now felt familiar. She slept peacefully throughout the night.

27

# No Place to Hide, No Friend to Save You

T HE SKY LOOKED DIFFERENT today. I stared up at pale purple clouds that faded into black. I wondered to myself if one of those clouds might be Privelion, or how I could possibly know what form he might be taking. I worried that if he were watching over me right now, he'd know my weakness is my friends. I looked over at them. They were all still sleeping. Jerome and Sadie were practically sleeping on top of each other. I must have been in my own world a long time. Last thing I remember is Sadie disregarding Jerome's advances toward her. I guess she finally gave in.

I stood up and stretched. It was far too early to head toward the Kleit community, but there was no way I could fall back asleep. I figured I could check if any of the Eyla were awake. I walked toward the Eyla cave. Upon entering, I recalled that the Eyla sleep in the water. None of them were awake, but it was quite the sight to see. Each pool of water had near twenty Eyla, their bodies all floating limply and many of them overlapping each other. I spotted Current, although I was shocked to recognize him when the Eyla all looked so similar to one another. I thought about waking him so we could have time to talk before late morning came, and with it, my departure. I decided against it.

I returned to the small hidden area between the outside of the cave and the branches of the Weeping Willow tree and decided it was worth admiring one more time before leaving the Eyla community. I lay down on the small patch of grass and allowed my mind to wander. I closed my eyes for what felt like only a moment, but when I opened them back up, significantly more light was seeping in through the leaves of the tree. I guess I was able to fall back asleep.

I slowly rose to my feet and rubbed at my eyes. I could hear the sound of chatter on the other side of the branches, informing me that several of the others were awake. Making out bits and pieces of their conversations, I gathered that they were looking for me and thought I might have left for the Kleit community without them. I came out into the open and made my presence known. My colleagues and several of the Eyla appeared to be relieved that I hadn't left yet. I certainly couldn't blame them. It was clear to me that Privelion was successful in gaining the compliance of the Kleit. I was sure that many of them would kill for Privelion, but I had equally growing confidence that many of them would kill for me upon finding out my status in the community... if my status should still exist.

"Zara!" Current exclaimed. "Please rethink going to the Kleit. If anything, go back to the Klaysta community! The Kleit are dangerous."

I shook my head firmly. "This is something I have to do, Current. They may not know it yet, but they are my family."

"What if this is a trap?" Sadie asked me.

"Then it's a damn good one," I responded. "Are you guys ready to leave?"

I got a thumbs up from Xavier. Sadie nodded. Jerome was too busy gazing into Sadie's eyes to even notice me talking to him. Judging from Marquette's lack of facial expression and response but direct eye contact, she appeared to be indifferent.

I walked to the entrance of the Eyla community, and the others followed. The Eyla came with to see us off. I let out a low-pitch quiet whistle, with complete confidence that it would result in a Gladiator at my feet seconds later. It did. However, to my surprise, it resulted in eight Gladiators lined up in a horizontal row in front of me. I looked at the eight boulders that had slid through the ground so quickly they developed a small-scale sandstorm. They had arrived and stopped in perfect unison. I wondered if my status as the daughter of a Kleit leader was somehow known to them, or if my whistle was simply on point. I had no time to further test those theories.

I straddled one of the two boulders in the middle and motioned for my friends to join me in doing the same. Their eyes were wide, and their jaws dropped at just the sight of the boulders. I couldn't wait to see their reactions to being lifted up by gigantic rock formations with legs.

"Now, on the count of three, we are all going to knock on the rock two times and then grasp it tightly. It is important that we all do it together," I instructed.

"Is this the same thing that knocked me over?" Sadie asked.

"Yepp!" I yelled out. *But it won't look like the same thing in a minute*, I thought to myself slyly. "One... two... three!" I called out. I knocked twice on the boulder in front of me, and it rose up simultaneously with Sadie's, Jerome's, and Xavier's. Sadie shrieked while Jerome and Xavier loudly gasped and uttered profanity. Apparently, Marquette didn't get the memo, as she was still straddling a boulder on the ground while the four of us were highly elevated atop intimidating creatures.

"Ah... no thanks!" Marquette called out, scrambling to her feet.

"Marquette, you have ten seconds to join us before we leave without you," I yelled to her.

Marquette looked back toward the Eyla and then forward toward us, hesitant to make up her mind. I told her she can either make up her mind or I will make it up for her. Twenty seconds went by with her being resistant.

"Can I ride on Xavier's with him?" Marquette asked.

"Nope!" Xavier answered.

"Jerome?" Marquette pleaded.

"I prefer not," Jerome responded.

"Marquette, I'm leaving in five seconds," I warned. "Five, four, three," I counted quickly. Marquette sat down on the ground straddling the boulder, closed her eyes, knocked twice, and held on tightly. The Gladiator rose to its feet. "See! Now that wasn't so bad," I pointed out.

"Uh huh," Marquette responded, with her eyes still closed.

"Alright, now I will guide mine, and yours will follow," I informed them, just as Tavion had informed me.

I slapped the side of the boulder, and the Gladiator took off running. Though it had been a short time since I rode on a Gladiator, I had somehow forgotten how freeing it felt to seemingly glide through the air. While my expression was one of energetic excitement and relaxation, the others did not look so composed. I could see varying degrees of terror on the faces of my counterparts when I looked back to check on them.

"Doing alright?" I yelled. They couldn't hear me over the sound of the wind blowing past them and the sandstorm clouding the air. I wrapped one arm tightly around the boulder and held out a thumbs up with my opposite hand to check for a visual sign that they were doing okay. They all nodded, except for Marquette who was holding on for dear life with her eyes still sealed tightly shut.

I wished I could ride along on the Gladiator all day, but before I knew it, we had arrived. Following the example that Tavion had set for me, I let out a high-pitch whistle, bringing not only my Gladiator but all five Gladiators to a halt. I let out a low-pitch whistle and the Gladiators all lowered us to the ground. While I had been inside the Kleit cave, I had never been to the Kleit community and didn't know what to expect. The Gladiators dropped us off at the land division where the desert sand met the forest grass.

"This is it," Marquette confirmed, recalling her horrid experience with the Kleit when they had disguised themselves as her husband, Damon.

"Please, let me go in first, and let me do the talking," I asked of the others. They nodded in agreement.

I walked forward toward a perimeter fence of stacked tree branches. Without another thought, I began to climb them. The branches felt like they were scraping up my hands as I climbed, but despite that, I kept moving. When I made it to the top, all I could see were trees. I wondered if they were really trees, or rather, the Kleit in disguise. I reached forward and pulled a low hanging leaf from one of them. It detached easily. I decided it couldn't be a Kleit. I climbed down the tree branches until my feet were touching the grass on the other side.

My anxiety heightened when I noticed the sun was beginning to go down. If I was already losing daylight, I would need to be strategic about every move to determine a way for myself and my friends to stay safe inside this community. I looked around, only to see thick tree trunks in every direction. *If only I could shapeshift,* I thought to myself. Perhaps my presence was a deterrent for the Kleit to show themselves. Perhaps they were already plotting to entrap or kill me. I heard a crackling sound come from behind me. I quickly turned to see one of Tavion's sons walking toward me. I wondered to myself why a Kleit would choose one of his sons to shapeshift into.

"Hi," it greeted me in a small voice.

"Hi," I cautiously replied, walking slowly toward it. "You don't have to be afraid of me," I informed. "I know who you are, and I am Silvia, daughter of Leto."

The small child slowly began to morph, developing black skin, elongated arms, an overly skinny torso, and slanted eyes. It didn't frighten me to see. If anything, I presumed this Kleit was frightened by me based on its initial choice in disguise.

"There we go," I praised. "Now, I know you can't communicate with me, but do you understand me when I say I am Silvia?" I asked. The Kleit nodded slowly, almost seeming to be looking through me. "Jeez, you must know more about me than I do," I conjectured out loud. "Is there a safe place here for me and my friends?" I asked.

The Kleit quickly shook its head no. I looked around and was not surprised. For anyone who couldn't shapeshift, it looked like this community had nowhere to hide. Still, we were here already, and I had to figure something out to get my friends safe entry and shelter.

"Well, my friends are standing right outside, and I need to bring them in here, okay?" I said, more as a statement than a question. The Kleit backed away slowly. "My friends won't hurt you," I assured the Kleit, "but I will need your help to protect them until the other Kleit know who I am," I asserted.

The Kleit continued to stand away from me but nodded in agreement. I didn't want to call out to the others for fear that the Kleit would hear me and initiate an immediate attack. I climbed the wall of branches once more until I was at the top of them and waved the others over. I remained at the top as they each climbed up to lend them a hand in helping them to the other side. Once they had all made it onto the inside wall of the branches, I climbed down with them. Sadie looked at the Kleit petrified. Her body resisted my hands on her shoulders guiding her toward it.

"Sadie, this is a friend," I informed her.

"How do you know?" Sadie whispered to me in a panic.

"I just know," I replied with a smile.

"So, what now?" Marquette asked loudly.

"Now, you can lower your voice!" I whispered harshly. I turned to the Kleit. "What do you know about Privelion?" I whispered.

Instead of responding to me, the Kleit looked behind me, and its slanted eyes grew wide. It pointed at something behind me. I looked and saw nothing. When I looked back at the Kleit, it was mid shape-shift, clearly morphing into the appearance of Tavion. It hurt me to see him again, even though it was only the image of him. It appeared that the Kleit was trying to tell me something through Tavion's image but couldn't find the words quick enough. I could tell the Kleit was alarmed by something by its complete misrepresentation of Tavion. It almost appeared as if Tavion was doing some sort of ritualistic dance. Quickly, the Kleit morphed into someone else. I watched as what looked like my sister rapidly opened and closed her mouth but did not release any words. The Kleit morphed again, this time into my mom. The second it finished morphing into my mom, it morphed into my dad. The second it finished morphing into my dad, it morphed into Dimitri. I watched in confusion and astonishment at the rapid transformations.

"I don't know what you're trying to tell me!" I exclaimed.

The Kleit morphed back into its original form and quickly pointed at the tree behind me. Clearly the Kleit had wasted its energy on the transformations, as that was all it took for me to understand. I lunged forward toward the Kleit, shouted for my friends to move back, and knocked the Kleit to the ground, rolling our bodies quickly to the side as a tree came crashing down, nearly landing on top of us. I scrambled to my feet and yelled for everyone to run. It didn't take long for us to realize there truly was no place to hide. Other trees came crashing down, missing us by a thread.

"What do we do?" I yelled to the Kleit who was running along with us. I was certain the Kleit was in no danger on its own, and yet, it was putting itself in danger to stay with us. I was thankful but also curious as to why it was taking the risk. It quickly motioned for us to get behind trees, directing us which trees in particular to stand behind. We did as directed, fully entrusting the Kleit with our lives.

By the time we realized that our trust may have been misplaced, it was too late. Hundreds of trees morphed more quickly than we could depart, and before we knew it, we were surrounded by Kleit. The Kleit who was standing by our side and initially seemed to be protecting us slowly backed into the crowd of Kleit. Clearly it was either no longer willing to take the risk for us or was in on this ambush from the start.

Several hands locked onto us and lifted us up into the air. No matter how much I struggled, I couldn't break free of their grasp. I yelled out my status as the daughter of the Kleit leader and demanded to be put down. My pleas were ignored. I didn't have to ask to know where they were taking me. I knew that they were following the orders of Privelion. I wondered if this might be a good thing. It would alert me to where Privelion is and what he is plotting, so long as I could stay alive long enough to make that information worth knowing. It wasn't worth the risk to me, but it seemed I would have no choice. I could hear Marquette sobbing and Sadie yelling out my name. I was in no position to help.

As we traveled further, my wrists and ankles began to hurt, being clasped onto tightly by the hands of the Kleit. Their Jell-O-like skin started to create a similar feeling to being tugged at by a tight rubber bracelet. I groaned in response to the aches in my body. I tried to look around at my surroundings to get a clue as to where they were taking us, but all I could see were the leaves and branches of the trees above me and the crowd of Kleit surrounding us. Jerome yelled out Sadie's name. I can't say I wasn't slightly offended that he seemed to only be concerned for her safety. Maybe I was also slightly envious. Deep down, I wished Tavion were with us to express his concern for me, but I wasn't sure he had any concern left for me at all at this point. I wondered if he might have even less concern for me now, knowing I was born to the Kleit tribe.

Oh, how I wished I could shapeshift. If I could turn myself into a Kleit right now and prove myself as one of them, they would surely drop Privelion's orders and hear me out. I tried one last time to yell out my position in their tribe. They did not react in the slightest and kept moving forward at the same pace. I closed my eyes, and tears seeped through my eyelids in frustration. I opened them hopefully when I heard clicking noises. It started with slow clicking from just one Kleit, and it led to rapid clicking from numerous Kleit as well as the crowd halting in their tracks. I looked around at them but couldn't tell what was going on. It was unclear whether they were stopping to rethink handing us over to Privelion, or for a different reason entirely.

I couldn't see it happen, but I assumed one of them shapeshifted when I heard a conversation of clicking turn to one of the Kleit speaking English. It was the voice of my sister. I felt so much comfort in the sound of her voice that I almost forgot to listen to the words. When it registered that this conversation might be the difference between life and death for me and my friends, I paid close attention.

"You need to put them down," the Kleit commanded, in my sister's voice.

"Why should we?" another one of them questioned, in the voice of Dimitri.

"Zara saved me, and she can save all of us," the Kleit asserted.

"I don't believe you," another one chimed in, with a voice that was unrecognizable to me. I figured they must have shapeshifted into a person familiar to one of my friends.

"Believe me or don't," the Kleit responded, "but she is..." The Kleit paused and shapeshifted into me prior to finishing the sentence. It continued, "Silvia, daughter of Leto."

There was a surplus of clicking and English that ensued. The Kleit that were holding me up set me down. Another Kleit shapeshifted into me. "If you're Silvia, prove it by shapeshifting," it demanded.

I looked toward my friends to make sure they were still safe. The Kleit holding them up had not yet set them down, but they did not appear to be in any harm. "I can't shapeshift," I informed them. "My father, Leto, used the full strength of his power to shapeshift me into a human. I am stuck in this form... forever." The Kleit quickly grabbed onto me ready to lift me back up. "Wait!" I yelled, "I can't shapeshift, but I can prove it!" I pulled the comm out of my pocket and pressed a few buttons, waiting anxiously for the person on the other end to respond.

"Hello?" a voice came through.

"Leto!" I was so thankful to hear his voice.

"I am with the Kleit. I need you to say something to them, anything, to prove who you are and who I am. They are trying to take me to Privelion!"

"I don't know what you are talking about," he replied.

"What do you mean?" I cried. "They are trying to take me to Privelion. He is going to kill me! You have to say something to prove to them that you are Leto, leader of the Kleit tribe!"

"I can't pretend to be something I am not. Goodbye, Zara," he replied. The comm began to beep.

The Kleit lifted me back up and carried me onward toward Privelion as they had planned. I couldn't fathom what reason the NASA administrator could have had to lead me astray. *Did he send me here to die?* I wondered. *Was everything he had told me a lie? But then how would he have known so much about the tribes?* Nothing made sense to me anymore, and I felt like I was back to square one, not knowing who I was. All that was left to do was wait in anticipation of my encounter with Privelion.

# 28

# ACT LIKE SUVIANS

THE SUN HAD GONE down and come back up by the time Zara and her friends were dropped off like packages on a doorstep. The Kleit tossed them onto the ground, leaving them with scrapes and pains that were sure to be marked by bruises. Immediately after dropping them off, the Kleit departed. Zara and the others looked around at their new surroundings. The sky was a pale pink, and in contrast to the red desert sand they had seen prior, they were now standing on top of light tan sand. It looked like there was nothing for miles in any direction. There wasn't a sound to be heard. There was no wind, and there was in fact an eerie stillness to the air. There was not one cloud overhead.

"Guys," Zara spoke slowly and nervously, her voice softly trembling, "we need to run as fast as we can in the direction we came."

"Why?" Sadie asked with equal angst in her tone.

"Because I've dreamed this, and it does not end well," Zara whispered, her voice still shaking. "Run!" she yelled.

All five of them bolted in the direction in which they were originally carried from. They ran as if their lives depended on it, because according to Zara, they did. From a bird's eye view, it would have appeared as if nothing was a threat for miles. Marquette slowed when she realized nothing was chasing them. The others fully trusted Zara and continued to run as quickly as they possibly could. Still, nothing happened. Zara began to question it herself, but the memory of her dream flooded her mind and willed her feet to keep moving.

It was almost unclear what came first, Marquette's scream or the excruciating sound of a bird squawking overhead.

None of them saw the bird coming, though it was gigantic and made ear-piercing noises. It was almost as if it had teleported there out of thin air. The bird dived down at an angle, likely traveling at 80 Kilometers per hour. Everyone ducked as the bird flew over their head, except Zara, who seeming to know the bird's exact path without looking, jumped as high as she could. It wasn't high enough. The bird dived beneath her feet, and her whole body fell stomach down on top of it. Zara tumbled hard to the ground as it slid out from underneath her. The bird flew high into the air, regaining momentum before circling back around to dive down again. When it came down the second time, it was clear the bird had no interest in anyone but Zara. It aimed directly for her once more. Zara's skin was ashy from the sand, and on the first fall, she had obtained several scrapes on her arm and a small one near her temple. She braced herself for the second fall as the bird came towards her with impressive speed. Though she didn't have high confidence that it would work, she did have a plan.

The bird once more was headed toward Zara's feet. As it approached, she jumped as high as she could, but this time, she intentionally lunged forward to not only fall onto the bird but grab onto it. Wrapping her arms tightly around the enormous bird's neck and chest, she was carried away by it high into the sky. Its squawking was so loud that Zara's ears started ringing in the intermittent periods of its silence. When it was silent, the sound of the wind took over.

Zara hadn't planned for the bird to take her this high. In fact, she had only planned to grab onto it. Thinking it would be caught off guard by her landing on top of it and latching on, she imagined it would give her the opportunity to wrestle it to the ground. Now, one hundred and fifty meters in the air, she had no plan at all other than to hang on tightly and survive.

The bird started zig zagging through the air, taking swift dips each time to maintain its speed. It appeared to be getting agitated with Zara. It dived toward the ground once more. Zara felt like she couldn't hold on much longer. She knew she would not survive another trip into the air with it and would have only one shot at releasing herself from this creature. Once the bird was not far from the ground, it leveled out to fly back upward. For a brief moment, it slowed to change its direction. Zara took advantage of the reduction in speed and quickly released her arms from the bird's body to roll onto the sand.

The bird quickly darted back upward into the air, but it was clear that the bird was not done with her. It circled around again. Zara realized that this would be an endless cycle. She wondered if it was fate that this play out just as her dream did, but as she clenched a handful of sand, she wasn't so sure. The sand in her dream was red, like the sand they had seen on a different part of Suvia. The sand beneath her was tan. The bird in the dream was marking her calf with Suvian abilities. The bird coming toward her seemed to be trying to do the same based on its aim each time it came down... unless it wasn't. Zara wondered if the bird was trying to replicate her dream for some reason, without actually having the same intended purpose. She had no time to determine what the purpose was, but believing the bird to be Privelion, she slowly rose to her feet and stood her ground. The bird in her dream was not Privelion, and she realized that this creature should therefore not be treated as the same. She decided that the best plan of attack was to treat it for what it was, a man from the Klaysta community who went rogue many years ago.

"Zara!" Xavier cried as the bird came toward her, "Run!"

Zara didn't listen. She stood still and waited for the bird to approach. When it was within probable earshot, she yelled to it. "Stop! I get the picture. You can hurt me. I am willing to talk to you!"

To her surprise, the bird did stop. Its gigantic body came to a halt in front of Zara and the others. Its enormous feet dug into the sand to slow down. Its wings spread wide and it squawked loudly again. Its chest was as red as an apple, and the rest of its feathering was pitch black. It looked at Zara with black beady eyes.

"Please shapeshift," Zara asked of it, "into your true form, just to talk."

For the first time in thirty-three years, Privelion shapeshifted back into his Klaysta body. The wings of the gigantic bird in front of them receded into nothingness, and two Klaysta arms stretched out in their place. The long black curved beak slowly shrank until it became a Klaysta nose. The beady black eyes turned to brown. The plump stomach shrank down into Klaysta abs. The thin bird legs thickened into Klaysta legs. Privelion stood tall, in the form of a Klaysta.

"This is what you wanted?" Privelion asked. "Don't be fooled by my true form," he warned. "I am no less dangerous than I was just moments ago."

"I don't doubt it," Zara agreed.

"You truly are Silvia," Privelion noted, almost in an accusatory way.

"What makes you so sure?" Zara asked.

"You anticipated that bird would mark you," Privelion explained. "It's why you jumped instead of ducked without even glancing behind you."

Zara nodded. "I am Silvia," she confirmed.

"And where is that father of yours?" Privelion laughed.

"Watching from afar," Zara assured him.

Privelion reached out and ran a strand of Zara's hair through his fingers. "He can't save you from afar." He smiled.

"I don't need saving," Zara replied. "What can I do for you to stop blackmailing my tribe?" Zara asked.

"You can do what Leto failed to do," Privelion responded, raising his voice forcefully. "You can convince your pathetic tribe to join me in my endeavors."

"If you're so strong, and if they're so pathetic, what do you need them for?" Zara asked.

"I am one being, with only three Suvian abilities," Privelion answered, "but if your tribe and the other tribes join me, I am the leader of thousands of beings that have seven abilities. Every being on every planet will be at my mercy and the mercy of Suvia!"

"I wasn't even raised on this planet," Zara informed him. "What reason could I possibly have to help you take over every planet?"

"The safe return of three Kleit children and the object I took that seemed so dear to the tribe all those years ago," Privelion offered coldly.

"How am I to know you haven't killed those children?" Zara inquired.

"I guess you'll have to trust me." Privelion smiled devilishly.

"I won't trust you, nor will I help you," Zara declined. "I will never join forces with you! I strive to protect Suvia, but not if it means destroying someone else's home, blackmailing the tribes, or using Suvian abilities with malicious intent," Zara barked confidently. "You're on your own."

Privelion was fuming by the time Zara finished speaking. If she wouldn't assist him in his plans, he had nothing left to say to her in his Klaysta form. His facial expression as a Klaysta turned aggressive as he began to shapeshift. His body extended horizontally into the form of a four-legged animal. His legs expanded until they were thick and cylindrical. His ears grew pointy and tilted back at an angle. His dark skin morphed into light tan fur. His nose extended by several centimeters and developed a jagged edge on top of it. Lastly, he opened his mouth to smile once more, this time with large sharp asymmetrical teeth. Only meters from Privelion who was now in the form of a Seltivor, Zara had to improvise. She knew she would be unable to outrun him. Zara ran underneath the Seltivor before it could react, knowing it would take it a minute to get its bearings and turn around. Her friends followed suit.

"What are we going to do? We don't have any weapons!" Sadie yelled.

"Act like Suvians!" Zara shouted. While continuing to run, Zara let out a low-pitch whistle, and more than enough Gladiators appeared at their feet almost instantly. "Quickly!" Zara demanded. "As we did before!"

While the Seltivor was getting ready to charge at them, each of them straddled a boulder and knocked twice. Gladiators quickly rose to their feet. Zara slapped the side of the boulder. The Seltivor charged. The Gladiators turned to face the Seltivor. The Gladiators stood side by side, creating a seemingly impenetrable wall, with Zara and the others vulnerably sitting on top of their heads. They charged faster than the Seltivor and headed straight for it. Zara and the others braced themselves for a head-on collision. Just seconds before that collision could take place, the Gladiators parted from each other. Three of the Gladiators zoomed past the Seltivor on its left side while two zoomed past on its right. The Seltivor couldn't react quick enough, having failed to anticipate the Gladiators' plan of attack.

The Seltivor turned to chase the Gladiators, but they were already long gone. He stopped and stood still, no longer engaging in the chase. Privelion was unruffled by the unexpected turn of events. Without a fret, Privelion shapeshifted back into the bird. He flew off above the dessert-like terrain, searching strategically for his escaped prey.

29

# A Change of Heart

THE GLADIATORS CONTINUED TO run full speed ahead without direction or guidance, seeming to be aware of the threat they escaped from. Zara pulled the comm from her pocket with one hand while wrapping her opposite arm around the boulder on top of the creature's head. She carefully hit the buttons necessary to initiate contact with Leto.

"Hello?" Leto answered.

"Are you going to tell me what's going on?" Zara yelled over the sound of the wind.

"Where are you? Are you safe?" Leto asked.

"Yes, no thanks to you. An explanation please!" Zara demanded.

"You needed to find Privelion, and I knew if I denied our relationship, they would bring you to him," Leto confessed.

"At what risk? I didn't even have weapons on me," Zara snapped.

"What?" Leto gasped. "Who travels on Suvia without weapons?"

"Someone that's from Earth!" Zara yelled into the comm. "Trust me, I won't make the mistake of traveling without weapons again, but you better not make the mistake of deciding the plan of attack for me again. You got that? You want to help me? Fine! But we do it as a team."

"Understood," Leto agreed.

"I'll get back in touch with you shortly!" Zara yelled. "Stay by the comm." She disconnected without waiting for another word from him.

"We're almost there!" Zara shouted to the others.

"Where are we going?" Marquette demanded.

"The one place Privelion would not expect, back to the Kleit," Zara responded.

When they arrived outside the barrier of trees, they climbed it again, experiencing a sense of déjà vu. Just like last time, they had no idea what they would be getting themselves into on the other side. Unlike last time, none of the Kleit were in disguise when they jumped over. There were hundreds of Kleit making clicking noises at each other, seeming to be fully immersed in a community discussion. When they saw Zara, they were silent and looked at her as if they were seeing a ghost.

"Privelion didn't kill you?" one of them asked after shapeshifting into the image of Zara.

It felt weird to Zara to speak with a clone of herself. "No," Zara replied. "He wasn't able to because I am Silvia, daughter of Leto."

"Give it up," a Kleit replied, after shapeshifting into the image of Dimitri.

"This time I will prove it," Zara assured them. Zara pulled out the comm and initiated contact with Leto again. Leto answered quickly. "Are you ready to tell the truth?" Zara asked him.

"Yes, of course," Leto promised.

"Tell them," Zara replied, holding the comm out for the Kleit to hear.

"She is speaking the truth," Leto informed them. "I am Leto... I was Leto, your leader. I failed you all, but I did it to protect my daughter, and in turn, she has returned to Suvia from her hiding place on Earth to protect all of you. I have forever sentenced her and myself to life in a human form. I did it for her protection. I did everything for her protection and ultimately, the protection of Suvia. You must trust her with your lives... and to prove my identity, I am the fourteenth leader of the tribe. My wife, and Silvia's mother, was called Aletti, and she died in a hunting accident. My closest friend was Lezin, and I hope you are there listening. Please let Silvia guide you, into a long-awaited retaliation against Privelion. If you don't, all of my endeavors the past few decades will have been for nothing, and for the first time ever, we will witness Suvia's downfall."

"Thank you, Dad," Zara responded, before disconnecting with Leto.

The Kleit were silent. They all seemed suddenly fascinated by Zara and swarmed around her to touch her skin, to smell her hair, and to ask her questions while in the forms of various disguises. Zara realized that they all seemed to have the same question: What would she do to stop Privelion?

The truth was, she had no idea what she would do. She was only human, and she feared that her only means of defeating Privelion would be through Suvian powers that she may or may not have. Even if she did have them, she had no idea how to control them or use them at will. All of the Kleit's eyes as well as the eyes of her friends were on her, waiting desperately for Zara to give them answers.

Zara did have one answer. Privelion was born to the Klaysta community, which meant if a hidden weakness existed for him, that is where it would be discovered. She relayed this information to the Kleit. Shapeshifting to speak with her, several of them agreed that it would be best if she goes to the Klaysta community to determine their next steps. They confided in her that they worried of her departure, now that they knew she was the only being that could protect them from Privelion.

Zara felt even more fearful of returning to the Klaysta community than she did of eventually facing Privelion again. The last encounters she had with the Klaysta were Kalari stabbing her and Tavion leaving her to be with Kalari. She did not feel welcome there any longer, but she knew if she wanted answers, she had no choice. A mixture of excitement and heartbreak arose in her as thoughts of Tavion came flooding back.

"So, it's a plan?" Jerome asked.

"It's a plan," Zara replied dryly. "Should we head there now?" she asked.

"Wait until morning," a Kleit disguised as her mother advised, putting a hand on Zara's shoulder warmly.

"Probably a good idea," Zara agreed. "Privelion is likely to be hunting us through the night."

"There is no place here to sleep, and it will be cold at night," a Kleit in disguise of Zara's father informed.

"We can build a fire," Zara suggested.

Xavier and Jerome went off to start a fire while Zara, Marquette, and Sadie stood awkwardly with the Kleit, not knowing what to say. The two groups looked at each other, the Kleit far outnumbering them and continuing to intimidate them, though it was no longer intentional. Zara thought of questions she still needed answers to about her origins. She debated bringing up her father and asking the Kleit what it was like to have him as a leader, but her lack of energy deterred her from conversing with them at all.

"I'm really hungry," Marquette informed them, breaking the silence.

"We get food at night," a Kleit disguised as one of Marquette's friends from back home informed them.

Sadie looked around. It was getting dark. "So, you'll be getting food soon?" she asked. Several of the Kleit nodded.

Zara began to walk away and proceed through the trees. "Let's go see how Xavier and Jerome are doing with that fire."

The Kleit dispersed to go hunt, agreeing to bring back food for their guests, though it was an unusual task for them. They explained to the humans that they typically eat the animals that they kill raw, immediately after slaughtering them. When they came back with small portions of animals the humans had not yet tasted, they encouraged them to cook the meat over the fire if they desired. After delivering them the food, the Kleit dispersed to give them space.

"This isn't as good as the food in the Klaysta community," Sadie whispered, after taking her first bite.

"Who cares!" Marquette exclaimed with a mouth full of meat. "It's edible."

"It's kind of chewy," Zara complained, discarding it after taking just two bites. Zara's stomach was growling, but even if the food were better, she doubted her ability to eat. She had a lump in her throat as she thought about returning to the Klaysta community that was making it difficult to swallow at all. "I'm gonna turn in for the night," Zara announced.

Zara lay down on the grass beside the fire, and the others joined her when they finished eating. Despite the fire, the grass was cold, as was the night air. Jerome and Sadie held each other while they slept, but the others shivered themselves to sleep. Zara couldn't wait for morning, but she also hoped it would never come.

30

# A POORLY TIMED DISCOVERY

S TANDING OUTSIDE THE KLAYSTA community, I couldn't bring myself to enter. I was quite sure Tavion wouldn't be there, as he would likely be out hunting, but I was certain that Kalari would be. It wasn't so much that I feared Kalari herself. It was more so that I feared Kalari would blindside me again.

"What if she makes another attempt to kill me?" I asked the others nervously.

"Hey," Xavier looked me in the eyes, "I'm not going to let that happen."

"But she has every right to," I said, staring off into space.

"What even compelled her to do that?" Jerome asked.

I bit my lip but didn't respond. I hadn't told anyone about my intimacy with Tavion, and I figured it was best to leave it that way.

"Look, you brought us here and said this is necessary, so let's go," Marquette snapped.

I nodded at Xavier and Jerome to move the boulder. It was the first time we were entering the Klaysta community unaccompanied by a member of the Klaysta tribe. In a way, it felt to me like breaking and entering. We walked through the tunnel that leads to the community and moved the boulder at the other end. When we passed through on the other side, numerous eyes were on us. Sadly, my identity as the daughter of a Kleit leader would hold no status in this community. If anything, it would have the potential to make us even more unwelcomed by the Klaysta tribe. I refrained from sharing what I learned about myself and asked the first Klaysta I saw about Tavion's whereabouts. They informed me that he left to hunt hours ago and would likely be back late.

"Kalari?" I asked.

One of the Klaysta pointed me in the direction of her tent while eyeing me up and down with a concerned look on their face. I had no intention of going to see Kalari. I only wanted to know her whereabouts so I would have a good idea of how to avoid her.

"Can anyone offer us a place to rest while we wait for Tavion's return?" I asked loudly to no one in particular. Everyone averted eye contact, not wanting to take us in. "What about Miravi?" I asked.

"Miravi is also out hunting," a Klaysta informed me. "It is mostly women and children here right now."

"Can we stay with you?" I asked of the woman who kindly gave us this information.

She looked at us hesitantly. "Do you have any weapons on you?" the Klaysta woman asked.

"None," I replied.

"You just need a place to rest until Tavion returns?" she confirmed.

"Yes," I spoke softly.

"Right this way." The woman led us through her tent and down the stairs into the cave area designated for her family. "You're in luck," she said smiling, "I have three children. There is a bed for me, my husband, and each child, which makes just enough space for the five of you. Feel free to lie down or just spend time in this space until Tavion gets back."

"I can't tell you how grateful I am for this," I expressed.

"Just... don't make me regret it," she said firmly.

"We most definitely will not," I assured her.

She left us alone, presumably so she could attend to parenting and the rest of her chores. None of us hesitated to hop onto the beds and warm ourselves with the pelts provided to us. After sleeping on cold grass and realizing we had taken our prior sleeping arrangements for granted, we had insurmountable gratitude for this improvement in our accommodations. It wasn't long before all five of us fell asleep.

When I woke up, I was dazed and disoriented. It took me a minute to recall where we were. The cave was dark, and it took my eyes a moment to adjust. Once they did, I was able to see that Xavier, Marquette, Jerome, and Sadie were all still soundly asleep. I turned onto my other side and found myself staring at two long legs. My torso sprung up, startled by the unexpected company. I looked up to see that it was Tavion standing over my bedside.

"I wasn't sure if I should wake you," Tavion whispered, "but Atrakia needs her space back for her family, and I think we should talk." I nodded in agreement. "You should wake the others. I'll only startle them," Tavion whispered.

I went to each bed one at a time to wake my friends up. I felt horrible, as this is the first time that they were able to lie down on a real bed in months. They looked so comfortable and warm. As expected, they were not happy to be awakened, but they seemed understanding that this wasn't our space to remain in.

"The guest cave you were staying in is empty," Tavion informed me, speaking in a slightly louder voice now that everyone was awake. "I'd like for your friends to go there and you and I to stay here for a moment to talk."

"I like that idea," I replied. I honestly couldn't think of a better idea myself. If we spoke in Tavion's cave, Kalari and the children would be there. If we spoke in front of my friends, they would find out what happened between me and Tavion and would no doubt have negative input. "Please go to the guest cave where we stayed before," I said to the others. "I will be there shortly." My friends left as requested, and Tavion and I were left alone.

"I heard you came here looking for me," Tavion stated in an accusatory tone. "I thought I made it clear that we need to be apart. Why didn't you stay with the Eyla?"

I laughed at his ignorance. So much had happened since I stayed with the Eyla, and he hadn't the slightest clue. "First of all, I didn't come here looking for you," I started. "I came here for answers about something. You just happen to be my main connection to this community, so I figured I could talk to you about what I am here for."

"Then what are you here for?" he asked.

"I need to know about a former member of the tribe," I replied.

"A former member?" he asked.

"Yes," I confirmed. "He went by the name of Privelion."

"Privelion?" Tavion repeated. "It has been many years since I heard that name. I was just a child when I learned of him and his grandfather."

"So, he is from this tribe?" I replied.

"He is indeed," Tavion responded, "but what does Privelion have to do with anything? He died a long time ago."

"He disappeared a long time ago," I corrected. "Privelion is the reason the Kleit are malicious. Privelion has developed the ability to utilize three Suvian powers as a result of chemical mixtures that he created shortly before his disappearance. He is using those powers, as well as the promise to return an object he stole and children he abducted from the Kleit, to manipulate them into joining forces with him. He is trying to build an army to take over other planets."

Tavion sat down on one of the beds. "Where did you learn of this?" he asked.

"That's going to be the hard part to explain," I answered. I took a deep breath. "Please don't hate me... I am Silvia, the daughter of Leto, leader of the Kleit tribe. My father informed me of my origins and gave me this information about Privelion. I have confirmed the information he gave me to be true. Privelion attacked me, and I witnessed him shapeshifting with my own eyes."

Tavion stood up and looked at me as if I were no longer recognizable. "I knew I should never have taken you in and offered you protection. You are one of them?" he barked at me. "And knowing danger is headed your way, you brought it here to my people... to my children!"

"I didn't know where else to turn!" I defended myself. "Privelion is from here, and I thought if I came here, I could figure out a weakness and stop him from harming any of the tribes."

"I can't trust you." He shook his head.

"I'm the same as I was since the day I arrived here, and you know that!" I cried.

"I know nothing about you," Tavion refuted.

"You know how you feel about me," I countered.

"I don't know what to feel about you," he reflected.

"Well, there's one way to find out," I stated boldly. I reached up to wrap my hands around his neck, guiding his face toward mine. He exhibited no resistance when our lips locked onto each other. He picked me up and lied me down on the bed, while gliding his lips along my jawline. He removed his clothing, and I removed mine. He climbed on top of me and ran his fingers along my skin.

"I've missed you," I whispered. A tear seeped out of my eye, and I let it fall, my arms locked down underneath him.

"I've missed you too," he replied, with a coldness to his tone.

It seemed like while his body could not resist me, his emotions were not on par.

"How do you feel about me? Right now?" I asked quietly.

"I have mixed emotions," he admitted.

"Do you love me?" I whispered. I felt so vulnerable and almost wished I could take back the question.

"We don't really use that word on Suvia," Tavion responded, "at least not in the Klaysta community. We care for one another."

"I didn't ask if you use the word," I clarified. "I asked if you feel that way about me."

"I think so," Tavion replied, tracing his fingers along the curvature of my body, "but I don't want to."

"I can tell," I noted. "I don't mean you any harm, and I would never wish harm to this community. I mean to protect your people, and any Suvian for that matter."

"Do you love me?" he asked.

"Without a doubt," I replied.

His lips reconnected with mine, and our bodies intertwined passionately. I felt nothing but love in our embrace, and for a while, nothing seemed to matter apart from the two of us. He picked me up from the bed with my legs wrapped around his torso and pinned me against the wall. Looking into his eyes, I felt like I could see a new truth. He didn't think he loved me. He did love me. He was just terrified to admit it, probably even more so now, knowing who I really was.

Who I was quickly began to change, both emotionally and physically. Emotionally, I felt like I was rediscovering myself. Physically, I felt like I was losing myself. Initially, I thought I was losing myself in Tavion, forgetting where my body ended and his began and feeling like we were one. I quickly realized I was losing myself in a far more catastrophic way.

My arms and torso felt like they were stretching, my legs felt like they were shrinking, and my vision felt like it was changing. I looked at the hair on my shoulder, and I watched as the ends lifted until all of it was completely out of view. Even in the dark room, I could see my skin turning black. Tavion's eyes were closed as he made love to me. His eyes shot open when he realized my skin no longer felt the same. Startled and disgusted by my appearance, he dropped me and pulled himself away. Hitting the floor didn't hurt me at all. It was as if my skin was elastic.

Right after falling to the cave floor, I began to change again. My arms and torso ached as I felt them shrink, my legs seemed to extend, my vision seemed to return to normal, and my hair fell back over my shoulders. I watched my skin turn from black to light tan.

"You really are one of them," Tavion acknowledged aloud.

"Was that a turn off?" I asked, trying to use humor in lieu of our fears.

"Yeah, kind of," Tavion laughed. "You don't seem surprised by what just happened," he noted.

"I did paralyze the Kleit on the spaceship," I said glumly.

"So, you're connected to a few tribes," he noted with more warmth to his tone.

"I guess."

Tavion sat down beside me on the cave floor and put his hand on my knee. "Have you experienced any other powers?"

"Yes," I replied. "I've experienced the powers of the Kleit, the Klaysta, and the Vultra." I paused before adding, "The same three as Privelion."

Tavion and I looked at each other with worry at the sudden realization of the connection. Before we could process it further, we both noticed my skin changing color again, although this time it was turning to a stone color, matching the shade of the cave wall. Before we knew it, my entire naked body was completely camouflaged against the cave wall and floor. Tavion's hand was still on my knee and he quickly slid it along my body, seeming to be worried that if he removed his hand, I would disappear completely.

Again, my body quickly returned to normal as the natural color of my skin returned. Tavion looked at me in astonishment. We realized then that not only was I distinct from Privelion, but that I could likely exceed his potential. Having experienced four Suvian abilities, I was now an anomaly. Tavion and I looked at each other excitedly, as if we had already won.

31

# No Weapons

Zara's arm was beginning to ache. She had been holding it straight out for ten minutes with unbroken concentration. Still nothing. Xavier, sitting on the floor of the guest cave in the Klaysta community, looked at her sympathetically, wondering how much longer she would continue on like this.

"You know, it's okay to take a break," Xavier suggested.

Zara paid him no attention. She couldn't afford to take a break now that Privelion was aware she had returned to Suvia. Any minute now, he might infiltrate the Klaysta community. She backed up against the cave wall and stiffened her body against it.

"She's still at this?" Sadie asked, as she and Jerome entered the tent and proceeded down the stairs.

"Yepp," Xavier responded unenthused.

"Can you guys be quiet please?" Zara asked. "I'm trying to focus." Right as she began speaking to them, her skin color began to change to match the color of the wall.

"Looks like the trick is to not focus," Xavier said aloud, bewildered by her success. Xavier, Sadie, and Jerome were all mesmerized by Zara's transformation, witnessing her use of a Suvian power for the first time. Marquette walked in just as Zara was transforming back. She was so startled by Zara's appearance, or rather lack thereof, that she tripped on one of the stairs and slid down three of the steps on her bottom.

"How did I do that?" Zara exclaimed. Sadie shrugged as if Zara had been speaking specifically to her. "And how do I do it again?" Zara asked aloud to herself.

"If you have access to several of the Suvian abilities, do you think you have the ability of the Tul tribe to bring beings back from the dead?" Xavier asked.

"I don't know, Xavier. Let me go test that ability," Zara remarked sarcastically.

"It was just a question," Xavier replied, more withdrawn.

"I'm sorry," Zara responded, "I am just really on edge. I think what would be best is for me to go test what I can do on my own." Zara quickly left the cave before anyone could protest.

When Zara exited the tent, she looked into the distance and immediately spotted Tavion putting out a fire. She walked toward him. As she did, she could smell the amazing scent of Velteis.

Zara laughed as she approached. "Now I know what Marquette was doing out here," she commented.

"Your other friends too," Tavion informed her. "I started to think you might starve yourself in there."

"Well, I didn't come over to you for the food," Zara admitted, "but now that I am here, it smells amazing."

"Eat," Tavion insisted.

Zara sat down and grabbed a piece of the Velteis. She didn't realize how hungry she was until she started eating. She practically swallowed the meat without chewing, causing her to stop eating intermittently to cough. Tavion sat down beside her.

"What's the plan?" Tavion asked.

Zara stopped eating for a moment and wiped her mouth with the sleeve of her shirt. "I was actually wondering if you'd come hunting with me."

"Sure," Tavion replied without a second thought. "When would you like to go?"

"Right now," Zara responded. She grabbed another piece of Velteis and stood up as she shoveled it into her mouth.

"Okay," Tavion agreed. "Let me go grab the weapons."

Zara shook her head. "No weapons."

"I beg your pardon," Tavion said, alarmed by Zara's request.

"No weapons," she repeated. "We are going to test my abilities."

"You must be out of your mind!" Tavion exclaimed. "Do you even have the ability to use your powers at will?"

"No," Zara admitted, "that's the problem. My powers seem to come when I am distracted, and for some reason I seem to be most distracted when experiencing an adrenaline rush, like when I was put in danger by the Kleit and when you and I... you know..." Zara trailed off with flushed cheeks.

"Zara, we aren't going if we don't bring weapons." Tavion spoke to her condescendingly, as if she were a child.

"Fine," Zara gave in. "You can bring them, but please refrain from using them except as a last resort."

Tavion nodded. "Deal."

The two of them grabbed the weapons and headed out of the Klaysta community. They walked through the desert together as they discussed the plan of attack against Privelion. Tavion informed Zara that her only chance at defeating Privelion would be to get all of the tribes on her side. Zara let that sink in, brainstorming ways to persuade them to join her in her pursuit.

"Let's start with a small animal?" Tavion asked, changing the subject to the matter at hand.

"The Velteis?" Zara replied.

"What is wrong with you?" Tavion exclaimed.

"What? Isn't that animal smaller than the Seltivor?" Zara asked.

"Well, it is smaller than the Seltivor, yes... but there are many smaller animals on Suvia that you haven't seen."

"Oh," Zara replied with naivety.

"You've got a long way to go," Tavion informed her.

"So, what animal should we hunt?" Zara asked.

"Let's start with a Moki," Tavion suggested.

"A Moki?" Zara asked. "That sounds cute. I hardly believe a creature with such a cute name would raise my adrenaline enough to..." Zara paused as she heard a growling sound and looked to her left to see a wolf-like creature headed toward them. "Is that a Moki?" Zara asked anxiously.

"No," Tavion replied. "That's a Rovlade."

"I see." Zara backed away slowly.

"Do you want a weapon?" Tavion asked, holding one out for her.

Zara looked at Tavion and realized he was giving her an "I told you so" gaze. She straightened her posture and stood her ground, remembering why she came out there in the first place. "No. No weapons," she replied.

"If you insist," Tavion said, sheathing the weapon.

The Rovlade lunged at Zara. "Agh!" she screamed. "Weapon! Weapon!"

Tavion nonchalantly withdrew a weapon and stabbed the animal mid pounce. It fell to the ground and began to bleed out. It went from heavily panting to whimpering, and after a short time, the sounds it made died out altogether.

"Can I ask you..." Tavion started.

"No," Zara interjected.

"But if we hadn't..." Tavion continued.

"I don't want to hear it," Zara replied. She turned away from Tavion, took a deep breath, and laughed quietly to herself.

"Why are you laughing?" Tavion asked.

"Because I'm clearly in over my head. Without you, I'd probably be dead right now," she responded.

"And that's funny?" Tavion asked.

"Kind of," Zara replied.

"Humans must have a warped sense of humor," Tavion hypothesized aloud.

"Oh, I'm no human," Zara corrected.

"Prove it," Tavion teased.

"I will," Zara replied, "but first, maybe we should practice on a Moki." Tavion burst into laughter. "What's so funny?" Zara asked.

"There's no animal here called a Moki. I made it up to boost your confidence when I saw the Rovlade coming toward us."

Zara tried to be angry but couldn't contain her laughter. Her laughter did not last long. Tavion withdrew a weapon and pointed it in her direction. Zara looked behind her for a threat. There was none. Tavion lunged toward her with a blade in hand.

"What are you doing?" Zara gasped.

"Something I am just now realizing I should have already done. I should have killed you the moment I found out you were a Kleit," Tavion hissed through his teeth.

"What? You know the Kleit are good, and you know I am different from them!" Zara exclaimed, taking a step back.

"I thought you were different than them, until I saw the way you looked at the Rovlade. You looked disgusted by it, as if it is beneath you. Now that I think about it, that is the same look you have given me ever since finding out your status as the precious daughter of a Kleit leader."

Zara shook her head. "This isn't you."

"I'm sorry, Zara, but I have to do this." Tavion rushed toward her with the weapon. Moments before he made contact with her, he collapsed on the ground and dropped the blade.

Zara looked down at him, angered and confused at his attempt to harm her. It took her a moment to realize that she was capable of harming him, but she chose not to. Instead, she held out a hand to help him up.

"Why are you helping me?" Tavion asked. "I just tried to kill you."

"I guess we have different goals," Zara responded, with a melancholy tone.

"No, we don't," Tavion replied with a smile. "Good job paralyzing me. Now let's try it again without the adrenaline."

"You were provoking me?" Zara yelled angrily.

"Yes, and if that is what helps you to rise up to what you need to be to defeat Privelion, I will continue to do so without apology," Tavion replied.

"Fair enough." Zara pouted. "Can we please practice something less intense now?"

"Paralyze me one more time first," Tavion demanded.

"I can't," Zara replied self-consciously. "The only reason I was able to before is because my adrenaline was off the charts."

"Maybe we can use a different form of adrenaline," Tavion suggested.

Tavion reached out to Zara and pulled her close, kissing her neck and biting her shoulder sensually. Zara began to feel the rush. Tavion's body stiffened, and he collapsed to the ground again. Zara felt bad, but she also felt a sense of pride in her success. She helped him again to his feet.

"As much as I don't want you to paralyze me again, we have to see if you can do it on command now," Tavion insisted.

"Okay..." Zara replied hesitantly. She focused intensely, but instead of Tavion falling to the ground, Zara's skin began to change color and blend with her surroundings.

"Wrong power," Tavion noted.

"Yes, I know," Zara replied, annoyed by her failure. She focused more intensely. Her skin began to lighten, and her hair began to shorten and turn blonde. She was able to stop herself mid-transformation. "This is hopeless!" she exclaimed.

"Tell me what's going through your mind," Tavion instructed.

"A lot," Zara replied. "I'm never going to be able to get these abilities under control, and if I can't access them, I'll be defenseless against Privelion. If I am defenseless against Privelion, he is most definitely going to kill me, and what then? What will Suvia be? How will my sister and my parents get through me not returning to Earth?"

"I think I see the problem," Tavion interjected. "You need to focus on one ability at a time and forget everything else. Your adrenaline must be a distraction for you from your constant thought process. If you can minimize those thoughts on your own, you will no longer be at the mercy of your adrenaline."

"In all my life, I haven't been able to stop thinking!" Zara replied with frustration.

"In all your life, you have been human," Tavion countered. "Now you are something else."

Zara and Tavion stopped talking, as they heard an animal in the distance. A Seltivor came charging at them full speed ahead. Tavion stepped aside, leaving Zara to stand alone.

"No weapons." Tavion nodded reassuringly.

Zara's adrenaline spiked as the Seltivor closed in on her. Her mind emptied of all other thoughts. The Seltivor exceeded her height sixfold, and the only thing that gave her the confidence to try to take down the Seltivor with her powers was Tavion standing by with the weapons. Nonetheless, she knew she had to try. As the Seltivor approached, it stood on its hind legs like a horse that got spooked by a snake, as if it were not tall enough already. Zara figured she should act quickly before it set its front legs down. She extended her arm, held up her hand, and let out a short yell like a judoka carrying out a martial arts attack. Instead of becoming paralyzed, the Seltivor became angered. Its front legs fell to the ground so hard that the ground shook noticeably.

"I think now would be a good time for the weapons!" Zara yelled.

Tavion withdrew a sword-like blade but shook his head firmly. "No weapons!" he yelled back.

Zara tried again to paralyze the animal. She extended her arm, held up her hand, and this time yelled even louder. The Seltivor's legs wobbled and began to fold in. Zara ran to clear the area for the Seltivor to fall. She heard it crash to the ground but kept running away from it.

"Where are you going?" Tavion yelled. By the time he asked, his voice was barely audible to Zara.

Zara continued to run until she was almost completely out of view. The Seltivor began to rise, and Tavion readied his weapon. Both the Seltivor and Tavion froze when they heard a thundering rumble that sounded like a herd of rhinos storming toward them. Tavion could see it from a distance. It was another Seltivor. Tavion began to run, knowing he would not stand a chance fighting two of them off simultaneously. The Seltivor stayed put, waiting for the other one to approach. When the second Seltivor grew close, it slowed down tremendously. It walked slowly toward the other one and made eye contact. The two Seltivor rubbed their jagged-saw-like noses together and then walked off. Tavion stopped running and watched as they departed.

"Zara?" he yelled.

There was no response. Tavion looked in all directions and didn't see her anywhere. He started in the direction he had seen her running off to, the same direction in which the other Seltivor had come from. He feared there might be more Seltivors up ahead and that Zara might have been attacked by one.

"Zara?" he called out again after walking further.

He heard a light breeze followed by a low rumble. He turned to look behind him and gasped. A Seltivor had somehow snuck up on him and was now close enough to touch. Tavion walked backward slowly. The Seltivor leaned its head down toward him but made no attempt to harm him.

"Zara?" he asked.

The animal's nose receded, and its body started to shrink. Its torso slowly shifted from horizontal to vertical. Its ears shifted forward, and its teeth grew less sharp. The fur all over it sank into the pores of human skin.

"You did it!" Tavion smiled.

"Not effortlessly..." Zara lifted her shirt to display a large gash just below her ribcage.

"What happened?" Tavion asked.

"After luring the Seltivor away with me, it noticed something off about my scent. Next thing I knew, the jagged knife-like-nose of it was inside of me," Zara informed him while she inspected the wound.

"You take less damage when transformed," Tavion acknowledged.

"I noticed that too," Zara replied. She pulled her shirt back down. "Anyways, I have full use of my powers now."

"Full use?" Tavion asked in disbelief.

"Yes. Watch." Zara proceeded to show Tavion that she could shapeshift, paralyze, and camouflage at will.

"What about the abilities of the other tribes?" Tavion asked.

Zara proved to Tavion that like the Klaysta tribe, she possesses the ability to see all beings. She noted that she could see her sister sitting cross-legged on her white patio chair, listening to music. Tavion confirmed.

"Rapid climbing? Underwater breathing? Bringing the dead back to life?" Tavion prompted.

"We can't quite test those here, can we?" Zara said, looking around at miles of desert sand. "Also, I think I'll leave bringing the dead back to life to the Tul tribe. There's no way to test that without wasting years of my life according to you."

"Good point," Tavion replied.

Tavion and Zara headed for the Eyla community to heal her wound and test her ability to breathe underwater. When they arrived, they developed a plan to travel to each of the seven communities and request their alliance in battle against Privelion. Zara ruled out the alliance of the Tul tribe, knowing they only help those within their community, that they do not have the skills necessary for battle, and that the skill they do have is far too time consuming to be an effective contribution toward Privelion's downfall.

Zara dipped herself into a pool in the Eyla cave and remained underwater for ten minutes to prove her fourth Suvian power. When she rose back up to the top of the water, she breathed normally, feeling no loss of oxygen. The Eyla were mesmerized by her ability and agreed without hesitation to join forces with her.

"Where to next?" Zara asked Tavion.

"Tuvon."

# 32

# TUVON

THE TUVON TRIBE BEING the furthest away, it took an entire day to get there. Though most of the travel was by Gladiator, Zara's legs felt as if she had been walking since sunrise. The bags under Tavion's eyes suggested that he wasn't in great shape either. Though it was late in the day, the sun remained high in the sky.

"When is the last time you traveled this far?" Zara asked Tavion.

"Never," he replied. "I never had reason to."

Zara was unaware that Tavion had never made contact with the Tuvon tribe. It didn't occur to her to be nervous until she realized that neither of them would have any idea what to expect. She felt a lump in her throat as they approached the mountains. A living being had yet to be seen.

"I think only one of us is equipped to navigate this territory," Tavion said, stopping in his tracks as they looked up at massive peaks.

If Tavion had said that to her days ago, Zara would have believed him to be speaking of himself. Now, she knew that she had to step up and navigate certain tasks on her own, despite being a foreigner to Suvia. She took a few steps forward toward the mountains and then turned around to look back at Tavion.

Tavion nodded with encouragement. "You can do this," he assured her. "I'll be right here waiting when you return."

Zara bit her lip anxiously and took a few steps back, as she decided it would be best to get a running start. She crouched down like a cross country runner preparing themselves at a starting line and then propelled herself forward. She ran as fast as she could but gained average speed for a runner at best. Her speed instantly adjusted when she grabbed onto the base of the mountain. As if she were a spider, she traveled up the mountain quickly and with ease. She felt intoxicated with adrenaline. Tavion looked up at her from the base of the mountain, having to squint for her to be in view. Before long, she was out of view entirely.

From the top of the mountain, Zara looked out into the distance. There must have been hundreds of peaks. Zara still didn't see any members of the Tuvon tribe. She figured they must live between the mountains at lower elevations. She climbed down with remarkable speed. Once she was at the base of the next mountain, she began to alternate between climbing and walking to weave between the mountains. Her face lit up with excitement when she saw smoke. Eagerly enhancing her speed, she headed towards it.

The closer she got to the smoke, the colder it got outside. Her arms appeared to be changing color. She put her hands under her shirt, worried that if they were exposed to the extreme temperatures for much longer, she might develop frostbite. She continued on toward the smoke, in hopes that she would find warmth or shelter. After making her way around three peaks, Zara found the source of the smoke. It was being expelled through a chimney of what appeared to be a cabin-like house, positioned between two of the mountains.

Zara walked toward it hesitantly. When she made it to the door of the small building, she pulled one of her hands out from underneath her shirt and knocked. Muffled voices on the other side of the door went silent, and then the door slowly creaked open.

"Veidle," a voice welcomed.

To Zara's surprise, she was able to understand their language. "Gizlar," Zara responded, equally surprised that she was able to speak the language. She wondered if she had access to all Suvian languages now that she had grasped the Suvian powers.

The door opened more fully, and a slim creature of average height was standing behind it. The creature had purple skin and pointed ears. Its eyes were iridescent, appearing to be yellow one minute and green the next. It had some sort of black geometrical pattern on its skin. Zara looked behind the creature to see several more that looked nearly identical.

"Greevlo vi glenz?" the creature asked. The creature was questioning Zara's appearance and how she made it to their home.

Continuing to speak their language, Zara informed them of her background as Silvia, as well as her identity from Earth. She asked politely if she may enter to warm up, explaining that her skin was not made for the cold temperature of the mountains. Though they didn't trust her, the members of the Tuvon tribe agreed to provide her with shelter temporarily while she explained her motives for being there. They shut the door behind her and invited her to take a seat on what looked like thick pillows on the ground.

Zara went on to tell them of Privelion and what was at stake for Suvia. As there wasn't a direct translation for some of the messages she needed to convey, she noted that she is a "protector". She explained that without the help of the tribes, she would be unable to protect.

"Govon?" one of the Tuvon asked.

"Ga. Govon. Protector," Zara replied.

A member of the Tuvon tribe stood up. He thanked Zara for the warning but respectfully declined to aid in battle. Zara presumed that he was the Tuvon leader. He went on to explain that the Tuvon tribe has always been neutral, and that they prefer to continue to mind their own business.

"Viltso giv glo," he stated. Zara translated his statement in her mind: *We are happy here.*

Zara asked if they will still be happy when Privelion takes control of all of Suvia. The Tuvon thought for a moment. He replied that his tribe will be happy whether Privelion takes over or does not, knowing that they chose peace and made what they consider to be the correct moral decision.

"Glistol volst?" Zara asked, looking around to see if any other Tuvon members had a different opinion.

"Vostle gard!" the Tuvon leader replied. He stated that he has spoken on behalf of his tribe and demanded Zara leave the mountains at once.

"Veit," another Tuvon said, rising to his feet. Zara looked at him hopefully. He informed her that he would like to join her. The Tuvon leader looked him up and down with disgust. He warned that if he goes with her, he will no longer have a home with the Tuvon community. The Tuvon that spoke up nodded in agreement. He turned toward another Tuvon who was still seated. "Grev!" he commanded. The Tuvon he spoke to shook his head no. "Grev!" he repeated. The seated Tuvon rolled his eyes and stood up. The rebellious Tuvon informed Zara that the two of them would be at her service.

As she went in alone and walked out with two companions, Zara considered her mission a success. She learned that the name of the Tuvon who spoke up was Gliv, and the name of his friend who agreed to accompany them was Garva. She guided the two of them back to Tavion, who was there waiting for her return as promised. After getting acquainted, the four of them set off for the Vultra tribe.

33

# VULTRA AND LISTUN

S MALL ROCKS IN THE stone archway reflected the sunlight toward us. Behind the archway was a stone bridge, crossing over a stream of unbelievably clear water. It was odd to see a stream of water up against the desert sand. Across the bridge was a stone building with four walls, like an upside-down box, with an open doorway on the wall facing the archway. The stone gave a very standoffish vibe that contradicted the open entryway. I half expected to see guards at the entrance, but the area was desolate. A small black bird of an unfamiliar species squawked above our heads and flew through the entrance before we were in reach of it. The entire atmosphere was eerie, though we hadn't set foot inside of the building yet.

When we came up to the building, we noticed stone statues lined up on each side of a hallway. It appeared there were no lights apart from the sunlight seeping in, and what was at the end of the hallway was a mystery we would only find out by walking through it. I walked in first. As I walked between the statues on either side of me, I analyzed them, noting that each one was unique. I also noticed that each one seemed to be either a Suvian being or a representation of a Suvian artifact. I recognized a statue of a Kleit, an Eyla, a Klaysta, and a Tuvon. I recognized several weapons I had used or seen Tavion use. I examined the beings I did not recognize, assuming they were members of the other tribes.

"Can you tell me which tribe each statue represents?" I asked Tavion, pointing to the three that were unfamiliar to me. Honoring my request, Tavion pointed them out.

He first pointed to and identified the statue of the Vultra. The Vultra were shorter than I had imagined, likely measuring to 152 centimeters. Their stomach was perfectly plump. Their eyes were further apart on their head than humans, and their nose was higher up. Their feet and hands appeared to be skinny and elongated. I blinked a couple of times while staring at the fingers on the statue, unsure if my eyes were deceiving me. They had four fingers on each hand, each finger equally spaced apart, and there seemed to be no equivalent on their hand to the human thumb.

Next, Tavion pointed to and identified the statue of the Tul. The statue towered over me by a meter. I walked towards it and put my hand up against the hand of the statue. My hand looked like that of a child in comparison. The eyes on the statue were closed, with heavy curvature to the eyelids. Thin lines underneath the bottom eyelids seemed to represent bags of exhaustion. The facial features of the Tul were very sharp, with a pointed nose, high cheek bones, and a square jaw. Long braids of stone started at the hairline of the statue and ran across the head, dropping down past the neck, with tips resting on the shoulders. Something about the Tul made it look elegant, and yet simultaneously wild.

Even if it were not process of elimination, I could have deduced that the third unfamiliar being represented was a member of the Listun tribe. The statue displayed only one vertical half of a body, presumably insinuating that the rest of the body was camouflaged. A thick muscular leg connected to a torso with defined abs. The torso connected to a broad shoulder, which connected to a thick neck, and above it, a chiseled face. The Listun appeared to be handsome by the standards of any species and appeared to look more human than any of the other tribes.

Seeing the statues of all these beings, I had almost forgotten who this sanctuary belonged to. I looked again at the statue of the Vultra. They didn't appear to be intimidating creatures, and I was intrigued by what I imagined was a very accurate representation of them. If it wasn't, they certainly didn't design it to do them justice. I imagined that they must be modest creatures to have designed their own statue with far less splendor than the statues beside it.

"Why do the Vultra have statues of other tribes?" I asked Tavion, unable to contain my curiosity.

"The Vultra are a very neutral tribe," Tavion explained. "They sometimes act as peacekeepers. That is why I thought they had paralyzed the Kleit that day on the spaceship. I thought they were protecting you from them. Little did I know you had all the capability to protect yourself."

I walked on in silence. It was still mind-boggling to me that I had the same powers as the beings on Suvia, and any time I thought about it, I became even more overwhelmed by the background I only recently learned I had. It all felt so surreal. I felt a headache coming on, and I couldn't tell which was pounding heavier, my head or my heart. I put my hand on my forehead as if the skin-to-skin contact would instantly alleviate my pain. I knew the only relief I would truly get would be from clearing my mind. I didn't quite know how to do that anymore.

"What's on your mind?" Tavion asked me, noticing me drifting.

There were so many things on my mind that I genuinely didn't know the answer to his question. I just shrugged and tried to come back to the present moment. "Do we have anything to worry about in approaching the Vultra?" I asked.

"No," Tavion replied.

"What about with Gliv and Garva?" I asked, pointing to the two Tuvon who had been walking silently behind us.

"No," Tavion assured me. "If going to seek help from the Vultra and the Listun tribe is what has your head in a spin, you can rest assured that the encounters will be peaceful."

I smiled half-heartedly and decided against correcting him about what was on my mind. Though I was curious about the tendencies of the remaining tribes, I was far more curious about the life I lived as a Kleit, the powers I acquired as a little girl, and the trouble I would be getting myself into using those powers in a fight against Privelion. Leto warned me that Privelion had been using his powers for more years than I had occupied my human body. I wondered how I could possibly go up against him, but I was certain I had no choice.

"We probably should have told the others when we would return," I said to Tavion as we continued walking through an impossibly long hallway. Our pace slowed as the sunlight shining in from behind us was now minimally effective at lighting our way.

"I didn't even tell Kalari," Tavion replied. I couldn't hold back the smile on my face that came from knowing Tavion was keeping secrets from Kalari to be with me. "But I will tell her when we return," he added. My smile faded.

"Will you tell her we were together again?" I asked.

"Yes, I will tell her we went to the Tuvon, Vultra, and Listun tribes together," he responded.

I shook my head. "I am asking if you will tell her we were together intimately." I looked behind me embarrassed to be speaking of it in front of Gliv and Garva, but I was put at ease by the fact that they had no understanding of English, further evident by their blank expressions.

"So she can attempt to kill you again?" Tavion asked. I had no words. "I can't see much of anything," Tavion noted. He extended his arms forward to ensure he wouldn't run into anything.

"I can still see," I informed him. Tavion looked at me with an expression of disbelief. "What?" I asked.

"Another power?" Tavion exclaimed.

I squinted at him curiously. "What do you mean?"

"You can see in the dark?" he asked.

"Oh, yes," I replied, "but it isn't a power. I have had good night vision since I was a kid. Plus, this is a lot lighter than the Kleit cave we were recently trapped in." I thought about what I had just said and wondered if my good night vision came from my other life in and out of caves as a Kleit child.

"We're coming up on something," Tavion alerted me.

"How do you know if you can't see?" I asked. I looked forward and realized it was now too dark for me to see as well.

"I feel a cloth," he replied.

"Gyahhhhh!" a voice yelled.

I was so startled that I jumped backward, nearly knocking Garva over. "What was that?" I exclaimed.

"Agar vidikin," a voice called out as a light turned on.

I blinked a few times as my eyes adjusted to the light. Before me was a short plump being like I had seen represented in the statue. It took me a moment of no one speaking to recall that there was a language barrier between everyone, and that I was the only one there who could translate. I spent roughly twenty-five minutes translating back and forth between Tavion, Gliv, Garva, and the Vultra who I learned goes by Igg. To an outsider, it might have seemed as if we were all family that had been acquainted with one another for years. After introductions, we all joked and laughed with one another as if we were long lost cousins. What should have been a short conversation became very drawn out through my translations, causing us to laugh even more at the absurdity of our roundabout conversation.

"All jokes aside," I said in the language of the Vultra, "we need your help." I proceeded to explain Privelion's threat looming over us and informed Igg that the help of all of the tribes would be necessary to combat Privelion. I disclosed my abilities to Igg, and to my surprise, he requested that I demonstrate by paralyzing him.

"I can't do that." I shook my head and cringed at the thought of harming him.

"You just said you could," he replied.

"Well yes, I am physically capable," I relayed in his language, "but I can't bring myself to do that to you."

"If you can, you will," Igg declared.

It didn't sound like a request anymore, and I didn't like the arising confrontation. I worried that denying his request would be a threat to the alliance I was hoping to build with him. Tavion, Gliv, and Garva all looked at me for clarification. I explained to them what Igg was asking of me, and they looked at me expectantly, waiting for me to do as I was told. I gulped nervously and extended my arm, pointing an open-faced palm toward him.

"Well come on now," Igg egged me on. My arm dropped to my side. Igg glared at me impatiently. "Do you want my help or not?" Igg asked me.

"I do," I replied, "but it turns out I physically cannot paralyze you."

"Hmm..." Igg began pacing back and forth. "Interesting..."

"What are you thinking?" I asked him.

"I am thinking you don't have what it takes to fight off an evil entity like Privelion," he jabbed.

"I paralyzed Tavion and a Seltivor!" I countered defensively. "Tell him!" I yelled at Tavion, still speaking the language of the Vultra.

Tavion stared at me blankly until I realized my mistake. "Tell him," I demanded in English. He continued to stare at me blankly. "Ugh, why can't you all speak the same language?" I snapped in English.

"You haven't told me what you would like me to..."

"I know! I know!" I cut him off. I changed my tone, realizing my harshness might not get me the outcome I needed with the Vultra. "Could you please let Igg know that I successfully paralyzed you and a Seltivor?"

"How would you like me to let him know that? I don't speak..."

I put my finger on his lips feeling incredibly annoyed with myself for the oversight. "From now on, I am doing all the talking," I announced. I repeated myself in the language of the Tuvon and the language of the Vultra. Everyone nodded in agreement, though Igg still looked at me, waiting for me to prove myself.

A thought suddenly came to me. "Paralyze me," I demanded of Igg.

"Paralyze you?" Igg asked.

"Yes. I am waiting," I grumbled. "Paralyze me."

Igg extended his arm and faced the palm of his four-fingered hand towards me. Nothing happened.

"Well come on now," I mocked with satisfaction. Igg slumped his shoulders and furrowed his eyebrows with noticeable aggravation. I apologized.

"It's not your fault," Igg replied. "I'm upset by my failure."

"I knew it wasn't going to work," I confessed. "I asked you to paralyze me to demonstrate that our powers are probably ineffective on one another since we possess the same ability."

"So, if you possess the same ability as Privelion..." Igg started.

"Then I will be invincible to his attacks!" I exclaimed, realizing his implication.

"But you won't," Igg noted.

"You're right," I acknowledged. "Privelion can still attack me by shapeshifting, but I certainly have an advantage." I stopped talking for a moment and thought about the further implications of this new information.

I quickly turned to Tavion. "Why hasn't Privelion used his Klaysta abilities to see where I am and what I am up to?" I asked him rhetorically. "Because he can't!" I explained without waiting for a reply.

I turned to Gliv and Garva and spoke in the language of the Tuvon. "Why is it that when I encountered Privelion, he made no attempt to paralyze me?" I asked them. "Because he can't!" I informed them.

I turned back to Igg and spoke dejectedly in the language of the Vultra. "Privelion knows he can't, or else he would have tried... and yet, he chose to attack me, knowing he is limited to shapeshifting." I was back to feeling hopeless. "He never planned to use those abilities on me, and he doesn't need to in order to carry out his plan. I have no advantage," I processed aloud in English.

"You do have an advantage!" Tavion exclaimed. "You have us. Are you guys in?" Tavion asked of Gliv, Garva, and Igg. Tavion looked to me to translate. I translated in the respective languages.

"Of course," Gliv confirmed. "If not, we would not have come with you this far."

Igg shook his head glumly. "I cannot help you," he informed me.

"Why not?" I asked, worried I may have offended him earlier with my mockery.

"I would like to help you," Igg clarified, "but I am afraid the Vultra tribe will be of no help to you. As I am sure you know, paralysis cannot be effectively induced from a distance. Privelion knows this and will purposefully maintain distance, not permitting an attack from us and putting us in harm's way if we are even in the vicinity. More importantly, we have just determined our powers are likely ineffective against him."

I thought about it and realized Igg was right. The risks of the Vultra helping in the fight against Privelion far outweighed the benefit, and their help would surely be useless altogether given this new information. "I understand," I assured him.

"I will have my tribe keep tabs on the battle, and we will certainly assist should our abilities become of use," Igg promised.

I nodded with gratitude. "Well, it was a pleasure to meet you, Igg." I reached out my hand to shake his. He looked at me curiously. I grabbed his hand hanging loosely at his side and shook it. Igg looked at Tavion for clarification of my behavior.

"Weird Earth custom," Tavion informed him.

"Yeah, I'm not translating that. Let's go," I insisted, walking back the way we had come.

Tavion followed me. Gliv and Garva followed closely behind him. Tavion looked back behind us and noticed Igg walking off in the other direction, further into the hallway. The light that Igg had turned on turned off, and Igg was no longer in view. We stopped in our tracks as our eyes adjusted to the dark.

"He's not coming?" Tavion asked.

I started walking forward again, cautious of my steps in the dark. "No, we will proceed without the Vultra," I responded. "I will explain on the way."

"On the way to where?" Tavion inquired.

"The Listun tribe," I responded. "We discussed this."

"Yes, but we didn't discuss leaving without the Vultra tribe," Tavion remarked playfully.

"Then we will discuss that on the way," I reiterated. While I appreciated him trying to lift my spirits, I wasn't in the mood for humor. As the fight with Privelion drew nearer, my mind wandered farther. I was beginning to feel detached from myself, and with that, detached from Tavion. I looked at him apologetically, but he sped his pace until it was me following behind him. Perhaps it was for the best that I was putting some emotional distance between us. Afterall, any interaction I had with him always ended in me feeling like a child, stripped of all control. If I wanted to overtake Privelion, I had to take back that control. If not, it would be the death of me. I shapeshifted into a Velteis and sprinted ahead until Tavion was back behind me. Then I returned to my true form. Tavion got the message. He submitted to me leading the way.

While I didn't know the directions to the Listun tribe, Tavion respectfully guided us from behind me. I had to give Tavion credit. I still perceived the Klaysta tribe to be very misogynistic, and I presumed it must be difficult for him to follow the lead of a woman. Then again, I wondered if he felt differently about me, being that I was not an Oranian woman.

After a while of walking, we decided to summon Gladiators to cut through the desert with speed. Gliv and Garva had never ridden on, nor seen a Gladiator. It took us some time to inform them what the process was and to mitigate their fears. Of all the tribes, they were by far the most sheltered.

Tavion informed me that the Listun tribe move around a lot, but that they can typically be found in a forest region where there are far more places to aid in their camouflage. There was one forest region in particular where Tavion anticipated them to be. I imagined it must look similar to where the Kleit reside. After what must have been hours, we arrived. Looking around at the vast number of trees and plants with hardly any space between them, I realized that the Kleit residence was nowhere near an accurate comparison.

"Do the Listun have any abilities other than self-camouflage?" I asked Tavion.

"No," Tavion replied.

"So, it is basically just a game of hide and seek?" I confirmed. Tavion nodded.

I took a step forward, and Tavion threw an arm out in front of me. "You do need to be careful though," he advised.

"Of what?" I asked. "Them jumping out at me?"

"No," Tavion replied. "Some of these plants are prickly, and some are poisonous."

"How do I know which are poisonous?" I inquired.

"You don't," he responded.

"Suvians don't study these things?" I scoffed.

I walked forward cautiously. The plants were so close together that I couldn't imagine avoiding any of them, even if I did know which were dangerous. I couldn't bring myself to enter, until I realized that I didn't have to. Anyone could enter, and I could be anyone.

I instructed the others to stay put as I held my arms straight out and morphed them into feathered wings. The rest of my body followed suit. Seconds later, I successfully shrank my body into the form of a small Sparrow. I stood on the ground, only able to see the feet of Tavion, Gliv, and Garva. I looked over my shoulder and admired my beautiful golden and dark grey feathers, seeming to shimmer in the sunlight. I pointed my beak upward to get a better view of the others. Their bodies looked ginormous. I couldn't tilt my head far enough to see their faces or what reactions they might have had to my transformation.

I looked back at the forest. My head moved quickly, and each time I turned it, I felt all twitchy. Looking at the forest from this new perspective, I saw clear pathways I would be able to move through without touching the plants and trees. I would still need to be careful, but it was certainly doable. I flapped my wings and flew forward into the forest.

It was difficult not to get distracted by the size of everything or the feeling of being in the air without gravity forcing me back to the ground. I flew around aimlessly at first while acclimating to my new form and practically unrecognizable surroundings. I realized a flaw in my transformation, in that I was unable to announce myself or make any attempt to verbally communicate with the Listun tribe. I would have to rely on my visual acuity, greatly enhanced by my new guise.

I flew through the forest quickly and hopefully with high spirits, checking every nook and cranny of the woodland. My enthusiasm fell when I saw nothing and no one. The Listun tribe were either here and in hiding or had relocated to a place that Tavion had not anticipated. Either way, I realized my endeavors were hopeless, and my wings began to feel heavy from the hard work of constant flapping. I wondered how birds kept this up all day.

I flew back to the others disappointedly and landed gently on the ground at their feet. I transformed back into my human form and informed them in English as well as the Tuvon language that I was unsuccessful in finding any members of the Listun tribe. Expressions of worry spread across their faces as they realized the implications of the news. We would only have the help of the Klaysta, the Kleit, the Eyla, Gliv, and Garva. While it seemed like a lot of beings to combat just one, we all feared that Privelion's extensive practice of three Suvian abilities would exceed our advantage of outnumbering him.

"You have the same abilities as Privelion and more," Tavion reminded me.

"I know," I replied, "but I fear his years of practice with those three powers will render any of my abilities useless."

"I know you can do this," Tavion assured me confidently.

"I'm glad one of us does," I replied, sitting down on the forest grass.

"We can do this," Gliv motivated me in the Tuvon language.

Hearing Gliv empower us as a collective reminded me that the weight of this war was not on my shoulders alone. We were in this together, regardless of our numbers.

## 34

# LOVE TRIANGLE

Z ARA AND TAVION STOOD outside of the Klaysta tunnel, hesitant to move the first boulder and enter the community. Gliv and Garva stood behind them, unaware of what was taking them so long. Zara was anxious about how her friends would react to her unexplained disappearance, especially after having kept them in the dark about her whereabouts once already. Tavion was terrified to tell Kalari about the trip he had taken, especially since he would need to explain Zara's involvement.

"What if we just don't go back in?" Zara asked Tavion. "We can just go back to the Kleit or the Eyla community and find refuge with them."

Tavion rolled his eyes. "You know I don't want to face this either, but we have to."

"Can I go with you to tell Kalari?" Zara asked.

"I truly think you have a death wish," Tavion replied.

"We'll tread carefully," Zara promised.

"One can only be so careful," Tavion responded.

Tavion motioned for Gliv and Garva to help him move the boulder aside. The four of them entered through the tunnel. Gliv and Garva were used to mountains and cabins, and they were mesmerized by all the changes in scenery. They were distracted by the lights on the tunnel wall, and even the wall itself. When they got to the end of the tunnel, Gliv and Garva assisted Tavion in shifting the second boulder aside.

Tavion and Zara half expected Kalari to be on the other side of the boulder, tapping her foot impatiently, waiting for their return. There was no one there to greet them, and none of the community members completing chores outside in the surrounding area seemed to be the least bit reactive to their return. Tavion started toward his tent, and Zara followed closely behind.

"Wait," Zara stopped him. "Can we tell my friends first?"

"That depends," Tavion responded. "Is this you trying to stall?"

Zara bit her lip anxiously. "Maybe a little," she confessed.

"Then no," Tavion replied, continuing toward his tent to speak with Kalari.

"But shouldn't we at least get Gliv and Garva settled?" Zara asked frantically.

Tavion squinted at Zara. He looked back at the two members of the Tuvon tribe. "Yes, I suppose you are correct. It wouldn't be right to have them present for this conversation, and I am sure they would like to get some rest." While Tavion knew Zara's reason for wanting to get them settled first was at least in part selfish, he genuinely believed she had a point.

Tavion guided Gliv and Garva to the guest tent that had been inhabited by Zara's friends. When they descended the stairs, they found the underground cave to be empty and tidied up, with the sleeping pouches hung up on the wall, and the chairs pushed in at the table. Zara's eyes widened with concern.

"Tell them they can stay here for the time being," Tavion instructed Zara.

"Where did my friends go?" Zara asked.

"How would I know? I've been with you," Tavion replied. "Let's solve one problem at a time."

Zara swallowed past a lump in her throat. "You can stay here for now. We will be back shortly," Zara translated to Gliv and Garva.

Zara followed Tavion back up the stairs without speaking a word, while worst case scenarios infiltrated her thoughts. They exited the tent and walked back towards Tavion's tent as originally planned. Zara looked around for her friends on the way but didn't see them outside either.

"You sure you want to come with me for this conversation?" Tavion asked.

"Yes, I'm sure," Zara replied.

Tavion led them through his tent and down into the cave. Kalari was in the middle of organizing what appeared to be clothing for their children. The two children were running around and jumping across the beds in a chase, tackling each other each time they caught up. Kalari looked at Tavion and then at Zara with no expression.

Kalari grabbed one of the kids by their shirt as they ran by. "Go play outside," she demanded. The child ran up the stairs, and the other child followed.

Kalari returned her attention to the clothes she was sorting. Tavion walked up behind her and put a hand on each of her shoulders. Kalari tilted her head to the side, leaning her cheek against his right hand. She closed her eyes, admiring the feeling of his touch.

"What is she doing here?" Kalari whispered.

"She needs our help," Tavion responded, "and we are going to help her."

"Seems like she has already helped herself to enough," Kalari said, turning towards him with tears in her eyes. Her eyes were red and puffy, with her eyelids only opening halfway.

Tavion wanted to explain to Kalari that he needed to go with Zara to the other communities in order to stop Privelion from taking over. He wanted to tell her that his relationship with Zara was one of necessity and not desire. He wanted to tell her that his relationship with Zara would end as soon as Privelion was no longer a threat. But he bit his tongue because none of that was true. He knew Zara could have went to the other communities alone, he was certain that his desire for her far exceeded his need, and he fantasized about a future with Zara that would outlast Privelion's reign.

Tavion could only think to speak three words that held truth. "I love her."

"Love?" Kalari gasped angrily. Tavion nodded shamefully. "Do you love me?" Kalari asked.

"I care for you," Tavion replied, his voice cracking with sadness.

Kalari bent down, looking like she was going to be sick. She fully extended her arm upward to rest her hand on the table beside her for support. Zara peeked around Tavion to get a better look at Kalari and make sure she was okay. Kalari began to hyperventilate.

"You… care about me," Kalari spoke between breaths. "It's crazy how those words sound so small in comparison."

"The way I feel about you is not small," Tavion assured her.

Kalari looked up at him, angered by his betrayal. "Get out!" she shouted. Tavion and Zara glanced at each other and respectfully headed for the stairs. "No. You stay," Kalari demanded. Zara turned around to see that Kalari was referring to her.

Tavion shook his head at Zara, but Zara obeyed Kalari. "Go look for my friends," Zara asked of Tavion. Tavion looked back and forth between Kalari and Zara, assessing the risk of leaving the two of them alone. Despite his fears of what interactions might occur with his departure, he trusted that everything would be okay. It put him at ease to know that Zara was more equipped to defend herself than she was during her last encounter with Kalari, and to know that Zara was not the type to cause unnecessary harm to anyone. He ascended the stairs and exited the tent.

Zara looked at Kalari hesitantly before slowly walking toward her and reaching out a hand to help her up. Kalari couldn't look her in the eye. The two of them sat down at opposite ends of the table and waited for one another to start the conversation. After a couple minutes of silence, Zara decided to start.

"I'm sorry," Zara apologized. "I never meant for any of this to happen."

Kalari looked up at the ceiling and wiped a tear from her eye before responding. "I believe you," Kalari replied, "but it did happen, and here we are."

"I've only ever been with one guy," Zara informed Kalari. "This isn't something I do. Just like you, I don't know what to say or how to navigate this."

Kalari nodded. "I've only ever been with Tavion."

"Do you love him?" Zara asked.

Kalari's body jolted as more tears came pouring out. "I care for him," Kalari replied with a shaky voice. "I must sound like such a hypocrite."

"No," Zara validated, "it's not wrong to want to feel loved by someone you care for." Kalari nodded and wiped her tears away. "Have you ever loved anyone?" Zara asked.

"Yes." Kalari smiled, still rubbing underneath her eyes. "I love my children."

"So, you know the feeling of love, and you know it isn't how you feel about Tavion," Zara reflected.

Kalari paused to think about what she wanted to say. She took a deep breath to collect herself. "Tavion takes care of me," she whispered to Zara. "Who will take care of me? Who will take care of our children if he leaves me for you?"

Zara smiled. "Is that all you are worried about?" Kalari nodded. "Tavion's not going anywhere," Zara assured her. "This is home, for him and for me." Kalari looked at Zara with one eyebrow lifted, clearly desiring further explanation. "I recently found out I was born to the Kleit tribe," Zara continued, "who are good beings that were manipulated into doing bad things. They were manipulated by a being who was born to the Klaysta community. Are you familiar with Privelion?"

"The boy who died many years ago?" Kalari asked.

"Yeah," Zara replied, "only, he is alive and threatening to take over Suvia and all other planets."

"Privelion is alive?" Kalari asked. "How could he possibly be that much of a threat?"

"He has three abilities instead of one," Zara informed her, "and he has been practicing use of them for more years than I have been alive in this human body."

Kalari blinked and looked Zara up and down, as if expecting to see through her skin to her true form as a Kleit. "I don't believe you are from here," Kalari replied.

"Well, I am," Zara responded, "and that's not all." Zara stood up from her chair and backed up against the cave wall, camouflaging herself against it until all that could be seen was her clothes. Kalari almost fell backwards in her chair, startled by Zara's shared ability with the Listun tribe. Zara willed herself to reappear. "I believe I have all seven abilities," she informed Kalari. "I have successfully tested six."

"Then why is Privelion a threat?" Kalari asked.

"He has had so many years of practice with the three most threatening Suvian abilities, and he knows the terrain of Suvia far better than I do," Zara explained.

Kalari nodded. "I understand."

Zara sat down in one of the chairs beside Kalari. "I am going to need all of the help I can get in the impending battle against him."

"I will help you, as will our tribe," Kalari responded. "What will you do when this comes to an end?" Kalari asked, subtly bringing the conversation back to where it started.

"If you'll have me, I would love to be a part of your family," Zara replied. "I won't take Tavion away from you, but I am also hoping you won't take him away from me."

"None of the others in this community would understand," Kalari noted.

"None of them have to," Zara responded.

Kalari shook her head and let out a breathy chuckle. "Welcome to the family," she announced, rolling her eyes at the absurdity of the situation.

Zara spent a few minutes speaking with Kalari more lightheartedly before her departure. After that, she set off to find Tavion to provide him with an update on Kalari and to see if he had an update regarding her friends. Zara looked around the community and didn't see any of them, so she decided to check on Gliv and Garva. When she walked down into the guest cave, she found that her friends had returned, and Tavion was with them.

"I filled everybody in," Tavion informed Zara. "Well, everyone except for Gliv and Garva."

"Where were you guys?" Zara asked.

"We went to try to fix the spaceship. It was a no-go," Jerome replied.

Zara nodded. "We are going to get you guys home," she reassured them.

"You guys? You won't be coming with us?" Sadie asked.

"I'm afraid not," Zara responded. The room grew silent.

"How did the conversation with Kalari go?" Tavion asked.

Zara walked over to Tavion and smiled. "The five of us are going to be a family," Zara informed him.

"And Kalari is okay with that?" Tavion asked.

"She is," Zara replied.

"Your family is on Earth, Zara," Xavier reminded her.

"I know," Zara responded. "Leto, my father, has cursed me with two homes. He has torn me in half between two planets, and I need to make a choice." Zara paused to hold back tears. "Zidia has always been fine on her own. She acts as if she needs me, but she doesn't. I know she will look after my parents, and I know you will look after her. I am needed here on Suvia."

"And if they ask about you?" Xavier inquired.

"You can tell them the truth, but they won't believe it," Zara answered. "They will think I died, and in a sense, I did. I am not Zara. I am Silvia. Zara no longer exists. She never did."

Sadie began to cry and grieve the loss of Zara. Jerome put his arms around Sadie to comfort her. Xavier refused to accept that there was any loss at all. He pleaded for Zara to return to Earth with them, but to no avail. Marquette stayed silent.

"Can I speak with you alone?" Xavier asked Zara.

Zara nodded. The two of them exited the cave together and walked to a secluded spot in the community. They sat down on the grass beside each other. Zara was happy to have a moment alone with Xavier. He was one of her dearest friends, and ever since they arrived on Suvia, she felt that they were growing apart. Even if they would soon be planets apart, she didn't want to lose her connection with him.

"What is it you wanted to speak with me about?" Zara asked. Xavier looked down at his hands nervously. "Come on, you know you can tell me anyth…"

Xavier leaned in and pressed his lips against hers. Zara's eyes stayed open while their lips connected, and while she didn't pull away, she also didn't kiss him back. Noticing her resistance, Xavier pulled away and apologized. Zara looked away from him, not expecting this awkward interaction. She thought for a moment, trying to process what had just happened.

"Zara, I am truly sorry," Xavier apologized again. "It's just…" he trailed off. "Have you ever thought about us?"

"Yes," Zara replied without a second thought.

"You have?" Xavier replied, taken aback by her answer.

"I have," she responded.

"When?" Xavier asked. "Why didn't you tell me?"

"Because I hadn't thought about it until we were on the spaceship coming here, and so many other things were happening, and by the time I could process any of this, your lips were on mine on a foreign planet that I now know to be my home. There is so much more going through my mind right now, like for starters, that I am not even human."

"You hadn't thought about it until we were on the spaceship coming here? Zara, I have been thinking about it for years."

"Is that all you got from what I said?" Zara asked. "Xavier, I am not human. Can you picture yourself being intimate with one of those Kleit?" He didn't respond. "Exactly," Zara continued, "any relationship I could ever have would have to be on Suvia. No one on Earth would understand what I am and where I came from. You push it aside and try to deny that part of my identity, but I feel that part of my identity growing like a virus inside of me. Don't you get it?"

"I love you," Xavier told her quietly.

Zara shook her head. "You love who you thought I was."

"You've been the same person for twenty-nine years," Xavier countered, unaware two additional years had passed during their travels.

"I haven't been a person at all. Not for one year." Zara stood up, ready to walk away from him.

"It hurts me to see you with him," Xavier admitted. Zara turned away but stayed put, trying to consider how he was feeling. "I just wonder if in another life," he continued, "you and I could have made something of this. I wonder if we could have been together."

"In another life, we probably were," Zara replied. She wiped a tear from her eye and walked back toward the tent to reconvene with the others.

35

# GOODBYE MY LOVE

B*EEP. EEP. EEP.* ZARA listened to the slow and steady beeps of the comm while she waited to hear her sister's voice. She traced the lines on the wooden table in the guest cave of the Klaysta community with her finger, lost in thought about what she might say. She knew she couldn't possibly tell Zidia that she wasn't her sister, or human, or from Earth... and yet... she felt the urge to tell her everything.

"Zara?"

"Zidia!" Zara smiled. "How are you?"

"I'm doing okay," Zidia replied. "I'm doing okay," she repeated, as if trying to convince herself. "I've just been worried about you."

"I'm doing okay too," Zara responded lightheartedly. "How is everything back on Earth? How are Mom and Dad?"

"Everything is very normal here," Zidia replied. "I've just been working and spending time at home. Dad made us a new coffee table and brought it over the other day. It's beautiful! Mom found a new TV show to binge."

Zara's face lit up as she learned everything was going well for her sister. "That all sounds great, Zidia."

"Yeah! Will you get to come home sooner because of everything that happened with the NASA administrator?" Zidia asked excitedly.

Zara paused. This was it. She had to decide right here and right now if she was going to tell Zidia the truth. She didn't have time to weigh the pros and cons.

The words came out before she could change her mind. "I don't think I'm coming home at all."

There was silence on the other end, followed by soft sobbing. "What do you mean?" Zidia asked. "What happened?"

"Suvia happened," Zara whispered.

"What?" Zidia asked between sobs.

Zara didn't think her sister heard her and debated changing her story to something more believable. She shook her head at the thought. She couldn't bring herself to lie to her sister, especially when she feared this might be their last conversation with one another.

"I'm not on Mars," Zara informed her. "This whole mission was a set up to get me to a planet called Suvia." Zara looked around the Klaysta guest cave feeling disconnected from reality and looking for anything in her surroundings that might help her to feel grounded. Part of her wished she hadn't asked the others to leave the room so that she could carry out this conversation with her sister privately. Zara knew that if she could just see someone from Suvia right now, it would ameliorate her feeling of alienation.

"Suvia?" Zidia asked.

It was weird for Zara to hear her sister say the name of the planet. "Suvia," Zara confirmed. "I was sent here by the man who impersonated the NASA administrator. His name is Leto." Zara went on to tell Zidia everything, down to the tiniest of details. Zidia listened attentively. When Zara was finished pouring out the truth to her sister, Zidia took a moment to process everything.

"Still there?" Zara asked.

Zidia sniffled on the other end of the comm. "So... I'm not really your sister?" Zidia asked.

"No matter what, you will always be my sister," Zara assured her, "but biologically, no. Ask Mom and Dad if I was adopted by them, and if they are honest with you, as I am now, they will tell you it is true."

"And you're not... human?" Zidia whispered, as if there were someone else beside her to keep the secret from.

"Correct," Zara replied, feeling odd saying these things out loud even though she had already verbalized and come to terms with it prior.

"Can you prove it?" Zidia asked, feeling like her sister was playing a cruel prank on her as she had done numerous times in their childhood years.

"Easily," Zara responded, "if you were here."

"What does that mean?" Zidia asked.

Zara got an idea. "Actually, you don't need to be here!" she exclaimed. "I can prove it to you right now, but I have to warn you, it is going to freak you out."

"Okay..." Zidia replied with concern.

Zara closed her eyes. "Zidia, walk to any room in the house, and don't tell me what room you are in," she instructed.

"Why?" Zidia asked cautiously.

"Just do it, and I will prove to you that I am not human."

Zidia got up and walked to the kitchen. "Okay, what now?" Zidia asked.

"Now, you are in the kitchen," Zara replied.

"Yeah, but what are you going to do to prove that... wait what? How did you know that?" Zidia asked. "Oh, I get it. You know how long it takes to get to the kitchen from the couch, and you know I'm usually on the couch when I talk to someone on the phone... or... whatever this device is."

Zara rolled her eyes impatiently. "Never mind that. Pick up an object, and don't tell me what it is."

Zidia went to pick up her cell phone but realized that it was an object that would be easy for Zara to guess. She looked around for something unique that Zara wouldn't think of. "Hang on," Zidia said to her sister, setting the comm down on the coffee table. She walked to the kitchen and grabbed a pair of scissors. Then she went to the living room and cut off a small thread from the carpet. She held the thread and the scissors in her hand and picked the comm back up.

"Zidia!" Zara exclaimed.

Zidia looked at the thread of carpet between her fingers. "What?"

"I can't believe you couldn't just pick up a piece of paper, or food, or the TV remote! Did you really just cut a piece of the carpet in the living room?"

Startled by the accuracy of her sister's accusation, Zidia dropped the pair of scissors from her hand and jumped back, the point of the scissors just barely missing her foot.

"Will you stop being reckless?" Zara exclaimed in exasperation.

"You saw that too?" Zidia gulped nervously.

"Yes," Zara replied.

Zidia looked around at the blinds. They were all closed. She looked around for cameras. There were none to be found. "Zara, tell me what's going on?" Zidia pleaded. "Do you have a way to spy on me from Mars?"

Zara threw her head back, tired of constantly having to repeat herself. "Zidia, I told you, I am not on Mars. I am on Suvia."

"Well, how are you doing that? How can you see me?" Zidia asked.

"I have Suvian powers," Zara informed her. "I can do a lot of things that I didn't even know were possible until I arrived on this planet."

"And the other astronauts? Do they have these powers too?" Zidia asked.

"No, because they are not from Suvia. I am," Zara explained.

"And you just happened to get sent to the planet you are supposedly from?" Zidia countered.

"I wasn't sent here by coincidence, Zidia!" Zara raised her voice. "I was sent here by Leto, who impersonated the NASA administrator, with the sole intention of getting me back to my home planet once I reached adulthood."

"Oh my..." Zidia sat down. "I believe you."

"It's about time! I've only had to repeat myself..."

"No," Zidia interjected, "I don't believe you because you have convinced me. I believe you because that man was in our home. I remember now. He gave us pamphlets." Zidia's mind flashed back to twenty-three years prior, seeing her sister's face light up as a total stranger inspired her to chase a dream she had never even considered until that day.

Zara nodded. "That man is my father."

"That's why I believe you," Zidia replied, "because it is all coming back to me, and he looked at you so lovingly and stopped by regularly to sustain your interest in space travel." Zara and Zidia both went silent, recollecting the experience that at the time seemed so innocent. "So, where do we go from here?" Zidia asked.

"This is my home," Zara replied. "It's not a matter of going anywhere. It's a matter of staying where we are."

"So, I won't see you again?" Zidia asked with tears in her eyes.

"I hope that one day you will," Zara responded, genuinely feeling torn between Earth and Suvia, "but for now, I belong here."

"What will I tell Mom and Dad?" Zidia asked.

Zara smiled, coming further to terms with her new identity now that she knew she had her sister's unconditional acceptance. "Tell them I am doing such an amazing job on Mars that NASA wants me to stay longer. Tell them I have all the provisions I need here and that I love them and miss them so much."

"Will we still be able to communicate with each other through this device?" Zidia asked with hopefulness in her tone.

Zara had left out every detail of Privelion's existence when she disclosed the truth to her sister. She wanted to promise Zidia that they would still be able to communicate but knew that the outcome of the impending battle lacked certainty. She thought for a moment about how to respond without giving her sister a reason to worry about her.

"Zidia..." Zara started.

"No, you know what, don't answer that," Zidia replied, sensing that whatever her sister was about to tell her would not be good. "Here's what I will do. I will hold on to this device every day, for the rest of my life. If you are able to contact me, I know you will, and if you are not, I will trust that you are happy and taking good care of yourself."

Zara sighed with relief. "This is what I love most about you, Zidia," she replied. "You always know just what to say."

Zidia smiled. "I love you."

"I love you too," Zara replied, "to Suvia and back."

The beeping of the comm signaled Zidia's disconnect. Zara pressed a few buttons and waited once more. Tavion entered through the flaps of the tent, descended the stairs, and sat down beside her at the table. Zara smiled and put her hand on his.

"Hello?"

"Dad?" Zara asked. There was a chuckle on the other end. "Sounds weird, doesn't it," Zara admitted.

"Very," Leto replied. "What brings you to contact me?"

"I wanted to thank you," Zara responded. "I know I have no memory of what you did for me leading up to my life as a human, but I hope to one day hear stories of our life together on Suvia. I can't express enough gratitude for your protection and the adoptive family that you chose for me on Earth. I feel so lucky to have three wonderful parents."

"Your adoptive parents chose you," Leto replied. "It is me and them that are the lucky ones."

"Thank you," Zara responded. "If it were not selfish, I would ask you to bring them and my sister here to Suvia. I would kill to be unified with everyone I love, but I know that wouldn't be right." Zara brushed her fingers along Tavion's skin, thankful to have at least one of her loved ones beside her.

"You are a brave girl, Silvia," Leto complimented.

Zara smiled. "Trying to be. If I make it out of this battle with Privelion alive..."

"When you make it out of the battle alive," Leto corrected. Tavion nodded, in agreement with Leto.

"... I will find my way back to you, whether that be on Earth or on Suvia," Zara declared.

"I know you will," Leto agreed confidently.

"I have a favor to ask of you," Zara informed him.

"Anything."

"I'd like to speak with Dimitri."

Leto hesitated. "Now I know you are probably angry with him, but you must understand, he was only a boy when I asked him to..." he trailed off as Zara started laughing. "What's so funny?" he asked.

"I'm not angry with him," Zara replied. "I really just want to talk to him. You have his comm."

"Oh, so the real reason you contacted me was to speak with him?" Leto responded.

"No, but I figured I could kill two birds with one stone." Zara chuckled.

"Kill two birds?"

"It's an expression," Zara informed him. "It means I can knock out both conversations at the same time. Can you please bring him the comm and get back to me?"

"Will do," Leto replied before disconnecting.

"What did your sister say?" Tavion inquired.

"Surprisingly, she believes me," Zara replied, "or so she says."

"You told her everything?" Tavion asked.

"More or less," Zara responded. "I left out the part about Privelion."

"Which part about Privelion?" Tavion asked.

"All the parts," Zara replied, slumping down in her chair.

"Probably for the best," Tavion noted supportively.

Sooner than expected, the comm started beeping. "Hello?" Zara greeted.

"Hey, Zar," Dimitri replied.

Zara tensed up a little at the sound of his voice. "Hey, is Leto with you?" Zara asked.

"Yes, we are both here," Leto replied.

"Okay, good," Zara responded, feeling comforted by Leto's presence.

"So, you're all filled in," Dimitri remarked.

"Yeah, I still can't believe you knew all this time," Zara responded.

"Since childhood," Dimitri noted, scratching his neck anxiously.

"You may be the best spy I have ever heard of," Zara complimented playfully. "I don't know how I spent so much time with you and didn't know it."

"Don't be too hard on yourself," Dimitri replied. "You might've guessed it if my feelings hadn't been real."

Zara laughed. Dimitri stayed silent. "Oh, you're being serious," Zara acknowledged.

"Yeah, Zar. I mean, I know I didn't have the best way of showing it..."

"Or any way of showing it," Zara chimed in.

"Or any way of showing it," he concurred, "but I really did grow to love you."

"Seems like a common theme lately," Zara replied, thinking of how things played out between her and Tavion, as well as her and Xavier.

"What do you mean?" Dimitri asked.

Zara looked up at Tavion with embarrassment. Tavion didn't seem to pick up on the fact that her comment had pertained to him. "Nothing," Zara replied to Dimitri.

"I understand that there won't be a future for us," Dimitri stated. "Leto informed me that you will be staying on Suvia indefinitely, but I want you to know that it really wasn't about the money. In fact, I stopped accepting Leto's money six years ago."

"It's true," Leto confirmed. "He told me to stop paying him and hasn't received a single payment from me since he was twenty-five years old."

"Really?" Zara asked, surprised by this information. "Why did it never feel real with you?"

"I guess I was just always insecure," Dimitri admitted. Zara's jaw dropped in shock. It was rare for Dimitri to admit any sense of vulnerability at all. "I knew our relationship was built on bribery and blackmail," he continued, "and I honestly didn't see a future for us, even when I wanted to. I tried not to be hopeful, and I know I was self-destructive at times, but only because I worried that if I made it the perfect relationship, it would hurt more to have it taken away from me."

"That honestly makes sense," Zara responded.

"Thanks, Zar. Listen, I'm sorry for the times I put you through hell. I know I did, and I regret it, especially knowing that's the last memory you'll have of me. In any case, I want you to know you always have a home with me. At the very least, I will always be your friend."

Zara's eyes welled up with tears. "This conversation is the last memory I will have of you," Zara replied. "I'm going to miss you..." She wiped at her eyes and chuckled. "...and I'm not just saying that."

"I'm going to miss you too," Dimitri replied. "I love you."

Tavion's head shot up at the sound of Dimitri's words. Zara leaned forward and put her hand on the side of Tavion's cheek reassuringly. "And I love you," she spoke to Tavion.

"I'm glad to hear you say that, Zara. I really am," Dimitri responded, clearly thinking her words were directed toward him. Zara and Tavion smiled at each other knowing otherwise.

"Zara, before we disconnect, I have good news for you," Leto informed her.

"What is it?" Zara asked.

"I can get your colleagues back to Earth," he replied. "I'm sure you've been trying to figure out a way to aid in their safe return, and being that it is my fault they got mixed up in the middle of this, I want to help."

"Yes!" Zara exclaimed. "That isn't good news. That is amazing news!"

"I have hidden on Suvia a replica of the device that brought us to Earth," Leto continued. "It is in the same location as the one we used all those years ago. Do you remember where I told you it was and how to access it?"

"Yes, of course!" Zara replied. "How does it function?"

"You must bring it to a very open part of the desert and set it on the ground," Leto instructed. "You will press the button on the top of the device, and you will have roughly fifteen seconds to clear the area."

"And if I don't clear it in time?" Zara asked.

"That's not an option," Leto responded.

"Understood," Zara replied.

"Be safe," Leto pleaded.

"I will," Zara assured him.

Zara disconnected on the comm and motioned for Tavion to follow her out of the cave. Her friends were waiting right outside of the tent. Zara didn't want to waste one moment, knowing the time they had left before Privelion's attack was scarce. Instead of filling them in on what she had learned, she motioned for them to follow her as well. Xavier, Sadie, and Jerome followed her without hesitation, while Marquette spewed out sarcastic comments and insults as usual as she trailed behind.

Zara led them to the Kleit cave, no longer concerned of its dangers. She stopped at the clearing and knelt down by the statue, knocking at the base of it exactly as directed by Leto. As anticipated, the stone slid down, revealing the secret compartment Leto had told her of. She grabbed the device within and sealed the compartment.

"Let's go," Zara instructed.

"Go where? Are you going to tell us what the hell is going on?" Marquette asked demandingly.

"You're going home," Zara informed them, "and it's not going to take months. It's going to take minutes."

"How the hell is it going to take minutes?" Marquette yelled in disbelief.

"Apparently Suvian technology is more advanced than ours," Zara replied.

"But they don't have bathrooms," Sadie countered.

The group followed Zara excitedly, enticed by just the hope of returning home. Zara led them toward the desert while explaining that though it will feel like minutes of traveling to them, they will be losing two years on Earth. She noted that they lost two already. Marquette sobbed as she realized her children would be four years older upon her return than when she had left them.

Once they made it to an open part of the desert, Zara set the travel device on the ground. She motioned for the others to clear a large perimeter. Zara knelt down, ready to press the button on the top of the device but froze when she heard the squawking of a large bird overhead.

"Privelion," Zara said aloud, shaking her head with disbelief and rising to her feet.

Zara didn't want a fight. Not here. Not with all of her friends and Tavion out in the open with nowhere to run. Zara knew if she made any use of her powers, Privelion would interpret it as her being ready for battle. She stood her ground in her human form and waited for the bird to approach.

The bird flew towards her at rapid speed and aimed low, as it did during their last encounter. This time, Zara made no attempt to defend herself, letting the bird knock her to the ground. She slowed her fall with her hands, which burned as they slid harshly across the sand. Her face hit the ground. She slowly stood up and wiped a drop of blood from her bottom lip.

"I'm not going to fight you!" Zara yelled. "Not yet."

Her words seemed to anger Privelion, as he flew to the ground and shapeshifted quickly into a Seltivor. The Seltivor crouched down and kicked sand back several times with one of its front legs, in preparation to charge at Zara. Zara walked toward the Seltivor, making her surrender clear.

"You know," Zara called out, "for someone who claims he has power, you sure aren't showing it by threatening someone who isn't going to fight back." The Seltivor continued to kick sand back, staring at Zara intensely with large black eyes. "Someone truly powerful would want a real fight," Zara assured him. "If you want to prove you are weak, you can kill me now. I will go down without a fight," she promised. "Or, if you want to show me your power and prove to Suvia that you are not a coward, you can fight me tomorrow. If you wait just one day, I will fight back!" Zara yelled. The Seltivor lifted itself upward and stilled. "What's it going to be?" Zara asked. The Seltivor took off running in the other direction. Zara closed her eyes, relieved, but aware that she had only bought herself one more day.

Zara hurriedly pressed the button on the travel device, worried that Privelion would change his mind and come back, or that another animal would see her and her friends in the open area and take advantage of their exposure. She ran as quickly as she could, away from the device and toward her friends. They all watched as the device expanded like a ginormous pop-up tent in the shape of a sphere.

"It's ready to go," Zara informed them. "As much as I want my time with you to last, we need to make this quick. We can't stay out here in the open."

"Please come with us," Xavier pleaded.

"Yes, Zara, please?" Sadie asked.

Zara shook her head no. "If I don't stay here and face Privelion, there may not be an Earth to return to."

"She has a good point," Jerome agreed.

Zara turned to Marquette. "Marquette, I'll miss you most," Zara teased, leaning in for a hug. Marquette backed away with a disgusted expression on her face.

"Thank you," Marquette said, "for finding me a way home to my family."

"You're welcome," Zara replied warmly.

"I'll miss you," Sadie cried, wrapping her arms tightly around Zara.

"I'm going to miss you too, Sadie," Zara responded, returning Sadie's hug. "You are like a sister to me."

"I don't want to let go," Sadie cried.

"Then don't," Zara replied. "You can let go of this hug, but hold on tightly to our friendship." Sadie nodded and released Zara.

Zara turned to Jerome. "Take good care of Sadie."

"You know I will," he replied. He hugged Zara goodbye.

Lastly, Zara turned toward Xavier. He looked down at the ground, unable to make eye contact with her. She took a step toward him and put her hand on his shoulder empathetically.

"I don't know how to say goodbye to you," Xavier whispered. He clenched his chest, feeling a heaviness weighing him down.

"What if we say something else?" Zara asked. "Like... until we see each other again?"

"You know as well as I that it's unlikely we will see each other again at all," Xavier retorted.

"I know you are one of the first people I will go to if I find myself back on Earth," Zara countered. "Just keep me alive in your heart. That's all that matters."

"I've learned that my heart is a painful place to keep you," Xavier replied, still hurt by her rejection.

"You'll forever be in mine. I can promise you that," Zara replied. She threw her arms around her best friend and let her tears seep through his shirt. He hugged her back, burying his face in her hair.

"Goodbye, Zara," Xavier said, letting go of her.

It hurt Zara to hear that word and in a tone that sounded so final. She couldn't bear the thought of this being the last time she saw him. Her pain led to a promise that she instantly regretted, knowing there was no guarantee she could keep it. "I will see you again," Zara assured him.

It appeared it wouldn't matter if she kept that promise or not. Her words didn't seem to spark an ounce of hope in Xavier. He walked glumly toward the travel device. One by one, each of her friends entered the contraption. Zara leaned in through the door of the contraption to inform them what buttons they would need to press on the control panel. While looking around the inside of the device, she cringed, feeling a sharp pain in her head. Suddenly, she had a flashback of looking down at two Kleit hands clasped on to each other: the hand of a father and child. Zara took a step back from the contraption, and only a moment later, it vanished.

# 36

# The Night Before

K ALARI AND TAVION INSISTED on holding a ritualistic ceremony for me in their community prior to battle. According to them, no one on Suvia had ever won in battle without having one. Skeptical as I was, I decided it would be best not to take any chances and to use all of the help I could get, even if that help was built on an unlikely superstition.

Kalari walked over to me and knelt down, with a pelt draped across her hands. It was hard for me to believe that someone who tried to kill me was now bowing before me in a gesture of honor and respect. I took the pelt from her hands and draped it around my shoulders as earlier instructed by Tavion. The rest of the Klaysta tribe, originally lined up in rows and watching attentively, joined Kalari in bowing to me. Tavion gave a speech in the language of the Oranians, which was immediately followed by everyone rising to their feet and engaging in a celebratory dance.

I felt like their queen during the ceremony and looked at Tavion, who was standing tall and confident like their king. Kalari joined the others in a celebratory dance, leaving just me and Tavion standing side by side. I moved closer to him for guidance, having carried out everything that was asked of me for the ceremony.

"What now?" I inquired.

"Now, you may stay and celebrate, or leave and strategize," Tavion said to me.

"What is the right thing to do?" I asked.

Tavion raised his eyebrows and looked at me expectantly, as if I should already know the answer to that. "What do you think the best warriors do?"

I nodded. "Meet me in the guest cave after this wraps up," I asked of him.

"I will," he assured me.

When I entered the guest cave, I was saddened by the emptiness of it. Gliv and Garva had joined the Oranians in celebration of the victory we hadn't achieved yet, and my friends had safely returned to a planet that I feared I might never set foot on again. I had neither the luxury to celebrate nor escape, but this did not concern me nearly as much as the feeling that I was in this alone. No matter how many beings were by my side, I was the only human. No matter how many beings agreed to join me in battle, I was the only leader. No matter how many times the others envisioned us winning, I only envisioned loss. I was glad to be in a room devoid of reflective surfaces, because I knew if I could see myself now, I would see a terrified woman who was briefly and intermittently faking confidence to cover up feelings of helplessness and defeat that were surely leaking into my expressions.

I sat down at the table to formulate a plan of attack against Privelion but quickly realized the location wasn't suitable for my preparation. I hastily left the cave, aware before even exiting the tent that daylight was departing as quickly as I was. The sounds of celebration still carried through the air. I weaved between tents and hurried along, so as not to be seen, worried that I would be talked out of going off alone the night before battle if anyone noticed me leaving.

When I got to the boulder, I panicked. There was no way I would be able to move it alone. I looked around in all directions to check if anyone was watching me. After confirming there were no bystanders, I began to transform. Midway through my transformation into Tavion, I realized I was not making good use of my abilities. Even if I did transform into someone muscular like Tavion, I had seen that it takes two to move that rock, and I realized my efforts would be useless. I transformed back and looked up. *Of course*, I thought to myself. I shapeshifted into a bird and flew high up into the air, flapping my wings furiously with excitement.

After flying over the wall dividing the Klaysta community from the open land, I could see the sun setting, with just a block of yellow and orange light hovering above the horizon. Dark grey clouds blotted out the rest of the light grey sky. The scenery was so breathtakingly distracting that I nearly shapeshifted back into my human form mid-air. I heightened my focus on the task at hand and flew a little further out before landing and morphing back into my human body safely on the ground.

I looked around. There was no sign of movement. Not yet. I sat down on the red sand, which was darkening to mahogany with the loss of daylight. I finally felt like I could think. I picked up a handful of sand and tried to concentrate on a single grain of it to clear my mind. The sand was cool to the touch and so vibrant in color. I slowly lowered my fingers until the sand was hidden in my palm beneath them. Then I squeezed my hand tightly into a fist and watched as the sand seeped through my fingers.

"If I hold onto it loosely, I stay in control of it," I said aloud to myself, staring out into the distance.

I thought about how that same concept applied to how I might outwit Privelion. If I let myself build with tension or become too fixated on one strategy, Privelion would inevitably slip through my fingers. I picked up another handful of sand and let it sit in my open palm. I brushed the sand off with the palm of my other hand and watched as it fell to its rightful place on the ground.

Once dropped, it was indistinguishable which grains of sand I had been holding. I thought about how each Suvian ability functioned optimally in specific environments. Like the sand, each being on Suvia was drawn to its rightful place. I wondered how I could maximize the potential of my allies when removing them from where they function best. It was like I needed the habitats to merge somehow, something that surely wasn't possible in the realm of physics. Then again, neither was shapeshifting.

The thought lingered. *Shapeshifting.* I wondered what the limitations were. I knew the Kleit had previously shapeshifted into trees. If they could do that, surely other environmental structures could be replicated. I pictured a mountain of 4,500-meter elevation in my mind and willed myself to morph into it. While my body quickly turned to a sizable rock formation, it wasn't nearly big enough to make up the mountain I had envisioned. The allied tribes had agreed to meet in the Klaysta community at nightfall, and I watched as the last gleam of sunlight slowly fell behind the horizon. I figured I ought to go back.

Though I had initially intended to come out here for a fight that would put my strategizing to practice, I realized it was unnecessary. I had a gut feeling that there was truth to the idea that loosely planning for this battle would lead to victory. Each tribe had a well-established niche. When the time came, I trusted that they would know what to do, so long as I could find a way to provide them with the means to do it.

When I arrived back at the Klaysta community, all eyes were on me. The Klaysta tribe, the Eyla tribe, the Kleit, Gliv, and Garva all fell silent upon my entry. There must have been well over a thousand beings, all packed into the small space designed to house only one community of Suvians. The noise of chatter picked back up, initially at a whisper, with the voices eventually rising to a crescendo. I made my way through the crowd, ignoring the countless number of pleas for my attention.

I turned in all directions in search for a familiar face. I didn't see anyone I recognized. I felt several hands with skin of varying textures tugging gently at my arms. The sound of voices was now constant, and I was hearing three different languages simultaneously. I needed a way to quiet them at once. I closed my eyes and shapeshifted into a bear, an animal that all but the Klaysta tribe had never before seen. I roared at the top of my lungs. The only noise that followed was the soft whisper of the wind. I shapeshifted back.

I looked around at the faces filled with shock, still attempting to find those I could identify. "Current?" I yelled.

The crowd separated to display a terrified Eyla, whose knees were shaking with angst. Current walked towards me nervously. "I am here, Zara," he replied with a trembling voice.

"Stand here," I commanded, pointing to the ground beside me. "You will translate to your tribe."

"As best I can," Current agreed.

"Tavion?" I called out.

Tavion parted the crowd, walked forward, and stood beside me. "You need to stop taking off the way you did," he said quietly to me.

"Now is not the time," I replied harshly.

Tavion looked away from me and straightened his posture. He nodded. "You are right. Carry on."

I examined the empty expressions of the faces in the crowd, now waiting on my cue for how to react. The Kleit's black skin and black eyes made them difficult to see in the night. In contrast, the purple skin of Gliv and Garva and the multicolored scales of the Eyla drew my eyes toward them. I squinted to identify who was where before addressing them.

"I want to thank you all for being here," I said loudly. I repeated myself in the language of the Tuvon and the clicking communication style of the Kleit. Current translated for me in the language of the Eyla. Many in the crowd nodded, and all were attentive. I continued, "If you don't know it yet, we are here to rise up against Privelion." I looked around for expressions of surprise or confusion and found none, although unease was an expression blanketed across the crowd. "You are all here willingly, and I can't tell you how much that means to me," I commended.

Garva raised his hand and spoke without permission. "I mean, I'm not exactly here willingly," he said to me in the language of the Tuvon. "Gliv kind of put me up to..." Gliv nudged Garva hard with his elbow.

"No one is to speak tonight unless I invite them to," I said bluntly. I carried on. "You each, as you know, have a unique Suvian ability. What some of you may not know is that I have all seven." I ignored the gasps and whispers from the crowd in response to my disclosure. "More information that may be new to you is that Privelion has three: the ability to shapeshift, the ability to paralyze, and the ability to see all beings. Now it may sound like I alone can defeat Privelion, but Privelion has been practicing the use of his three powers for thirty-three years. I have been practicing for days. While I have the tools to succeed, I cannot do this alone. Your help is essential to reclaiming your power and stripping Privelion of his. If we fail, not only is Suvia in jeopardy, but every inhabited planet in existence as well." I looked out at the crowd, clearly hanging on my every word. Many leaned forward with anticipation of what I might say next.

"Any questions?" I asked.

"I have a question," Tavion replied. "Have you thought of how we will strategize?"

Current and I translated Tavion's question, and I spoke my answer in the other languages prior to responding in English. "I have thought a lot about it," I replied. Tavion let out a sigh of relief. "And we won't."

The crowd went wide-eyed, and whispers picked up again. "What do you mean we won't?" Tavion asked angrily.

"Calm down," I replied, directing my instruction at both Tavion and the crowd. "Our strategy is to not strategize. Privelion can see all beings, apart from me and the Klaysta. This means that if the rest of you practice exactly what you plan to do in battle, Privelion will be capable of seeing it, and he will strategize accordingly. We do not want him to have that foresight. You can think of what you will do, and I can tell you what you can do, but do not practice at all."

I clicked my tongue at the Kleit to communicate what I would need from them. "I need you guys to replicate the environments that these guys thrive in," I informed them, referencing the other tribes. "Can you do that?" I asked. They confirmed that they could. "What are the limitations?" I asked. "Can you shapeshift into water? A sky-high mountain?"

With the clicking of his tongue, one Kleit responded to me. "It is possible if we shapeshift together."

"I am learning," I replied. "Tell me how that works."

"We can replicate a shape we are trying to portray with our bodies, and if there are enough of us," he paused to look around at the others, "which there are, we can become the shape we are portraying."

"Do not practice it or demonstrate to me, but are you positive it will work?" I asked.

"Without a doubt," the Kleit assured me. The surrounding Kleit nodded in agreement.

"How do you shapeshift into water?" I asked, purely out of curiosity. "Never mind," I said before they could respond, "I don't want to know." Something about the idea of them transforming into a liquid freaked me out, especially after seeing the black puddle that they form after breathing their last breath. I quickly changed the subject. "You have two responsibilities in this battle," I informed them. "Make sure the others have access to replicas of their natural environments, and shapeshift into large beings when needed to defend me."

"Sounds easy enough," a Kleit replied.

I laughed anxiously. "Oh, how I hope you are right."

I moved on to the Eyla. "I've seen you guys flip out of the water with such impeccable speed and force. Use that to your advantage, and when the time comes, I will need you to be my healers." A few of the Eyla who were already familiar with me from our trip to the Kleit cave wrapped their arms around me one at a time in a caring embrace.

"We are with you," Current informed me in his usual scratchy and high-pitched voice. "Whatever you need."

I moved on to the Klaysta tribe and hugged Kalari. "Weapons," I declared to them. "Weapons, weapons, weapons. You all are my hands-on combat. You have weapons, and I know you know how to use them."

"Well, the men do," Kalari corrected.

"Right..." I thought about what role the women could have, and I could think of no place for them in this battle. "The Oranian women will stay," I commanded.

"But I need to be there for you," Kalari objected.

I shook my head no. Tavion was already planning to join me in battle, and I couldn't imagine leaving their kids orphaned should anything go wrong. "You will stay with the kids."

"I have a friend who will watch the kids. Whether you like it or not, Zara, I am going to be there," Kalari asserted.

I nodded in coerced acceptance. "Fine, Kalari," I replied tiredly. I turned to Tavion. "Tonight, teach Kalari how and when to use each weapon," I commanded. Tavion agreed to comply with this task.

I walked over to Gliv and Garva and spoke to them in the language of the Tuvon. "The Kleit will build you mountains in the middle of the desert where the battle will take place," I informed them. "Your job is to climb to the peak and warn us when Privelion is approaching."

"That's it? That's all you want from us?" Gliv asked, seeming to be almost insulted by the diminutiveness of the task.

"Unless you can think of other ways to use your ability to aid in battle," I replied. "Just don't practice anything," I reminded them.

I departed from the middle of the crowd to stand before the collective group once again. "I have given all of you a role," I announced. "I am not asking you to follow it to a T. In fact, I am requesting quite the opposite. You all have spent your whole lives using your respective abilities, and I won't specify to you how you should use them now in battle. You all have my full trust, and I hope that is mutual. Work with each other, help the other tribes, and together we will conquer this." Waves of cheers corresponding with each translation echoed through the crisp night air. "Let's get some rest," I insisted. "Privelion will surely be awaiting our early arrival, and we do not want him coming for us or catching us off guard. We want full control of the environment in which the battle will take place." I made eye contact with the Kleit as a subtle reminder of their responsibility to create that environment.

The night before the battle ended with a large feast of both Seltivor and Velteis. While it was typical in the Klaysta community to eat around the campfires, there were far too many beings to accommodate, leaving everyone to find a place on the grass to eat and mingle within their tribes. I sat down on the grass, staring up at the moons, not yet having swallowed one mouthful of food. Tavion sat down beside me with a surplus of meat piled high on a makeshift wooden plate. He held out the plate and offered some to me, but I politely refused. There was a knot in my stomach, and a lump of anxiety invaded my throat, making it difficult to swallow.

"Do you think this is going to work?" I asked Tavion.

Tavion paused before answering. "Well, there isn't much of a plan."

"Do you think not having a plan will work?" I asked, feeling desperate and unsure of myself.

Tavion looked around at the others scattered about on the grass. They were immersed in conversation and laughter and were happily devouring their meals. "Zara, I don't know," Tavion replied. "All I know is whatever happens, you have done something amazing here tonight. In my lifetime, this many tribes have not congregated in one place. Because of you, we are united, not as separate tribes but as Suvians." Tavion wrapped one arm around me and put the plate back in front of me with his opposite hand. "Now eat. You will need it for strength and energy."

I smiled coyly and took a large chunk of meat off the plate. "Thank you," I replied. "It brings me so much joy to see everyone unified. I am hoping this will be the beginning of a new chapter."

# 37

# Until One of us Dies

T HERE WAS AN EERIE stillness to Suvia the morning of the battle. Not a bird flew overhead, nor did any animals make themselves known. It was as if Suvia had frozen in time and would only resume at the battle's conclusion. Accompanying the stillness was an intense silence that was only broken up by the footsteps Gliv and Garva were taking as they walked toward the mountain the Kleit had constructed for them.

When they arrived at the mountain, their movements grew louder, as they climbed at a seemingly impossible pace toward the peak. The others were watching intently from their already established positions. The environmental set-up looked more unnatural than anything any of them had ever seen, including the Kleit who had immeasurable practice forming unnatural environments. There was a large lake in the middle of the desert. There was a forest beside it. The base of a massive mountain was less than one hundred meters from the nearest edge of the lake.

"I think we got something!" Gliv yelled in the language of the Tuvon, after running down to the base of the mountain where he could be heard. Garva stayed at the top to keep watch. From Garva's viewpoint, a quick moving speck was traveling through the desert in their direction. The speck turned to two specks, with one traveling on top of the other at the exact same speed. Zara squinted but could not yet see anything. Garva continued watching. As the travelers came closer, Garva could not make out the rider but realized the being beneath it was a Gladiator. Assuming based on the size ratio of the rider to the Gladiator that Privelion was riding toward them in his true form, Garva sped down the mountain as quickly as possible to provide the tribes with a final warning of his arrival.

Zara yelled out an expression of gratitude and commanded Gliv and Garva to return to the peak of the mountain. They did as instructed. The Klaysta stood at the forefront of the battlefield and prepared their weapons, creating a partial blockade to protect the more defenseless Eyla tribe positioned behind them. Privelion approached and dismounted the Gladiator.

Privelion looked around, analyzing the surroundings. He was neither fearful nor impressed, only observant. "I'm feeling generous today!" Privelion announced, glaring smugly at Zara. He repeated himself in the languages of the other tribes, making it apparent that Zara wasn't the only one with that ability. "I will give you all one last chance to join me without a fight," he continued. "If you should turn down my offer, your death will be inevitable."

Several members of each tribe looked around, worried that they may lose members of their community to fear. While fear was present in each of them, it overcame none of them. After receiving reassurance of the loyalty of their counterparts, every single one of them stayed silent and turned their attention back to Privelion.

Zara took a step forward to speak on their behalf. "I believe their silence speaks loudly."

"So it does." Privelion frowned.

Privelion shapeshifted so quickly into a Seltivor that some of the tribe members thought twice as to whether his transformation was instantaneous. He charged forward, and Zara was sure that she would be his first target. The Klaysta readied their weapons, and Zara prepared to shapeshift. She stopped herself when she realized her certainty was misguided. She was not Privelion's first target. Privelion made a sharp turn before reaching her and sprung into the forest, knocking down trees as he passed through and forcing those trees back into their true forms as Kleit. Privelion knew the Kleit could experience pain, even in their shapeshifted forms. He tilted his head while continuing to run through the forest, slicing many of the trees with the jigsaw-like bladed nose of the Seltivor body he occupied. The trees that got scathed quickly shapeshifted back into Kleit, crying out in agony and attending to their injuries.

Outside of the forest, Zara was contemplating aloud whether to enter. "I have to do something," she insisted to Tavion and Kalari, who were urging her to stay put.

"In the forest, you will be vulnerable," Kalari assured her. "There won't be a clear sightline, and you won't have as much protection."

"This doesn't make any sense!" Zara ran her fingers through her hair frantically, staring out at the trees. "Why wouldn't he come straight for me?"

"I am guessing he is determined to get revenge on the Kleit for betraying him," Tavion replied. "Or perhaps he is trying to distract you with worry."

"Successfully," Zara noted in frustration. "I'm going in."

Before Zara could take a step, she sighted three Kleit in their natural forms coming out from between the trees. They appeared to be gravely injured, with one of them crawling and two of them grasping desperately at their torso. Zara watched as one by one, they melted into puddles of black goo on the grass.

Zara was enraged, partly at Privelion for causing their death and partly at herself for having done nothing at all to stop it. As quickly as she could, Zara shapeshifted into a Seltivor to be evenly matched, not pausing to think about the potential repercussions of that transformation. At the greatest speed she could achieve in the massive body, Zara bolted into the forest despite protests from the others behind her, which all too quickly faded into the distance.

As Zara ran through the forest, her enormous form led to unanticipated harm and destruction. Her body forcefully rammed into trees that were housing the bodies of the Kleit, causing them to shrink and morph back before falling to the ground. Zara came into the forest with such speed that she couldn't stop herself until it was too late. After realizing what she had done, she came to a halt, burdened by the fact that Privelion had already outwitted her. He chose that form for a reason, and she chose it mindlessly. Zara began to fear that she was an encumbrance in this battle, as opposed to an asset. Her mind was clouded, and Privelion seemed to know how to keep it that way.

Zara quickly abandoned her form as a Seltivor to return to her human form and ensure the Kleit she rammed into were okay. Privelion didn't have a moment of doubt that Zara would be weakened by her protectiveness. Having already planned for her careless display of affection, he charged back through the trees, heading straight for her. The forest rumbled at each stride the Seltivor took in her direction. Zara backed away slowly, but there was nowhere to run, nor hide. She found herself with her back against a tree. At least, she thought it was a tree. Unexpected by both her and Privelion, two arms wrapped around Zara and quickly spun her until the being attached to the arms was standing face to face with her, their back toward Privelion.

The being quickly spun themself back around to face Privelion, grabbed a weapon that had been hidden behind their back, and stabbed the leg of the Seltivor with a long spear-like blade that Zara had not yet seen on Suvia. Privelion was too caught off guard by the unforeseen ally to react.

"I'm Vortil... of the Listun tribe," the unsolicited helper informed Zara in his native tongue. "If Privelion knew we were coming, he would have avoided this, you know," Vortil claimed as he pressed the blade of the spear-like weapon further into the Seltivor's leg.

"We?" Zara asked. Several others from the Listun tribe stepped out from the trees in response.

"What's happening to him?" Zara asked, noticing that the Seltivor looked stunned.

"I'm sure you know from your affiliation with the Klaysta tribe that Suvian weapons are often filled with poison," Vortil replied.

"So, he'll die?" Zara asked. "Just like that? It's over?"

"Not quite," Vortil replied. "In our tribe, we do not kill, not even for food. We survive off the foods of the land."

"Then that brings me back to my first question," Zara reiterated. "What is happening to him?"

"He will go into a rapid but short state of delirium," Vortil explained. "I suggest you act quickly." Vortil quickly pulled the weapon out of the Seltivor's leg. The Seltivor slowly turned away from them and started limping.

"Hurry!" one of the Listun urged the others. They ran quickly to get ahead of Privelion, and Zara followed. They created a perimeter around Privelion with weapons at the ready. The Seltivor turned in all directions, its eyes seeming to flutter back and forth. It shook its head violently and blew a thin layer of mucus out at the Listun in the process. Suddenly angered and seeming to come to its senses, it charged forward, nearly trampling a few of the Listun who managed to move to the side just in time.

"A short state of delirium?" Zara asked, throwing her hands into the air in frustration. "I didn't realize it'd be that short."

"It's not," Vortil assured her, pointing at the path the Seltivor had taken.

In a dazed and confused attempt to evacuate the forest, Privelion had bolted forward blindly, failing to realize that the Kleit had vastly expanded the lake. By the time he noticed that he was headed straight for it, it was too late. He fell into the lake, shooting a tremendous amount of water into the air in the process.

The Eyla in the water quickly dispersed to not get stuck underneath the animal's enormous body. The Seltivor's body subsequently began shrinking, as Privelion unwilfully transformed back into his true form on his way to the bottom of the lake. The Eyla flooded back in toward him as he morphed to the size of a Klaysta. They tore off their body jewels and strung them around Privelion, in an attempt to trap him at the bottom of the water to drown.

Meanwhile, roughly fifty Gladiators stormed through the desert, carrying members of the Vultra tribe on their back. Now that Privelion was temporarily immobilized, they were able to test whether their powers would be of use to make him stay that way. The Vultra commanded the Gladiators to a halt at the edge of the lake, dismounted them, and jumped in. The Vultra, unable to breathe underwater, took turns quickly swimming to the bottom to further paralyze Privelion and assist the Eyla in trapping him.

One of the Vultra climbed out of the lake, after a struggle to hoist his plump stomach out of the water. Zara recognized this Vultra as Igg, who she had become acquainted with the other day. Zara quickly jogged toward him for an update of what was happening underneath the water.

"We are in the process of keeping him immobilized and trapped," Igg informed Zara.

"I thought we determined your abilities would have no effect on him!" Zara exclaimed, excited and relieved to hear otherwise.

"We thought the same," Igg replied.

"Perhaps he hasn't used the ability to paralyze in thirty-three years, since it caused the death of his grandfather..." Zara contemplated. "If he had been using that ability since then, what other reason would he have had for withholding it during his attacks against us?"

"That would explain why our ability is effective against him," Igg added in agreement. "Perhaps frequent use of the power is what offers one the immunity to it."

While Igg and Zara were collaborating, Privelion was plotting. He didn't care that the Eyla had him trapped. In fact, it is what he wanted. After getting all of the Eyla in one place, huddled like a school of fish over his body, he shapeshifted into a Minnow and swam free from the trap, weaving between the Eyla toward the water's surface. When he reached the Eyla that were closest to the surface, he morphed into one of them, cleverly disguised in the crowd. Only one Eyla saw him transform. The two of them made eye contact before quickly racing to the water's surface.

When the two Eyla got out of the water, Zara ran to them. "What's going on down there?" Zara asked. "Do you still have him trapped?"

"No!" one of the Eyla exclaimed before the other could speak a word. "He shapeshifted into one of us and raced me to get out here so he could trick you," the Eyla revealed, pointing to the one standing beside him.

"He's lying!" the other Eyla cried. "He's Privelion! I watched him transform under the water."

Though Zara didn't know if it were possible, she closed her eyes, focused, and willed herself to turn into a military tank. Her bottom half started transforming first. Her legs hardened and changed color before merging into each other and expanding outward and upward. Before long, her human torso was being held up by the base of a tank, but something didn't feel right.

"What are you going to do?" one of the Eyla asked frantically, watching as she transformed. "Kill us both?"

"No," Zara replied, "just you." Zara had grown too familiar with the peculiar voice of the Eyla to be deceived by Privelion's attempts to replicate it. Zara tensed her upper body, willing it to transform, but it would not. She was beginning to feel nauseous and fatigued.

The Eyla smiled an eerie toothless grin before shapeshifting and confirming Zara's accusation. "You don't seem to know what's happening to you." Privelion roared with laughter.

Zara's body began to transform back, her ability beginning to slip entirely from the grips of her control. Zara fell to the ground in her human form and looked up at Privelion, panting heavily. "Enlighten me," Zara snarled, enraged, but helpless at his feet.

Privelion knelt down and put his pointer finger underneath Zara's chin, lifting it upward to force her eye contact. "Suvian energy is on a budget darling, and yours is spent." He spit impudently at her feet.

The Klaysta closed in on Privelion, preparing to eject sharp blades from their weapons. Unlike the Listun weapons, all Klaysta weapons were designed to kill. Just as several of them brushed their finger against the trigger of their weapon, Privelion threw his arms outward, sending what seemed like a wave of energy through the air. This wave was made visible by the ripple effect of a sandstorm that moved outward from his arms and across the desert floor. With just that single motion, every being on the battlefield apart from Zara and the Vultra became paralyzed. Seemingly with ease, Privelion transformed into a small rocket and shot up quickly into the sky.

By the time Privelion was high above them, movement was restored to those who were still on the ground. The Vultra summoned Gladiators and took off as quickly as they could, knowing that they were of no further use to stopping Privelion. The Klaysta tribe rose to their feet, taking a moment to fully recuperate. Zara looked up and saw an already darkening sky become overcast.

"Thirty-three years ago, he..." Zara began to say, feeling a bout of déjà vu coming on from the story Leto had told her.

Zara was silenced by a crackling thunder, followed by the sight of a single lightning bolt that struck the sand only a few meters from her feet. Zara looked up, attempting to find where the cloud ended and met clear skies, but that bisection was nowhere in sight. Zara had no idea where to run. She stood her ground in a panic, praying the next lightning bolt would not strike her, nor her allies.

"How does he have the necessary energy for this?" Zara yelled over the sound of thunder.

"He must have some way to harness and store it that we don't!" Tavion yelled back.

The next lightning bolt struck much further from Zara this time and did not come close to hitting anyone. Thunder roared through again. A third lightning bolt struck even further from Zara, almost hitting one of the Klaysta. Zara noticed the lightning was striking predictably, relatively along the path of an invisible line, further and further away from her. Thunder again. Lightning to follow. Same pattern. Zara looked out into the distance of the line, suddenly realizing that she should have no relief that the lightning was striking progressively further from her, as it was getting progressively closer to the lake.

"No!" Zara shouted at the top of her lungs. She sprinted toward the lake with tears clouding her eyes. "Get out!" Zara yelled to the Eyla and the Kleit. "Get out! Get out!" Zara cried hysterically. "He's coming for the water!" The Eyla responded quickly, swimming as fast as they could toward land. "Get out!" Zara yelled again, still running toward them. The Eyla lifted themselves out of the water, in large groups at a time, until only a few of them were left in the water.

The Eyla that got out were lending helping hands to lift the few remaining out of the water when thunder boomed again, and an individual lightning bolt came down in what almost seemed to appear as slow motion. Heads turned upward, watching the lightning come down in a vertical path, in a line directed straight toward the center of the lake.

Current, the only Eyla yet to evacuate, also saw it happen in slow motion. A bright white bolt of electricity coursing through the air. Zara mouthing the word "no", hunching over, greatly disheveled, with her hands near her face and tears in her eyes. The water illuminating a fluorescent blue, matching the color of the Eyla's eyes. The background fading, and everything turning to white.

The ear-piercing cry coming from Zara told stories of pain and heartbreak that no one could ever accurately replicate with words. She watched as the bolt of lightning branched out through the water, merged with Current's body, and illuminated it, giving it a tragically beautiful glow, further amplified by the way it lit up Current's multicolored scales. All at once, the light vanished and Current, unresponsive, sunk down to the bottom of the lake.

Zara rose to her feet. While she felt utterly destroyed, she knew she didn't have time to grieve. Lightning continued to strike, narrowly missing the target each time. Privelion grew frustrated with each failed attempt. Though his energy reserve was far greater than Zara's, it was nevertheless finite, and he realized he was expending it wastefully. The day had gone, and night had replaced it. He changed his plan of attack, lest sunrise be his downfall.

The sky cleared of the dark cloud and appeared even darker on its own. Privelion vanished from sight. Zara bit her bottom lip hard and sobbed uncontrollably, seeing Current's body being electrocuted over and over again in her mind. She looked toward where the lake had been, and a massive body of black goo was in its place. For a split second, she could swear it was illuminated water once more. With a blink of her eyes, the mere outline of the black goo was hardly visible in the night. The Eyla and the Kleit joined Zara in releasing tears of loss, while the Klaysta and the Listun tribe stayed silent, empathetic to their pain.

The ground rumbled and Zara, startled, looked up into the eyes of the massive beast now charging at her. It was the biggest Seltivor she had seen, possibly exceeding the size of any true Seltivor on Suvia. Zara stood her ground. The beast grew closer. The Klaysta readied their weapons. The beast ran faster. Zara stood still, not making any attempt to stop him. Instead, she closed her eyes and listened to the sound of his footsteps trampling the ground. One, two, three, four. One, two, three, four. One, two, three, four. One, two, three, four. Like the beat of a drum. Zara silently counted out the sequential rumbles as the creature's feet predictably hit the ground. The Seltivor was only meters away. Kalari fired her weapon. Privelion ducked. Zara fell.

Kalari's weapon flew over the Seltivor's back and landed point down in the sand. Zara's body shrank more quickly than anyone could fathom. She became a boulder, far lower than Privelion's line of sight. Privelion continued running toward where she had stood only a moment ago, unsure of where she had disappeared to. Zara listened and waited. Within seconds, he was standing above her in confusion. The Klaysta fired more weapons. Privelion remarkably dodged them. What he failed to dodge was the weapon that shot up from underneath him: A Gladiator, nearly three times his size.

The Seltivor's body was flung into the air and came crashing toward the ground. Klaysta quickly cleared the area in preparation for his impact. The Seltivor skidded on its side across the sand, sending a dusty fog through the air that infiltrated everyone's airways. Zara, protected by a body of rock, was the only one unaffected. In the Gladiator's body, Zara lunged forward.

The Seltivor stood on its hind legs and slammed the front of its body down full force onto the Gladiator's back. The Gladiator fell to the ground, unharmed, but pinned beneath the Seltivor's feet. The Seltivor leaned its head down and opened its mouth wide, displaying sixteen jagged teeth. It closed its mouth hard onto the Gladiator. A loud crunching sound followed, and the Seltivor cried out in pain. It opened its mouth, now bloodied with nine of the sixteen teeth cracked. Privelion worried about the damage that may have caused, even to his true form. He realized that he had picked the weaker of the two animals, and yet, he couldn't bring himself to transform. No. He refused to display any sign of weakness or failure.

Determined to let his rage overshadow his weaker form, the Seltivor leveled its back and stood tall over Zara before doing something that no real Seltivor had ever done nor could do. He jumped high into the air and slammed down on the ground. Not once, not twice, but over and over again. The Earth rattled, and the sand in the air made it difficult to see anything or even breath, leaving Zara unprotected by her allies. It was just Privelion and Zara. Seltivor and Gladiator. Visually and functionally, everyone else disappeared.

As the Seltivor repeatedly slammed down on the ground, its feet landed in slightly different spots each time, sometimes crashing onto the sand and sometimes directly onto the body of the Gladiator. With each fall of the Seltivor's body, there was a crack in the Gladiator's, surely causing deep damage that Zara could only pray to recover from.

After a while, the Seltivor's jumping slowed. Privelion was exhausted and rapidly losing momentum. The Gladiator, still lying on the ground, glanced up at the sun rising up from the horizon, realizing they had fought through the night. The others had evacuated to a distant perimeter to rid their airways of the sandy dust that was just now beginning to clear.

The Seltivor tiredly stopped jumping altogether and began to walk away victoriously from the Gladiator's immobile body, certain that the battle was over. The Gladiator, badly injured but determined to prevail, slowly rose to its feet and thrusted its body forward at the Seltivor. The two bodies crashed hard to the sand and slid, neither having the energy to move at all after coming to a stop. The two of them shapeshifted back to their true form simultaneously out of great fatigue, with Zara lying directly on top of Privelion. Being that Privelion's body matched the general height and build of Tavion's, Zara for a moment found comfort in her unintended physical contact with her enemy's Klaysta anatomy. It was a period of serenity after so many hours of torture. It was a period of acceptance after so many hours of hatred. It was blissfully disturbing. It was rightfully short-lived.

As the sun shined higher and brighter in the sky, Privelion's energy seemed to return with full force, as evidenced by him sliding out from underneath Zara and briskly jumping to his feet. Zara lay helpless on the ground, with three cracked ribs, a bloodied lip, and bruises covering her pale skin. All she could bring herself to move were her eyes as she watched Privelion stand over her body minaciously.

Privelion looked up at the bright sky and smiled. "I'm going to finish this, Silvia," he said to her, with a sinister smile.

Zara looked up at the sky as Privelion had, quickly coming to a revelation. "You harness energy from the sun," she processed aloud.

Privelion's smile widened. "And now there is plenty of it."

"But how?" Zara asked, possessing nothing more than curiosity in her final moments at his mercy.

"The chemicals I created don't just give me multiple Suvian abilities," Privelion informed her jauntily. "They absorb sunlight, affording me the energy and capacity to maximize those abilities."

The tribes were running towards Zara and Privelion as quickly as possible, realizing it was safe to return and seeing that Zara had not risen to her feet in quite some time. Privelion looked out into the distance and watched as they came closer. He chuckled. "Your friends think they can save you," he said, with an insincere tone of pity. "They don't see you as I see you, already dead." Privelion shapeshifted into a Seltivor and lifted a leg into the air, ready to deliver one final blow to Zara's human body.

The Klaysta, arriving just in time, prepared their weapons and fired at the Seltivor. The Seltivor's leg came down to the side of Zara, just missing her face, and it wearily stumbled over her. Though the Seltivor was losing its balance, it was not falling to its death as the Klaysta would have anticipated.

"What's happening?" Kalari yelled over the rumbles of its footsteps.

"A chemical reaction," Zara replied. "It seems to be reacting harmfully with his energy source, and yet, it seems to be protecting him from death."

"It's all we have!" Kalari cried.

"Deplete his energy!" Zara commanded. The Klaysta fired more poison-filled weapons until the Seltivor fell to the ground with an overwhelming feeling of enervation. His true form emerged once more. He looked down at his skin, which was pierced by seven weapons. One by one, he pulled them out of his flesh, unable to remove the poison they had transmitted and recover the vitality he had lost.

The Klaysta tribe stood over Privelion's body with several more weapons pointed at him. "This fight is over," Tavion informed him. Privelion nodded and put his hands up in the air in a gesture of surrender.

Kalari turned to Tavion for guidance. "Kill or capture?" she asked.

Before Tavion could respond, Privelion swiftly pulled his leg forward and snapped it back across Tavion's ankles, knocking Tavion off his feet. Tavion fell and dropped his weapon between Privelion and himself. Privelion quickly grabbed hold of it, aimed, and fired.

Zara looked down at her abdomen, the weapon deeply penetrating her flesh. Her vision blurred, and her other senses seemed to intensify. She could swear she felt the individual grains of desert sand against her back. The smell of her own blood grew stronger and instantly nauseated her. She could practically taste the vomit that had not been expelled from her body. Voices echoed and merged together. All at once, her senses faded into nothingness, and her eyelids fluttered and closed, permitting the final wash of blackness to consume her.

Tavion ran to Zara's side and grabbed hold of her hand. He put his other hand on her neck and desperately felt for her heartbeat. There was a ringing in his ears, drowning out the sounds of chatter and sobs from the crowd behind him. He hung his head over her as tears dropped down from his eyes and landed on her cheek. He looked up at the others and shook his head. Tavion looked back at Privelion vengefully. This battle was far from over, though Zara would no longer exist to see it through.

# Epilogue

G REEN PLANTS OF VARIOUS species occupied nearly all of the walking space around a square perimeter of the room. The room smelled of lavender and fresh bamboo. The walls were bright chestnut in color, with slim planks of wood intersecting perpendicular to each other in a design seemingly similar to oriental architecture. The center of the room was clear of everything, save for a pale red ceremonial rug with a light tan intricate design and the wooden floorboards beneath it.

Five elegant, and yet simultaneously wild beings arched their spine, hunching their shoulders over the rectangular carpet in front of them. Their pointed noses flared with each deep breath. Their heavily curved eyelids felt weighty with each blink. The frayed hair extending outward from their braids caused itching along their shoulders.

In front of them, a body lay still. A body of a woman. This woman did not ask for their help, nor did she have the tribal affiliation that privileged her with it. Not a single being asked for their help on her behalf. Not a single being was present when her body was discovered. Just a woman, alone in the desert, abandoned, with not the flow of air to pass in and out of her lungs.

These beings knew this woman. Her legend had preceded her. She was the protector of the land, with not a soul left to protect her outside of their community. She was the giver, with no desire nor anticipation to receive. She was the strength that never looked down upon weakness. While their ability was life-consuming, they would make the sacrifice for the protector of life itself. They considered her more worthy of resuscitation than any and all members of their own tribe. They were nearly certain that with the recovery of her life would come the great reduction of death, and for that reason, they had all the determination in the world to revive her.

# ACKNOWLEDGMENTS

T HEY SAY IT TAKES a village to raise a child. While it didn't take quite so many helping hands to make this book possible, the helping hands that did contribute made a village of a difference. I thank my older brother for his assistance with ideas, a plot outline, and critiques. I thank my best friend for her assistance with proofreading *Suvia* in its entirety. I thank Lance Bernstein for his brilliant artwork that brings the cover of *Suvia* to life. I thank the other published authors I have connected with, not only for welcoming me into the industry with open arms, but for providing me with tips and suggestions for formatting, publishing, and distribution. These are the people that made up my village and helped me construct a road that led to *Suvia*. With gratitude, a most deserving acknowledgment to my readers. I am eternally grateful for your support.

# About the Author

Alison was born and raised in the suburbs of Minnesota. She holds a bachelor's and a master's degree in specialized divisions of Psychology. Her education has given her an outlook on life and relationships that permeates the interpersonal dynamics of the characters in her writing. From a young age, Alison has had great enthusiasm for the written word. Having written countless poems, songs, and short stories as a hobby over the years, Alison was elated to introduce *Suvia* in 2022 and make her debut as a Novelist. Outside of writing, Alison's greatest joys are spending time with friends and family, listening to a wide array of music genres, and watching romantic comedies and action films. Alison is confident that *Suvia* is only the beginning to a long career in the writing industry. With several more projects in the works, Alison plans to release works of fiction in the genres of Mystery, Contemporary Literature, Fantasy, and Poetry. Alison's greatest hope for her written work is that she will inspire the world with the written word, inspire producers in the film industry, and find overall prosperity in doing what she loves.